SHADOWS of LANCASTER COUNTY

MINDY STARNS CLARK

Doubleday Large Print
Home Library Edition

HARVEST HOUSE PUBLISHERS
EUGENE, OREGON

This Large Print Edition, prepared especially for Doubleday Large Print Home Library, contains the complete, unabridged text of the original Publisher's Edition.

Cover by Dugan Design Group, Bloomington, Minnesota

Cover photos © Tom Laman / National Geographic / Getty Images; David R. Frazier Photolibrary, Inc. / Alamy; Stockxpert

The author is represented by MacGregor Literary.

SHADOWS OF LANCASTER COUNTY

Published by Harvest House Publishers
Eugene, Oregon 97402

ISBN-978-1-60751-699-6

Printed in the United States of America

This Large Print Book carries the Seal of Approval of N.A.V.H.

**For Shari Weber,
who helps me in ways too
numerous to count,
meets challenges with
grace and strength,
and lives God's truth every day.
I'm honored to call you my friend!**

ACKNOWLEDGMENTS

I am deeply indebted to:

John Clark, for always, for everything.

Emily and Lauren Clark, for patience and understanding and inspiration.

Kim Moore, for putting up with me—cheerfully!—over and over and over.

All of the amazing folks at Harvest House Publishers.

Thanks also to:

ChiLibris, Alice Clark, Colleen Coble, the members of my online advisory group CONSENSUS, Aaron Dillon, Traci Hall, Traci Hoffman, Karri James, Aaron Jarvis, Benjamin Jarvis, Laura Knudson, Kristian, Tobi Layton, Chip MacGregor, Tom Morrissey, Gayle Roper, Ned & Marie Scannell, Tami, Abby Van Wormer, Sisters in Crime, Shari Weber,

Richard & Janet White, and
Stacie Williams.

Special thanks to Erik Wesner, author of
www.amishamerica.typepad.com.

Finally, thanks to J.K. Wolfe, MD, and Harry Krause, MD, outstanding physicians who generously brainstormed with me as I attempted to blur the lines between medical reality and what-if fiction. Any inaccuracies—not to mention flights of fancy—are purely mine.

ONE

Bobby

I'm dead. The powerful engine gunning behind him drowned out every other thought. He held on to the handlebars of the borrowed motorcycle, crouched low on the leather seat, and accelerated as far as he dared. When the dark car struck his rear tire the first time, he managed to hang on through the jolt, though just barely. Regaining control, he crouched even lower and gripped the handlebars more tightly, adrenaline surging in the piercing cold. In vain he searched the blackness ahead for an escape, for some point of diversion where the motorcycle could go but the car pursuing him could not. Caught on the wide curve of a hilly highway, there were no shoulders here, and no way to know what lay in the darkness off to the right beyond the metal guardrail. Worse, he knew he couldn't swerve back and forth on the blacktop to dodge the next hit, because moves like that on a motorcycle would end up flipping the bike and high-siding him whether the car rammed into him again or not.

A second jolt came just as the guardrail ended, a collision that nearly managed to unseat him. Barely hanging on, he regained his balance, scooted forward on the leather seat, and took a deep breath, conscious of the vehicle still roaring aggressively behind him in murderous pursuit. In a choice between certain death on the road and possible survival off of it, he steeled his nerves and made the decision to leave the pavement no matter what he might run into. Holding on tight, he shifted his weight and angled the handlebars to the right, veering into the unknown darkness. The action was punctuated by a series of bumps and jolts as his tires went from blacktop to gravel to crunchy brown grass.

Let it be a field, God. Let it be somebody's farm.

The headlamp of the borrowed motorcycle was strong, its beam slicing through the February night air to reveal the unfamiliar terrain he had driven himself into. Before he could discern what lay ahead, however, before he could even slow down or adjust his direction or see if the car had tried to follow, he spotted the looming gray mass in front of him—a solid, four-foot-high cement retaining wall. He knew this was the end.

The sudden stop flung him heavenward, propelling him in a broad arc across the night sky like the flare of a Roman candle. As he went, he thought mostly of the ground far below him, the frozen and unforgiving earth that was going to greet him by shattering his bones or snapping his neck upon landing. He prayed for the latter, less painful option.

Let it end quickly, God.

As his trajectory continued, his limbs instinctively flailing against the void, his mind went to one person: his younger sister, Anna. He hoped beyond hope that his message would get to her, that she would understand what he wanted her to do. For a guy who didn't even own a computer, he found it vaguely ironic that the last thought that raced through his mind just before certain death was of an email. But the message he had sent her was the only chance he had, the only hope that Lydia and Isaac might still be protected. That one email was the only way his desperate efforts might save his wife and son and the unborn child Lydia was carrying.

Let it end quickly, God, he prayed again just before impact. *And please, God, please guide Anna to the truth.*

TWO

Anna

The nightmare started up again last night.

That was the first thought that struck me as I turned off the alarm. Somewhere in the early hours of the dawn I had gone there in my sleep for the first time in many months. Now as I sat up and swung my legs over the side of the bed, I couldn't understand why it was back, this nightmare that had plagued me off and on for the past eleven years.

Why now? Why last night?

Sometimes all it took was an external cue, like a house fire spotted from the freeway. An Amish character flashing across the television screen. A news report about a dead newborn baby. But I hadn't experienced any of those things lately. There was simply no reason for the nightmare to have returned like this, out of the blue.

Standing up, I traded my nightgown for shorts and a T-shirt and then padded into the bathroom. As I stood at the mirror and brushed my teeth, I tried not to relive it again now that I was awake, but I couldn't help it.

The dream was always beautiful at first: rolling fields that look like patchwork on an Amish quilt, cars sharing the road with horses and buggies, colorful laundry flapping in the wind. But then there was the farmhouse, the rambling old farmhouse. Without electricity or curtains, as I came closer the windows would turn into dark, empty eyes staring at me. My nightmare always ended the same: black to orange to hot white. Sirens. Screams. The acrid stench of smoke, of terror, of unspeakable loss. When I woke up, guilt would consume me like flame.

Wishing I could spit out that guilt along with the toothpaste, I rinsed my mouth and then reached for my hairbrush, attacking my long, blond hair with vigor.

It happened a long, long time ago.

You paid your dues.

All has been forgiven.

Telling myself that over and over, I swept my hair into a ponytail, turned out the light, and headed downstairs. In the kitchen, judging by the mess on the counter and the fact that the door was ajar, I realized my housemate was already up and doing her exercises on the back porch. Kiki was always trying out some new fitness trend, the latest and greatest plan guaranteed to shed pounds and inches by the second. I had given up long ago trying to convince her that if she would just come jogging with me a few times a week, she would eventually achieve the results she so desperately sought. Still, I thought as I put away the juice carton and wiped off the counter, on days like today I was glad I could jog alone. I needed the quiet to clear my head and wash away the last remnants of my nightmare.

Once the kitchen was tidy, I grabbed a bottle of water from the fridge and opened the back door the rest of the way; a warm ocean breeze wafted in to greet me. I stepped out onto the uneven slats of the porch and let the door fall shut behind me as I inhaled the salty sea smell of morning. Gorgeous. As someone who had grown up in snowy Pennsylvania, I knew I'd never get used to the year-round warm weather and sunshine of Southern California.

"Howdy," Kiki said cheerfully. She was doing stretches on the far side of the porch, past the square of rotten boards near the door. "Wanna see my new Piloga move?"

"Piloga? What's that? Some cross between Pilates and Yoga?"

"No, it's named after the founder, Manny Piloga. He teaches the fifty-plus class down at the Y."

I smiled, glancing at my watch. It was early yet; I could spare a few minutes to encourage her efforts—not to mention that a quick chat might help distract me even further from my nightmare. As Kiki sat on the wooden floorboards, I reached for a folded aluminum chair that was propped against the wall and told her to be careful on the floor lest she get splinters in her bottom.

"Aw, I've got so much padding, I probably wouldn't even feel it if I did," Kiki laughed, adjusting the waistband on her pajamas and stretching her legs out in front of her.

"Hey, I saw that guy at the grocery store flirting with you yesterday," I reminded her as I sat in the chair. "He didn't seem to mind a little extra padding at all."

"That's 'cause he works in the deli department. He likes it when the scales weigh in heavy."

I rolled my eyes again, refusing to laugh at her joke, but she laughed loud enough for both of us.

"Okay, check out the ab work I've been doing," Kiki said as she leaned back, arms jutting forward parallel to the ground. Slowly, she raised her legs into the air and held them there. "I can stay like this for three minutes, just long enough for you to tell me about your date last night. A fancy dinner at Harborside, hmm? He must have had something in mind. Maybe a certain question he wanted to pop?"

"Good grief, Kik, it was just our third date."

"Sometimes true love can speed things along. I got engaged to my Roger during our first date—and we were happily married for twenty-five years before he passed, God rest his soul."

"Yeah, well, you were one of the lucky ones. Very impressive stance, by the way."

"Thanks. Manny says it strengthens the core."

I opened up my water bottle, took a sip, and looked at my housemate, who also happened to be my landlord, coworker, and best friend despite the twenty-one-year difference in our ages. As she maintained her bizarre position, I thought about yesterday evening, about my third and final outing with Hal, or as I had come to think of him, Hal-itosis.

"We decided not to see each other anymore."

She let out a long grunt, though I wasn't sure if it was from exertion or exasperation.

"'We' who? 'We' him or 'we' you? Or do I even have to ask?"

"Well, like you expected, he did take me to Harborside for a reason. He told me he wants to get more serious."

"Exclusive dating serious or engagement serious?"

"I have no idea, Kik. His exact words were 'I think it's time we should take this to the next level.' I didn't even want to know what the next level was. I suggested he would be happier with someone who enjoys day-old-coffee breath."

A loud laugh burst from Kiki's mouth. "You didn't say that!"

"No, I didn't. But I thought it. I just told him I didn't think it would be fair to him, because I wasn't interested in a long-term relationship."

"Yeah, right."

"I'm *not* interested in a long-term relationship . . . with him."

"Uh-huh." She was quiet for a long moment, but her silence was louder than words.

I looked her way to see that she was still holding her pose, though beads of sweat were now forming along her hairline.

"What?" I demanded. "What is it you're not saying?"

"I don't know, Anna, it's just that you're so picky about who you're willing to go out with, which is fine. Not every fellow who comes sniffing around a pretty girl is worth her time or attention. But how come the ones who make it through the first elimination never get to the next round?"

"What am I, a game show?"

"You know what I mean. How come every one of your relationships ends this way, with you breaking it off just when the guy wants to get more serious? How can you be so sure one of these fellows isn't The One?"

I shrugged, wondering how I could explain. I kept dating because I hoped someday to find the man who would make me forget all about Reed Thornton. He had been The One, as far as I was concerned, but I had lost him eleven years ago when the fire that burned in my nightmares had also extinguished my dreams with him. Even though I hadn't seen or spoken to Reed since, I still thought of him often, no matter how hard I tried not to. Somehow, I had yet to meet the man who could even begin to compare.

"I'm not waiting for the perfect guy. I just want a guy who's perfect for me. If I can't find that, I'd rather be alone."

With a loud groan, Kiki finally collapsed, breathing heavily as she lay sprawled on the floor. I glanced at my watch. I needed to get moving soon if I wanted to get in a full run before we needed to leave for work. Still, as Kiki recovered from her efforts, I could tell she had more to say.

"Go ahead, Kiki. Don't hold back now."

With a chuckle, she rolled on her side and propped up on one elbow.

"Fine. You're a very private person, Anna, and I know you have trouble letting people in. But if you want to find someone, stop giving up so soon. True love starts when you open yourself to chances."

Chances? It had been a long time since I'd allowed myself the luxury of chances. Once I broke with my past seven years ago and created my new self, my new identity, my whole life had become one big chance. Back then, finding Mr. Right was the least of my worries—especially because my heart was broken from all that had happened with Reed. As time went on and I finally escaped from my past and found peace in my new life here in California, the daily risk factor had greatly lessened. Maybe it was time to take a few chances in life.

"Thanks, Kiki, I'll think on it," I said as I stood and moved toward the steps in my bare feet. "Gotta run for now though, or we'll be late for work."

Careful to avoid more rotten boards, I made my way down one side of the steps to the sandy beach.

"Without shoes?" Kiki asked, moving into position for another exercise.

"Yep, and no sunscreen either," I said, grinning. "See? I can take chances."

I turned, my bare feet digging down into the sand, and took off. My movements were awkward until I reached the damp packed sand near the water. There it was easier to run, easier to find traction in the gritty ground. I tucked in my elbows and sprinted along the water's edge until I could feel my heartbeat pounding in my chest. I slowed to a jog and ran farther than I had intended, which was not a wise choice given my bare feet. I would pay for this later, but for now it just felt good. It was calming. Sometimes I thought God used the sand and water and my quiet morning runs as a special gift for me, just to keep me sane.

At the jetty I turned around, picked up the pace, and headed home. As I jogged, I thought about Reed and how loving him had spoiled me for any other man. In the years since I last saw him, I had probably built him up in my mind to be far more special than he actually was. I decided it wouldn't hurt to remember that he wasn't perfect, that in fact he had at least one very serious flaw I knew about—and probably tons more I had never had the opportunity to discover. Maybe I really did need to take a chance or two. Maybe I should stop cutting off every single relationship the moment it began to get serious. Here I was waiting for someone to come along who instantly lit that spark inside of me the way Reed had, someone who made me feel as though the world ceased to exist beyond the intensity of his gaze. But maybe I wouldn't ever find that again. Maybe I should learn to settle for less—either that, or decide to stop looking and find contentment in being single the way Kiki had after her husband died.

As I neared her ramshackle beachfront house, I slowed my run to a walk, fingers to my wrist as I studied the second hand on my watch. Pulse rate was good, lungs open and clear, leg muscles burning nicely. Too bad the soles of my feet were throbbing.

I climbed up the side of the steps, grabbed the empty glass Kiki had left on the porch, and carried it through the open back door to the kitchen. I decided to stop thinking about my love life for now and focus on getting ready for work. I hoped Kiki had finished showering and I could take my turn right away. I wouldn't have time to blow-dry my hair, but at least I could put on some makeup in the car.

"Hey, Kik, you out of the shower yet?" I yelled.

"One more minute and then it's all yours," she called back, her voice echoing from the bathroom directly above the kitchen.

My stomach growling, I grabbed an energy bar from the pantry and another bottle of cold water from the fridge before leaving the kitchen. I had just unwrapped the bar and taken my first bite when the phone started ringing. I hesitated at the bottom of the stairs, listening as it went to the machine, knowing I didn't have much time to spare.

"We're not here, leave a message!" Kiki's recorded voice said cheerily from the box on the kitchen counter. That was followed by a beep and a long silence.

"Annalise?" a woman's voice finally uttered, sounding very far away. "Is this the number of Annalise Jensen?"

Annalise Jensen? I hadn't heard that name for years, not since I left Pennsylvania behind, moved west, and became Anna Bailey. Quickly, I dashed to the machine, heart pounding and praying that Kiki hadn't overheard.

"I hope this is the right number," the voice continued in a lilting accent. "I guess I leave a message and wait and see."

One glance at Caller ID confirmed that the woman was calling from Dreiheit, Pennsylvania. I didn't recognize the number, but I recognized the voice and its familiar Pennsylvania Dutch lilt. I steeled myself and answered, closing my eyes as the past came rushing toward me through three thousand miles of telephone line.

"Don't hang up," I said, turning off the machine. "It's me. I'm here."

"Annalise? Is Lydia. Lydia Jensen." My sister-in-law.

"Lydia? How did you get my number?"

I had given this number to my brother in confidence and told him to keep it somewhere private, never share it with anyone—not even his wife—and never use it himself except in an extreme emergency.

"Bobby gave it to me last night. He said to call you if anything went wrong. Otherwise I would never . . ."

I struggled to listen as Kiki started making clunking noises overhead. What was she doing up there, a tap dance?

"What was that last thing you said?" I asked.

"So sorry. You cannot hear me *gut*? I am calling from my sister's farm, out behind the milk house."

I held a hand over my other ear, closed my eyes, and tried to focus, picturing my sister-in-law standing in one of those Amish phone shanties that looked more like an outhouse than a telephone booth.

"It's okay. What is it, Lydia? What's wrong?"

She exhaled slowly, and as I waited for her to explain, I tried to calm my pounding heart and push away a feeling of impending doom.

"I am calling about Bobby. He . . . he is *verschwunden.* Missing. He has gone missing, Annalise. I am so frightened for him. I do not know what to do."

I cleared my throat, genuinely surprised to hear that my brother had abandoned his wife and child. He had always seemed so happily married, but maybe there was trouble in paradise.

"Um, it's Anna now, not Annalise," I corrected, leaning over to reset the tape on the answering machine, erasing the part of her message that had been recorded before I picked up. "Anyway, so he left you? Like, moved out?"

"No, no, nothing like that. Is complicated to explain."

"Go on," I said, stretching the cord as far as I could to get to the fridge. At least I could make lunches as we talked.

"Well, it started last night. Bobby was working late at the lab, and little Isaac and I had choir practice. When we got home from church, there was something wrong with the apartment. The lock on the door was broken, and it looked like someone had been inside, going through our things."

"What do you mean?" I asked, setting a pack of sliced ham and some condiments on the counter.

"Closets and drawers were half open. Items were emptied out of baskets. Our belongings were intact, but they were *ferroontzled*—uh, like messy, out of order. Like someone had been here looking for something."

"Were you robbed?" I asked, wondering what that had to do with Bobby's decision to leave. I grabbed a loaf of whole wheat from the bread box and began assembling our sandwiches.

"I did not think so. I could not find anything that was missing. Still, I was about to call the police when the phone rang. It was Bobby. Before I could even tell him about the apartment, he said for me to take Isaac and get out of there, that we were in danger. He said for us to go to my sister's farm and to wait there until he contacted us. When I told him about the broken lock and the *ferroontzled* apartment and everything, he was even more upset. I told him I was about to call the police, but he said, 'Don't call the police, Lydia. Just go right now. *Go.*' "

"Did you?"

"*Yah,* he was so insistent, we left right away. Bobby had already talked to my brother Caleb and told him to watch for us, and for him and my brother-in-law

Nathaniel to protect us from harm once we arrived."

"Protect you from harm? Why?"

"I have no idea. I do not understand any of this. I was just glad that Caleb has a cell phone so that Bobby could call us back once we got there—"

"Wait," I interrupted. "You're telling me an Amish boy has a cell phone? Since when is that allowed?" I had only been gone from Pennsylvania for seven years, but I couldn't imagine that in that time the Amish community had gone from having no phones in homes to letting their kids run around with cell phones in their pockets.

Lydia hesitated and then explained.

"Caleb is nineteen, not such a boy anymore. He is on *rumspringa* right now, so the rules for him are bent a bit. He is not allowed to use the cell phone in the house, but in this case an exception was made so Bobby could call back."

Rumspringa, I knew only too well, was that time in every Amish teen's life when they were allowed extra freedom and more access to the outside world. The whole point was to let them see what was "out there," what they would be giving up—and what they would be gaining—if they chose to join the Amish church and commit to a lifetime of living by Amish rules. Bobby and Lydia's romance had begun during her *rumspringa,* and in the end she had chosen to forgo Amish baptism, leave the faith for a less restrictive denomination, and marry a man the Amish considered an outsider, an "Englisher." At least she had made her radical decision prior to baptism. Had she been baptized Amish first and then left the faith, she would have been punished through shunning. As it was, though no one in the Amish community had been happy about her decision, at least they were allowed to have contact with her and her husband and children and could remain somewhat involved in their lives.

"So did he?" I asked, trying to get back to the point. "Did Bobby call you again?"

"*Yah,* soon after we arrive at the farm, Bobby called on Caleb's phone to make sure we had arrived safely. I asked him what was going on, but he said it was a long story and that he would explain everything as soon as he got to us in just a few hours."

"And?"

"And those few hours came and went, but Bobby never showed up. Now it is almost ten fifteen in the morning and we still have not seen or heard from him since that phone call last night."

"So he's a few hours late—"

"Nine hours, Anna. Almost nine hours since he should have gotten here, twelve hours since his phone call!"

"Maybe he fell asleep at his desk. Maybe he was really tired and went to the wrong farm by mistake." I didn't add that it would be an easy error. All the Amish farms in Lancaster County had always looked the same to me.

"No, it is not like that. Something has happened to him. Something terrible. I know this."

Putting the sandwich fixings back into the fridge, I took a deep breath and held it for a moment. I felt bad for her, but I didn't know what she expected me to do. Though my brother and I emailed occasionally, I hadn't spoken to him in weeks—maybe a month, even. He and I had always shared a special bond, especially since the fire and its aftermath, but that didn't mean we stayed in constant touch.

"Lydia, I don't know what you want from me."

"I have no idea, Anna. I just know I need your help—and Bobby specifically said for me to call you if something went wrong."

"But how can I help from way out here? I don't have any way of knowing where he might be."

"This is what you do, *yah?* You find people who have gone missing?"

"Yes, I'm a skip tracer. But—"

"Your brother has gone missing. Please, Anna. Please, help me find him before it is too late."

THREE

Turning around, I leaned against the counter and looked through the kitchen window at the glistening sand and the blue-gray expanse of the Pacific Ocean beyond. I thought how very far I was—both literally and figuratively—from the gentle plains and rolling hills of Amish country back home.

"That is not all," Lydia added before I could form my response, and from the tone of her voice, I could tell the situation was about to get more complicated.

"Okay, then wait a second," I said, once again almost unable to hear thanks to the clunking noises Kiki was making upstairs.

I couldn't fathom what she was doing, though from the bumps and scrapes, it sounded as though she was rearranging the furniture. If so, that was a good thing as it meant I'd still have a chance at carpooling. I asked Lydia to give me the number she had called from, explaining that I needed to switch our conversation over to my cell phone. We hung up, and immediately I retrieved my cell from the charger, turned it on, and called her back.

"Sorry about that. Go ahead with what you were telling me. There's more?"

"Yes. All night, I have been thinking about the apartment, about the mess that had been made, about our things. I worried that whoever had been there *did* take something." She hesitated, and as I waited for her to go on, I assembled our lunches into brown paper bags and set them near the door along with my purse, keys, and sunglasses. "Bobby has a metal box filled with all of our important papers: birth certificates, marriage license, things like that. Early this morning I started thinking about that box, that maybe they took our papers, our information. A woman at the bridal shop where I do alterations had identity theft once, and I worry that we might have that too. So when Caleb went over to the apartment a while ago to fix the lock, I asked him to bring back that box. I knew it had been gone through, because last night it was open on the floor in front of the cabinet."

"And?" I prodded, leaving the kitchen and moving through the living room toward the stairs.

"And Caleb brought me the box and everything was there, even our Social Security cards. Even the credit card we keep for emergencies. Only one thing was gone. I am so sorry, Anna."

I paused halfway up the stairs as her words sunk in. *Why was she sorry?*

"It was a sealed envelope. Inside was your new name, your address, your phone numbers. When Bobby put it in there years ago, he told me what it was but said I was never to open it unless something happened to him and I needed to contact you. That envelope . . . it is gone, Anna. Someone took your information. If he had not given me this number last night over the phone, I would have had no way to reach you."

"Lydia, hold on a minute," I managed to say.

"*Yah,* sure."

As she waited, silent, at the other end of the line, I walked slowly up the rest of the stairs, trying to understand the implications of what had happened—and what I could do about it now. I needed to think.

When I reached the top, I took a deep breath and knocked on Kiki's door, intending to tell her I was running late and she would have to go to work without me. Getting no response, I crossed the hall to my own room and reached for the knob. It twisted, but the door wouldn't swing open.

"I'm sorry, Lydia. Keep holding," I said into the receiver. Then I tucked the open phone in my shorts pocket so I could use both hands and a hip to work open the door that was always getting stuck. More than anything, I needed to sit in the privacy of my room, finish this call, clear my head, and *think.*

"Come on," I whispered, jiggling and pushing until the door finally broke free.

As it swung open, I stepped inside, startled when my foot caught on something—something big and warm and lying on the floor. Before I could stop myself, I was falling. My knees and hands hit the ground as the phone shot from my pocket and skittered across the room. I turned to see what had tripped me and gasped. It was Kiki, lying on the floor, her eyes closed, her face covered with blood.

Trying not to scream, I turned back around, and that's when I saw him, a man standing across the room dressed in black and wearing a ski mask. At his feet was my open cell phone.

Without a word, he reached down with a gloved hand and gave the phone a push so that it slid back across the room to me.

"Finish your conversation and hang up," he said softly, his voice menacing and unfamiliar. "Don't do anything stupid."

I swallowed hard, trying to find my voice. Slowly, I picked up the phone, weighing my options.

"Anna?" Lydia's voice was saying over the phone line. "Anna, are you still there? Please do not be too upset. I do not know why anyone would go to such desperate measures to find you after all these years. I just wanted you to know that someone might call you."

I tried to reply, but my voice was lost somewhere deep in my throat. I swallowed again, watching with wide eyes as the man pointed a gun straight at me.

"Anna? Are you there?" Lydia persisted. "I'm sorry, but I suppose it is possible that someone might even come looking for you."

I cleared my throat and took a deep breath.

"You may be right about that," I said finally into the receiver. "More than you know."

With the man's gun still pointed toward me, I somehow managed to conclude my call, promising the distraught and confused Lydia that I'd be in touch as soon as possible. As I disconnected, I wondered if I was cutting off the one chance I had to scream for help and be heard. Then again, how could she possibly help me from an Amish farm three thousand miles away?

"Who are you?" I asked as I put the phone in my pocket and tried not to sound as scared as I felt. "What have you done?"

Instinctively, I reached for Kiki's wrist and felt for a pulse, which was faint but still there. Turning my attention to her face,

I pushed back her hair to find the source of the bleeding. I expected to see a bullet wound, but instead it looked more like a gash, the result of being hit in the head by something hard and sharp edged, probably the butt of his gun.

"Your friend didn't want to cooperate," the man said. "Maybe you can learn by her example."

He took a step closer, and as he did, I stood, anger and adrenaline pumping through my veins.

"What do you want?"

"I think you know what I want," he replied, his eyes boring into me through the holes in the ski mask. "I'm here for the rubies. The whole set."

"The *rubies*? What rubies?"

He took another step toward me, with something like excitement flashing in his eyes.

"The Beauharnais Rubies. I know you have them."

He might as well have asked me for the Hope Diamond or the Crown Jewels. I had no rubies in my possession—and no idea what he was even talking about.

"I don't know what you mean," I said

earnestly, stepping backward and nearly tripping again over Kiki's body. "I drive a car that's held together by duct tape. I have less than a hundred dollars in my checking account. Do you really think I'd be living this way if I had something as valuable as rubies?"

"Who knows why anyone lives as they do?" he replied. "Get them. Now."

"This is crazy," I said, shaking my head. "You're crazy. You have the wrong person, the wrong house."

He spoke evenly, cocking his gun.

"Your name is Annalise Bailey Jensen, currently going by the name of Anna Bailey. You are the sister of Robert 'Bobby' Jensen, the daughter of Charles Jensen and a descendant of Peter and Jonas and Karl Jensen, among others. I'm in the right house, and you're the right person. Now hand them over." Whoever this guy was, he knew more about my family tree than I did. But what he was asking for was ridiculous. I had never owned any rubies—and doubted I ever would.

Looking around, I tried to decide what my chances would be if I made a run for it. He was tall and looked strong under the form-fitting black shirt—though the ski mask could become a bit of an impediment. Unfortunately, as he spoke his steps had closed much of the gap between us.

"I'll ask you one more time, and then I'll have to get serious," he said, coming to a stop in front of me and resting the gun barrel against my temple. "Where . . . are . . . the . . . rubies?"

Our eyes met and held. At that moment, Kiki let out a small whimper, stirring on the ground between us.

That was enough to make him glance down for just a second. In a flash, I reached out and pulled the bottom of his mask downward, so that the eye holes were somewhere around his chin. Afraid he would start shooting blind, I turned around and dove low through the door and then rolled toward the stairs.

By the time I got to my feet and was halfway down the stairs, one explosive shot had rung out and he was just bursting through the bedroom doorway himself, mask on straight and eyes blazing.

I reached the bottom two and three steps at a time, hesitating only for a moment at the sight of the front door. That way was closer, with a greater chance of spotting someone outside who might help me. Still, I made the decision to run to the back door, pausing long enough to knock down chairs and a small table behind me as I went, in the hopes of slowing him down.

I was fast, but he was faster. By the time I was through the living room and the kitchen and had reached the back door, I could feel him grab for the back of my T-shirt, catch hold for a moment, and then lose his grip. Shouting for help, I flung open the door, ran onto the porch and turned immediately to the right, jumping over the most rotten section of boards. Directly behind me, just as I hoped, the man made the mistake of stepping in exactly the wrong spot. With a resounding crash, one hard step broke through the porch floor and sent him falling into the crawl space below.

I had known that if my little plan worked, it would buy me some time to get away while he struggled back out of the depths. What I hadn't counted on was that his gun would go flying as he fell, and that I would be able to recover it from where it landed on the sand.

It wasn't until I was standing on the side

of the porch, gun pointed down at the hole, that my hands began to shake. Soon my entire body was trembling so fiercely that I was afraid I might drop the gun.

"Freeze or I'll shoot," I yelled, meaning it.

"Help me," the man cried in a wavering voice. "Please!"

I thought he was trying to trick me somehow, but when I leaned slightly forward to peer down at him, I saw why he was so upset. His right leg had been impaled on what looked like a jagged piece of rebar.

"Don't move or you might bleed to death," I told him, reaching for the cell phone in my pocket. "I'm not kidding."

I managed to dial 911 and sound fairly coherent as I explained the situation, leaving out only the strange bit about the rubies. I ended by describing the intruder's painful predicament and saying I was now in possession of the gun, and it didn't look as though this guy, whoever he was, was going anywhere.

"Tell him not to move," the operator said as she activated emergency services.

"She said don't move," I repeated, feeling guilty for the satisfaction in my words.

Once I was assured police and ambulances were on the way, I hung up the phone, bent forward at the waist, and put my hands on my knees, trying to catch my breath. I wanted to run upstairs and check on Kiki, but I didn't dare leave my prisoner here alone, impaled leg or not. I had seen too many scary movies to know that the moment the bad guy was down and the heroine thought she was safe, that's when he would spring back to life and nearly do her in.

"Anna? Hey, Anna!"

I turned to see one of our neighbors striding briskly across the sand, a retired old gentleman from two houses down whom everyone called "Colonel." I'd always thought that was his nickname because he bore a striking resemblance to the face on the bucket of fried chicken, but at that moment I could only hope he had earned it in the military instead.

"What's all the ruckus? Was that a gunshot I heard?"

I tried to tell him what happened, but as soon as I started explaining, I burst into tears. Somehow, through my hysterical babbling, he was able to put two and two together. Drawing himself up to his full height, clad in a T-shirt and Bermuda shorts with black socks and sandals, he took the gun from my trembling hand and assured me the cavalry was near and the situation was under control.

"Cover your ears," he added. Then, to my surprise, he pointed the gun toward the sky and pulled the trigger.

Within seconds, several of his cronies came spilling off of his deck and heading our way across the sand.

"The Screaming Eagles of the Hundred and First Airborne at your service," he said with a salute. I was so relieved, I planted a big, teary kiss right on his cheek.

"Can you keep this guy prisoner until the police and ambulance get here?" I asked, wiping my damp cheeks with the back of my hand.

"We stood at Bastogne in the Battle of the Bulge. I think we can handle a burglar with a stick through his leg," the Colonel said, reaching out and removing the ski mask from the man's head. The face his action revealed was sweating and flushed red under greasy black hair. I didn't recognize the guy, though I studied his features now to make sure I'd never forget him again.

"Thank you, Colonel," I whispered.

Tears still streaming down my face, I gave a grateful wave to the advancing troops and went inside, desperate to see if Kiki was still alive.

When I reached the bedroom, I knelt down at her side, noting that she hadn't moved and that the pool of blood surrounding her head had grown. I again pushed back her hair, revealing a face that seemed unnaturally pale.

Hands trembling, I gently lifted her wrist and felt for a pulse, but this time I wasn't quite sure if I could feel one or not. I leaned forward, my tears dropping into her hair, and begged her to hang on just a little longer. Despair clenched at my insides, and I felt sick at the thought that once again someone might die because of me.

Not knowing what else to do, I got up and crossed the hall to her bedroom, the obvious site of their primary struggle. With a wave of nausea, I looked at the mess surrounding me, realizing that all those noises I'd heard while I was on the phone with

Lydia were the sounds of Kiki trying to fend off a madman.

Remembering that madman, I went to her back window and opened it, leaning out into the bright sunshine to see what was happening below. Obviously, the old guys had the situation well under control. In fact, they seemed positively energized, pacing back and forth on the sand and taking turns holding the gun on the prisoner. One of them had run home to grab a camera, and I watched as he creakily lumbered back across the sand, waving it in the air. Seeing that, I pulled myself in and closed the window, hoping that those would be the only photographs taken here today. After all I had done to disappear and start over, I couldn't take the chance that the media might somehow get hold of my image and blow my hard-won privacy right out of the water. Worse, I didn't even want to think how they would twist this situation around.

When the police and emergency services arrived soon after, it was to find me sitting beside Kiki, holding her hand and crying. The paramedics were gentle but efficient, checking her out and then stabilizing her, all the while assuring me she was indeed still alive—for now. Once she was loaded up in the ambulance and it had driven away—followed closely behind by the one carrying our injured intruder—I was able to let out my breath. I pulled myself together, went into the living room, and sat on the couch, ready to answer the policemen's questions. I tried not to look at the mess that had been made when I knocked things over in an attempt to slow down my attacker.

The detective in charge wore a neatly pressed suit, its smooth surfaces providing a stark contrast to his wrinkled and weatherworn face. He introduced himself as Detective Hernandez, and he seemed professional and compassionate as he questioned me. Jotting down notes on a small pad as we talked, he had me go through the scenario over and over, pausing each time to verify exactly what the intruder had said to me. When the detective asked me how to spell "Beauharnais," I replied I had no idea.

"B-o-r-n-a-y-s?" I suggested. "Really, I

don't know. I've never heard that term before."

He seemed to take me at my word, and for a brief moment I felt guilty for being less than honest in the beginning, when I had given him my fake name rather than the real one. But then I thought of other policemen in the past, ones who were far less compassionate, less trusting, and my heart hardened. This man had all the information he needed.

As Detective Hernandez and I were talking, I glimpsed through the window a news van pulling up in front of the house, probably tipped off by one of the Screaming Eagles who wanted his heroic moment to make the twelve o'clock news. Seeing my expression, the detective turned to look. I watched over his shoulder as the van pulled to a stop between two police cars.

"Can you make them go away?" I asked softly.

He turned back toward me and shrugged.

"I can keep them off the property, but I can't stop them from doing a report."

Heart pounding, I considered the situation in full as I watched a sharply dressed woman hop out of the passenger seat of the van. She was their on-air reporter, no doubt.

"Is there a problem?" Detective Hernandez asked me, sounding vaguely suspicious.

Summoning my nerve, I turned my attention from the scene outside to the man in front of me.

"I'm a former . . . celebrity," I said, using the term loosely. "You know how embarrassing it can be when someone who was, um, famous in their youth gets caught on the news as an adult. Especially living in this ramshackle old house . . ." Glancing over his shoulder, I spotted the driver opening the back of the van and pulling out camera equipment.

"I knew it!" the detective replied softly, grinning as he searched my face. "I knew you looked familiar. Who were you? I mean, *are* you? Who are you? You were on some sitcom, right?"

"I went by a different name back then," I answered truthfully.

"Let's see. If you were just a kid . . . What was it. *The Facts of Life*? *Growing Pains*?"

"Please, help me out, okay? Right now

the last thing I need is to be on the TV news."

"Mork and Mindy? The Cosby Show? Doogie Howser?"

"Please?"

He seemed to consider my request, and then he finally snapped his notebook closed.

"No problem," he told me. "I think we're done here anyway."

To my vast relief, he took charge, stepping outside to steer the news crew to the back porch. As they went, he came inside and rounded up his men, who also seemed ready to go.

"I'll tell the news crew to get out of here once they're done filming the old guys," he said, handing me his business card. "Call me if you think of anything else related to this case."

"Will do. Can you thank the Colonel and his friends for me? Tell them I'm too distraught to come outside and thank them myself just now."

"No problem."

I waited as he gathered his things and then walked him to the front door, thanking him again for everything.

"Just doing our job, ma'am," he winked, but as he stepped outside, he gave it one more try. "*One Day at a Time*? *Family Ties*? *Gimme a Break*?"

"Yeah, give me a break," I echoed, closing the door behind him before he could realize it was a request, not the answer to his question.

With the door locked and bolted, I headed upstairs to change into a shirt and slacks. I wasn't sure how long the crew might be filming, but I thought I could seize the window of opportunity to slip out the front door and get away from here unseen. The paramedics had told me which hospital they were taking Kiki to.

I just hoped I would get there before it was too late.

FOUR

STEPHANIE

November 14, 1828

My Dearest Son,

It is with the greatest of urgency that I write to you.

With the appearance of this package today, I can assume that your adoptive parents have now informed you of the identity of your true parentage. In my original agreement with them, this news was to be withheld until the date of your eighteenth birthday. However, circumstances have dictated that I act now, despite the fact that you are only sixteen. I apologize to you and the Jensens for not waiting until the established date, though given recent events in Nuremburg, I feel certain that they understand the need for expediency. Surely a young man of sixteen is old enough to digest and comprehend all of this information.

In any event, the shocking news your guardians have given you about your rightful parentage is true. Enclosed you will find proof, including your *geburtszeugnis*, as well as the listings from the *Adelsmatrikel* and from the *Almanach de Goth*. Please note that in both the *Adelsmatrikel* and the *Almanach de Goth* you are listed without name, as "son, stillborn." This deception was necessary at the time, as I am sure you will come to understand. In addition, I have included the guardianship agreement I conducted in secrecy with the Jensens three days before you were born.

Also enclosed is one perfect pair of ruby-and-diamond earrings. Until now these earrings have been kept in the royal vault along with the other six pieces that comprise the full set of the Beauharnais Rubies, a gift given to me by Napoleon upon the occasion of your birth. I send these earrings to you as proof of their provenance and yours, and as proof of my sincerity. Please keep them hidden in a safe place until such time as you can return to the palace and rejoin them with the full set. On that day, I shall put on these jewels for the first time since receiving them and wear them with pride, standing beside you, my son, as you assume your rightful place in a long line of nobility. Only then will the true heir be known and the evil plottings and actions of your stepgrandmother and her son will be brought to light.

Please be in readiness, as I will summon you at the appropriate time.

With deep and abiding love,
Your mother, SdB

FIVE

ANNA

My brain was so addled by my encounter with the intruder, the subsequent questioning by the police, and the appearance of the media that I was almost to the hospital before it dawned on me to contact Kiki's mother, a spry little septuagenarian who lived nearby. I called her on my cell phone as I turned into the parking garage, and she arrived at the hospital so quickly that she almost beat me to the reception desk. Together we waited for news of Kiki, and we were finally told that she was conscious but resting and that they had given her twelve stitches to the scalp. They were still awaiting the results of her CAT scan, but the preliminary diagnosis was a grade 3 concussion. She had also lost a lot of blood. According to the nurse, they would probably keep her overnight for observation and to give her a transfusion, and then release her to go home tomorrow.

When we learned that only blood relatives would be allowed in to see her, I was actually relieved. Overwhelmed with guilt for what had happened, I wasn't sure if I could face Kiki just yet. I kept thinking about how she had struggled for her life upstairs while I was right there, downstairs, talking on the phone. Why hadn't I realized something was wrong? That man was there for me. Whatever he wanted, it was my fault he had come, my fault Kiki was now in the hospital.

Feeling sick at heart, I told Kiki's mother to give her my love, and then I left and made my way to the car. My steps were heavy and slow, tears threatening behind my eyes. Could I ruin any more lives than I already had? Was I destined to be a danger to everyone who knew me? I took a deep, shaky breath and tried to calm down. Once I got in the car, I forced myself to sit there for a few minutes, soaking in the warmth and the silence until my emotions were under control. I could keep the tears at bay if I tried hard enough, but the guilt wasn't going anywhere. Kiki had been nothing but a loyal friend to me, and in return I had never entrusted her with the truth about my past, had never told her who I really was. The only person out here who knew that was Norman, our supervisor at work, and only because he figured it out himself, not because I had told him.

Thinking of Norman, I knew he would be wondering where Kiki and I were, but I'd rather tell him what had happened to her in person than have him see it on television or hear it over the phone. I decided to go to the office. If I really did need to search for my brother the computers there were far better for that than my little laptop at home.

I started up the car and headed out of the parking garage, remembering the day Norman and I first met, seven years ago, when I showed up at the office in answer to a want ad, one that had said "Experience preferred but not required." Our interview had gone very well and Norman wanted to hire me, but being the skip tracer that he was, he couldn't in good conscience do so without first figuring out why certain parts of my application didn't add up. As an old pro up against a rank amateur, it hadn't taken long for him to trace out my real identity. Now he was the only person out here who knew the truth, who understood that Anna Bailey was really Annalise Bailey Jensen, a member of the notorious group that the press had once dubbed the "Dreiheit Five."

Eleven years ago, the media had made us out to be nothing less than monsters, when in fact what we were was a group of reckless teenagers who had made a stupid mistake, accidentally setting fire to an Amish farmhouse. That fire ended up killing a mother and father and their newborn child—and leaving the couple's other five children as orphans. Though we had been tormented by the press and convicted by the courts, at least the Amish community had forgiven us. Still, all the forgiveness in the world didn't change the fact that because we were careless and foolish, lives were lost. Norman knew that, and yet he had been willing to offer me the job anyway, saying everyone deserved another chance in life.

I got a hunch about you, kid, he had told me at the end of our second interview. *Considering how hard you tried to hide your own paper trail, I bet you got a special gift for this kind of work. You'll do fine.*

And I had, I thought as I turned onto the main road. I had done just fine here. My job didn't pay very well, but I loved it anyway, loved the folks I worked with, loved the challenge of being a skip tracer, of tracing down people who were missing.

Merging into traffic, I headed downtown. I tried dialing Lydia's number several times as I drove, feeling bad that I'd had to cut her off so abruptly before. She didn't answer, so when I reached the office I gave up for the time being, found an empty spot in the employee parking lot, and made my way into the building and through a familiar maze of corridors toward our department. In the metropolis that was Kepler-West Finance, the room where Kiki and Norman and I worked was definitely located on the wrong side of the tracks. Far from the shiny front entrance or the sleek administrative wing, our tiny section was tucked away on a lower level in an interior corridor with no windows or natural light. Still, what we lacked in ambiance we made up for in efficiency and effectiveness. Our trio functioned like a well-oiled machine, with Norman at the helm, me doing most of the computer work, and Kiki doing most of the footwork. In the seven years I had worked there, we had traced everything from criminal-level bail jumpers to absconding millionaires—but I never thought I'd be hunting down my own brother.

Norman was fighting with the coffee machine when I appeared in the doorway, but when he saw my face he seemed to forget all about it and focused on me instead. Obviously, he could tell something was wrong.

Fortunately, we were there by ourselves and could talk. I told him what had happened, glad at least that this time I was able to get through it without crying. He listened intently, asking questions when necessary, handing me a box of tissues when I was finished.

"I'm all right," I said, giving the box back.

"I'm not," he said, pulling out a tissue and blowing his nose. "Poor Kiki! She's over in the hospital right now, when it just as easily could have been the morgue!"

I let him pace and moan for a bit, grateful he was the kind of person who deeply, truly cared. While he recovered, I fixed the coffeemaker and started a pot going, and then I made a cup just the way he liked it, with lots of cream and two packets of sweetener. I needed to tell him that beyond dealing with the morning's break-in, there was also the matter of a family emergency I needed to handle. As I gave him his coffee, he offered me the day off, saying he felt sure I needed it after such a traumatic morning. I replied I would appreciate that a lot, especially if I could stay here in the office for a while first and use the computer to handle a personal matter.

"Whatever you need," he said, taking a seat at his desk. "Just let me know if you want any help."

"Thanks, boss. Actually, I'd like to pick your brain for a minute, if you don't mind."

Rolling a chair over to his desk, I told him the rest of the story, about my missing brother and everything Lydia had said. He listened intently, nodding once in a while and jotting down a few notes. He made me go through the attack again as well, but when I got to the part about what the intruder said, he stopped writing and looked up at me.

"What kind of rubies?" he asked.

"He pronounced it 'bor-nays rubies.' Does that mean anything to you? Have you ever heard that term before?"

Norman shook his head, contemplating. "If he brought up your family tree like that, though, it must be something that was passed down through the generations."

"Yeah, but I don't think he had the right family tree. He got my brother and father right, but then he named people I've never heard of. Peter? Jonas? Karl? I don't know who these men are. He must have me confused with someone else."

"How far back have you traced your roots?"

"What do you mean?"

"Ancestry, genealogy, all of that. Do you even know the names of your great-grandparents or your great-great-grandparents?"

I shook my head, realizing he had a

point. How could I be sure these names weren't connected with me if I didn't know anything beyond a few generations?

"Have you spoken to your parents? They might be able to help," Norman suggested.

"My parents are on vacation right now. I wouldn't even know how to reach them."

"Don't they have cell phones?"

I explained that the phones wouldn't work where they were right now, that my parents were avid bird-watchers and were currently on a three-week hike across New Zealand, pursuing Yellow-Nosed Mollymawks and Wedge-Tailed Shearwaters.

"Are they scientists?"

"No," I replied, adding that once my dad took early retirement, his favorite hobby of bird-watching had become an obsession. Ever the good sport, my mother indulged him as best she could, though when he announced his plans for this trip, she nearly beaned him with his own binoculars. "His idea won out, but next year he has to go with her to a scrapbooking convention."

"Well, then, talk to your eldest living relative, a grandparent maybe," Norman persisted. “Sometimes people are surprised by the wealth of information that old folks carry around in their head. You could sit and talk with a great-grandmother for example and learn all sorts of things about *her* great-grandmother—and much of the rest of the family too.”

I thought about that, slowly shaking my head. On my father’s side, there were no old folks left. My great-grandparents were long dead by the time I was born, my grandmother died of cancer when I was twelve, and my grandfather had passed just a year after that from an aortic aneurism. I told Norman as much, and he suggested I do a little genealogical work of my own anyway. He was convinced that the Beauharnais Rubies were some sort of family heirloom, and if I traced back the family tree I should be able to find the point at which they had probably been handed down to some other branch.

“What do you want to bet some distant cousin is running around in those rubies right now, while you’re the one getting attacked by mistake?”

“Maybe so.”

“Or, for all you know, the man who showed

up at your house this morning *is* a distant cousin, one who thinks you got the rubies instead of him! No telling what the whole story is, but I think this would be the best place to start. You might also get a lot more information once the police have had a chance to interrogate the guy."

That was true, though I knew it might take a while before he was out of surgery and coherent enough to be interrogated. In the meantime, I decided to focus on finding my brother. Considering the timing, his disappearance and my break-in were likely related somehow.

I thanked Norman and rolled back to my desk. From there I opened several different applications on my computer and then dialed the number of the phone shanty yet again. Lydia answered this time, apologizing that she hadn't been able to hear the phone before. I apologized as well for taking so long to get back to her, but for the sake of time I didn't recount the morning's trauma in full; I simply gave her an abbreviated version. Mostly, I wanted to know if she'd ever heard of the Beauharnais Rubies, but she sounded as clueless as I was.

"Any word yet from Bobby?" I asked, changing the subject.

"No, Anna. Is like he simply disappeared from the face of the earth."

"He's out there somewhere," I said, "but if I'm going to hunt him down, I need all of your personal account numbers, including his Social Security number."

"*Yah,* I can do that. I still have the box of our important papers."

She promised to call me back in a few minutes, so while I waited I began Googling the term "Beauharnais Rubies." I tried every spelling I could think of—bornays, barnhaze, bernaze, bernais—but no matter what entry I typed in, it came back with nothing even remotely relevant. Whatever that man had wanted, I sure wasn't going to figure it out easily.

When Lydia called back with the information, I pulled up my usual skip tracing form, thinking I might as well go about this in my standard, systematic way, even if it was my own brother I was looking for. As always, I began by entering "known data." Of course, the form didn't ask for the things I *did* know, such as how Bobby loved the way his son Isaac's hair reflected a million shades of reddish brown in the sun, or how he much he enjoyed hanging out with his Amish buddy who trained race horses, speeding around the track on horseback at breakneck speed. Instead, the form wanted data I didn't know so well, such as any current and former mailing addresses, his credit history, his job title. These things I got from Lydia, who read them off from the papers one by one.

It wasn't that Bobby and I didn't keep up with the basics, I thought as I typed in a credit card number. He and I usually spoke on the phone once or twice a month, and I was always bugging him to get a computer at home so we could communicate more often via email. But after the fire and all that happened in its wake, my brother and I had stopped talking about unimportant stuff, such as job titles and life facts, and tended more often to discuss feelings and thoughts.

When you share a tragedy that way, you find yourself living a different sort of bond.

Once Lydia had given me every piece of information she could find, I thanked her and told her I would call back in about an hour, hopefully with some good news, though deep inside I feared it may be the opposite. My main concern was that the man who broke into my house this morning had confronted my brother in a similar manner last night—but that Bobby hadn't managed to escape from him the way I had. With that thought in mind, I started my trace by calling the Lancaster and Chester County, Pennsylvania, hospitals, morgues, and police stations to see if they had encountered anyone matching Bobby's description, dead or alive. The answer was no across the board, so after I had exhausted every possible avenue of that sort, I turned to the data Lydia had given me and began running credit card checks.

What I found was both interesting and confusing. Judging by his expenditures, Bobby's day-to-day life, financially speaking, was so predictable, so simple, it was boring just to read about it. Late last night, however, all sorts of strange activity had suddenly taken place with his accounts. From what I could tell, between the hours of ten and eleven p.m., Bobby had made strange ATM withdrawals, rented a car, bought an airline ticket—to Las Vegas of all places—and changed his name, address, and contact information on various bills and accounts all over the map. Either his identity had been stolen and someone else had done all this, or Bobby had done it himself in an attempt to obscure his path and disappear. In my expert opinion, the types of things that had been done seemed to indicate the latter.

While this maze of hits and misses left me baffled and confused, it also made me feel hopeful. If these transactions were really conducted by Bobby himself, then at least I could conclude that his disappearance had been self-orchestrated. I still didn't know why he would have done such a thing, but at least that was better than learning he had been the victim of a crime and was lying somewhere unconscious with no one around to help him.

"Bobby, what's going on?" I whispered, trying to put myself into his mind-set, wondering what he would do if he found himself in some kind of trouble. Running possibilities around and around in my mind, I initiated an ISP search so that at least I could find the computer of origin, the place where he had been sitting when he made all of those strange computer maneuvers last night.

As in any good skip trace, diligence and careful research would win out in the end. At least that was what I told myself as I pressed onward, my fingers flying across the keyboard, my heart inching toward despair.

SIX

Some digging was required, but in the end it turned out that Bobby had done all of his online activity from an Internet café in Exton, Pennsylvania, last night between ten and eleven p.m. That at least locked him in to a specific place and time. Just to be sure the person at the keyboard had been him and not someone else, I contacted the café and spoke to the manager, who was very accommodating. She had been on duty last night, and she distinctly remembered a man coming in around ten and staying for about an hour. According to her, the guy was "really good looking," in his early thirties, with curly brown hair and green eyes. She said he had bought a black coffee with an extra shot of espresso, but he was already so tense she couldn't imagine why he needed it.

"I thought about talking him out of it," she said, "like a bartender refusing to serve a drunk, you know? But I figured it was none of my business."

"Was he alone?"

"Far as I could tell. He went outside to use the pay phone a couple times, though."

Bobby didn't own a cell phone, so I felt sure that was how he had called Lydia to tell her that she and Isaac were in danger and that they should go to the farm. But danger from what? From whom? Despite his flurry of subterfuge, what was this all adding up to, anyway? Now that I knew he wasn't lying on the ground somewhere hurt and alone, I kept glancing at the clock, feeling more and more stupid for wasting several hours on a fruitless hunt for what was likely nothing more than some temporary domestic drama that would soon play itself out with or without my help. It wouldn't have been in character for him, but maybe my brother had created the whole "danger" thing as a ruse to buy himself time to get away from his wife.

If that's what was going on here, it wouldn't be the first time Bobby decided to drop off the face of the earth. Years ago, the day his parole ended, he had taken off and hitchhiked his way across the country. For a while it felt as though he had simply vanished, but somehow, eventually, he made his way back home, where he learned that Lydia still loved him and had been waiting for him all that time. They were married soon after, and as far as I knew, he had been a steadfast and very-present husband ever since.

I was about to take a break when the phone rang, startling me. Glancing at the screen, I saw that it was Lydia.

I hoped she was calling to say that Bobby had finally returned and all was well, but instead, as soon as she started talking, her voice caught in a sob.

"What's wrong, Lydia?"

"I just had a talk with Haley."

"Haley Brown?" Haley had been my best friend all through high school and was one of the Dreiheit Five, as was her husband, Doug. Once I moved away and started over, we had lost touch, but I knew I would always consider her a good friend, a member of that small group who shared the common bond of tragedy and its aftermath.

"*Yah.* I have been calling all around, to see if any of our friends have seen Bobby. When I called the Browns I got Haley. I think I found out more than I wanted to." She sobbed again, and I bit my lip, listening intently as she got herself under control and continued. "Haley said yes, that Bobby came to their house last night."

"That's good, actually. What time?"

"Around eleven thirty. Which means he went over there about an hour and a half after he called me the second time."

"Okay, so there's one piece of the puzzle," I said, making a note on the time line of my skip tracing form. The timing made sense: He had called Lydia at ten p.m. worked on the computer until eleven p.m., and then made it to Haley's house by eleven thirty. "Is that unusual for him to go over there that late? Are the four of you still friends? Don't you get together sometimes?"

"Sometimes, *yah,* if Doug wants to show off his new boat or his new motorcycle or his new jet ski, and then Bobby cannot get there soon enough. These men and their fast vehicles, *ach.* Give me a horse and buggy any day." Lydia was exaggerating, as I knew she had traded in her horse and buggy for a Volkswagen Beetle the day she left the Amish order to marry Bobby. "Anyway, while it might not be unusual for Bobby to go to the Browns' house, it was unusual for him to show up in the middle of the night, uninvited."

"They still live in Hidden Springs?"

"*Yah,* in that big fancy place Haley's father gave them. Anyway, Haley said that when Bobby got there, he was very agitated. Doug was not home yet, but Bobby did not even ask for him. He just knocked on the door and when Haley answered it, he said he needed to borrow some money, as much cash as she had on hand."

"Did he do that often? Borrow money from your rich friends?"

"Never," Lydia said emphatically, and then in a less certain tone she added, "that I know of, anyway."

"So what happened? Did she give him some money?"

"*Yah,* she told him to wait there and she went back to the bedroom safe and took out eight thousand dollars. *Ach,* imagine that. She had eight thousand dollars in cash in a box in her room!"

I didn't reply, but I knew that probably added up to a year's apartment rental for Lydia and Bobby. Not exactly pocket change.

"Anyway, she said he was so agitated she did not ask questions. She just told him to pay it back when he could. He said okay and thanks, and then he left."

"So why—"

"There is more. After he was gone, Haley glanced at the security cameras to watch him drive away—and instead she saw movement in the backyard. She said Bobby must have stolen the keys to Doug's motorcycle while she was getting the money from the safe, because as she watched on the security monitor, he went into the detached garage and took Doug's motorcycle. Then he rolled it out of the back gate."

"What? Bobby stole Doug's motorcycle?"

"Haley said she thought it was odd and just kind of curious, or maybe even funny, like a practical joke. She trusted that Bobby would bring it back eventually."

"But he hasn't brought it back yet?"

"No."

"Okay, so we've got an atypical encounter with a friend, a loan of cash, and a stolen motorcycle. Is that it?"

"No, there's more," she said, her voice growing more shaky again. "Haley said that Doug never came home last night. For a while, she thought maybe Bobby had taken the motorcycle for Doug, so that the two of them could sneak off on a late-night joyride. But then Doug did not come home and Bobby did not come back and finally she fell asleep, still waiting. By this morning, he had not shown up at all and she was furious."

"So now Doug is missing too?"

"No, Anna. Doug is not missing. Doug is dead."

Dead? That was not news I had expected to hear!

"Dead? How?"

From the corner of my eye, I could see

Norman turning my way. As Lydia answered me with a story about Doug's body having been discovered this morning on a construction site, apparently after having fallen quite a distance from a higher floor, I put a hand over the phone and whispered, "Not my brother. Someone else."

I made noises of sympathy over the phone, feeling oddly detached from the news that one of the members of our notorious little group was no longer among the living. Before the fire, Doug and I hadn't been all that close. Back then, he only had eyes for Haley, whom he eventually married, and all my attentions were turned toward his friend Reed. After the fire, of course, going through the same nightmare of court appearances and testimonies and sentencing hearings, most of us grew much closer. Though I hadn't spoken to Doug in several years, I knew we had shared a strange kinship nonetheless. Now he was dead. The selfish part of me, the part I was ashamed of, knew that this news would give the press yet another opportunity to trot out the old story of the Dreiheit Five and splash it across the latest issues of countless tabloids, newspapers, and magazines just as they had done eleven years ago.

Back then, the story of the Dreiheit Five was too good to let go, too full of potential, so the media had continued to exploit it, over and over, for far too long. What should have remained for the most part local news caught the interest of the nation, probably because the victims had been Amish. After that, no matter what we did or where we went, photos of our five faces—Reed's, Doug's, Bobby's, Haley's, and mine—began showing up in the tabloids, on the covers of newsmagazines, on the front pages of the newspapers. Quickly, we went from being five friends who were hanging around one night and made a tragic mistake to the focus of articles like "Wild Teen Party Turns Tragic, Kills Amish Family." The press's version of events wasn't at all true, but it made for great headlines. Now those headlines would be back. In an effort to cover Doug's death and funeral from every possible angle, the press would no doubt hound us all and ruin our recovered lives just to sell a few more issues.

Trying not to think about that for now, I decided that Doug's death had a number of implications, none of them good. I took a deep breath, trying to organize my thoughts and figure out how Doug's death related to Bobby's disappearance—and what stealing a motorcycle had to do with it. Norman was hovering nearby, whispering an offer to help, so I asked Lydia to hold on for a minute.

"Sure," I said to Norman gratefully, jotting down the make, model, and plate number of Bobby's car on a slip of paper. Handing it to him, I asked him to run a trace on the vehicle and see if it had been wrecked or towed or involved in any sort of accident last night. My thinking was that at least a car crash would explain the need for alternative transportation—and it would give us another piece of the puzzle, pinpointing Bobby in a specific time and place. While Norman ran the vehicle search, I returned to my conversation with Lydia, asking her if she and Isaac were still safe.

"*Yah.* Nathaniel and Caleb, they have to milk the cows and work the fields, so they asked a neighbor to come and stay with us.

That neighbor brought his son and brother and cousin, so we are well protected."

"What about all of their cows and their fields?"

"They do not work farms, they have jobs in town. Today is their day off, so they come here to watch over us."

And that, in a nutshell, was what it was like to be a part of an Amish community. *You need help? You need me to come over and stand watch for you? On my one day off this week when I had a million and one things to do and all sorts of plans? No problem. I'm there.* That was one of the things I had always respected most about the Amish. They cared. They filled needs in their community, even at the cost of tending to their own individual needs.

"Do they get in trouble, hanging around with you?"

"Why?"

"Because you left the order and all. Aren't they supposed to limit socializing with you?"

"Anna, you know I was not shunned. I chose to leave the order before baptism."

"But your family—"

"My family is to be in the world, not of the world. They are to limit contact with me, *yah,* but not cut it off completely. And if their friends and neighbors are willing to do me and my son a favor, they will do it. That is the Amish way. You know that."

I did know that. In the year following the fire, I had the opportunity to see and experience the Amish community at work, up close and personal. Their grace in action ended up being one of the few positive elements to come out of the entire experience.

Taking a deep breath, I gathered the papers that were spread on my desk in front of me and decided to tell Lydia what I had learned so far about Bobby's activities from last night. When I described the strange series of online actions he had taken at the Internet café, she sounded as perplexed as I was, especially when I mentioned the reservation to Las Vegas. Trying to find a reason for that flight, I asked Lydia if Bobby ever gambled, but she said absolutely not. In answer to my questions, she also insisted that they did not have any friends in Nevada and that Bobby had never gone there before, not for a convention or a jaunt with the guys or anything.

"And you're sure he doesn't have a secret gambling problem?" I persisted.

"I am certain he does not. We have never even gone to Atlantic City, which is much closer than Las Vegas."

"No missing money or hidden bank accounts or pawnshop tickets showing up in his pockets?"

This time she was quiet for a moment.

"Lydia? What is it?"

"I . . . I did find a ticket from a Harrisburg pawnshop in one of his pockets when I did the laundry. But I do not think that it has to do with gambling. He has just been very . . . thrifty lately. When I asked him about the ticket, he said that the high cost of gas has been hurting our budget, and so he pawned some things to help make ends meet." She went on to list the sorts of things he had pawned: his old trumpet, a power drill, some candlesticks that had been a wedding present. Lydia said she hadn't noticed the items were missing because they had all come from the storage locker in the basement of their apartment building.

"Hmm," I said, not sure how to reply. Obviously, Bobby had been keeping something from Lydia, otherwise he would have told her about the pawnshop voluntarily, rather than waiting until he got busted. "How about your cousin, the one who trains race horses? Any chance he's been acting as a bookie on the side, taking bets on those horses?"

"I am not sure what a 'bookie' is, but Silas is as honest a man as they come. Bobby does not have an interest in betting over horses anyway. He just likes to go fast—on almost anything. Fast cars, fast horses, fast motorcycles, whatever gives him good speed. He is your brother, Anna. You know this about him. Even as a boy, he loved to ride his bike as fast as he could down the hills here, remember?"

I did remember.

Norman was waving at me to get my attention, so I asked Lydia to hold on.

"I ran the plates," Norman told me, "but your brother's car hasn't been seen, cited, or recovered in the last twenty-four hours."

I thanked him for his help, and as he returned to his computer, I thought of what my next step should be. I had done the basic skip trace from behind my computer. There were still other avenues to pursue, of course, from exploring complications at Bobby's job to probing his various hobbies and interests and contacts. This was usually where Kiki took over, doing the kind of investigating that required a lot of face-to-face contact, pounding the pavement, watching for clues. She was so good at that sort of thing, not just because she was smart and observant, but also because she came across to other people as nonthreatening and disarming. Given her age and gender and personality, she was a natural at eliciting information.

I, on the other hand, was much more comfortable with a computer screen than I was with people. It wasn't that I was shy; it was just that I was always on my guard, always waiting for someone to recognize me, always ready to bolt if they got that curious look on their face and asked me if we'd ever met before. Still, given the current situation, I couldn't see that I had any choice. Now that I had done all I could to solve this riddle from my office here in

California, the next obvious step was to go to Pennsylvania and try to pick up Bobby's trail from there.

My heart heavy, I said as much to Lydia now. She jumped right on it, obviously relieved and eager for my on-site help.

"You are welcome to stay at the farm with my family," she assured me. "I know you can find him more easily if you are here, Anna. More than that, I worry that danger may eventually come your way too, now that someone has your contact information. You will likely be safer here."

I decided to be completely honest with her.

"Remember I told you I had a little run-in this morning?"

"*Yah.* Some man came to your house to ask for rubies?"

"Sort of. You have so much to worry about on your end that I didn't want to add to your problems, but if you want to know the whole story, he broke into my house, knocked my roommate unconscious, and threatened me with a gun. I'd say danger has already arrived."

That set her off on another bout of crying,

and once I got her calmed down, I told her I needed to go but I would call her back in exactly half an hour, after I had a chance to look at flight schedules and availability.

After I hung up the phone, I simply sat there in silence for a long time, closing my eyes and trying to accept the inevitable. I had no choice but to go home. My brother was in big trouble right now; I felt it to my bones. Whatever was happening with him, it wasn't good.

What do I do now, God? I prayed silently, knowing the obvious answer. *Go to Pennsylvania.*

I thought of my pitiful little savings account, hovering right around seven hundred dollars total, with nothing else in reserve except a hundred in checking and a single credit card with a three-thousand-dollar credit limit—one I never used except in the case of an extreme emergency.

I can't afford this, I reminded my heavenly Father, as if He needed reminding. More than that, my going back there would surely catch someone's eye, and soon the media would slam down on me full force. My new look and new life would be discovered—and no doubt destroyed.

Go to Pennsylvania anyway.

I thought once more of the Amish, of how they cared, how they filled needs in their community without thoughts of tending first to their own. Bobby was my community, my closest living relative, and he needed me. Somehow, he needed me.

"Okay, God," I whispered, a surge of emotion filling my eyes with tears. Despite everything, I would go back home and straighten things out. Wiping my eyes, I turned to my computer and began to check for flights to Philadelphia. This would be the first time I would return since I had fled seven years ago. With a sick feeling in the pit of my stomach, I just knew that by the time this was all over, everything I had done to make a break and start over was going to be for naught.

Fingers trembling, I was glad at least to find some cheap seats on a few red-eyes leaving tonight. I chose the flight that would connect in Vegas, so I would have a few minutes to do a little sleuthing there. After clearing some time off with Norman and getting his assurance that he would keep an eye on Kiki in my stead, I booked the flight and paid for it, and then I opened my email for the first time today, to send a general "I'll be out of town" note to my local friends.

I was so distracted by all I needed to do that I almost missed it. There in my list of incoming mail was an email from Bobby himself, sent to me at ten forty-two ET last night, with the subject line "Urgent." I opened the note, holding my breath as I read:

Hey, Bobanna,

Remember a while back when you said that if you could do one thing over again using the knowledge you have now, you'd do it differently? I'm following your advice. Please communicate accordingly.

Bobby

I sat back, swallowing hard. "Bobanna" was his nickname for me. That much of the note I understood. As for the rest, I couldn't have been more perplexed. One thing I could do over again? Knowledge I have now? I shook my head, trying to clear my brain.

Sadly, though he had sent me this urgent note and was counting on me to follow up with it, I didn't know what he was talking about. I didn't remember any such conversation. What did he mean?

I simply didn't have a clue.

SEVEN

I spent the next two hours wrapping up pending cases while Norman took a closer look at the reservation Bobby had made for a flight to Las Vegas. My boss had connections I didn't have—connections with transportation officials and airline employees that sometimes netted him information not available to the average skip tracer. I tried not to eavesdrop as he called in some favors on my behalf, but I couldn't help but notice the triumphant gleam in his eye when he finally hung up the phone.

"All right, kid. Pull up a chair and I'll

explain my theory. You said it looked like Bobby was intentionally trying to disappear. Stands to reason, then, that most of what he did on the Internet last night was to create a big, confusing mess that would be difficult to track back out. Right?"

"Right."

"All those account changes were for subterfuge and confusion, to buy time while he slipped out of town. Are you with me?"

"Yes."

"To my mind, the flight reservation and the rental car were also part of that subterfuge. He booked that flight to make it look like he went to Vegas, but in fact I don't believe he got on the plane."

The stuff Norman was giving me was like Skip Tracing 101, the most basic steps of How to Disappear.

"That was my thought too, at first," I replied. "But you're leaving out one important element: the ATM withdrawal. If Bobby didn't take that flight, then how did he manage to withdraw a hundred dollars from his checking account at an ATM machine in the Las Vegas airport this morning, twenty minutes after the flight landed?"

Norman narrowed his eyes and studied my face.

"If this were a stranger you were tracking, Anna, you'd know the answer to that question."

I sat and looked back at him for a long moment before realization dawned.

"Someone else is involved here," I whispered.

"Yes, that's my assumption. That other person was either on the flight and made the withdrawal on Bobby's behalf when they got off the plane, or they were already out in Vegas and just came to the airport at the right time and did it then. Either way, I don't think that withdrawal was made by your brother. I don't think he ever got on that airplane. I heard you asking your sister-in-law about Vegas and gambling and all of that, but I think you're wasting your time. He never went to Vegas."

I sat back and thought about the implications of a second person. I wanted to give my brother the benefit of the doubt, but the more I was learning, the harder that was becoming.

"According to my source at the airline," Norman continued, "your brother checked in the for the flight at the Philadelphia airport. That much is in the computer. What's not in the computer is that second verification, the one that pops up when a boarding pass is scanned in at the gate as the passengers are getting on the plane."

"So Bobby checked in at the departures desk but never made it onto the flight itself?"

"Exactly."

"What about heightened airport security and all of that? Aren't there rules now about airplanes not being able to take off if they're carrying luggage that doesn't directly correspond to a passenger?"

"That's the procedure, yeah. But Bobby didn't check any luggage. Apparently, he was carry-on only, so the flight was cleared for takeoff without him."

I thanked Norman for his hard work, my brain spinning. Maybe he was right. If this were a stranger I was tracking, I would have been thinking much more clearly and might have thought about things such as whether he had a girlfriend or if he was involved in illegal activity. But because it was Bobby, my much-needed on-the-job cynicism was missing from this pursuit. If you couldn't think the worst of someone, how could you ever make the mental leaps necessary for following their trail?

Returning to my own desk, I shut down my computer and cleared off my desk, ready to head out of town. There was one task left to do, so with a heavy heart I pulled out the card the detective had given me this morning and dialed the number on it.

When I told Detective Hernandez who was calling, his voice sounded oddly strained this time, and I soon realized why.

"You weren't on *Gimme a Break.* You weren't on any sitcom, were you? In fact, the reason you looked familiar isn't because you were a child star at all, but because you were notorious in a completely different way."

"I never said the words 'child star.' I just said that I was famous when I was younger. You made that leap yourself."

"Let's see," he continued, ignoring my protest, "we've got reckless endangerment . . . involuntary manslaughter . . . I've got your mug shot up on my screen right now. I seem to recall your face being all over the nightly news back then. I knew I had seen you before."

"That's not relevant to this."

"Oh, I think it is. At the very least, you might have mentioned all of this to me this morning, Ms. Bailey. Or, excuse me, Ms. Jensen."

"Why? That was in a different state, and it happened a long time ago."

"Still, considering the situation, knowing you have a police record might have helped."

Pulse surging, I felt a sudden rage build in my chest. When I spoke again, my words were even and firm.

"If you bothered to read that record, Detective Hernandez, you'd see that I was a juvenile when it happened. I got house arrest and probation. It's not as though I went to prison."

"Maybe not, but someone who tends to . . . omit . . . pertinent information and misrepresent themselves makes me nervous."

I rested my forehead in my hands and took a deep breath, feeling that old familiar rush of despair and claustrophobia that always came upon me when yet another person wouldn't give me the benefit of the doubt. It was hard enough to deal with the guilt I heaped upon myself, but I really didn't need other people adding to it—especially when they filtered in the press's ridiculous version of the events that occurred that fateful night so long ago.

"If you bothered to read any of the details of my arrest, you'd know I was not involved in a malicious criminal act. We were just a bunch of kids who were caught up in a terrible tragedy." He didn't reply, so I continued. "I was only seventeen when it all happened, but the minute I turned eighteen a month later and the press could legally reveal my name and image, I was done for. The press coverage was brutal and unrelenting. When that news van showed up at the house this morning, it felt like history was about to repeat itself. It's just my poor fortune that some random intruder chose my house to invade. The present situation has nothing to do with the past, and I was in no way obligated to tell you I had a record. Keep in mind, Detective, that this time I'm the victim here, not the criminal."

My face was burning hot by the time I finished my little speech, and I was surprised at the venom I heard in my own voice. I had worked hard to let the anger and resentment go, but now, when I was challenged, it was obvious there was still more angst buried deep inside. I wondered if I could ever rid myself of those old feelings entirely.

At least the detective backed off a bit after that, the tone of his voice growing less suspicious. Finally, I was able to get to the first reason I was calling, to find out where the situation stood with the intruder. Detective Hernandez said that the man had gone through surgery around noon and was currently resting. The doctors thought he would be kept there for a day or two, at which point, barring any medical complications, he would be released into police custody.

"Were you able to question him? Did you find out more about why he did it and what he wanted?"

"We ran his prints, but they didn't tell us anything. As far as questioning him, we've asked the questions, yes, but he's not answering. He knows he has the right to remain silent, and that's exactly what he's doing, for now at least. We'll be in a better position to interrogate him once he's in our custody."

"You should have talked to him when he was under anesthesia."

"Yeah, right. Try taking that into a courtroom."

I needed to go, and I wanted to end this call. For now I chose not to give Hernandez the news about my missing brother. Though Bobby's disappearance and my intruder might somehow be connected, I wanted Detective Hernandez to concentrate on my break-in as a single, isolated crime without unnecessarily clouding the issue. Considering his attitude about my police record, as soon as he heard that Bobby may in some way be involved, I knew he would jump to all the wrong conclusions.

Instead of mentioning Bobby, I just asked if the house was still a crime scene or if I would be allowed to straighten up and pack.

"We're all finished there—though you might see some yellow caution tape around the back porch because of the hole. You'll need to get that taken care of before someone else gets hurt."

"Will do."

When our excruciating phone call was over, I hung up, got out my purse, and turned to Norman, who had also neatened his desk and looked as though he was ready to leave. He was insisting that I let him come home with me, for safety's sake, and then also give me a ride to the airport. Knowing I needed help, I put up only a minor fuss but I didn't refuse.

We headed out, my car leading the way, and were at the beach house within twenty minutes.

As we parked our cars and walked to the door, it struck me that once Kiki understood the details of the situation, she might ask me to move out. I couldn't imagine what the impact of that would be for my life. Besides the fact that she was a great housemate—easygoing and fun and nonintrusive—I literally couldn't afford to live anywhere else. Except for this house and a small pension from her late husband, Kiki was as poor as I was, but she rented me one of the spare bedrooms for a pittance, and I made up the difference by doing most of the cooking and cleaning—an arrangement that had worked out well for both of us. Without that deal, I would be sunk for sure.

Trying not to think about that for now, I unlocked the front door and we stepped inside, though Norman insisted on going first. His posture rigid and ready, he checked out every room in the house, including the pantry and all closets. At his age, I doubted he could fend off a criminal if one popped up, but it was very sweet of him to look, nonetheless. When he spotted the bullet hole in the wall in my room, he let out a low whistle. I wasn't bothered by the bullet hole nearly as much as I was by the big bloodstain on the floor. Once Norman went downstairs, I quickly used bleach and rags to clean it as best I could.

I didn't have any idea how long I would be in Pennsylvania, so I threw together one suitcase's worth of clothes and shoes, toiletries, and a blow-dryer. I also packed up my laptop, taking the time to print a few pictures of Bobby first.

When I got downstairs, Norman was on

the phone. After he hung up, he explained that his son would be here first thing Saturday to fix the back porch, fill in the bullet hole upstairs, and replace the wood flooring in my bedroom that had been ruined by Kiki's blood. Before I could figure out how I was going to afford all that, Norman added that the labor would be free—though we could reimburse them for the supplies later, once Kiki's insurance claim went through, if we wanted to.

I thanked him profusely as I locked up the house and we carried my bags to the car. Driving toward the airport, Norman at the wheel, I tried calling Kiki at the hospital. I got her mother, who said that the CAT scan had come back normal except for a concussion, as expected, and that Kiki would be staying with her for a while after she got out of the hospital.

When I was finished with the call, I tucked away my phone and asked Norman to check on Kiki while I was gone and tell her about the house repairs.

Traffic was light, so the trip to the airport went smoothly. Norman and I said our farewells at the curb, and then I was on my own, checking my bags and making my way through security. By the time I reached the gate, I had an hour and a half to kill, which was good as there were a few things I needed to take care of before takeoff.

EIGHT

STEPHANIE

November 21, 1828

My Dearest Son,

I do not understand your reaction to the letter I sent to you. How can you refuse to participate in what is to be your absolute destiny? Royal blood flows through your veins, my child! It is your duty to put down your farm implements and take up the scepter very soon. Enclosed is another piece from the Beauharnais Rubies, this time the Coronet, as yet more proof of my devotion to the cause of restoring you to your rightful place.

You cannot know what was sacrificed for this moment! To impress this upon you, I am including with this letter pages written by my own hand sixteen years ago in the months before you were born. In reading my journal now, I see that I was a vain and frivolous girl, but my hope is that you will look beyond the trivialities to the love I held for you even before your birth, as well as come to understand why I made the decisions about you that I did.

This is not a mantle you can refuse! As you read the following entries, my hope is that you will understand that truth above all.

All my love,
SdB

JOURNAL
March 5, 1812

I fainted at court today, prompting Karl to summon the palace doctor. I told my husband not to worry, that no doubt my condition was caused by the unseasonably warm temperatures heightened by the new turban I wore. It was a gift from The Emperor, who says turbans are all the rage in Paris these days. I am not sure why, as I found the thing to be quite hot and uncomfortable—but I do love to be in fashion. And oh, how I miss Paris!

In any event, after a private conversation with the doctor and a modest examination, he has confirmed what I have been suspecting since January: I am with child again, likely due to give birth in the fall. Oh, how I hope to give Karl a son this time!

Princess Amelie is but nine months old today. Though her smile gives sunshine to me in this otherwise gloomy palace, her existence does little to secure my position or validate my marriage to Karl. Luise works hard to make certain I am not happy here, and I know she acts from jealousy and disdain.

Once I give birth to a male heir, all will change.

NINE

ANNA

Finding an empty area not far from my gate, I pulled out my cell phone and calculated the time in Pennsylvania. It was ten thirty p.m. on the East Coast, which would make a phone call at this hour rude but not ridiculous. I decided that one of my first goals should be to find out more about Doug Brown's death. Given the timing and Bobby's strange appearance at Doug's house that very night, I knew there had to be a connection of some kind. In the past I would simply have asked my father to look into it for me. As a code inspector for the township, he had worked closely with the local police and was always up on town gossip. Now that he had retired and moved away, however, I would have to depend on someone else, maybe some old buddy of his who still worked in Hidden Springs and had an ear on the goings-on there.

I thought of Mr. Carver, one of the few men who had stuck by my dad's side and given Bobby and me the benefit of the doubt when he and I were arrested, tried, and convicted for our crimes. Back then, our whole family had been thrust into a very difficult situation, but at least we all found out who our real friends were—and there weren't very many of them. From what I could recall, Mr. Carver had remained steadfast through all of it. I called information and got the man's home number in Hidden Springs. He answered on the third ring, his voice warm and familiar.

After apologizing for calling at such a late hour, I jumped right in, telling him who I was and saying that ordinarily my father would have been the one making this call, but he was currently on vacation in New Zealand.

"New Zealand?" he cried. "What's the old bugger doing way out there?"

I explained briefly about the bird-watching and then said I was headed to Pennsylvania to find my brother, who was missing.

"According to his wife, Bobby disappeared last night, and then today I heard about Doug Brown's death. Considering that they were good friends, I thought it might help me in my search for Bobby if I could learn more about what happened with Doug. You were always such a good buddy to my dad. I was hoping it would be okay to impose on you with this call, to see if maybe there was anything you could tell me about the situation just so I could have all the facts straight."

Mr. Carver sounded happy to hear from me, but he wasn't sure how much help he could be.

"Of course, there has been a lot of talk rolling around the township building, gossip and whatnot. You know how those things are. It would probably be easier to discuss this in person. Did you say you were in town? Why don't you come on over right now, and I'll get Letha to heat us up a couple pieces of peach pie?"

I thanked him, saying I was on my way but I wouldn't be getting into Philadelphia until morning. He suggested we meet in a coffee shop once I had arrived, an offer for which I was extremely grateful. I told him my flight would be in around seven and that I could be in Hidden Springs by nine.

"Actually, would you mind meeting somewhere else, somewhere not quite so close to my office? Just to keep tongues from wagging."

"Name the place and I'll be there."

He suggested a coffee shop near Valley Forge, so I jotted down the address and agreed to meet him there at nine in the morning unless my flight was delayed, in which case I would call as soon as I landed. As we ended the call and I tucked my phone away, I said a silent prayer of thanks that at least one thing had gone right thus far.

Glancing at my watch, I saw I still had time to accomplish several necessary errands before my flight would begin boarding. First stop was an electronics store, and I was relieved to find one in the same terminal as my gate. There, I bought a disposable cell phone, the kind that can be used and then tossed. It was for Lydia, so I could reach her more easily over the next few days. This phone shanty business was for the birds.

After that I went right next door to a jewelry store. Bypassing two busy salespeople, I sought out the oldest, most experienced-looking person there and waited as he finished with a transaction. The woman in front of me dropped her jacket, and as I picked it up and handed it back to her, it dawned on me I was heading to Pennsylvania in the dead of winter and I hadn't even thought to bring a coat.

"May I help you?" the salesman asked as his customer walked away.

Putting aside my concerns about a coat for now, I gave the man a warm smile and asked if he had ever heard of anything called the "Beauharnais Rubies."

"Yes, of course," he replied, not missing a beat. "Right over here we have some lovely Burmese ruby pendants. We have gems in pear shape, marquis, oval . . ."

Before he became too excited about making a sale, I explained that I didn't want to know for shopping purposes. I was just asking him as an experienced jeweler for research purposes.

"And not *Bur-mese*," I said. "*Bor-nays.* Have you ever heard that term? Is that a type of ruby?"

He said that hadn't heard the word per se, but he suggested that "Beauharnais" might be the place where they were mined.

"Rubies are found in Thailand, Sri Lanka, Vietnam, Madagascar . . . Perhaps Beauharnais is over in that region." He went on to say that "Beauharnais" could also be the name for a new form of synthetic ruby. "These rings, for example, are made from Verneuil rubies. Very lovely, and much more reasonably priced than their Burmese cousins."

He was still trying to make a sale, but I couldn't afford to even *look* at the rubies, much less buy any. I thanked him for his help and said I needed to be on my way. He was very gracious, apologizing that he hadn't been able to answer my question. He then suggested that I contact a gemstone or jewelry museum and ask someone there. I thanked him, wondering why I hadn't thought of that myself.

As I left the store, I let my thoughts return to the coat problem. I knew I would never find one for sale in an airport shop, not in and among the sunscreen and the "So Cool in So. Cal." beach towels. Swallowing my pride, I made my way to the Lost and Found department and asked what they did with older items that had never been claimed.

"They go in there," he said as he pointed to a large canvas bin on wheels, one that was practically overflowing with items. "Help yourself."

I had no problem wearing used clothing, and in fact much of my wardrobe had come from Goodwill. But I always thoroughly cleaned my purchases before I wore them. Here, I knew I wouldn't have that luxury. Gritting my teeth and trying not to think about germs and body odor, I went through the cart until I found a cute little navy peacoat with matching gloves stuffed in the pockets.

By the time I reached my gate a second time, I had only a short wait. I found a seat near the window, put down my things, and stared out at the busy ground crew. Taking a deep breath and letting it out slowly, I let my mind drift to Bobby's email.

Remember a while back when you said that if you could do one thing over again using the knowledge you have now, you'd do it differently?

I had no recollection of saying that, but obviously it must have come up in some conversation a while back. I tried to think of what we could have been talking about at the time, but nothing that came to mind made any sense. It wasn't until I was boarding the plane that it struck me what Bobby might have been talking about: Disappearing.

I vaguely remembered a telephone conversation we'd had about six months after I started working as a skip tracer, when I explained how much of my on-the-job training could have helped me do a better job of erasing my tracks and starting over. Had I been in hiding from a mafia don or a violent ex-boyfriend, I probably would have gone to the trouble to redo what I had already done but in a much more knowledgeable fashion. As it was, the only reason I had gone into hiding in the first place was to remove myself from the constant scrutiny of the media, and as long as the tricks I had used continued to prevent any aggressive journalists from tracking me down, my escape was sufficient.

Still, I remembered saying to my brother, *if I had to disappear all over again, my approach would be so much more sophisticated now. I've learned how to erase a paper trail so thoroughly I don't think anyone could ever find me.*

Filing onto the plane now, I decided that must be it. From what I could recall, we had talked about it for a while as I had laid out the three steps a person could take to start a new life and thoroughly break away from an old one: misinformation, disinformation, and reformation. I didn't remember Bobby finding the topic particularly fascinating, but I had told him about it anyway, probably to show off all of my newfound knowledge. All of those tricks he had done on the computer last night had likely been learned from me, during our conversation.

The problem, of course, was that Bobby's email ended by saying I should "communicate accordingly." Unfortunately, I didn't know how that would be. I must have mentioned some secure way a person could communicate back and forth with those who had been left behind, but for the life of me, I could not remember what it was. My mind flitted from leaving a written note in a designated spot to renting a bogus PO box in another city to leaving a message under a free online email account created just for that purpose. There were lots of ways to send and receive secure communications—or at least nonsecure communications in places made secure simply by the fact that no one would ever think to look there. But I didn't know what method Bobby was using, and without any clear direction, poking around and trying to figure it out could take weeks.

Closing my eyes for takeoff, I silently prayed that God might help dig that entire conversation from the recesses of my brain and bring it more fully to mind. I prayed also for a safe flight, for Kiki's recovery, for Lydia's peace of mind. Most of all, I prayed for Bobby.

Wherever he is, whatever he needs, please keep him safely in Your hands until I can find him.

TEN

Bobby

The pain was like nothing he had ever known. The knowledge that he survived the crash was of no comfort, considering that he couldn't get to Lydia and Isaac. He couldn't get anywhere at all.

He opened one eye, wincing at the pain that simple action caused to the other eye, which was swollen shut. It took every ounce of energy he had just to look around the dark, damp chamber. The small space smelled of earth and rust. No, not rust. Blood.

His blood.

He wanted to try and pull up on the one

good leg, but he knew the waves of pain and nausea would likely put him back down again in a flash. For the hundredth time since the crash, he mentally cataloged his injuries, the cuts and gashes, the ribs that were surely broken, the bone that was still jutting out below his kneecap, the flap of skin that hung over one eye. Every movement was like reliving the pain of the crash all over again, but he knew that if he didn't do something drastic, something to get out of here, he would die—as would Lydia and Isaac if he didn't make it to them in time.

He closed his eyes and laid his head back against the dirt, trying to be grateful for small blessings. At least he had some blankets. At least he had water and even food, of sorts. At least he had a flashlight, though he didn't dare use it often, for fear that the batteries would run out. Because of the cold, there weren't likely to be any snakes in here, nor even any spiders.

The mice were a different story.

He had been lying in this prison, this death chamber, for two days now, by his count. He wasn't sure of that, though, as the fever that raged through his body had also been messing with his mind. In his nightmares, thousands of rats swarmed over him, gnawing at the open flesh at his knee. Then he would awake and hear the tell-tale squeak of mice near his head and start screaming, batting at them with his hands, kicking them away with his good leg.

No one heard his screams, though. No one came to save him, not even Anna. Instead, he was alone. All around him, things were dark and cold and without life.

Much like he was beginning to feel.

ELEVEN

ANNA

Two questions rolled around in my head for most of the flight, so finally I took out pen and paper and wrote them down:

Was Norman right about Bobby's reservation to Las Vegas being bogus?

Why had Bobby needed Doug's motorcycle when he had a perfectly good car?

No matter how much I thought about it, I could not make sense of either act. As we landed in my connecting city and pulled into the gate right on schedule, I tucked away the pad and pen and got ready to disembark, those questions still prominent in my mind. I glanced at my watch as I walked off the plane, glad I had time to do a little poking around before my next flight.

According to the record I had pulled from Bobby's credit card, last night he had purchased a one-way ticket from Philadelphia to Las Vegas for a late-night flight that would have gotten him here around seven this morning. Considering Lydia's insistence that Bobby had no known connection to this city or to gambling or Nevada, I hadn't known what to think—and now that I was here in Vegas, I was starting to believe Norman's theory that Bobby had bought the ticket as a ruse only.

Still, somebody must have made that trip in his stead, because a withdrawal from his checking account had been made from an ATM machine in this airport at seven eighteen a.m. Who was it? A friend? A girlfriend? Obviously, that was one of the biggest concerns I had run across thus far. We already knew that Bobby had been keeping some things from his wife. Was it really that big of a leap to wonder if he had been cheating on her as well? I was having trouble coming up with any other feasible explanation, but I was determined to give Bobby the benefit of the doubt.

Out in the main lobby, I located the ATM machine in question. If I were in law enforcement, I could have requested a copy of the machine's surveillance video and gotten an actual look at the person who had made the withdrawal. That wasn't currently possible, however, so instead I just stood there at the machine for a moment, trying to picture the scene of what had really happened here in my mind.

There wasn't much to see, I had to admit. After that one withdrawal—which had taken the balance in Bobby and Lydia's checking account from $120 down to $20—there had been no other activity on that card. There had also been no charges on Bobby's credit card for anything in Vegas, not hotels or rental car or meals.

Are you here, Bobby? Are you in Las Vegas?

I turned full circle to look at the people around me. Despite the late hour, there were vacationing tourists, business folk, exhausted-looking parents, overactive children, soldiers in uniform. There were no signs of my brother, no one-dimpled smile, no handsome green eyes, no "Hey, Bobanna!"

Feeling strangely disappointed, I headed back to my gate, wondering what I had thought I could find here just by locating that ATM machine. Had I really expected Bobby to be standing next to it, waiting for me? It felt silly to admit, but in a way I think I had, despite Norman's more experienced opinion. Pathetic.

Back at the gate for my connection, I found an empty seat in the waiting area and sat, still working through scenarios in my mind. By combining the two questions into one, at least I was finally able to come up with a theory: What if Bobby had needed the motorcycle *because* he booked the flight? If Bobby had been doing everything he could to make it look as though he flew to Las Vegas, it stood to reason that he would have driven to the airport and parked his car in a prominent spot in airport parking. That way, if someone were hunting him down, not only would they know he'd bought the airline ticket to Vegas, they would also find his car sitting there at the airport, waiting for his return.

What more proof could one need that Bobby really had taken that trip? Somehow, he had even gotten someone to make a cash withdrawal from the ATM in Vegas for him, further proving that he was there.

But if he was only making it *look* as though he had taken the flight, then putting his car in airport parking left him with a big problem: How was he going to get back home without his car? He would need some sort of transportation, but a car rental would be reflected on his credit card whether he paid cash for it or not. He couldn't afford to buy a used car—not that he could have found one in the middle of the night anyway—so he was left with essentially two choices: a shuttle or the train. Neither one would get him all the way home to Lydia's sister's farm in Dreiheit. But the train would get him to Hidden Springs, I realized, where Doug and Haley Brown lived less than a mile from the train station.

Pulse surging, I closed my eyes and tried to picture Bobby's actions from last night. My guess was that after leaving the Internet café in Exton, he had driven to the Hidden Springs train station and parked his car there. Then he had jogged to the Brown's house, borrowed money from Haley and took the motorcycle, then drove it back to the train station and parked it there. Switching back to his own car, he drove to the Philadelphia airport and parked in long-term parking, checked in for the flight, and then left the airport via train and took it back to Hidden Springs. There, he got off the train, climbed onto the motorcycle, and took off. To anyone else, his actions would have seemed nutty, but that was the sort of complicated ruse I had described to him years ago, when I was telling him how I would disappear if I could do it over again.

If my theory was correct, then the question that remained was why hadn't he gotten to Lydia when he said he would? Why hadn't he come to her sister's farm as he had promised?

Rolling those questions around in my mind, I boarded my connecting flight. I was glad to see that the two seats next to mine were empty, so once the flight was underway, I stretched out and made myself as comfortable as possible. Slowly, I drifted off to sleep, hoping I wouldn't wake again until it was time to land in Philadelphia. I had a busy day ahead of me, and I needed all the shut-eye I could get.

The night didn't go quite that smoothly, but I did manage to grab several hours of sleep off and on, punctuated by a lot of shifting and resettling. At six a.m. sharp, the cabin lights came on, the morning beverage service rolled through, and then we began our descent. With money as tight as it was, I had been hoping for a free breakfast, but the best I got was a tiny, plastic-wrapped cheese Danish with my coffee.

Walking off of the airplane and into the Philadelphia airport felt familiar, of course, but it didn't give me the feeling that I had come "home." Instead, as I walked up the long corridors, along the moving sidewalk, and then down the escalator to the baggage claim area, it just seemed more like déjà vu, as in "been there, done that." I made a quick stop in the restroom to freshen up, and by the time I reached baggage claim, the bags were starting to come out. I grabbed my dinged-up black suitcase as it rolled past, but I didn't head straight for the rental car area just yet. First, I went over to Ground Transportation and checked the train schedules to see if my theory held water. Sure enough, Bobby would have been able to go from the Philadelphia airport to Hidden Springs by train, with just one quick switch at 30th Street Station.

I would have to take a shuttle to pick up my car, so I stepped outside, not thinking, into the January winter air. I gasped, shocked at the depth of the cold. I didn't remember it being this freezing here. I quickly pulled on my coat and gloves, feeling foolish. I might as well have the word "Californian" stamped on my forehead. At least the shuttle was prompt, though once I was at the car rental company and inside their heated building, I had to take it off again as I waited in a slow-moving line.

There was a seating area over to one side with a television flashing pictures but no sound, and underneath that a coffee service and a small tray of donuts. I took a pass on the donuts, but the coffee smelled good. As I awaited my turn, trying to decide whether to make a cup now or after I had finished my transaction, one of the images on the television caught my eye and nearly stopped my heart: It was a photo of Doug Brown's face, smiling at the camera. That image dissolved into a picture of Bobby, with his name across the bottom and the words "Sought for Questioning." I wanted to run over and turn up the sound to hear what was being said, but I didn't dare. Instead I just stood there watching as Bobby's face faded into a reporter talking into the microphone. Then, much to my dismay, the next image shown was the famous photo of the group that the press had dubbed the "Dreiheit Five." There we were, all five of us: Bobby, Doug, Reed, Haley, and me. In the photo, we were frozen in time, walking down the steps of the courthouse together, the guys in suits, Haley and me in dresses. The first time I saw that photo was in an article in *Newsweek* magazine, with the heading "Final Hearing for Wild Teen Party-Turned-Nightmare."

The camera then zoomed in to our individual faces, lingering on each one for a moment. When they got to mine, I literally couldn't breathe, standing there gazing at the eighteen-year-old girl with the sad face and the short, dark hair. Self-consciously,

I smoothed my bangs toward my eyes, while wondering if my face was distinctive enough that I would be recognized immediately despite the change in hairstyle and color and the fact that I had aged eleven years since then. Frantically, I dug in my carry-on for my sunglasses, and I was slipping them on just as I heard the woman at the counter say "Next?"

She must have thought I was a little bit nuts, considering that I never met her eyes or even looked up for the entire transaction. Nevertheless, she rented me the car I had reserved, the cheapest last-minute rental I could find. After I loaded my bags in the trunk, I got in the car and just sat for a while, trying to recover from the shock of seeing my old self on TV.

I didn't want to be here.

I really, really didn't want to be here.

But what else could I do? My brother was obviously in trouble and needed my help—and to be honest, I was probably better suited to finding him than anyone else on earth. It wasn't just my professional experience, my knowledge of skip tracing, that made me perfect for the job.

It was that I knew my brother, I knew how he thought, how his mind worked. If anyone could find Bobby, I could.

Reluctantly, I started up the car and pulled out from the lot, following the signs for 95 South. Almost on autopilot, I took that for several miles before moving to the Blue Route, which would bring me to Valley Forge without having to pass directly through downtown Philadelphia. Glancing at the dashboard clock, I was glad to see that I should make it to my nine o'clock meeting on time, even if I ran into some rush hour traffic along the way.

As I drove along, I listened to the news on the radio, but the story told me nothing I hadn't figured out by watching the photos flash by on the television. Turning off the radio, one photo kept coming back into my mind, the picture of the five of us leaving the courthouse. We were so young then, so burdened by what we had done. In the years since, we had each taken a different path to self-forgiveness. Bobby had lost his way for a while but eventually ended up where it had all begun, there in Dreiheit with Lydia. Haley and Doug had found solace with each other, though from what I understood their marriage wasn't exactly a resounding success. According to Bobby, Haley spent most of her time at the bottom of a bottle; Doug had consoled himself by spending her father's money. I had managed to carve out a life for myself once I started over in California, though it was nothing like what I had pictured when I was younger.

Then there was Reed. As the oldest one in the group, he had suffered the harshest penalties, in more ways than one. After the fire, he had spent three months in the burn unit at the hospital. When he was released from that prison, he moved onto the next. Convicted of reckless endangerment, involuntary manslaughter, corruption of minors, and a misdemeanor drug charge, he was sentenced to a year in jail and three years of probation.

His road had been the toughest, and yet in a way, he had managed to bounce back more thoroughly than any of us. After the fire, Doug and Bobby both gave up their dreams of medical school and, in fact, never even finished college. But Reed stuck it out. When he got out of prison, he returned to medical school, earned his degree, and then went into research.

Nowadays, from what I understood, he lived in Washington, DC, and worked in the field of DNA—not just the science of it but also legislation and ethics. Somehow, Reed had managed to become a success in the work world despite having a police record, something not easy to do. Reed's family was very wealthy, so I had always figured they used their money and influence to pave the way, both by convincing the medical school to let their son back in once he got out of prison and by helping him land a prestigious position once he was finished.

I hadn't seen Reed Thornton since the day he was sentenced. He already had a guilty verdict from the jury, and the only hope we were able to hang onto between that and the sentencing was that the judge would take into account the fact that Reed had no prior offenses, he was a first year medical student with good grades, and he had acted heroically at the scene of the fire, running inside and saving a child before nearly being consumed by flames himself. It was obvious he had already been through physical agony; did he really deserve to spend several years in prison for what was essentially an accident?

I would never forget the first thing Reed did when the sentence was announced. After absorbing the news that he was to spend the next year of his life in prison followed by three years of probation, he simply turned around and looked at me. With his beautiful blue eyes, he looked at me, his expression a combination of fear and sadness and regret. As I met and held his gaze, I thought about what he and I could have been to each other, about how it had been love at first sight as far as I was concerned, how it had taken all summer of hanging around together and getting to know each other for him to discover that he had feelings for me in return. Finally, I thought about that one kiss we had shared, that single kiss that had held such promise and ended up being the last good moment of the worst night of my life.

I will always love you, I said with my eyes, hoping he understood. Then the bailiff took

Reed's arm and led him out of the door of the courtroom, and I was truly alone.

I had never seen him since.

Seeing his youthful face on the television screen today had brought it all back, the grief, the yearning, the loss. Bobby kept me posted on everyone, and according to him Reed had never married. Moving into the right lane for the exit that was coming up, I wondered if he was happy now, if he enjoyed his work, if he had a good life.

Most of all, I wondered if he still thought about me as often as I thought about him.

TWELVE

Stephanie

May 20, 1812

I am pleased to report that though I am now five months with child, the Empire waist remains in fashion. This news is very helpful to me, as such a style is perfectly suited to my growing shape. I have kept the royal dressmakers busy this month, but I feel confident that my new gowns will suffice through the fall.

Upon return from his most recent travels, Karl presented me with a copy of *La Belle Assemblée* and several yards of rose-colored silk fringe. I do believe that my husband finally has a growing fondness for me, for how else would he have arrived at such thoughtful gifts so well suited to this transplanted Parisian? Last night I dreamed of Versailles, and today my heart yearns for the beautiful gardens of home.

Other than Karl's recent kindness, life at the palace is still quite disagreeable. This morning I came upon Luise and her son, Leopold, whispering in the salon. Upon realizing that I was there, they gave no greeting but simply turned and departed. Their snubs continue to sting.

Someday, perhaps I will come to understand what my husband's grandfather saw in Luise when he chose to take her as his second wife—in a morganatic union at that. I find her unattractive inside and out, and Leopold has inherited his mother's bitter and vindictive manner.

At least the palace is large enough that I am able to pass days at a time with only minimal interaction. I long for the day, however, when peace is made between all members of this family. I do not want my child to be born amid the whispers and snubs of such domestic distress.

THIRTEEN

ANNA

Mr. Carver, my dad's old friend, was waiting for me when I walked into the coffee shop in Valley Forge. He was sitting in a booth by the window, and I spotted him as soon as I came in the door. He gave me a smile and a wave, and I joined him at the table.

We talked about the weather, me saying how cold it was outside and him replying with a chuckle that actually it wasn't all that cold right now; it probably just felt like it because I wasn't exactly dressed for the weather. He was right, of course. I had on a light cotton short-sleeved shirt under my peacoat. As soon as I got to Lydia's, I was definitely going to have to borrow some sweaters.

After making small talk and placing our order, Mr. Carver got right down to business. He lowered his voice and said he had agreed to meet me here for two reasons: Because my father had always been a good friend to him, and because he didn't like the way the situation was unfolding, how everyone seemed to be jumping to the conclusion that Bobby had something to do with Doug's death.

"Your brother's a good boy," he said. "I know he could never kill someone on purpose, especially not a friend. People like to forget that that fire was an accident."

Mr. Carver said that the police weren't using the word "murder" yet, but that Bobby was being "sought for questioning" in the "suspicious death" of his friend Doug. All signs pointed to guilty, which was bad news for Bobby, wherever he was.

Bobby and Doug both worked for the same parent company: Wynn Industries, the large pharmaceutical firm owned by Doug's father-in-law, Orin Wynn. According to Mr. Carver, Doug had last been seen on Wednesday night as he left his job at the Wynn Industries building in Hidden Springs around eight. Apparently, he then had driven from there to the town of Exton, which was about fifteen minutes away, and gone to the new Wynn Industries headquarters, a ten story building still under construction.

The time of death wasn't certain, but at some point between eight and midnight, Doug fell from the eighth floor to the ground floor lobby and was killed instantly. Mr. Carver said the building had a ten story atrium, but that not all of the guardrails had been installed yet, and the eighth floor had none at all. There were no signs of struggle up there, and in fact the whole area had been swept clean of the construction dust that seemed to coat almost everything else in the building. At some point after he fell, a heavy box of tiles fell as well, landing on the ground next to his body, denting the floor and shattering into pieces.

Mr. Carver said the police weren't sure if the fall was an accident or if Doug had been pushed, but for the time being they were proceeding with the assumption that it was a push—and that Bobby had been the one doing the pushing.

"But why Bobby?" I asked, utterly dismayed.

Mr. Carver replied that Bobby's fingerprints were found on Doug's body and on the handle of the main door to the building, both inside and out.

"I'm sorry, but there is no way my brother could have killed Doug," I said adamantly. "Fingerprints may prove he was there, but they don't prove he pushed a friend to his death."

"Now you see why I agreed to meet with you. They're saying Bobby is the primary suspect because of the fingerprints, but between you and me, I think their conclusion has less to do with fingerprints than it does with Bobby's past police record. You know how it is. Once a criminal, always a criminal."

My stomach churning, I asked Mr. Carver to continue. He went on to talk about Doug's wife, Haley, who was saying that Bobby showed up at her and Doug's house around eleven thirty that same night, asking for a loan. She had given him eight thousand dollars in cash and sent him on his way, after which Bobby had snuck into the back shed and stolen Doug's motorcycle. Bobby's fingerprints were found on the key cabinet near the front door where the motorcycle key was stored, so Haley's theory that he grabbed the keys while she was gone from the room seemed to be correct.

"That's all I've got," Mr. Carver said, shaking his head sadly.

I sat back, wiping my mouth with my napkin though I had hardly eaten a thing. Bobby's disappearance had suddenly taken on a whole new level of complexity, leaving me with a sick feeling in the pit of my stomach.

"What do you think happened that night?" I asked. "How do you think Bobby was involved in Doug's death?"

Mr. Carver shrugged, pausing to eat another bite of his breakfast before answering.

"Well, Bobby was obviously in the building in Exton, but I'd be willing to bet that he was never up on that eighth floor. I mean, why would he go to the trouble to sweep up the dust and erase their footprints upstairs but not bother to wipe his prints off the front door handle? That's just dumb, and Bobby's not dumb."

"No, he's not."

"Personally, I think Bobby either saw Doug fall or he got there after he had fallen. There were two of Bobby's fingerprints on Doug's wrist, right here," he said, indicating the underside of the wrist, slightly to the left, "and on his neck right here," he continued, placing his fingers under his chin and to the right. "That's what you do when you're checking for a pulse. You put your fingers there, on the wrist, and if you can't feel anything, you put your fingers there, on the neck."

Instantly my mind jumped to yesterday morning, when I had done the very same thing with Kiki as she lay bleeding on the floor.

"The cops tend to follow the pulse theory as well, but they say it's just as likely that Bobby checked Doug's pulse not in the hopes that he was still alive, but to make sure that he was dead."

Mr. Carver shook his head ruefully.

"That's why I agreed to meet with you, Annalise. I'm hoping you'll be able to figure out the real truth here and not jump to conclusions just because Bobby happens to have a police record."

"Unfortunately, when you have a police record, people are always jumping to conclusions. It's the nature of the game. All five of us have learned that the hard way."

We chatted a bit longer, and when the check came I reached for it, knowing that I should pay since Mr. Carver had come here at my request. He insisted on taking care of it, though, and I didn't put up much of a fight. I just tucked my wallet away, grateful for his chivalry.

Parting ways in the parking lot, I thanked Mr. Carver profusely. He went to shake my hand, but I gave him a hug instead, saying I was glad my dad had good friends like him we could count on.

"Yeah, well, you need to keep it quiet or I could get in trouble," he said. "But what's the point of knowing all the gossip that's going around the police department and the township building if I can't share it once in a while?" With a laugh, he opened my car door for me and said to take care.

As I pulled out of the parking lot, I had the odd sensation that someone was watching me. I kept an eye on my rearview mirror for a long time to see if I was being followed. Though it didn't seem like it, I continued on my way thinking that with one man dead and another missing, it would be wise for me to remain vigilant.

Back on Gulph Road, I thought about the three towns of Dreiheit, Hidden Springs, and Exton—all of which had played a part in the strange events that had taken place on Wednesday night. Exton was located in Chester County along Route 30. Hidden Springs was about 15 miles northwest of there, just before the Lancaster County line. Dreiheit was another 20 miles southwest of Hidden Springs, below Lincoln Highway on the road toward Quarryville. All together, the three towns formed a sort of wide triangle.

Hidden Springs was the town that Bobby and I originally called home, the place where we grew up and went to school for all twelve grades. We had also spent a fair amount of our childhood in Dreiheit, visiting our grandparents. Other than an occasional shopping trip to the mall, though, we had no personal connection to the town of Exton at all.

Still, considering that that was where Doug had been killed and Bobby had gone online at an Internet café the same night, I decided to hop on 202 South and head toward Exton first. I wanted to get a look at the building where Doug died, if for no other reason than to orient myself to the happenings of that night. According to Mr. Carver, the new Wynn Industries building was located about a mile from the intersection of Route 30 and Highway 100, so I went there now, surprised to see the number of stores and other businesses that had sprung up around the Exton Mall. I turned onto 100 and drove until I spotted a ten-story building looming up on the right. Fortunately, there was a gas station to the left, so I pulled in there instead, for fear of being seen. I couldn't have used more than a gallon or two of gas since picking up my rental car at the airport, but I pulled up to the pump anyway and took my time topping off the tank, using the opportunity to observe the construction site across the street.

The building was the tallest thing around, and once it was completed it would be a striking structure of glass and steel, very fitting for the cutting-edge pharmaceutical company that it would house. The grounds around the building were filled with the detritus of construction: mounds of dirt, stacks of building materials, a small crane, and other machinery now sitting idle. The whole property was encircled by temporary orange-net fencing, and from where I was standing I thought I could see a strip of vivid yellow police tape across the main door to the building. A number of cars were parked near that entrance, not just police cars but a few high-end vehicles as well. I had a feeling they belonged to some of the Wynn Industries executives, who were likely keeping an eye on the situation. Haley's father owned the entire company, so I felt sure it did not bode well that his son-in-law had fallen to his death in their very own building.

I was just closing my gas cap when a Channel 6 Action News van came rumbling up the road and turned onto the property. Heart pounding, I quickly slapped the lid shut, got back in my car, and started it up. Tucking my credit card into my purse, I drove away, wondering how much longer it would be before the media found out I was back in Pennsylvania and on the case.

My next stop was Hidden Springs, the town I would always call home even though my parents had sold the house and moved to Florida a few years ago. I went the back way, cutting across the countryside via a series of turns so familiar that it was as though I were driving on autopilot. I finally reached the old neighborhood and turned onto the street where I grew up. Our house was halfway down on the right, a three-bedroom ranch style. Pulling over to the side of the road and idling for a few minutes, I thought how much smaller the house looked now than it had when I lived there.

Modest as it was, this had been a nice house to grow up in, with a neighborhood full of kids and an elementary school just a few blocks away. I never really made friends with Haley Wynn until middle school, but by the end of the eighth grade we were practically inseparable. Once I saw her gigantic, fancy home on the wealthy side of town, mine was never good enough again. I probably tormented my poor parents for the next few years, wanting to know why

Haley's family had a pool and we didn't, why Haley's father made lots of money and mine didn't. I received several lectures about the benefits of being a civil servant, but they were all lost on me. As long as Haley had a TV in her bedroom and a walk-in closet filled with the latest fashions, civil service could never trump private entrepreneurship in my book.

Thinking of Haley now made me feel kind of lost and sad. I felt guilty for having let our friendship fade away, especially knowing what I did about her unhappy marriage and her problems with alcohol. Maybe I could have made a difference in her life. Maybe I should pay her a visit right now.

Summoning my nerve, I put the car in drive and headed across town to the home that had been given to Haley and Doug as a wedding present from her father. I had been there only once, a few days before I left for California seven years ago, but I had been duly impressed. Almost as big as the house she had grown up in, it had come complete with a pool and pool house and a detached three-car garage, the whole thing a stunning example of

Pennsylvania stone-and-wood Colonial. Nestled on several acres in the costliest neighborhood in town only served to make it more impressive.

"This place is so huge you guys are going to lose each other," I had said to Haley with a laugh when she gave me a tour.

Sadly, I thought now, losing each other was exactly what had happened. I wondered how it felt to be widowed at only twenty-nine.

Turning into their neighborhood, I had second thoughts about showing up unannounced. Doug's body had just been discovered the day before, so Haley was probably overwhelmed right now, dealing with funeral arrangements and out-of-town relatives, not to mention working through her own grief. On the other hand, a visit from her old best friend might be just what she needed most at the moment—not to mention that hearing her story firsthand would help in my investigation.

I continued driving there, but when I was half a block away, I could see that her home was surrounded by the media, with three different news vans parked outside. Heart pounding, I put on my brakes and then quickly pulled into someone else's driveway, turned around, and drove away.

Of course they are camping out there, I thought as I raced out of the neighborhood. This was a big story, with ties to another, older big story that simply refused to die. My stomach still in knots by the time I turned onto Lincoln Highway, I decided I would try to connect with Haley later, via phone.

For now, I needed to move on to Dreiheit, the very town where, on that fateful August night in 1997, an Amish farmer and his wife and their newborn baby died—but five other people essentially lost their lives as well. As I crossed into Lancaster County and turned onto a winding, picturesque road, I thought in detail about the tragedy that had so deeply marked the turning point in all of our lives.

FOURTEEN

The story actually began when Bobby and I were just children. Though we lived with our parents in Hidden Springs, we often visited our grandparents in Dreiheit. They owned a gorgeous old stone home on about five rolling acres there, and as children Bobby and I loved to explore the grounds and play with Grete and Lydia Schumann, the Amish sisters who lived next door with their parents and grandparents and baby brother, Caleb. Their whole family was just so different, so sweet, that I used to come home from our visits there and try to talk my parents in becoming Amish too.

Our grandmother died of cancer the year I was twelve and Bobby was fourteen. Her illness had been so prolonged that her death hadn't come as much of a surprise, but we were all stunned when an aneurism took our vibrant grandfather's life just one year later. As my father was their only child, he inherited the beautiful old family home in Dreiheit that had been passed down through several generations of Jensens. Though our parents would have liked to keep the house in the family, they couldn't afford the cost of maintaining it. As sad as it was, our family had had no choice but to clear out the century-old, Federal-style stone mansion and put it on the market. Mr. Schumann expressed an interest in buying the land, which worked out quite well because the Realtor was able to sell just the house to an architect who had property along the Susquehanna River and had been looking for a uniquely beautiful structure to move there. Once the deal was sealed, Bobby and I missed our grandparents terribly, of course, but we also missed their gorgeous home in Dreiheit, not to mention our Amish friends from the farm next door.

Over time, as Haley Wynn and I grew closer, I began to go back to Dreiheit occasionally with her. Her parents were divorced, and though Haley lived in Hidden Springs with her father, who had primary custody, she spent many weekends in Dreiheit with her mother, who lived in a little cottage about a mile away from the very place where my grandparents' house had once stood. Though her small home was a far cry from the grandeur of the old Jensen homestead that was no more, it was still nice to visit the town I loved so much there in the heart of Amish country. As we grew older and got driver's licenses—and Haley's father gave her a car—we continued the tradition, driving out to Dreiheit for the occasional weekend of fun and relaxation at her mom's. A hippie-type who had long wavy hair and wore peasant blouses, Mrs. Wynn was not a typical suburban mother. Once we started high school, she began insisting that I was old enough to call her by her first name, Melody, and that I make myself completely at home whenever I was there. She had an organic garden out back, one that was so prolific that it was like having our own personal produce stand. Though Haley was allergic to tomatoes, I loved nothing more than to pick them right off the vine, wash them, and eat them like apples.

As nice as Haley's mother was, though, I liked her father better. Melody was pleasantly laid back, but Orin Wynn had the sharp mind, quick wit, and boundless energy of a hugely successful entrepreneur. I was used to boring, mostly trivial conversations around my family's dinner table at home, but whenever I was invited to dinner at Haley's with her and her dad, the conversations were challenging and fascinating—and never predictable. On one evening we might debate the merits of capitalism versus socialism or name the Ten Places We Most Wanted to See in Our Lifetimes. When Haley and I were in our junior year of high school, I was eating over when the conversation turned to Bobby, who was in his first year of college at the University of Pennsylvania.

"That's rather impressive," Mr. Wynn had said, adding that UPenn was a top-notch school and a member of the Ivy League. When he learned that Bobby was in pre-med, hoping to continue on after graduation at the medical school there, he stopped cutting his steak and gave me a nod. "Do you know if he has plans for next summer? Because we're expanding our research extension out in Lancaster County. We'll have a few openings for summer interns in the DNA lab, if he's interested."

I had no idea if Bobby was into DNA work or not, but I told Mr. Wynn I would ask him.

"We've already filled one spot with a fellow down from Harvard, a first-year med student named Reed Thornton. There are still two spots left though, so have your brother give me a call."

Have your brother give me a call.

It was just a chance remark, a kind offer from a family friend, but it would end up being the seven words that were the beginning of the end for all of us.

Mr. Wynn owned Wynn Industries, a huge pharmaceutical company based in Hidden Springs. I didn't think his offer of an internship was any big deal, but when I called Bobby at school a few days later and conveyed the conversation to him, he was beside himself with excitement.

"DNA is where the future is!" Bobby

cried. "Of *course* I'm into DNA work, you goofball."

Bobby had contacted Mr. Wynn immediately and arranged an interview, and about a month later he learned that he had been hired. The third internship went to a student from yet another Ivy League school, a guy from the Midwest named Doug Brown. That June, as soon as the semester was over, Bobby packed up the things from his dorm room and moved them out to a rental in Dreiheit, where the lab was located. Unlike the other two interns, Bobby was already very familiar with the town and its environs from the years of visiting our grandparents there.

A few weeks later, Haley and I drove to Dreiheit to spend the Fourth of July weekend at her mom's. We decided to pay a visit to Bobby at the lab while we were in town, and though I enjoyed seeing his workplace and meeting his boss, the brilliant Dr. Updyke, Haley had been more interested in one of Bobby's fellow interns, the one from the Midwest named Doug. Haley and Doug hit it off immediately, and by the time the fireworks went off on the night of the Fourth, they were making a few fireworks of their own.

Soon they were officially a couple, the guy from Harvard had arrived and stepped into his position as the senior intern, and Haley was talking about staying in Dreiheit for the whole summer. Once she found a job at the local ice cream parlor, it was a done deal. Her job was a lot of fun, and when another opening became available soon afterward, she started bugging me to come out and apply for the position myself and spend the summer at her mom's with her. I was already bored with the random babysitting jobs I was getting at home, so I took her up on it. Haley was thrilled, as she was hoping to play matchmaker with me and the intern I hadn't met yet, Reed Thornton, whom she described on the phone as a "major hottie" and exactly my type.

When I first met Reed, I thought Haley had made an understatement. He wasn't just a "hottie," he was, in fact, the most gorgeous guy I had ever seen. He seemed attracted to me as well, at least until my big-mouthed brother stepped in and pointedly referred to me as his "seventeen-year-old *baby* sister." Reed, who was twenty-one at the time, quickly seemed to lose interest, though he was still very nice to me. Instead of having the romance I would have liked, Reed and I became good friends instead. The five of us—Reed, Doug, Bobby, Haley, and I—ended up spending a lot of time together that summer. We would work all day, and then in the evenings we would go to the local tourist traps or drop in on the occasional *rumspringa* party or just spend time hanging out at Haley's mom's house. Melody worked in agriculture and was fascinated with the potential of exploring plant DNA, and she loved to pick the guys' brains about their research with human DNA at the lab. Their conversations were often way over my head, but I loved to listen anyway, simply because Reed was so incredibly smart.

Just as Haley had predicted, that summer was great fun. The men were brilliant and funny and loved to tease, and of course Haley and I enjoyed being around older, more mature guys for a change. The more time I spent with Reed, the harder I fell for him, and soon I was convinced I was absolutely in love, though he still treated me more like a sister than anything else. Reed may have been oblivious to my charms, but Bobby certainly noticed the vibes I was giving off. More than once he warned me not to fall too hard for Reed, saying there were things about him I didn't know and would not like. I just assumed Bobby was being an overprotective big brother, and I ignored most of his advice. As the summer progressed, I continued to make a shameless play for Reed, and he continued to treat me like a close friend.

To everyone's surprise, the real romance of the summer ended up being not me and Reed or Haley and Doug, but Bobby and an Amish girl named Lydia Schumann. The Schumanns were the ones we had played with as children, who lived next door to our grandparents. As kids, Lydia and her siblings had taught us Dutch Blitz and taken us sledding and pretty much showed us how much fun you could have without a television set or sophisticated toys of any kind.

Bobby and Lydia were the same age, and as children the two of them had been positively unbeatable in any game we played. They both loved pulling practical jokes and weaving fantastic stories and rounding up every possible person for pickup games of stickball. When our grandparents died, my brother and I had felt sure we'd never see the Schumann kids again.

Once Bobby began his internship there in Dreiheit, however, one of the first families to walk through the door of the lab was Lydia's. A rare genetic disorder ran in her family, and her mother, Kate, who was pregnant, had come in for some genetic testing. Around her family Lydia acted quiet and shy, but when Bobby saw her that weekend at a *rumspringa* party, she was anything but. Still mischievous, fun, funny, and smart, she was now also beautiful as well. They fell in love almost instantly and began spending every possible moment together that they could.

Lydia was nineteen at the time, the age when she should have been preparing for baptism into the Amish church and marriage to some nice Amish boy. Instead, she had fallen for Bobby, and she had begun to seriously question whether she was going to be baptized as Amish or not. The stakes were high, and she knew it. If she went ahead with a baptism and later changed her mind, she would be shunned by the Amish community forever. If, instead, she made a break with the church now and never was baptized at all, she could remain in contact with her family and would not suffer the complete social ostracization that shunning created. Either decision would lead to serious consequences and could not be taken lightly.

Bobby and Lydia continued to date the rest of the summer, but the more in love they grew, the more frustrated he became with not being able to see her except on weekends. Amish parents usually looked the other way on Friday and Saturday nights when their kids were on *rumpspringa,* hoping that a little taste of freedom and a brief exploration of the outside world would be all they needed to make the decision to remain Amish for the rest of their lives. It was a little harder to pull off sneaking out during the week, but Lydia was determined to start trying. Because the family had no phone, however, she and Bobby had to come up with a system of communication for the weeknights that he didn't have to work late and wanted to see her.

It hadn't taken long for Bobby to figure out how to get a signal to Lydia. Her bedroom was the only one in their house with a view of the family's back fields; the rest of the bedroom windows were obscured by a row of maple trees. Because she could see so far, Bobby bought a pack of fireworks, and to signal her to come out and meet him, he would simply drive around to the back of their farm—on the property that used to belong to our grandparents—and shoot one off. Eventually, he changed to Roman candles because they didn't make as much noise and they contained six flares in a row. That was almost always enough to get her attention, and whenever she saw those bright orange streaks across the sky in the distance, she would quietly get dressed and slip outside and run down the long, straight rows of the cornfield until she reached him at the other side.

Usually, they didn't even go anywhere. They would just spend time together out there in the darkness, sometimes late into the night. On cooler evenings, they would make a small fire or bundle up inside Bobby's truck. Despite the risks of dating a girl who was off limits, we all thought it incredibly romantic that Bobby and Lydia had each fallen for their childhood friend. Their clandestine meetings were made even more special by the notion that the very ground they were sitting on had once belonged to his family and now belonged to hers.

One night near the end of the summer, Bobby was planning to meet Lydia as usual. That time, however, the rest of us had nothing better to do, so we asked if we could come along, maybe build a fire in their fire pit, roast marshmallows, and just hang out. It was a beautiful night and it sounded like something fun to do. We all piled into Bobby's big truck, making one stop on the way for Doug, who wanted some beer.

Out at the farm, I could see why Bobby enjoyed being there. In the place where our grandparents' house once stood, all that remained were the front and back cement steps, the basement, which was now open to the elements, and their old garage, in which Lydia's father now stored some farm equipment. Otherwise, Mr. Schumann hadn't done much with the property, so the graceful old trees that used to shade our grandparents' front lawn were still there. Our old rope swing even hung from the tallest of those trees, though the rope had nearly rotted away.

When we arrived, Bobby sent us out into the yard to gather sticks for the fire. As we did that, he pulled out a Roman candle from his secret stash in the back of the truck and shot it off so that Lydia would know to come. Doug wanted to shoot some off too, just for fun, but Bobby lied and said he didn't have any more. I knew he did, and I knew where he kept them in the truck, but I didn't say anything because I felt sure the reason he didn't want Doug playing with them was because they would make us too noticeable back here. One Roman candle could come and go without attracting too much attention. A whole bunch of Roman candles could light up the night sky and draw the neighbors—or maybe even the police.

While we waited for Lydia, Bobby directed us to the fire pit, which he and Lydia had constructed with a circle of rocks and some sand. The guys started our little bonfire while Haley and I chose the perfect sticks for roasting marshmallows. We spread a couple of blankets on the ground around the fire. At that point, Lydia joined us, out of breath from her dash across the field but happy to see the whole gang.

For the next hour we all simply sat around and talked and laughed and roasted marshmallows. Over the summer of hanging out with this group, I had become used to seeing the two couples hang all over each other while Reed and I kept a platonic distance. That night, however, he seemed to sit a little closer, let his hand linger on my hand a while longer. I had long ago given up hope of his being interested in me, but it was still fun to see him flirt back for a change.

When Bobby and Lydia excused themselves, we knew they were going off to find a little privacy. At that point, I wasn't sure how far they went when they were alone, but I hoped that their faith gave them the strength to resist going too far.

According to Haley, she and Doug were not having sex even though he wanted to.

As I watched the two of them finish off one six-pack and start into another, I wondered how drunk she would have to be before her boundaries flew out the window.

Eventually, Reed reached for a beer too, though when he offered me one, I declined. At seventeen-almost-eighteen, I was pretty much a good girl. I was a virgin, didn't drink, had only tried smoking once, rarely cursed. It wasn't that I enjoyed being known as a Goody Two-shoes. It was just that I happened to take to heart the behavioral elements of my Christianity. When I accepted Christ at thirteen, I had accepted the whole package: to be like Him, to learn about Him, to worship Him, to love Him. As far as I was concerned, the kids I knew who went a little wild sometimes never really enjoyed it beyond the moment anyway, and sometimes, most times, later they were really sorry. Puking in the toilet, they were sorry. Trying to get the smell of smoke out of their hair before going home, they were sorry. Seeing the little line in the tiny window turn into a plus sign, they were really, really sorry. To me, it seemed easier—and smarter and certainly more

Christlike—to just not go there in the first place. I didn't freak out if my friends crossed the line, but I wasn't going to cross it with them. Fortunately, except for Doug's drinking, our whole group was pretty tame anyway.

As the tamest one of all, I usually wasn't given a hard time by these guys because they knew my limits and seemed to respect them. But for some reason, that night Doug started teasing me, calling me a party pooper. Haley, who was supposed to be my best friend, soon joined him. To their mind, it was all in good fun, but they were drunk and that made it obnoxious and a little too aggressive. I looked to Reed for help, but he just smiled and said, "I can't see how one beer could hurt."

Much to my amazement, I found myself pressured into a corner. I was very uncomfortable, but on the one night that Reed had finally shown some interest in me, I really didn't want to blow it by looking like a prude—or worse, like a little kid. That was why I said what I said next. Later, if I could have taken it back, I would have—a thousand times over, I would have.

"Hey, guys," I said in a desperate attempt to change the subject, "I know where Bobby keeps all those Roman candles. He was lying to you, Doug. He's got a whole case in the back of his truck."

The night took on a life of its own after that. Doug and Reed forgot all about teasing me and ran to get the fireworks instead. For the next fifteen or twenty minutes, they managed to shoot off half the box. Doug even threw a handful in the fire to see what would happen. Unfortunately, they still went off, only the shots came out horizontal rather than vertical. Laughing hysterically, we all jumped and ducked to avoid the orange fireballs as they shot past.

The whole time the guys were playing around, I kept expecting Bobby to come running out from the shadows and tell them to stop. He never did, though, and we later learned that was because he and Lydia were in the garage. He testified later that they could hear us laughing but they didn't see the flashes of light because the door was firmly closed.

When Doug grew tired of shooting off Roman candles, he scooped Haley into his arms and began kissing her aggressively.

She seemed to return his passion, and after about a minute, they whispered something to each other, joined hands, and just like Bobby and Lydia had done, they disappeared into the shadows.

That left me alone with Reed. We sat beside the dwindling fire and talked about the fact that the summer was almost over and how sad we were for it to end. He talked about his family back home, the rich parents who were more interested in their next vacation than they were in their own son. I talked about how eager I was to finish high school so I could get started with college.

"Yeah, it's easy to forget you're just seventeen," he said, suddenly focusing in on me with those blue eyes. "Sometimes, Annalise, I just don't know what to do about you . . ."

With one hand, he reached up and gently brushed the hair from my face. What happened next was the fulfillment of the dream that had hounded me the entire summer. Slowly, Reed leaned forward, and then he kissed me.

Heart racing, I kissed him back, placing a hand on his muscular shoulder. I loved him so much, in the way that only seventeen-year-old girls can love. I wanted the hearts and the flowers and the words and the promises. He was the man of my dreams, and he was kissing me.

Afterward, he touched his warm lips to my cheek and my forehead and then he simply pulled me close. We sat there like that, beside the fire, silently holding on to each other, not saying a word. I would have been happy to stay there forever, but after a while I realized that the gentle caresses his hands were making on my shoulders and back were gaining energy, were moving wider and lower and more to the front. I was trying to think how to calm his ardor without sounding like a child when he suddenly pulled away, chuckling softly.

"Like I said, it's easy to forget how young you are sometimes. Sorry about that. I shouldn't have kissed you."

"Don't be sorry," I said, looking up at him, knowing that not only was he the most handsome, sweetest, greatest guy I had ever known—he had also found the wherewithal to act like a gentlemen in the face of his most desperate passions. "I've been dreaming all summer of your kiss."

He chuckled again, shook his head, and then utterly destroyed the moment by scooting further away, reaching into his pocket, and pulling out a joint.

To say that I was surprised was an understatement.

"This'll help us cool down," he said, and then he lit it, took a deep drag, and held his breath as he passed it to me.

Maybe I was naive back then. Maybe it shouldn't have been that big of a shock, but I didn't do drugs, and I didn't think he was the kind of guy who did either. Slowly, as he held out that joint, I realized that all the good things I had thought about him weren't true. He wasn't the greatest guy in the world. He wasn't the man of my dreams. Finally, I understood what Bobby had been hinting at all summer that Reed was a pothead.

This time I didn't need a diversion to avoid being pressured. I just shook my head and told him no thanks. I tried to play it cool, but after a minute my eyes filled with tears. Heartbroken, I got up and ran to Bobby's truck hoping Reed would follow me and apologize. Maybe he would say he was just kidding, it was a joke, it was a fake. But as the sweet, acrid smell of marijuana smoke reached my nostrils, I knew it was no joke. I turned around to look at Reed, who had simply laid down on his side, elbow bent, head propped on his hand, and continued to smoke as he stared at the fire.

At that point, my sadness turned to anger. I was mad at all of them, at Bobby and Lydia for going off and probably having sex in a dirty old garage, at Haley for betraying me and getting drunk and acting like a slut, at Doug for trying to pressure me into drinking, at Reed for showing his true colors. And, I was mad at myself for having been such a Pollyanna. Done with the lot of them, I climbed into the truck and slammed the door, deciding I would stay there until everybody was ready to go. Despite my rage, at some point I must have fallen asleep.

The next thing I knew, I was lying across the front seat, the door was open, and someone was tugging at my foot. I opened my eyes, surprised to see Reed standing there beside the truck, his hand pulling at my shoe. I sat up, and immediately I knew that a fair amount of time must have passed, because he was as high as a kite.

"Something's wrong," he said, his eyes heavy-lidded, his body leaning side to side.

"What?" I snapped, still angry.

"Something's wrong. Over there."

Blinking, he pointed, and in the direction of the Schumann's home I could see an odd red glow. I got out of the truck and stood on the doorframe, getting higher to see better. From there, the "something wrong" was clear.

The Schumann's house was on fire.

FIFTEEN

The next hour was a blur. As Reed stood there looking stoned, I began shouting for the others. Doug and Haley, still half drunk, clothes askew, came running from the shadows as Bobby and Lydia emerged from the garage. All four of them spotted the fire at the same moment, and then we all made a mad scramble to get to the farmhouse.

"The truck will be faster!" Bobby yelled, so we all jumped in the back and he took off driving along the edge of the cornfield, finally slamming his brakes to a stop in the Schumann's backyard.

Like many Amish farmhouses, the Schumann's place was a series of additions and expansions each joined at one corner, creating a stairstep effect. From what we could see, the part that was on fire was the furthest section out, the addition that had been built for Lydia's grandparents when they were still alive, a sort of in-law suite known among the Amish as a *Dawdy Haus.* That was an incredible relief, because as far as I knew, currently no one was living in that part of the home.

Still, if we didn't act quickly, the fire could spread to the rest of the house. We moved as fast as we could, Lydia leading us to the source of water and showing Bobby how to use the pump so it would flow through the hose. I called for help from the phone shanty out back and then ran around the house, trying every door until I found one that was open. I ran inside yelling, with Lydia and Reed right behind. Between the three of us, we found Lydia's seven-year-old brother, Caleb, and her six-year-old sister, Rebecca, and got them out the front door and onto the lawn safely. The children were both in their nightclothes, and they stood there shivering in the heat, watching wide-eyed as the *Dawdy Haus* was consumed with flame.

"Is this everyone?" I screamed to Lydia over the roar of the fire.

"No! I don't see Ezra or my parents!"

Once he heard that, Reed ran back inside to search for them while Lydia herded the other two siblings around back to help throw buckets of water onto the fire. When fire trucks pealed in the distance, I ran toward the road to flag them down. Obviously, I wasn't thinking clearly, because by that point the flame had grown so large that there's no way they could have missed it.

Three trucks responded to the call, and soon the place was swarming with men and women in firefighting gear. We were told to move back and stay out of the way while they tried to do their job. It wasn't until then that I realized Reed had never come back out of the house. Lydia was already frantic, insisting that her parents and little brother were still in there somewhere. I grew just as frantic. Joining in her cries for help, I begged them to save Reed and prayed furiously for his safety.

Another five minutes passed before he finally emerged. Like a phoenix from the ashes, he came stumbling from the house, the unconscious body of Lydia's three-year-old brother, Ezra, in his arms. He handed the child over to a professional and then simply fell forward onto his face on the lawn. His entire back and both arms were black, and for a moment I thought he had put on a jacket. Then I realized what I was seeing wasn't a jacket at all. It was his skin.

I didn't remember much after that, though eventually the fire was brought under control and Reed and Ezra were whisked away to the hospital. Lydia's parents had not turned up, and with a lot of hushed whispers, Caleb and Rebecca were sent home for the night with some of their Amish cousins—though Lydia refused to leave until her parents were found. Police appeared on the scene, and we had to repeat the story of what had happened over and over. No one knew how the fire had started, but at least the firefighters had managed to stop the blaze from traveling much further than the washroom that connected the main house to the *Dawdy Haus*.

Finally, in the early hours of the morning, our worst fears were confirmed when the charred remains of Lydia's mother and father were discovered. At first, no one understood why they had been in the *Dawdy Haus* because their bedroom was in the main house. It wasn't until the police announced that one more body had been found on the scene that it all made sense. That third body was a tiny one, not much more than six pounds, and apparently had been only a few hours old.

I didn't understand at first but later it was explained to me that Mrs. Schumann and her husband had obviously gone out to the *Dawdy Haus* that night because she had been in labor. That was how the Amish often did it, giving birth to their children at home with only a midwife in atendance, sometimes not even telling the other family members what was happening until the next morning, after the child had been born, cleaned up, and placed neatly in its cradle.

Later, Lydia would struggle greatly with guilt, knowing she should have sensed that her mother was in labor when she refused lunch and dinner and had spent much of the day out of sight, supposedly resting. Worse, after Lydia had snuck out and run across the back field to meet up with the rest of us that night, Mrs. Schummann had likely been in the throes of delivery, giving birth out in the *Dawdy Haus* so that the younger children would not be disturbed by her cries of pain.

When all was said and done, the whole situation was a horrible tragedy for Lydia and her family. We all wondered how the fire had begun, whether from an overturned lamp, a spill of oil, maybe a leaking propane tank. What we didn't expect was what the fire inspector finally announced after walking in a clump of dried grass along the back wall. Judging by several small cardboard cylinders found nearby, the source of ignition had been sparks from a Roman candle.

Those of us who had been out of the back field when it happened understood that *we* had burned the house down, *we* had killed Lydia's parents and her newborn sibling.

We did not attempt to hide what had happened, nor did we lie or make excuses. We were honest immediately, saying we had been in the back field shooting off Roman candles earlier. Upon hearing our confession, the police immediately proceeded to the scene, to see if it could have been possible to set the house on fire from so far away.

Once they got there, of course, they found a bunch of empty beer cans as well as several roaches, a roach clip, and some rolling papers near the fire pit. They also found the casings from several dozen spent Roman candles, and all sorts of burn marks in the nearby trees and cornstalks—probably from the Roman candles that had shot out sideways from the fire. Upon further examination, evidence of sexual activity was found in the garage and out behind the big oak tree. We later learned that when Reed's clothes were cut away from his body at the hospital, a small baggie of marijuana had been found in the pocket.

Suddenly, what had looked like a tragic accident quickly turned to a crime scene, not to mention a scandal of monumental proportions. The five of us—Bobby, Lydia, Doug, Haley, and I—were arrested. Along with Reed, who would be in the hospital for a good while yet, we were charged with everything from reckless endangerment to involuntary manslaughter. Once we had been processed and Haley and I were identified as juveniles, the others were charged with corruption of minors as well.

Of course, our parents and their lawyers were on top of things quickly. One by one, we had all been released by morning. Considering her limited involvement and the extenuating circumstances, Lydia's charges were dropped. The rest of us weren't so lucky. For the next several months, our lives became a haze of depositions, media bombardments, trials, and sentencing hearings. In the end, we each had our own cross to bear.

Convicted of reckless endangerment and involuntary manslaughter, Haley and I were both sentenced to a year of house arrest and a year of probation.

Convicted of reckless endangerment, involuntary manslaughter, and corruption of minors, Bobby was sentenced to six months in jail and a year of probation.

Convicted of reckless endangerment, involuntary manslaughter, corruption of minors, and public drunkenness, Doug was sentenced to eight months in jail and a year of probation.

Convicted of reckless endangerment, involuntary manslaughter, corruption of minors, and a misdemeanor drug charge, Reed got a year in jail and three years of probation. As the oldest one there, the judge had come down hardest on him.

For the rest of our lives, we would all have to live with the knowledge that our actions had caused the deaths of three innocent people. Beyond that, the worst part for me and Haley—worse even than the claustrophobia of house arrest, the humiliation of probation, the constant invasion of privacy by the media—was the way the kids in our high school reacted. At first, because of our age, our names weren't released, but rumors spread like wildfire and soon everyone knew who the two minors in the Dreiheit Five had been. After that, people we had thought were friends turned their backs on us. Girls gossiped about us. Boys taunted us—or came on to us, thinking we were big-time partiers. The stoners even made a few overtures of friendship, which would have been funny if it weren't so sad. "Slut" was painted on our lockers. Roach clips were left on our desks. Condoms were put on the antennas of our cars.

Even the teachers who had so highly praised my schoolwork the year before could now barely look at me.

Everyone assumed the worst.

No one gave us the benefit of the doubt.

Through everything, all I kept thinking about was that here I was—a virgin who had never smoked, never drank, never took drugs—being accused of all sorts of things by people who had done far worse. Their judgment was relentless.

With house arrest, we were allowed to go to school and to work, but that was it. My bedroom slowly became my prison and my safe haven, all at the same time. By the end of the year, I chose not to stand for graduation. Instead, I received my diploma in the mail, and then I cried for three days.

The only thing that helped me hang on to my sanity were the letters that came in a steady flow from the Amish community. Somehow, they knew how badly we needed to hear that we were forgiven, that we were being prayed for, that life was going to be okay. Even Lydia and her siblings wrote, though little Ezra's letters weren't much more than scribbles on the page. Rejected by our own community, we were embraced by the very community we had wronged. When my house arrest ended, I actually got in my car and drove to Dreiheit and made myself stand there in the back field of the Schumann's property and contemplate all that had happened that fateful night. I wanted to curse God and turn my back on Him for good, but in the midst of my hurt and rage I could not forget the kindnesses that had been shown to me by the Amish in His name.

Finally, I had simply knelt down on the ground and surrendered, asking God to come back into my life, fill me with peace, and make me whole again. Thinking of the Amish and how quick they had been to forgive, I knew that I also had some people I needed to forgive—like rotten friends and insensitive teachers and cruel strangers. I had to forgive intrusive reporters and unethical tabloid publishers and gossipy neighbors. When I finally opened up and let all of it go—all the hatred, all the shame, all the resentment—then that huge, aching, empty place inside of me immediately began to fill up with something else, something much bigger than any problem this world could throw my way.

I had given up to God my resentments and He had given me back His peace.

As the sun set in the sky that day, I had heard the sound of footsteps and opened my eyes. When I looked up, it was to see a young, bearded Amish man heading my way, trailed by two preteens, also Amish, who seemed concerned by the sight of me kneeling there crying. As they got closer, they recognized who I was, and they insisted that I come up to the house with them. Flanked by Lydia's younger siblings Caleb and Rebecca on one side, and her older sister's husband, Nathaniel, on the other, I accepted their invitation and went into the home that my actions had helped to burn.

Though the *Dawdy Haus* had not been rebuilt, otherwise, the place looked the same. All evidence of the fire was gone, the washhouse repaired, the smoke damage to the main house taken care of. Inside, I was met by Lydia, who simply wrapped her arms around me and held on to me for a long time. We all cried then, but they were good tears, tears of healing.

Sitting there at their table, sharing a meal, catching up with all that had happened in the last year and a half, I had learned more about how Lydia's older sister, Grete, her husband, Nathaniel, and their baby, Tresa, had moved into the farmhouse soon after the repairs had begun, and with Lydia's help had taken over the raising of their younger siblings. Aided by the whole Amish community, what was left of this family had managed to pick up the pieces and go on. I knew they missed their parents, but they seemed to be okay in spite of that. Most importantly, they seemed to harbor no ill will whatsoever, not toward any of us.

In the months that followed that heart-healing encounter, I found myself spending more and more time out in Lancaster County. Haley's mom gave me a key to her house and let me come and go—something I did far more often those days than did her own daughter, who wanted to be left alone and seemed to be assuaging her pain in other ways. Conversely, I found more healing and restoration by allowing myself to feel the embrace of the Amish community. I accepted every invitation that came my way—for meals, for family gatherings, even for an Amish hymn sing. Throughout all of it, I was gaining strength and courage and the confidence that had been stripped away from me in high school.

When my probation ended, I went away to college out of state, ready at last to start fresh.

I was in for a rude awakening.

The problem I found was that no matter how much I wanted to leave the past behind and move on, as long as people continued to recognize me, that simply wasn't going to be possible. There were whispers as I passed by. There was the occasional proposition and catcall. Still, I managed to rise above most of it and endure my freshman and sophomore years.

In the fall of my junior year in college, Bobby and Lydia announced their engagement. I went home for the wedding, a sweet, simple affair in Dreiheit that I hoped would mark a new beginning for both of them. The reception had been held in the fellowship hall of their church, and I made the regrettable mistake of conversing with a woman who sat down next to me at one of the tables. She was extremely warm and friendly, and soon the two of us were chatting away like fast friends, something I didn't do very often with strangers.

Eventually, she asked me the inevitable question, what did it feel like to be back in Dreiheit, to see my brother and Lydia tie the knot despite the heartbreak in the aftermath of the fire. Usually, I deflected such questions, especially from people I didn't know. But she was so kind, so open, and my emotions were already running high from being back in town and from seeing my brother get married.

Needing someone to confide in, this time instead of avoiding the question, I answered it honestly. I told her exactly how it felt, how I worried that Bobby was marrying Lydia more from guilt than love. I talked about the night of the fire and how it had been completely twisted by the press into something much more sinister than it actually was. I talked about my life since, how I wanted to move on but every time I tried, someone was there to remind me, to harass me, to make false assumptions about me.

"If it hadn't been for the way the Amish responded," I had told her, "with grace and forgiveness and love, I never would have survived these past few years. In fact, given the torment I suffered in high school, if not for them I would probably have killed myself. Thank the Lord, the embrace I felt from the Amish community was probably the only thing that helped me find my way through."

The evening ended well, Bobby and Lydia headed off on their honeymoon, and I went back to college.

One week later, I was in the checkout line at the school bookstore when I saw the new issue of a nationally published tabloid. On the cover was a photo of my face, and along the bottom the words "Saved from Suicide by Amish Embrace." Heart pounding, I bought the issue, ran outside to a secluded place behind a row of bushes, and vomited.

Later, alone in my dorm room, I sat down on the bed and forced myself to read the article. I knew before I even started it that it had been written by the woman who sat next to me at the wedding reception. For the most part, she had taken what I told her and turned it into a sympathetic piece about how hard it is to get on with your life once you have been convicted of a crime. But the quotes she chose to use verbatim all made it sound as if I were blaming everyone else in the group for what happened, as if I didn't deserve the punishment I had received, as if I had done no wrong. Worse, my comment about how I probably would have "killed myself"—purely an expression of speech—she had treated as literal. Apparently, after talking with me she had interviewed several doctors and a psychiatrist, and the article was full of comments about suicide and death and depression.

Half of the people on my campus hadn't known who I was before, but now it seemed that all of them did. After a week of sympathetic glances, snide comments, and a flyer about "Are You Considering Suicide?" anonymously slid under my dorm room door, I gave up.

With the last shred of dignity I could muster, I marched down to the administration building and dropped out of school.

Back home, feeling even more infuriated and violated by the experience, I decided to sue for false representation and illegal audiotaping. The author and publisher settled out of court, but of course the money I won did little to erase the damage that had been done. In fact, almost every penny of it was used to reimburse my parents for the legal fees that had been incurred during my criminal trial—so while I was able to break even, I ended up with only a few thousand dollars left over.

At that point I began to take steps to create a new identity for myself, a new life, far away from the tragedy and the past and the media that had so defined me since the fire. I had been growing my hair out for the last year, but now I dyed it blond, changed my name, obtained a new ID.

Then, with just those several thousand dollars to my name, I packed up my car, told my parents goodbye, and drove to California. Once there, I worked my way up the coast until I found a town I liked and a decent job. After one week in the skip tracing department at Kepler-West Finance, my coworker Kiki saw that I was looking for a cheap apartment and asked me if I would like to rent a room in her house instead. We worked out the details and I moved in, and I had been there ever since. Like Norman, Kiki knew I had made a break with my past, changed my name, and started over. Unlike Norman, though, she didn't know why—and to her credit, she never once asked. She simply took me for what I was and became my friend.

At that point in my life, I really needed a friend.

Now Kiki was in the hospital with twelve stitches sewn into her forehead, and my carefully constructed world was about to be blown to bits. As I reached Dreiheit and turned onto the road that would lead me to the Schumann farm, I took a deep breath to ask God to keep me safe and prepared for all that lay ahead.

SIXTEEN

As I neared the farm I shouldn't have been surprised to see a news van parked at the end of the driveway. I called Lydia and told her about it and asked if we could meet elsewhere.

She suggested we go to her and Bobby's apartment, explaining where I could find the hidden key to let myself in.

"You go first, and I will wait a bit and then come there myself and join you. That way, if the news people follow me, they will not realize that you are already in there."

I had only been to their apartment once

before, so Lydia reminded me of the directions and I headed off, glad to see when I got there that the place was deserted. Their apartment was in downtown Dreiheit, two blocks from Main Street in a small complex of ten units. I parked my rental car in the nearly empty lot in a space marked for visitors and then walked to door 108. The key was hidden in the light fixture just as Lydia had described, so I easily got it down and used it to let myself in. As I did, I thought about the break-in that had happened here night before last, and I wondered if their intruder here and the man who had broken into my house in California were one and the same person. A shudder ran through me at the memory, and I had to remind myself that he was still hospitalized and in police custody.

Once inside the apartment, my heart raced as I gingerly checked each of the rooms to make sure I was indeed alone. To be extra careful, I peeked in all the closets and under the beds as well. As I did, I could see what Lydia had meant about the place being out of order somehow, but I was still impressed by how neat and clean it was overall. Knowing what a slob Bobby had been growing up, I felt sure all the credit went to Lydia.

Their apartment was comfortable but small, with a galley kitchen and breakfast nook, a living room, one bathroom, and two bedrooms. There was a crib in the master bedroom, and it wasn't until I saw it that I remembered Lydia was pregnant. The poor thing. Here she was going through all this at a time when trauma was the last thing she needed. I tried to calculate how far along she would be by now, but I couldn't remember when Bobby first told me she was expecting. Four months ago? Six months ago? Whenever it was, it had been a while, so she must be due to deliver soon. I felt guilty for how little I knew about their life. What kind of sister was I?

Worse, their son, Isaac, was my nephew, and I didn't even know how old he was. Judging by a row of photos that hung in the hallway, he looked to be about six or seven. No, actually, I realized that he had to be at least eight, because the last time I saw him was seven years ago when I came to Dreiheit to say goodbye, just before I moved away to California. At that time Isaac was still in diapers, not yet walking. Judging from the pictures I was looking at now, he had grown into an adorable little boy.

Once I finished my search and knew no bad guys were in hiding, I returned to the living room to wait for Lydia. More photos lined the top of the television, and I walked over to take a look. Most of them were candid shots, taken outside in nature: Isaac grinning down from his perch in a tree, Bobby waving from a Jet Ski, Lydia holding Isaac's hand as they strolled through a pumpkin patch. They were all so engaging, and I was glad that when Lydia left the Amish order she had left behind their ban against photographs as well. As far as I knew, none of the local Amish communities allowed photographs of people, feeling that would violate the Bible's commandment against making graven images.

I picked up the last picture on the row, the one that seemed to be the most recent. It was a family portrait, and judging by the autumn leaves in the background, I guessed that it had been taken at a photo studio just a few months before. In the picture, all three of them were smiling, and I could make out a small baby bulge under Lydia's maroon corduroy jumper. Isaac sat in front, and his impish grin reminded me so much of Bobby when he was a boy. Except for that smile and the trademark dimple in one cheek, Isaac was all Lydia, with the same long eyelashes and delicate features.

To look at that picture, they seemed like one big happy family, their smiles genuine, their pose comfortably affectionate. Who could know whether that was an accurate representation or not?

I was just putting the picture back in place when I heard the front doorknob jiggling, and then the door swung open and a large man stepped inside. Still jumpy from my encounter with the ski-masked intruder, I was about to scream when Lydia walked in behind him.

"Anna!" she cried, setting down the bag she was carrying and then waddling quickly across the room to give me a long, fierce hug. I was startled by the intensity of her greeting—not to mention the girth of her pregnant belly that protruded between us—but I hugged her back, realizing as I did that I was genuinely glad to see her.

The man who had come with her disappeared into the back without a word, which seemed odd. Judging by his defensive posture as he went, however, I realized he must be some sort of bodyguard. He was gone for a short while, and then he returned and announced that all was clear.

Lydia released me from our hug, and as we pulled apart I gave her a questioning look.

"Let us go to the kitchen and I will explain everything," she said.

Picking up the bag she had brought in, she led me to the breakfast nook set in the curve of a bay window. I took a seat there, asking if the man who had remained in the living room was a friend.

"No, he is a professional," Lydia replied, setting the bag on a nearby counter and unloading its contents. "I believe such a thing is very expensive, but this is being paid for by Mr. Wynn."

I wasn't sure why Hayley's father had become involved here, but I was glad to see that Lydia was being protected by someone who obviously knew what they were doing.

"What happened to the Amish protection brigade?"

"The men who guarded us yesterday

had to go back to work today, and Caleb and Nathaniel need to spend their time out with the cows, not inside the house with the women and children. Mr. Wynn offered protection last night, so this morning I took him up on it."

"I don't understand," I said. "Why Mr. Wynn? What does he have to do with anything?"

Lydia let out a long sigh as she continued to unload the bag.

"I called Haley again last night, to see how she was doing and to tell her that you were coming. Her father was there when I called. She was resting, so I spoke with him instead. When I told him you had been attacked, he pointed out that between your attack and Doug being dead and Bobby going missing, it sounded to him like maybe someone is out to get the Dreiheit Five."

"The Dreiheit Five? Why?"

"We could not come up with any reason. But right then Mr. Wynn decided to hire a bodyguard for Haley just in case, and since Bobby had already said Isaac and I were in danger, Mr. Wynn insisted on hiring a guard for us too, probably because he knew I could not afford it. He did not know how to reach you, but he told me to extend the same offer to you when you came."

"That's awfully nice of him, but I'll decline for now," I said, trying to hide my dismay at Lydia's big mouth. She had no business telling Haley's dad that I was on my way or that I had been attacked. Mr. Wynn was a good man and an old friend, but it still wasn't Lydia's place to share my business with anyone. "You didn't tell anybody else I was coming, did you?"

"Just my sister so she could ready a room at the farm."

If the sister knew, the kids likely knew, and soon word would spread through the Amish grapevine and eventually be out all over town. Great.

"Of course," Lydia continued, "I had to insist that the guard not carry any weapons. There can be no guns on the farm, not to mention that when Bobby shows up, I do not want him accidentally shot."

I didn't comment, but I was savvy enough to know that the bodyguard now stationed in the living room was not unarmed. I hadn't seen any telltale bulge at his side, but I felt sure he had a gun on him somewhere, probably in an ankle holster.

"What about Reed?" I asked, my pulse suddenly surging. "Has he been warned? Has anything bad happened to him?"

"I guess he is okay or we would have heard otherwise. Mr. Wynn was going to call him last night after he talked to me. At least Reed can afford to hire his own bodyguard if he wants one. He is some big shot down in Washington, you know. I think he is very successful." Lydia unwrapped some foil to reveal a large square of cornbread, glancing at me. "You want lunch, *yah?*"

My face flushing with heat for no reason, I nodded. My appetite had returned since sitting in the restaurant with Mr. Carver, and now I realized I was famished. Lydia opened various containers she had brought and served up two plates with a hearty-looking beef stew and a colorful pile of carrots and peas.

"You look so very different with the long, blond hair," Lydia said, glancing my way again as she put one of the plates in the microwave. "Is very stylish, very . . . how you say . . . sexy, *yah*?"

She giggled with the word "sexy," and I

was reminded of the sheltered nature of her upbringing. She hadn't been Amish for years, but in many ways, she hadn't changed at all. Then again, I thought as I watched her push the buttons on the microwave, in some ways she had become a regular, modern woman.

"Thanks," I replied. "I didn't do it to be sexy, just unrecognizable. I really don't relish the thought of seeing my face splashed all over the news again."

"I know, I know. The reporters, they are respectfully staying off of my sister's land, but with their long-range cameras pointed right at the house, we have had to close all the blinds for fear of being photographed inside. The children are going stir-crazy not to be outside."

"Outside, are you kidding? It's freezing out there."

"*Yah,* but they are used to it. They like to get bundled up and play stick ball in the yard." She pulled one steaming plate from the microwave and put in the next.

"How are all the kids, Lydia?"

"They are *gut,* thank you."

"How about Grete? I've always felt so

sorry for her, that she had to become a mother to her younger brothers and sisters when she was barely an adult herself. Are she and Nathaniel still doing all right?"

"Oh, *yah.* Grete was no stranger to hard work, and she has done well with the kids. She and Nathaniel have been good stewards of the land too, keeping the farm profitable."

"That's a relief. And your siblings are really okay?"

Lydia considered my question for a moment.

"I think Caleb could have used the stern hand of a real father, but Rebecca and Ezra are fine."

"Did Grete and Nathaniel ever have any more children of their own, or were their hands already full raising your siblings?"

"They wanted more, but Tresa is the only child of theirs born without the disorder that runs in our family. Three other times Grete carried a babe to term, but they always died soon after delivery. Is not unusual around here. The Lord gives and the Lord takes away. Like you said, she already had her hands full anyway."

Lydia busied herself with setting the heated plates of food on the table, and adding napkins and silverware. As she did, I thought about the incredibly high incidence of genetic disorders that existed among the Amish. From what I understood, it had to do with the fact that the Lancaster County Amish usually married within the community, so their gene pool grew more limited—and more prone to genetic mutations—with each generation. According to Bobby, progress was being made all the time in the prevention and treatment of many of the common Amish disorders, though I wondered how close they were to finding a cure for the disorder that prevented Lydia's sister from being able to deliver healthy, surviving children. At least Lydia hadn't had to worry; by marrying a man who wasn't Amish, she had altered the direction of her own genetic fate.

She joined me at the table and bowed her head in silence. I thought maybe she was waiting for me to pray, but after a moment she softly said, "Amen," opened her eyes, and began eating.

"Amen," I echoed, feeling foolish as I

remembered that that was how the Amish began every meal, in silent prayer.

I ate the delicious stew as Lydia caught me up on the latest development with Bobby's situation.

Looking embarrassed, Lydia told me she had called Bobby's office this morning, to see if they knew anything of his whereabouts. According to the office manager, they hadn't seen Bobby for days, not since before he was suspended.

"Suspended?" I asked, nearly dropping my fork.

"Yes, Anna. I was very shocked to learn that two and a half weeks ago, Bobby got in trouble at work and was given a three-week suspension without pay. He is supposed to start back on Monday, if he shows up by then. Why he never told me this, I do not understand."

"Did they say why?"

"No," Lydia replied, looking as if she was on the verge of tears. "They say that is between him and Dr. Updyke. Mostly, I was just mortified that I did not know about any of this, even though I am his wife."

"I don't understand," I said. "Do you mean to tell me that Bobby hasn't been to work in two and a half weeks and you never noticed?"

"That is correct. If he had stayed at home or laid on the couch or spent time with us somehow, then I would have known. But my husband left this apartment every morning at the same time as usual and come home at the end of the day at the same time as usual. I do not know where he has been going or what he has been doing every day, but the office manager swore to me that he was not coming in to work." Lydia blinked, and two tears ran down her cheeks. "Bobby loves me," she said intensely. "I do not know why he did this strange thing—or why he thought he could not tell me about it—but I trust him. I believe in him. Whatever he has been doing, I know that all will be made clear in the end."

We sat there together in silence as I thought about what she said, and I could feel myself growing furious with Bobby. It was one thing not to tell his wife that he had been suspended from his job; it was quite another to carry out the elaborate pretense of a regular nine-to-five job, day after day, for almost three weeks.

"Did you ask to speak with the doctor? Surely he could tell you why Bobby was suspended."

"I have called several times, but always he has been busy or out."

I was reminded of the disposable cell phone I had bought at the airport. After loading the number into my own phone, I gave it to Lydia, who thanked me profusely.

Returning to our conversation, I asked Lydia about where she thought Bobby may have been going every day, but she had no idea.

"Sorry to be so personal," I said, "but I need to know about your marriage. Were you happy? Did Bobby lie to you often? Given what you know now, do you still believe there's no chance that he has simply abandoned you?"

Lydia was quiet for a long moment, and my questions must have killed her appetite because she pushed her plate away as she sat there thinking. Finally, she answered me, pretty much telling me exactly what I had expected to hear. According to her, she and Bobby were still deeply in love. Lydia insisted that he was happily married, that he adored spending time with Isaac, that he very much enjoyed his job at the lab, and that she had no doubt he intended to live there with her and Isaac forever.

"He was especially excited about the new baby. I cannot tell you how many nights he lay next to me in bed simply holding on to my tummy, whispering sweet words to our child. A man who does that has no intention of leaving. You have to believe me on this, Anna."

"Okay," I replied. "I am going to proceed on the assumption that everything you've just said is true. But if I find out about even more secrets that Bobby was keeping from you, I won't be surprised—and you shouldn't be either."

SEVENTEEN

We were just finishing our lunch when we heard a knock on the front door.

"Are you expecting anyone?" I whispered.

Lydia shook her head as she got up from the table.

"Ma'am?" the bodyguard said, leaning into the room. "Looks like a woman in her fifties, blond hair, holding a package?"

I told Lydia I would stay in the kitchen if she wanted to see who it was. Nodding, she followed the bodyguard out of the room, and I listened as she opened the front door and carried on a conversation with someone whose voice sounded very familiar. Straining to listen, I finally decided it was Melody Wynn, Haley's mother.

I wondered why she was here and not with her daughter at this difficult time, but Haley and her mother had a strange and complicated relationship that had never made much sense to me. To hear Haley tell it, even though her mother had given up her career as a plant biologist to become a stay-at-home mom when Haley was born, she hadn't been very suited to the role. Rather than dote on her little girl, Melody had spent most of her time doting on the plants in the massive greenhouse she had built in their backyard. Haley grew up feeling neglected and lost, the poor little rich girl who rarely got much of her mother's attention. Her father's attention, on the other hand, was adoring and absolute—on those rare occasions when he managed to get home on time. Lost between a mother who was there in body but not in mind and a father who was there in mind but not in body, Haley basically raised herself. When we first met, she was the most independent, self-sufficient kid I had ever known. That was one of the things I had liked most about her, though it took a while for me to understand the depth of pain behind that independence.

Her parents had divorced the year before we met for reasons Haley didn't divulge for a long time. All I knew at first was that her father had been the one to get custody of their only child and her mother had moved out to a little cottage in Dreiheit and gone back to working full time with an agricultural research firm—a position that seemed to suit her much better than that of full-time mom. Eventually, Haley confided that her mother had been engaging in casual affairs for years, and when Mr. Wynn found out about it, he had immediately filed for a divorce.

By the time Haley and I started high school, those wounds had healed a bit, though it seemed to me that Haley and her mother were more like friends than parent and child. Melody was always very warm and friendly with Haley, but then again she was that way with everyone, her house an open door. When Haley and I came on our weekend visits, it felt as if we were checking into a dorm with a housemother rather than staying with someone's actual mom. It was around that time that Melody took to wearing diaphanous, earthy dresses and letting her hair grow long, and privately I nicknamed her "The Floater," because she was someone who floated through spaces, lost in her own little world, oblivious to the pain inside her own child.

Now in the living room, Melody was peppering Lydia with questions about Bobby, and I felt bad for her. Lydia was such an earnest, honest person that I knew she was finding it hard not to admit that I was here to investigate his disappearance—and that I was in the very next room. I decided to make it easier for her. I rose and walked to the doorway and stood there for a moment, looking past the bodyguard to study my old best friend's mother. Melody still wore her hair loose and wavy and blond, though just to her shoulders now rather than halfway down her back. Her face may have seemed a little older, but she was still beautiful.

"Are you sure I can't help with anything?" Melody was asking. "How about Isaac?

Does he need a sitter or rides to school or anything?"

"Thank you, no. Isaac will be staying home from school until we know what is going on."

"What about your job at the bridal shop?"

"I am not scheduled to go in until next Wednesday, so I suppose I will wait and see what happens between now and then."

"Well, please let me know if—" Melody's voice stopped short when she spotted me. "Oh, I'm sorry. I didn't realize you had company. I won't hold you up."

"Melody," I said, stepping forward. "It's me. Annalise. Well, I go by just Anna now."

The expression on Melody's face went from confusion to surprise. With a squeal, she ran across the room and wrapped me in a hug, holding on as fervently as Lydia had earlier. For the next few minutes, she went on and on about how different I looked. I told her the opposite, that she hadn't aged a day, that she was still as stunning as ever.

Melody repeated many of the same questions to me that she had asked of

Lydia, expressing her concerns about Bobby and her sadness about Doug. In turn, I asked about Haley and how she was doing.

"I have no idea," Melody replied mournfully. "When she couldn't find her husband, she kept calling me for help, but once he turned up dead, all she wanted was her father. I don't know why I should be surprised. She's never let me be there for her before. She wouldn't even let me go with her to the funeral home."

Lydia and I glanced at each other, neither one of us sure how to respond. I hadn't spoken to Haley in years, so I was hardly in a position to comment. Melody seemed to sense our discomfort, because she changed the subject yet again and asked me how long I would be in town and where I was staying.

"Anna will be with me, at my family's farm," Lydia volunteered.

Melody squinted her eyes and leaned toward me, lowering her voice.

"You do know the Amish don't heat their bedrooms, right?" she asked. I did know that—though I had forgotten until she reminded me. "If it gets too cold for you over there, let me know. There's always room on my couch. Maybe Haley could come out too. It could be like old times."

I thanked her for the offer, thinking how oddly Melody's mind worked. Old times? Haley's husband was dead! My brother was missing and was being sought by the police for questioning in his death! Yet somehow The Floater thought we could sit around and eat granola and gab about cute boys.

"Thanks. I'll keep that in mind," I replied, though I doubted I would take advantage of her offer, even if I had to wear footed fleece pajamas to bed. Not only did I feel that I needed to remain close to Lydia for safety's sake, I also knew that if Bobby turned up on his own, he would more than likely show up at the farm.

Melody had to go, but as we said our goodbyes I asked her to please not tell anyone I was in town.

"I know the press will find out eventually," I explained, "but I'd like to keep it quiet as long as I can."

"Can I tell Haley at least? I know she'll want to see you."

"Lydia already told her I was coming.

But if you do speak to her, tell her I drove to her house today on my way here, but there were so many news vans parked out front that I turned around and left. I hope we can figure out a way to get together that doesn't include the media."

Melody put a hand on my wrist and looked deeply into my eyes.

"Please do, Anna. Even if Haley doesn't want her mother around, she still needs her friends. Services for Doug won't be for a few days yet, so give her a call and try to find a way to make it happen before then, okay?"

"Okay," I promised, and with a final hug and a goodbye, Melody was gone.

As Lydia closed the door behind her, I said that if she didn't mind, what I'd like to do next was listen to the messages on their answering machine.

"*Ach,* the machine!" she cried, obviously forgetting that their messages had likely been piling up since she had left here Wednesday night. Rushing to the machine, which sat on a corner table in the living room, she was shocked to see she had twenty-two messages. "I cannot listen. Please, Anna, do this for me and just tell me what you hear. Unless it is the sound of my husband's voice telling me where he is, I do not want to know."

Glad to be left on my own, I told her that was no problem.

"*Gut.* You focus on this. I will wash the dishes and pack up the things Isaac and I need."

I asked if she could loan me some warmer clothes, especially sweaters, and she said that would be no problem.

Grabbing my skip tracing forms and my laptop, I sat down and took a look at their machine, noticing as I did that the bodyguard repositioned himself near the door, right within earshot. Feeling uncomfortable, I wondered if part of his job description included listening to our conversations or monitoring our activities—and reporting back to the man who was paying for his services. I couldn't fathom why Mr. Wynn might want to do such a thing, but just to be prudent I unplugged the machine, carried it to the privacy of Isaac's bedroom, shut the door, and plugged it back in. Settling down on my nephew's the little bed, I listened to the messages that had come in over the last few days.

The first message of any importance had come from Doug on Wednesday evening at 6:58 p.m.: *Hey Bobby, it's Doug. Give me a call ASAP. I'm still at the office but use my cell, not the office line, okay?*

A second message from Doug showed up at 8:40 p.m. This one was especially disconcerting and sounded even more urgent than the first: *Bobby, it's Doug again. Listen, man, we need to talk. I've got the, um, info you wanted, including some you didn't expect. Call me back on my cell the second you get this message. I'm in the car now, driving to the construction site in Exton. You know where that is, right? I should be there in about fifteen minutes, so if you can't reach me on the phone, just come on out there and find me. We really need to talk right away.*

Next was a call that had come in at 11:58 that night. It was Haley, and she sounded drunk: *Bobby? It's Haley. Man, I saw what you did after you left. I don't know if you're stupid or crazy, but you better get that motorcycle back here before Doug comes home, or he's gonna kill you.* The phone made a few clunks and then she spoke again. *'Course, if you're with Doug now and the two of you are out on some joyride or something, then I'm gonna kill both of you. Do you guys have any idea what time it is?* The message ended after that, though from the various sounds that followed, she'd had a little trouble hanging up the phone.

Ten minutes later Melody called, saying Haley was trying to track down Bobby and had asked her to help since she was there in Dreiheit: *Bobby, can you call her when you get in? She wants me to go over to your place and bang on the door, but I'm already dressed for bed so I'm not going to do that. Just call her as soon as you get this, okay? Doesn't matter how late, just call.*

Next was Haley again, the next morning. That time she sounded sober but hung over, and very, very angry. She was looking for Doug and/or Bobby, demanding to know where the motorcycle was and why her husband had never come home. She called twice more during the next hour, each time sounding a little less angry and a little more worried.

At 10:12 a.m., Melody called, saying that Haley was having a fit trying to locate Doug or Bobby: *She still wants me to go to your apartment and bang on the door, but I don't think anybody's home. Bobby or Lydia, when one of you gets in, would you please call me? Haley is practically frantic.*

At 12:15 p.m. the same day, there was a brief message from a man with a deep voice: *This is the Exton Police Department, trying to locate a Mr. Robert Jensen. Would you please contact us at your earliest convenience?* The man went on to leave his name and phone number.

At 2:45 p.m., the Dreiheit police had also called looking for Bobby and asking that either he or his wife please call them back as soon as possible. After that, there were a number of messages from various reporters and a few nosy friends who wanted to know what was going on, but nothing else of any importance.

No calls had come in from Bobby at all.

Lydia came in twice while I was working, the first time to get some of Isaac's clothes, the second time to see how much longer I would be because she wanted to get back to the farm before dark, especially because it was supposed to start snowing any time now. Glancing at my watch, I was shocked to see that it was almost 3:30 in the afternoon—and in Pennsylvania in January it would likely be dark within an hour.

Before we separated, I wanted to reconstruct the events of Wednesday evening from her point of view one more time. Lydia said that she and Isaac had left for choir practice around six and returned a little after nine, to find that while they had been gone not only had Bobby run by the house to grab dinner and leave her a note saying that he would be working late, but also, apparently after he left again, the apartment had been broken into by someone else, someone who had poked around but seemed to have taken only one thing, the envelope containing information on how to find me.

Just minutes after Lydia and Isaac had arrived after choir practice and discovered all of this, Bobby called to tell her that they were in danger and that they needed to leave immediately. She had done as he said, racing to her sister's farm. Though she had sent her brother Caleb over yesterday to fix the lock on the door and retrieve her box of important papers, she hadn't returned to the apartment herself until this afternoon, when she met me here. At no point during any of that had she ever contacted the police about the break-in nor filed a missing persons report on Bobby. When I asked why, she seemed confused and said that once I was on the case, it had never crossed her mind to do so.

"Not even after you heard about Doug's death?" I asked. "What if the person who broke in here was the same person who killed Doug? The police need to be notified."

When I said that, Lydia put her head in her hands.

"I do not think as you do, Anna," she cried. "So much evil around, so many confusing things. I just assume when Bobby finally comes home, he will explain it all to me. I thought this would be over by now."

She seemed so upset and remorseful

that I didn't press the issue. I just suggested that she head over to the Dreiheit police station on her way home and file a missing persons report on Bobby. Against my better judgment but knowing it was the right thing to do, I also advised her to bring them the message tape.

"When you are ready to come out to the farm," Lydia said as we were leaving, "call me on the cell phone you gave me, and I will tell you if the reporters are gone yet."

"Are you sure this isn't too much of an imposition on your sister and the rest of the family?"

"Of course not, Anna. My family is your family."

Once the bodyguard had checked to make sure no reporters or bad guys were lurking outside, we walked to the parking lot, and as we parted ways, I gave Lydia my most encouraging smile.

"You hang in there," I said. "We may have a lot of questions right now, but I promise you, I will stick with this until I find him."

Tears filled Lydia's eyes.

"I am just so scared for him," she whispered. "Thank you, Anna. Thank you for being here."

I didn't reply but merely nodded, knowing that if I tried to speak I would start crying as well.

EIGHTEEN

Stephanie

June 7, 1812

Despite the winds that carry hints of warmer weather from the south, I have taken to strolling each afternoon around the grounds of the palace. The doctor tells me that such activity can lead to a healthier pregnancy, easier delivery, and a more robust child. As this thinking is quite unconventional, I began these endeavors with some trepidation, but of late have come to anticipate them greatly. Now each day, after dispensing with my duties of the morning and taking lunch and a nap, my attendants prepare me for an outdoor afternoon stroll, though they are also skeptical and look upon this action in a somewhat condescending manner.

June 20, 1812

The doctor's advice has proven true, for I feel much healthier than I did when I was in my seventh month with Princess Amalie. I stayed mostly in bed that time, as per the normal conventions, and I felt sickly to the very end. This time, however, I find that I grow stronger each day despite the bulging belly that protrudes from the folds of my gowns.

My confidence in the doctor's advice has been increased by the frequent sightings of one of our tenant farmer's wives, a lovely young woman who seems to be with child also, and perhaps in the same month in which I find myself. I have seen her numerous times on my walks, and each time, though her stomach also protrudes from the folds of her much plainer gown, she is forever working: hanging laundry, feeding chickens, even carrying tools for her farmer-husband—and all of this with a toddler often propped on her hip! Taking the evidence of her obviously robust health and my own good humour, I now firmly believe that fresh air and hard work can be healthy for a woman who is with child.

July 3, 1812

Against all propriety and convention, I have taken to speaking with this young tenant farmer's wife, whom I see daily now on my afternoon strolls around the grounds. Her name is Priscilla, and she is a twenty-four-year-old Amisch woman who moved here with her family from the Palatinate about ten years ago. Up close, her face is fair and lovely, though her hands are gnarled from hard work and look like those of a much older woman. As I suspected, her child is to be born at approximately the same time as mine, and she confirms that she has also felt a distant kinship with me when she spotted me strolling the grounds with my bulging midsection. Though I know it is frowned upon by the palace, society, and even my own attendants, I intend to visit with this exceedingly pleasant young woman again.

NINETEEN

ANNA

Next stop for me was the laboratory where Bobby worked. The whole suspension thing was very disconcerting, especially considering how hard he tried to hide it from his wife. My brother was such a good worker, a smart guy, and an agreeable person that I couldn't imagine what he might have done to get himself in such big trouble in the workplace. I was determined to find out, however, even if that information was confidential.

It had been a long time since I pulled into the parking lot of the Wynn Industries Research Extension—or as it was locally known, the WIRE. The headquarters in Hidden Springs was huge, but their branch office out here in Dreiheit wasn't all that impressive. The building it was housed in was so rectangular and unremarkable that it had always reminded me of a grocery store from the outside. The inside, however, was another story. I had only seen the interior offices a few times, but they were impressive indeed, filled with all sorts of strange and fascinating machinery as well as men and women in white lab coats bending over microscopes or working with test tubes and beakers. Many years ago, before the fire, Bobby had dreamed of becoming a doctor and working in a place just like this. To this day he still said that the summer he spent working here as an intern was the most professionally fulfilling period of his life. After the fire, once he gave up his biggest dreams, he had still managed to carve out a good life for himself, one that kept him in the medical field by working as a phlebotomist, collecting Amish blood samples for the lab's genetic research.

Located just a few blocks from downtown Dreiheit, the building sat back from the road and was flanked on one side by an insurance company and the other by an auto repair shop. I pulled into the half empty parking lot and went in through the main entrance. At the reception desk in the lobby, I asked for the office manager but was told she was already gone for the day. I then asked for Dr. Updyke but was told that he would be leaving soon and wouldn't have time to see me.

"Is there anyone in authority here I could speak with?" I asked, my voice catching the attention of another woman who was walking past. She hesitated, turning to look at me.

"I'm sorry. You'll have to come back tomorrow," the receptionist said.

Behind her, the other woman gave me a pointed look and gestured with her head toward the door.

"Okay, then. I'll do that," I replied, turning to go out the way I had come in.

Outside, I sat in my car and watched the building until that other woman emerged from a side door, bundled up in a coat. Again, she caught my eye, and then she started walking toward the auto repair shop. I waited a beat before getting out of the car and following her.

"It was the hair," she said when I caught up with her. "I didn't recognize you at first because of the hair. How are you doing, Annalise?" At my questioning expression she added, "You probably don't remember me, but I worked the front desk back when your brother was just an intern here."

"Oh, right," I said, the memory vaguely coming back to me.

"I guess that's why you've come? To ask about your brother's suspension? Rumor has it Lydia didn't even know."

"What can you tell me about it?"

A few snowflakes started to fall as we walked toward the end of the block. She explained that Bobby's suspension had come as a shock to everyone. Prior to that, he had been a model employee, never in a bit of trouble, and extremely popular with both the doctors and the staff. She said they weren't told what happened or why he had been suspended, only that the word had come down from Dr. Updyke himself, and it seemed to be over some issue between the two of them.

"Does Bobby work closely with the doctor?" I asked. I knew he liked the man and respected his work, but my impression was that Bobby's job was primarily done with patients.

"Not really. Bobby handles all the blood draws, both inpatient and outpatient, so his work usually keeps him in the small front lab or on the road. Still, he and the doctor have what I guess you would call a friendship. Bobby likes to pick his brain, talk medicine and research and all that stuff. I have no idea what happened, but from what I understand he's supposed to come back to work on Monday. Of course, now that he is missing, I guess that's not likely to happen."

"What's the gossip about his suspension?"

"People are saying everything from an OSHA violation to a problem with paperwork. Personally, the only thing I can think of that might have landed him in this much trouble would be some sort of mix-up with the blood samples. It's anybody's guess really, and Dr. Updyke isn't talking."

We reached the corner at the end of the block, and my companion turned around and began walking back toward the office. I knew I didn't have much time left to ask all the questions running through my mind. Before I could think of what to ask next, she spoke.

"How's Lydia?" They said she called here today looking for him, and that was the first she had heard of it."

Rather than give her an answer, I responded with another question.

"Would it have been unusual for him not to tell her something like that?"

"I don't know what you mean."

"Have you ever sensed that Bobby was the kind of person to keep secrets from Lydia?" Thinking of the mystery person who made the ATM withdrawal in Las Vegas, what I really wanted to know was if she thought he could have been having an affair. I didn't want to plant that idea in her head, however, so I didn't ask my questions outright.

"Are you kidding? Honey, that man is the perfect husband. He was probably just too embarrassed to tell her, not to mention he didn't want her to worry about the lack of a paycheck."

"That makes sense."

As we neared the parking lot she hesitated, pointing to a black Cadillac that was pulling around from the back of the building. "That's Dr. Updyke. I'd better go. I don't want to get in trouble."

Before the car had even made it halfway to the front of the building, she was off, trotting toward the door and out of sight.

As the car slowly approached, I moved directly into its path, waving both hands in front of me until it pulled to a stop. Rather than step around to the driver's side, I went to the passenger's side and knocked on the window. I was determined to have this conversation no matter what it took.

"May I help you?" the man inside asked after lowering the window.

Quickly, I reached a hand in, flipped up the lock, and opened the door. Before he could stop me, I was sitting beside him, holding out my hand for a shake.

"Anna Jensen, sir. Bobby's sister. I need to talk to you right away."

"Apparently."

"I'm sorry to be so pushy, but the situation is kind of desperate."

"Well, I desperately have to pick up my

son from swim practice in exactly ten minutes. But you're welcome to ride along. I can drop you back here after we get him."

"Sounds good to me," I said, buckling my seat belt. As he pulled out of the parking lot and onto the road, he asked if this had to do with Bobby's suspension.

"Yes, sir. I'm not sure if you've heard, but two nights ago Bobby disappeared. I'm trying to find him, and I'm hoping you can tell me a little bit about what was going on with him here at work. That might give me some idea of where he may have gone."

Dr. Updyke ran a hand over his wavy salt-and-pepper hair. I could tell he was carefully forming the words of his reply.

"I'm afraid the nature of his suspension is confidential, but I assure you it had nothing to do with his disappearance."

He turned onto the main road and headed toward the high school. More snowflakes were falling now, and I couldn't help but admire the beauty of the landscape. As we passed houses and farms, I fell into the old habit of looking for power lines and curtains, the two telltale signs for whether or not an Amish family lived there.

If a home had neither—especially if there were dark green blinds or shades in the windows—then it was a good guess that the home was an Amish one.

"Dr. Updyke, may I be frank?"

"You already hijacked my car. I think frankness is a given."

"I know that a lot of high-level, top secret research goes on at the WIRE. Is there any chance that Bobby could have been abducted because of something he was involved with at work? By any chance was he working on some project that would have endangered him that way?" I was only thinking out loud, but considering the high stakes of cutting-edge medicine, I thought it might be an avenue worth pursuing.

"I think you've seen too many movies, Ms. Jensen. It's true that we have a state-of-the-art laboratory, and we are involved in some very exciting research, but trust me, none of us is in danger because of it."

"There's a lot of money to be made in the field of DNA."

"There will be one day," he replied. "For now, primarily, it's still a big puzzle we're all trying to figure out."

I asked about the general nature of their work, and though he didn't give specifics, Dr. Updyke did a pretty thorough job of explaining the goals of the lab and the possibilities that existed in the future both for Wynn industries and in the field of DNA research in general. By the time we reached the high school, I could see why Bobby was so fascinated by this man. When I was a teenager, I considered him as nothing more than a science geek; now, as an adult, though I didn't understand everything he was saying, I was still impressed with the clarity of his goals and the compassion with which he described the more successful results.

As we pulled to a stop near the flagpole, a young man broke away from a huddle of teenagers and ran to the car, his breath making steam in the cold air. He opened the door to the backseat, tossed in his backpack, and plopped himself heavily inside, slamming the door.

"Hey, Pops, I got a one ten on the hundred meter breast!"

Dr. Updyke surprised me by swinging his arm over the back of the seat. I thought he was going to slap his son, but instead their hands met in a loud high five.

"That's great, son. If you can repeat that on Saturday, you'll be in good shape."

"That's what Coach said."

With a nod to me, and not a hint of curiosity about who I was or why I was there, the boy pulled a pair of earbuds out of his front pocket, stuck them in his ears, and turned on an iPod. Smiling, I glanced at his father, who winked at me, beaming with parental pride.

"Sorry. I guess we need to teach Michael Phelps here a few manners."

"That's okay. I was his age once myself."

"Oh, I remember," the doctor said as he turned out of the high school and headed back up the road we had come down. "I think you were, what, seventeen when we met? At the lab, we used to call you and Haley Wynn the Giggle Twins."

His mention of Haley made me think of Doug.

"Dr. Updyke, do you think there could be any connection between Bobby's disappearance and Doug Brown's death?"

"I'm sure I wouldn't know. Given their connection, I suppose it's possible."

"Connection . . . of working for different branches of the same company? Of both having been in the Dreiheit Five?"

He shrugged.

"I just meant their connection of friendship. Who knows what might have happened to either of them?"

"I might be able to figure it out if you would tell me why Bobby was suspended."

"No can do," he said firmly.

We rode along uncomfortably for a minute until he turned off the main road and drove slowly up the block toward the lab. The snow was starting to stick now, and this less-traveled road had already turned a grayish-white.

"At the very least, can you describe the nature of Bobby's offense?"

"Sorry."

"Look, I can either get the truth from you, or I'll just have to check out all the rumors about it that are floating around the office. Your choice."

Dr. Updyke put on his blinker and turned into the parking lot, which held only a few cars at this point. Now that the sun had dipped below the horizon, the entire scene felt rather creepy.

We pulled to a stop directly behind my rental car, but I paused before getting out, one hand on the door handle. I looked at the doctor expectantly, and finally he spoke, glancing toward his son and then lowering his voice.

"Fine. I caught your brother trying to access restricted information. We have rules that are very well established, and policies that must be followed to the letter. He broke the rule, and so I had no choice but to enforce the policy. That's the most I can tell you."

"Any idea why he was doing that?"

The doctor hesitated, glancing again at his son, who was oblivious to our entire conversation. I thought Dr. Updyke was going to answer my question, but instead he simply shook his head.

"I have no idea," he said, looking me straight in the eye, and for the first time in the entire car ride, I had the distinct impression he was lying.

I also knew, without question, that our conversation was over for now. I thanked him very much for his time, pausing just long enough to write down my name and cell phone number on a piece of paper.

"If you get any ideas," I said, handing him the paper, "or have any other thoughts on the subject, please don't hesitate to call me."

With that, I quickly transferred from his warm luxury vehicle into my cold little rental car. I watched his taillights as he drove away, and I couldn't help but think that the piece of paper with my phone number on it was probably going directly into the trash. He had no intention of speaking with me again.

Making sure to lock the car doors, I started up the engine and sat there for a minute, trying to decide where to go next. Putting on the headlights, they illuminated the snow that fell between me and the ugly blond brick of the building in front of me. Looking at this place, a person would have no idea of the level of research going on inside. Despite what the good doctor had said, I had no doubt that abduction or even murder was not unheard of in high-tech industries such as DNA research. I just wished I knew more about the field in general. For the first time ever, I felt guilty for having tuned out my brother's voice every time he went on and on about his work.

I thought it would be helpful to speak with someone who was knowledgeable about DNA research, just to verify the things that Dr. Updyke had told me, and to get a second opinion on the possibility that Bobby's disappearance could have had something to do with his job.

For a moment, I thought of calling Reed Thornton down in Washington. Given that he was a medical ethicist working in the field of DNA, he could have told me everything I wanted to know. Putting the car in gear, I backed out of my parking space and headed for the main road, thinking that as much as I would have loved to hear the sound of his voice again, I knew I shouldn't call him. I had spent so many years trying to forget him that talking to him now would be like an alcoholic with many years of sobriety suddenly tossing back a stiff drink.

TWENTY

Snow was falling more steadily now, and though I had hoped to get so much more done today, I didn't want to be driving on slick roads in the dark, especially considering that I was completely out of practice. As I held on to the steering wheel with both hands, I realized I hadn't even seen snow for seven years. Despite the reason for my being here and everything I had gone through to get here, I allowed myself a few quiet minutes to simply take in the beauty of the snowfall all around me. There was something about Lancaster County in the winter that belonged on a postcard. Maybe it was the size of the Amish farms—small by necessity because of the limitations their religion imposed on the types of farm machinery they were allowed to use. Whatever made it so quaint and picturesque, the sight of the rolling hills and rambling homes was only made more beautiful with the addition of snow.

At least the road wasn't very crowded, which was a good thing because I was going well below the speed limit. The headlights of the car directly behind mine were too bright, and judging from the bluish tone, likely halogen. I tilted my rearview mirror just enough to keep them from blinding me and kept going, my grip on the steering wheel firm.

When I was about half a mile from the farm, I pulled over into a busy parking lot of a hardware store where it looked as though they were doing a brisk business with snow shovels and sidewalk salt. I had a few quick phone calls I needed to make in the privacy of my car, but I didn't want to talk on the phone while driving.

Sitting there in the parking lot, as well-bundled people rushed in and out of the store, I took a deep breath and dialed the number for Kiki's cell phone. If all had gone according to plan, she would now be out of the hospital and safely ensconced at her mother's house.

When Kiki answered the phone, I felt a surge of emotion, a mix of guilt and sadness and relief. In turn, her voice was oddly strained, though I didn't know whether that was a side effect of all that she had been through or whether she was upset with me.

As we talked, it became clear it was the latter. I asked her to describe the attack from her perspective, which she did, but when I began sharing mine, she stopped me, saying that Detective Hernandez had already told her everything. She also had never heard of the Beauharnais rubies.

"He told me a whole lot, actually," she said, and as I waited for her to go on, the tension coming through the phone line was palpable.

"Go ahead, Kiki. What is that you're not saying?"

She had me hold on while she shooed her mother from the room. Coming back on the line, I could hear the hurt in her voice.

"Look, Anna, I know there's a lot about your past I don't know about, and that was always fine with me. I figured you had an abusive ex-husband or you testified in a big trial or something. I always figured you'd trust me enough someday to tell me what your big secret was. But now that I know you're an ex-convict . . . I don't know. I'm not sure what to think."

Closing my eyes, I pinched the bridge of my nose and tried to form the right reply.

"First of all, it's true I was convicted of a crime. But I was only seventeen at the time. House arrest followed by probation hardly makes me an ex-con."

She didn't sound convinced, and I felt furious with Detective Hernandez for passing his prejudice along to her. The more I thought about her reaction to all of this, I felt myself growing angry. Kiki knew me. She knew my heart. Was she really willing to toss out all of that based on the malicious slurs of one person?

"You know what?" I said finally. "I don't want to talk about this any more. If you want the whole story, I suggest you get some copies of *Time* or *Newsweek* from August through December of 1997. Trust me, they had something about us at least once a month for that entire period."

"You're kidding."

"No, I'm not. Why don't you get yourself a copy of those news magazines and read what the media had to say. Then, if you feel like hearing the truth, why don't you give me a call?" I knew my voice was sounding harsh, so I softened my tone as best I could. "I love you, Kiki, and you're one of the best friends I've ever had. But if you're going to throw away our friendship based on one man's version of events that happened eleven years ago, then you're not the friend I thought you were. Call me when you're ready to hear my side."

Hands shaking, I disconnected the call.

As I sat there in the parking lot and tried to calm down, I just kept thinking how a person's entire world could change in a matter of minutes. Between Bobby's disappearance and this single incident with the intruder, everything about my life was starting to fall apart. Whether Kiki and I were going to be able to mend this rift and continue being housemates remained to be seen.

I wanted to call Detective Hernandez to see what was going on with his investigation, but I didn't trust myself to talk with him right now as I knew I might say something I would regret. Instead, I simply called Lydia on the phone I had bought for her and told her I would be at the farm very soon, unless it was still surrounded by reporters.

"No, they are all gone. I think the snow scared them off."

"Good. I have more to do, but it'll have to wait until tomorrow."

She said that the bodyguard had left for the night, once the men had come in from milking. The women were just about to put dinner on the table, so my timing was perfect. We concluded our call and I pulled out of the parking lot, right behind an Amish horse and buggy.

Already the road felt slicker, and I didn't even bother trying to pass it; I was glad to have an excuse to go so slow. Cars began to pile up behind us as we made progress down the road, but soon I again was bothered by bright lights in my rearview mirror. When I reached up to make another adjustment, I realized that they looked like the same lights that had bothered me before: too bright, and with a bluish tinge.

Was someone following me?

It might have been a coincidence, but I didn't think there were that many cars on the road with halogen lights. If it hadn't been snowing, or if I had been more confident on the road, I might have done a few maneuvers just to see if the car stayed with me. As it was, I didn't have much choice but to continue to my destination. At least once I got there I would be surrounded by people and presumably safe.

The car behind me turned onto a side road when I was about a block from the farm, which made me feel a little better. Once I got there, I turned onto the long, paved driveway and pulled up to the house that had played such a pivotal part of my past.

In the dark it was hard to see if it had changed much, but it didn't look as though it had. Other than the *Dawdy Haus* being gone, it was still a collection of neat, white buildings, some of which were connected at the corners. The yard was dark, but within the glow of my headlights before I turned off the car, I glimpsed a big wooden swing set, a long clothesline, and a square area where a vegetable garden must grow in warmer months.

The front door opened as I was getting out of the car, and an Amish man stepped out, followed by Lydia, who was carrying a flashlight.

"Anna, we are so glad you are here," Lydia said, waddling over to give me another hug.

As they came closer, I realized that the "Amish man" with her was about nineteen, and that he must be Caleb, Lydia's younger brother. He had really grown up. Taller than me by several inches, the black felt hat he wore made him look even taller. He was clean shaven, a sign he was not yet married. Once Amish males married, I knew, they grew out their beards, though they continued to shave their upper lips, as mustaches were not allowed.

"Welcome, Anna," he said in a deep voice, reaching out to shake my hand.

"Caleb, is that you? I can't believe it. Last time I saw you, you barely came up to my shoulder."

He was quite a handsome young man, with a sparkle in his eyes and a ruddy complexion that bespoke of the hours he spent doing farmwork every day, even in winter.

"*Yah.* Much time has passed since then."

I popped open the trunk of my rental car and he pulled out my suitcase, handling it easily, as if it weighed nothing at all. The three of us trudged inside, where I was greeted with more hugs and handshakes and smiling faces.

Though my nose had picked up that old, familiar tinge of manure outside, inside the house smelled like heaven, a mixture of roasting meat and baking bread and something like apples with cinnamon. One by one, I greeted the whole family: Lydia's brother-in-law, Nathaniel, who still wore small round spectacles and had a bushy beard; her older sister, Grete, who now served as a mother to the other siblings; Rebecca, who had transformed into a lovely young woman; Ezra, who looked to be about fifteen, and Tresa, Nathaniel and Grete's daughter, a cute preteen wearing the traditional white *kapp* and blue dress. Last to say hello was Isaac, my nephew.

He whispered something to his mother, and she nodded her head.

"Yes, this is your aunt. But do not whisper in front of others. It is rude."

Politely, Isaac stepped forward and held out his hand for a shake. As he did, I felt a surge of emotion so strong I was afraid I might cry. This was my nephew, for goodness' sake, my brother's son, and I had not seen him since he was an infant. Now he was eight years old. All at once, the years that had passed since then—the years I had worked so hard at creating a new and separate life—suddenly felt wrong somehow, almost foolish, as if I had lost sight of what was really important in life. Swallowing hard, I took Isaac's hand and shook it, but then I asked if it would be okay if I gave him a hug too. Blushing, he nodded, and I pulled him into my arms for a quick squeeze. I would have liked to hold on longer, but I didn't want to make him uncomfortable.

"You have your mom's face and your dad's smile," I said as we pulled apart. If a boy could be described as "pretty," then that's what he was, with delicate features and gorgeous long eyelashes. He was also tall for his age, with Bobby's lopsided grin and a single dimple in his cheek. Without a doubt, in about five or six more years, the girls were going to be flocking to him like flies to shoofly pie.

I was glad that the kitchen was nice and warm, not to mention well lit, thanks to a big lamp that hung over the broad table. Against the wall sat a wood-burning stove, which gave heat to the entire room; near that was a sitting area, illuminated by a floor lamp connected to a propane tank under its round, wooden base.

After the enthusiastic greeting, everyone returned to what they had been doing when I arrived. The women were getting dinner on the table, and once I had taken off my coat and hung it on the peg by the door, I offered to help. Grete said that dinner was under control but that Isaac could probably use a hand picking up a pile of wooden blocks from where he had been playing with them on the floor near the wood stove. I was happy to oblige, and I plopped down next to him on the floor. As we worked, his shyness seemed to dissipate, and the more vocal he became, the more he reminded me of Bobby. Despite a few odd expressions I assumed were rooted in the Pennsylvania German dialect, he did not have his mother's lilting accent at all but instead sounded like an average American kid.

By the time dinner was served, the blocks were all put away and my nephew seemed fully at ease with me. At dinner Isaac insisted I sit beside him, which thrilled my heart. Maybe in that special way kids have he could sense my need to bond with him despite the years we had already lost.

I was astounded at the sheer quantity of food that was heaped upon platters on the table: pork chops in sauerkraut, homemade bread, noodles in butter, and a variety of vegetables that the family had likely grown and canned themselves. After a silent prayer, everyone dug in, and even the women scooped up generous portions of butter for their bread. I had forgotten how heartily the Amish ate, especially the men, who had built up an appetite working the farm all day. No one in this family was overweight, though I had to wonder about their cholesterol levels.

The meal passed so pleasantly that about halfway through I simply allowed myself to sit there and take it all in. How could I have forgotten what it was like to be in an Amish kitchen and listen to the gentle banter, the politeness of the children, the sweet teasing of the husband and wife?

As we ate, I kept thinking of the day after the fire, when I was consumed with fear and guilt and rage and heartache over all that had happened the night before, not to mention the uncertainty of how everything was going to play out, legally speaking. My prayers during and immediately after the fire—prayers that God would spare Lydia's parents and keep Reed safe as he tried to find them inside the burning house—had been fervent and heartfelt, but by the next day I had decided that perhaps God hadn't cared enough to answer those prayers. With Reed in the hospital suffering from third degree burns and Lydia's parents both dead along with their newborn baby, I even began to question the existence of God altogether.

I remembered vividly the next day, when Bobby and I were finally released from custody. As we walked out of the police station flanked by our parents and their lawyer, we passed through a gauntlet of photographers and reporters shouting questions and snapping pictures. At the parking lot, we came face-to-face with a small group of Amish men who had been waiting by my parents' car. I thought they were there to condemn us or call out accusations, but much to my shock, when we got to them, they simply asked the press to give us some privacy and waited in silence as one by one the media retreated—one of the few times the press had acted with dignity throughout the entire ordeal.

"We have come to let you know that we forgive you," one of the Amish men said finally, looking from me to Bobby. "The deaths of the Schumanns was a terrible tragedy, yes, but we harbor no ill will. Speaking on behalf of the victims' family and the entire community, you have our forgiveness."

"Please to let us know if you have need or want of anything," another one added.

We were touched and surprised, though it was only the first of many similar such acts that would take place over the next few months. Eventually, when I got up the nerve to ask an older Amish friend how we could have been forgiven so fully, so instantly, she quoted a verse from Matthew, the one that said if we forgive men their trespasses, our heavenly Father will also forgive us. I knew it wasn't that simple, but at least it was a place to start.

Even though the general public saw the Dreiheit Five as nothing less than amoral monsters, the Amish community embraced us at every turn, sitting in the courtrooms at our various trials, even asking the judges for leniency in sentencing. I hadn't understood where they managed to find such generosity of spirit, but I kept thinking all along that if Christ Himself had been there, He would have done those things too. Just seeing God's love in action like that was enough to break through the wall that the fire had erected in my heart and eventually lead me back to Him, back to my faith, back to a private rededication of my life and a renewed faith that had grown steadily ever since.

According to Lydia, to many of the Amish she knew, living the way they did was more about preserving their culture and heritage than it was about true faith. I wasn't so sure about that. Among the Amish who embraced us so wholeheartedly, what I saw in their actions was nothing less than vivid evidence of the Holy Spirit alive in their hearts. I may not have understood their willingness to live life as they did, but I respected it, and I knew they were walking, talking examples of Christ's love at every turn. Years later, after the Amish school shooting, the nation would be shocked at the Amish forgiveness extended to the killer and his surviving family, forgiveness that was swift and complete. I, however, had not been surprised at all. I knew they would act as they did because I had once benefited from the same thing myself. Now here I sat in the very kitchen of the house I had helped to burn down, sharing a meal with the children of the couple I helped to kill. If that wasn't a true example of Amish grace, then I didn't know what was.

"Don't eat yourself full, Ezra," Grete scolded her younger brother as he took a third helping of noodles. "There's cake back yet."

"We can make snow ice cream too, *yah*?" Ezra asked.

"Please?" added Isaac. "I put out the . . . s-squares . . . like you said."

"The squares?" Lydia asked, looking at her son with sudden concern. "The cookie sheets, you mean?"

"Yeah. I put them out in the clear, where they'll fill with . . . w-white cold."

A look passed between Lydia and Grete, one I didn't understand. For a long moment, everyone at the table was silent and oddly uncomfortable—everyone except Isaac, who reached out to take another helping of bread. As he did, he knocked over his glass of milk.

"Schushlich!" Nathaniel said, quickly rising to grab a towel.

A few sentences passed between him and Grete, though in the Pennsylvania Dutch dialect I didn't understand. From their tones and body language, however, I gathered that she was trying to calm him down, telling him not to make such a fuss over spilled milk. She and Lydia cleaned it up, and after taking a deep breath, Nathaniel sat down and returned to eating his meal. I didn't know Nathaniel that well, but his reaction had surprised me. I thought he was more easygoing than that.

"So how do you make snow ice cream?"

I asked, trying to fill the uncomfortable silence that followed.

"You take clean snow and add to that milk and vanilla and sugar," Lydia explained, forcing a smile. "Have you never done that before?"

"I may have, as a child. Actually, come to think of it, you guys are probably the ones who taught Bobby and me how to make it when we were just kids."

As soon as I said Bobby's name, everyone around the table again grew silent. This time, even Isaac seemed aware of the tension.

"Aunt Anna, do you know where my daddy is?" he asked me suddenly.

"Not exactly, but I have some good ideas about where to look for him."

"Is probably a good thing Daddy is not here tonight, though, or he might eat up all the snow ice cream, *yah*?" Lydia added, smiling at Isaac and forcing her voice to sound lighthearted.

We got through the rest of the meal without incident, and soon the older men were bundled up and off to the barns to tend to the cows before bedtime and the women were at the sink, washing all of the dishes by hand. Again, they wouldn't let me help, and in a way I was grateful. Their movements were efficient, born from years of going through the same motions night after night. I knew my way around a dish-washer, but it had been a long time since I'd washed dishes by hand, so I was glad I wouldn't have the chance to embarrass myself.

Isaac and I cleared and wiped the table instead, and then we went over to the sitting area where he asked me to read to him. I was happy to oblige, but between the warm kitchen, the heavy meal, and my lack of sleep last night, after a few picture books I could scarcely keep my eyes open.

When the men returned bearing two cookie sheets heaped with snow, I was spared from having to read any more. By the time the ice cream had been made and consumed, I was definitely ready for bed.

Fortunately, so was everyone else. At the stroke of nine, Nathaniel read aloud from a German prayer book, and then Grete doled out flashlights. Lydia led me upstairs to the room I would be using, which couldn't have been more than forty degrees. Caleb had already placed my suitcase on a chair in a corner, and once Lydia lit the kerosene lamp on the bedside table, she pointed out the stack of sweaters she had left for me on the bed, said goodnight, and excused herself to join Isaac in the room next door.

Using the lamplight and the flashlight, I went through my clothes, trying to find comfortable layers to sleep in. As I did, it struck me that without any electrical outlets, I wouldn't be able to charge the batteries in my phone and my laptop overnight, as I usually did. I turned them both off, hoping the power they still had in them would hold until I had a chance to get to some electricity. Carrying a pile of clothes, I used the bathroom at the bottom of the stairs to brush my teeth and get changed, grateful at least that the Amish in this community were allowed to have indoor plumbing as long as they drew from a well or a cistern and not the municipal water supply. Finally, I came back up and crawled into the bed, blew out the lamp, and pulled the heavy covers up to my chin. Though I could almost see my breath in front of me, somehow I managed to fall asleep almost immediately.

I didn't stir again until after midnight, when a noise awoke me. Startled, I sat up in the bed, trying to get my bearings in the pitch-black darkness.

TWENTY-ONE

The sound was coming from outside, a clicking noise that sounded like a door lock or a gate latch. I slowly lifted the green shade that obscured the window and peeked out, holding my breath.

The snow had stopped falling and the clouds had given way to a crystal clear night sky. Amid sparkling stars, the half-moon shone down on a winter landscape, the ground covered in a blanket of pristine white snow. Movement caught my eye, and sure enough I watched as someone stepped out from the shadows of the house and began running across the back field. It was a man, obviously young and fit from the way he moved, dressed in a leather coat and jeans. On his head was a dark knit cap with ear flaps that hung loose from the sides, the strings blowing behind him as he ran.

I grabbed the flashlight from the bedside table and crept to the room where Lydia slept, next door. At least she and Isaac were both safe, gently snoozing away in the twin beds there. I reached out and shook Lydia's shoulder, careful not to shine the flashlight in her eyes. Once she was fully awake and seemed coherent, I explained what I had seen.

"We need to check on everyone and make sure they're okay," I said breathlessly.

Her response was odd, as she seemed more annoyed than frightened. Sitting up, she swung her legs out of the bed, pulled on her slippers, grabbed her own flashlight, and turned it on. As she got up and bravely led the way out of the room and down the stairs, the reason for her irritation soon became clear. First stop was Caleb's room, which was empty, though it smelled strongly of aftershave. The corner of a trunk was peeking out from under the bed, and Lydia slid it out and opened it up to reveal what looked like several folded pairs of jeans, some shirts, and gift set of Axe deodorant and cologne.

"The man you saw, by any chance was he wearing a leather jacket and jeans?"

"Yes, and a knit cap with ear flaps."

"*Yah,* that was no stranger, that was Caleb. No doubt he is off to visit with his English buddies or his fancy girlfriend."

I stood up straight, exhaling slowly. Of course. Caleb was on *rumspringa,* and it was a Friday night. As I pictured the movements of the man running through the snow, I realized that it had, indeed, been him. Lydia put the trunk away and we returned upstairs, her movements angry and swift.

"You can't be too mad at him," I whispered as I followed along behind. "You were doing the same thing when you were his age."

She waited until we were in my bedroom with the door closed before she replied.

"This is different!" she hissed. "I asked

him specifically not to slip away from the house until Bobby returned or we knew what was going on. He is supposed to be guarding us, not running out to be with other people. He is so irresponsible! Always, he is bucking against everything, fighting every rule, every request."

She paced as she talked, and I could tell she needed to vent. I sat on the bed, pulling a blanket over my lap to keep from shivering.

"At least Nathaniel's still here," I whispered, gesturing toward the wall. He and Grete were sleeping two rooms over, but even from that distance we could hear the vague rumble of his snoring. "We're okay."

"That's not the point, Anna," Lydia said, finally stopping her pacing to sit next to me on the bed. "Things with Caleb are . . . so complicated."

I pulled the blanket up my chin, our breath making vapor as we spoke.

"When he argues, he uses me as his example," Lydia continued, shaking her head. "As one who left the Order, I could be seen as a very bad influence on my younger relatives. He does not know the position he puts me in when he says things like 'I am going to do what Lydia did' or 'I do not know what is so wrong about taking the path Lydia took.' Too much of that, and the bishops might not let me keep coming around. *Ach,* I am so mad at him right now, I could scream."

I reached out and patted her hand, wishing I could think of something to say that would make her feel better.

"Have you told him that he needs to stop talking about you that way?"

"*Yah,* but it makes no difference. He is hardheaded and says what he wants in the heat of passion. Besides, he does not understand how different his motives are from what mine were when I was his age and decided to break away."

"He's not taking a pass on baptism out of love for his Englisher?" I asked.

"What do you mean?"

"Like you did, for Bobby."

Lydia looked at me in the dim glow of our flashlights, her eyebrows knit together.

"This is what you think I did? That I left the Amish Order because I was in love with your brother?"

"Didn't you?"

She shook her head slowly, looking at me in surprise.

"No, Anna, that is not how it was at all," she said earnestly, turning her body to face me fully. "I made the decision not to be baptized before Bobby and I even started dating."

"You did? Why?"

She continued to shake her head, as if she could shake away the surprise of my misunderstanding.

"Is hard to explain. Did you know that the *Ordnung* prohibits Bible study? The bishops say that to do such a thing could make a person prideful, because it might give them special knowledge."

"I didn't realize that," I said, remembering that the *Ordnung* was the unwritten set of rules that the Amish community was required to follow.

"Maybe it was the rebel inside of me, Anna, but when I was told not to study my Bible, that only made me want to do it more. When I was seventeen, I began reading one in secret. Instead of letting the bishops tell me everything I was supposed to believe, I studied the Bible so I could decide what to believe for myself. Of course, much of what I read confused me because it contradicted what I had been taught in the church."

"Like what?"

"Like, the *Ordnung* says that it is prideful to be certain of one's salvation, so they are required always to wonder if they will get into heaven, never to know for sure until after death, never to feel good enough in the eyes of God. But then I came to verses like in First John where he says that he has written "these things 'so that you may *know* that you have eternal life.' I decided on this issue the Amish were wrong. Long before I got involved with Bobby, I went to the bishops and quoted that verse and asked them why I was not allowed to have this assurance if God had promised it to me right in His Holy Word. They refused to answer my question but instead wanted to deal only with my 'disobedience' for having studied my Bible in secret. Right then, I knew that if I was going to be the person the Bible told me to be, then I would have to leave the Amish faith and find a church that was more willing to let me think for myself. When Bobby and I started dating, I had not yet made it official, but I already knew I was not going to be baptized as Amish."

"I had no idea, Lydia. I guess with the timing and everything, I just assumed you left for love."

"Is okay. It may have looked that way. When my parents died in the fire, I kept my decision private for as long as I could because I did not want to leave home yet. I knew I needed to stay close for a year or two longer to help with my siblings. When I turned twenty-one, though, after much pressure to be baptized, I announced my decision, and then of course I had to leave home. It was very hard, the hardest thing I have ever done. But soon Bobby came back into my life, and he still loved me, as I still loved him, so that helped me stay strong. We were married soon after, and I never was sorry."

Tears filled her eyes, and I wondered if she was starting to doubt whether Bobby had been the husband she thought he was, now that we knew he had been keeping secrets from her.

"My brother Caleb," she added, wiping

at her eyes, "he does not do this thing out of a desire to know God. He does it from a desire to have freedom and independence. I worry that he is involved in things that have taken over his will and made him both headstrong and weak, all at the same time."

I considered her comment, wondering what she meant.

"Maybe in the old days," she continued, "when the world was a simpler place, maybe then *rumspringa* was a good idea. Turning a blind eye to teenage shenanigans is one thing, but these days, raising up children to be completely innocent of the world and then looking the other way as they go out into that world is crazy. The lure of drugs, sex, and the wild parties . . . You remember what it was like."

"Oh, yeah," I said, thinking of the several *rumspringa* parties we attended that fateful summer. What usually started as a fun gathering with a little music out in somebody's back field would always degenerate once somebody showed up with a couple of kegs. From what I saw, it seemed like the Amish kids were often the wildest, getting dangerously drunk, pairing off and slipping away, everyone smoking. We learned to get to the parties early and not stay too long. Despite Haley's relationship with Doug and my attraction to Reed, Haley and I liked going mostly so we could flirt with the cute Amish boys, who were sort of forbidden fruit as far as we were concerned. Though most everyone dressed like regular American teens at those parties, we always knew which ones were Amish by their white foreheads, the result of wearing hats every day as they worked the fields.

"*Ach,* my heart aches for Caleb. Who knows what he is mixed up in out there?"

We were both quiet for a minute.

"Well," I said finally, breaking the silence, "back when you were Caleb's age, after the fire, everyone thought you had been hanging out with a wild bunch of partiers too—when in fact, our little group of friends was completely tame for the most part. The circumstantial evidence from that night made things look much worse than they were. Your brother's activities could be just as innocent, you know."

"Maybe."

"Are you worried about drugs?"

"*Yah.*"

"Do you have any evidence?"

"I do not know. Last month, Bobby saw Caleb down at the Quarry," she said, referring to the older, more run-down portion of town, a place drug dealers were known to frequent.

"Not the Quarry," I said, a shiver running through me as I pictured it. Not only did I now understand her concerns about Caleb, I also began to wonder if this might have something to do with Bobby's disappearance.

Ten years ago, a Philadelphia-based drug ring had gotten a foothold among some of the Amish youth in this region, and though law enforcement had cracked down pretty hard on the whole thing, I had to wonder if it had started up again—and if Bobby may have been involved somehow in an attempt to help Caleb. It would have been just like my brother to act first, without regard to his personal safety.

Of course, I didn't say as much to Lydia, though she may have been thinking the same thing herself. We wrapped up our conversation and Lydia returned to her room to go back to sleep. Before I turned off my flashlight to do the same, however, I grabbed a pen and my skip tracing form and scribbled on the back of the last page. Quickly, I jotted down a list that seemed to be growing longer all the time. Headed *Reasons Bobby Might Have Disappeared,* so far it had four items:

1. Something to do with the rubies, whatever they were.

2. Something to do with the Dreiheit Five, though for what reason I couldn't imagine.

3. Something to do with his job. Bobby had a low-level position in a high-tech field, and he was currently under suspension, a fact he had hidden from his wife.

4. Something to do with Caleb and drug use. I wasn't going to tell Lydia this, but if my investigation had not progressed significantly in other directions by the same time tomorrow night, I intended to follow Caleb and see where he was going on his little midnight run.

I felt more in control once my thoughts were down on paper. Shivering in the cold, I turned off the flashlight, rolled toward the wall, and tried to get back to sleep. It was things like this that confused me about the

Amish faith, as I couldn't fathom how sleeping in these kinds of temperatures brought one closer to God—unless it was all that time they must spend in prayer, asking for warmer weather.

I managed to get back to sleep and stay that way for the rest of the night. But when I awoke the next morning, the room was even colder, and I was starting to worry if too many nights of this in a row might make me sick. I decided to give Melody Wynn a call—not so I could move over to her house, but just to see if I could impose on her hospitality long enough this morning to take a shower in a well-heated bathroom. After pulling my hair up into a ponytail, I grabbed my stuff and headed downstairs to the kitchen.

It was gloriously warm in there, heated by the woodstove and the cooking. All of the window blinds were wide open, and the sun reflecting off of the snow outside bathed the room in a brilliant light. I had expected to find the whole family in there, but the room was empty. At the sink, it looked as if someone had abandoned the job of washing dishes halfway through.

Suddenly, the door at the far side of

the sitting area opened and Grete came walking in. She had something small and square in her hands, but the moment she saw me, she gasped and whipped it behind her back.

"You gave me a fright!" she said, forcing a laugh. There was no smile in her eyes, however.

"Sorry about that."

She remained awkwardly frozen in place, so out of courtesy I finally turned away and walked toward the alcove to put my stuff near the door. From the corner of my eye, I watched as she quickly stashed whatever she had been hiding in a large ceramic canister. After doing that, she walked to the sink and plunged her hands into the soapy water, obviously picking up right where she had left off. Though I was dying to see what was in the canister, I didn't dare look. Instead, I walked over to the woodstove and stood in front of it, warming my hands.

"Where is everyone?"

"Isaac wanted to go sledding before the snow melts, so Lydia and Tresa took him to the hill out back," Grete said as she rinsed a plate and dried her hands. She was polite but not effusive, telling me that she had kept a plate warm for me on the stove. It was only a little after eight, but I quickly realized that the rest of the family had likely been up for several hours and had long since eaten.

She carried the plate to the table and set it down next to a clean set of silverware, insisting that I sit and have breakfast. I sat, but as I regarded the full plate in front of me, I wondered how I was going to find room in my stomach for more food when I was still stuffed from last night's dinner. Not wanting to be rude, I did the best I could, picking at the ham and eggs and biscuits to make it look as though I had eaten more than I really had.

Grete returned to her work at the sink, quietly moving through the job with the same efficient motions I had observed last night. Thinking of whatever lay hidden inside the jar, I asked if she was okay. She looked at me, her shoulders slumping, and she exhaled in frustration.

"I am sorry if I seem a bit distracted this morning. I do not know why it bothers me so much, considering that it has been happening every weekend lately."

"What's been happening?"

"Caleb," she said, using the same frustrated tone of voice Lydia had used last night. "The longer he stays on *rumspringa,* the more *agasinish* he becomes. He went out last night, which is fine. It was a Friday. But now here we are on Saturday morning with cows that need milking and a wagon that needs repairing and stalls that need mucking, and where is Caleb? Who knows? He chose not to come home last night."

My eyes widened.

"You mean he disappeared?"

"No, he did not disappear. I know exactly where he is. He is running around with his friends who have jobs in town and have the weekends off. Those boys may have a lot of extra money and time to get themselves in trouble, but Caleb's work is here on the farm, with Nathaniel, even on Saturdays. Because Caleb is not here, Rebecca and Ezra had to do his chores this morning on top of their own. We are all *feraikled* with him."

"So when does he usually show back up?"

"Oh, we will probably see him at tomorrow night's hymn sing, charming all the girls and making everyone laugh and acting like he did not abandon his work and his family for the entire weekend."

I took a final bite of my breakfast, thinking about the difficult road life had handed to Grete. To be saddled with an entire family at such a young age had to have been overwhelming, even with such extensive support from the community. To my mind, she was being far too hard on herself, obviously seeing Caleb's behavior as a result of something she and her husband had done or didn't do. I couldn't say as much to her, but as far as I was concerned, considering the loss they all had suffered at such an early age, if these kids made it to adulthood as good, healthy, well-adjusted individuals who loved God and each other, then Grete had more than done her job, whether they ended up Amish or not.

"Don't beat yourself up about a little rebellion," I said. "God can soften even the hardest heart, but in His time, of course."

"Of course."

With a nod and a smile, Grete turned her attention to the inside of the pantry. Taking advantage of the moment, I carried my plate to the trash can and quickly dumped my leftovers before she could notice how very little I had eaten. Bringing my plate and glass to the sink, I gave them a good washing and rinsing, and then I dried them and put them away.

As I admired the handmade cabinets, I noticed the ticking clock over the stove, which reminded me I needed to get moving. I kept thinking about that jar, but Grete wasn't likely to leave the room until I was out of there.

"I feel bad that I just keep showing up for meals and then leaving," I said, "but I really need to run. I have so much to do that I probably won't be back until tonight. If there's no snow, I probably won't even make it back for dinner."

"Please, you go. Find my sister's husband. We are here if you need us."

I thanked her, taking a moment to look out the front window, toward the road.

"I'm assuming that with the blinds up and the kids outside, that means there aren't any reporters or photographers out there today?"

"Not yet anyway."

"This is a good time to make an exit,

then," I said, thanking Grete again for the breakfast and the hospitality.

She waved away my thanks and started shooing me out the door, so I bundled up in my coat and scarf, grabbed my bags, and left. Outside, from somewhere in the distance, I could hear the squeals of the children. I put everything into the car, but before I got in I headed toward the squeals to let Lydia know I was leaving.

What I saw as I rounded the corner of the washhouse warmed my heart, a cozy scene of a young mother and her son and niece running up a tiny hill, piling onto various "vehicles," and sliding down on them in the mushy snow, an endeavor that was more comical than successful. Tresa, dressed in her black Amish cape, was using a wagon of some sort, though in the place of the wheels were blades that looked like snow skis. Isaac, wearing jeans and a ski jacket, had a brightly colored store-bought plastic sled, the kind Bobby and I always liked best when we were kids.

My smile dimmed just a bit when I spotted the bodyguard standing nearby, because his presence reminded me of the situation we were currently in. With that in mind, I gave Lydia a quick wave and called out that I would be in touch later. She waved back, and I headed to my car and took off, thinking as I did so how easy it was to be lulled into the peace and calm of an Amish household. Where everything had felt so urgent before, after one night with this family, I had already begun to feel as though I had all the time in the world, that no problem was too big for God and time to handle.

While that was true, I knew it wouldn't hurt to get my game back on and get busy finding my brother.

TWENTY-TWO

STEPHANIE

July 21, 1812

I have discovered a confection so enticing that certainly its very existence must be a sin: tiny, individual apple pastries that Priscilla calls schnitz pie. When I passed her in the fields today as I made my rounds, she shyly offered up a basket of this delicacy. One bite and I was convinced I have tasted heaven here on earth. I have asked for the recipe to give to the palace chefs, but she claims it was simply learned from her mother without thought to measure or timing. I asked how she came to make apple pastries in July, well before the fall apple harvest, and she explained that schnitz pie is made from dried apples, not fresh.

As I know I will see her again, I asked that she prepare more of these in the future, though not so often as to make me grow even heavier than this child in my womb is already making me. Between myself, my attendant, Priscilla, her toddler Francis, and Priscilla's shy husband, Samuel, we finished the whole basket of delights. Next time, I will save at least one to bring back to the chef, in the hopes he could take that sample and approximate it in his kitchen.

July 30, 1812

I continue to be refreshed and delighted by my walks, strengthened by the physical exertion, and much reassured by my daily encounters with Priscilla. I do believe we have formed a genuine friendship, and I will be sad to see this friendship come to an end once my child is born. Perhaps it is for the best, as propriety would never allow the wife of the Duke and the wife of a tenant farmer, an Amisch woman no less, to meet under any other circumstance.

August 5, 1812

Today while visiting with Pricilla, I expressed my deep regret at having to terminate our friendship once our respective children are born. Certainly, she understood why our relationship must end, though she did offer up some hope by reminding me that my husband's family has shown great kindness to her people in the past. In particular, she spoke of how just eleven years ago my husband's grandfather, the reigning Duke at that time, abolished many of the old, unfair laws that had caused so much grief and hardship to the local Amisch community. Because of his kind actions, Priscilla said, her family had moved here to the fertile land of Baden to become tenant farmers, where they had thrived and multiplied. Surely, she said, the grandson of a man so tolerant of her religion might see fit to allow his wife such a minor daily social interaction as I have found on these walks.

I reminded her that it was my own husband who reinstated one of those old, abolished laws just last month, when he removed the exemption of her community's males from the military.

She agreed and we were both downcast for a while until she suggested that we each continue to pray that my husband, Karl, would grow into the role of a benevolent ruler more in keeping with his grandfather's rein—and that the men in her community would not be forced to take up arms when their religion so strictly forbids it. I added that my most fervent prayers would be for the continuance of our friendship and the opportunity to persist with these daily walks even when I no longer had pregnancy and doctor's orders as my excuse.

TWENTY-THREE

ANNA

With all the trips I had made to Haley's mother's house as a teenager, I had no trouble finding it now. Technically, Melody lived in a neighborhood, though her driveway began where the road ended, curving completely out of sight behind a stand of trees so thick that the house could not be seen from the street, even now in the winter, when many of the limbs were bare. I turned onto the winding driveway, glad that the snow had already turned to slush, and took it all in as I went, surprised at how much of the property she had allowed to grow wild in the years since I had been here. Deep woods seemed to encroach on all sides, and though there was a tidy row of bushes along the front of the house, otherwise it didn't seem as if she had done any pruning or neatening of any kind to the various forms of vegetation that had once graced the yard.

The cottage itself was small but cozy, with two bedrooms and a single bathroom. I parked the car, grabbed my stuff, and headed to the front door. Melody greeted me with a warm hug, and as we pulled apart, I couldn't help but notice the view of the backyard, visible through the center hallway that led to the living room.

"Wow," I said, walking toward that room now, where the windows gave a panoramic view of the outside. Directly in the center of the backyard was a huge crabapple tree, one that she had planted when Haley and I were teens. Looking at it now made me feel old, for it had grown tall and wide, its form beautiful, its branches spreading out perfectly to every side. "I can't believe how much that tree has grown. I remember when it wasn't much taller than I am now."

"I know. I used a lot of compost with it, and of course the soil is a rich loam with a the perfect pH for crabapple."

She pointed out a few other new features she had added to the yard, including a small pond and fountain. I was afraid she might launch into an extended discussion of her various plants and shrubs, but instead she simply suggested I go ahead and take my shower.

I did as she said, grabbing a towel from the closet in the hall and then letting myself into the bathroom. As I opened the door, waves of heat embraced me like a sauna. Delicious.

I would have loved to indulge myself with a long-drawn-out shower, but I thought that might be rude, so I showered and dressed as quickly as I could, turning off the space heater as soon as I was finished. After using a portion of my towel to wipe the fog from the glass, I put on my makeup and fixed my hair. When I finally emerged from the bathroom, I felt like a new person.

"I can't believe anyone could suggest such a thing," Melody said as I was walking up the hall, and a for a minute I thought she was talking to me. When she continued, I realized she was on the phone. "Honestly, people can be so stupid!"

She was in the kitchen, so I tiptoed up the hallway, intending to give her a wave of thanks and tell her I was leaving. Before I got there, however, she spoke again.

"Having a good life insurance policy on your husband doesn't make you a murderer!"

I froze, realizing she must be talking to Haley.

"Tell them unless they want to bring official charges, you're not talking. And get a lawyer in the meantime. Ask your father to hire the best in the business."

I was trying to decide what to do—stand there and eavesdrop or return to the bathroom and pretend I hadn't heard anything—when she suddenly concluded her call.

"What? Sure, fine. Keep me posted. Bye."

She hung up the phone and all was silent. I waited for the count of ten and then continued on to the kitchen doorway.

"Hey, thanks so much for the shower," I

said nonchalantly. "Guess I need to get rolling."

"Wait," she replied. "I was just talking to Haley. You won't believe this, but she's now a suspect in her husband's death."

I moved into the room as she described their phone call. Apparently, the police had learned of a million-dollar life insurance policy that had been taken out on Doug just last year—and Haley had made the mistake of trying to cash in on it less than an hour after she was told he had died.

"Less than an hour?" I asked. "No wonder the police were suspicious."

"Yes, well, Haley wouldn't have wished Doug dead, but I feel sure that that policy was the first silver lining that popped into her mind."

Knowing how fond Haley was of money, I had a feeling that was true.

"It's her own fault," Melody continued as I joined her at the table. "Frankly, I don't think Doug was murdered at all. I think his fall was an accident. But Haley kept making such a big deal out of the whole motorcycle thing, and then with

Bobby's disappearance and all that, she kept saying, 'Make sure it wasn't a murder. I think it might have been a murder.' Once the police started looking at it that way, she turned out to be one of their biggest suspects. If she had kept her mouth shut, she wouldn't be in this position."

"Has she been charged?"

"No. And if I know Orin, he'll make sure she never is. That man would move heaven and earth to protect his daughter. I have no doubt he'll have some of the top lawyers in the country on the case by noon."

She had that right.

"Speaking of Orin," I said, hoping it wasn't tacky of me to change the subject at such a difficult time, "I wonder if I could ask you a couple of questions about Wynn Industries, specifically the extension out here in Dreiheit, the WIRE."

She seemed startled by my request, but she nodded.

"Sure. What do you want to know?"

I told her about Bobby's suspension and my conversation last night with Dr. Updyke.

"This is only one of several completely

different avenues I'm exploring," I explained, "but I have to wonder if Bobby's disappearance could have been connected with something going on at the lab, maybe with Dr. Updyke himself. Do you know much about the research that goes on there? Is there any chance Bobby could have been abducted—or even killed—because of something he knew, or something he did that was related to the lab in some way?" She stared at me blankly, so I added, "You know, like are the WIRE's secrets valuable enough to cost a life? I just don't know anything about the world of DNA research."

Melody stood and went to the breadbox, pulling out an Entenmann's coffee cake. Before I could decline, she had cut two pieces and plopped one of them on a paper towel in front of me.

"Let's see," she began, sitting back down at the table. "What can I tell you? The world of DNA research, as you put it, is all about potential. With what's been discovered so far—and I'm talking about all over the world, not just at the WIRE—scientists have enough information to be able to see where they're going to go eventually, but not enough information to get there yet. Does that make sense?"

"Not really."

"Okay, then I'll be more specific. By studying human genes and the nature of DNA, scientists know that someday they'll be able to cure a huge number of ailments not with pills or surgery, but through simple gene therapy. The body will repair itself. They know it's going to be possible; they just haven't perfected how to do it yet."

"Is that what they're working on at the WIRE? Manipulating genes?"

"I would imagine, among other things. Scientists love the Lancaster County Amish because most of them descended from the same small group of ancestors. To that, add the fact that almost no one ever joins the Amish religion from the outside, so it's very rare for new genes to be brought into the mix. Consequently, researchers can study Amish DNA more easily than they can study the genes of your average person. The same thing holds true in Iceland, in certain Jewish sects, and really anywhere that breeding is essentially closed to outsiders. It's called the

'Founder Effect,' and scientists find it useful because when you have an entire society with very similar DNA, it's much easier to see which genes are the ones that are causing problems."

Melody tore off several pieces of her cake and lined them up on the table as a visual aid.

"Let's say these five people are all Amish, so their DNA is very similar. Now, let's say this one is born with cystic fibrosis. Put simply, to figure out the gene that's responsible for cystic fibrosis, all they have to do is compare the DNA of all five and see which gene is radically different in this person than in the other four, which would indicate a mutation. Or, instead of a mutated gene being present in this one guy, maybe there's an important gene that the other four have that this person is simply missing, which can also cause problems. One by one, researchers have been able to isolate a huge number of genes that are related to genetic disorders by studying and comparing Amish DNA. Finding the gene is always the first step in creating a cure."

"What if Dr. Updyke discovered the next

step in creating a cure? Maybe he made a big breakthrough that nobody knows about yet? Wouldn't that be valuable?"

Melody popped the five pieces into her mouth, one after the other.

"It's more complicated than that," she replied after chewing and swallowing. "Researchers already know how to do gene therapy. The hard part is getting the altered gene to go into the body and into the correct place and do what it's supposed to do once it gets there. Some experiments have been more successful than others, but it's going to be years before they have figured it all out. There are too many variables—and not just one answer. Each discovery is one little piece of a massive jigsaw puzzle, so nothing he could have discovered would be big enough in and of itself to put someone's life at risk. Someday, yes, DNA is going to be a very lucrative field. Right now, I feel sure that places like the WIRE only lose money. The eventual payoff that everyone hopes for is probably worth the cost, but I can't think of a single thing at this point that would be worth abducting or killing over."

I considered her words, wishing I knew more about the science of it.

"Look at my field, for example," she continued. "A lot of my friends have made a fortune manipulating the DNA of plants, because that's simpler and much further along than human studies. From tomatoes with a longer shelf life to peaches that are more fragrant to potatoes that have added calcium, whatever the market will bear, that's what's being done in plant biology."

"So when does your fortune come rolling in?" I teased.

"Probably not for a long time, not that it matters. I'm working in the field of edible vaccinations." She went on to explain that she and the fellow researchers at her company were trying to find a way to insert the vaccines into the DNA of plants.

"One of the problems in the Third World is keeping vaccines refrigerated until they can be injected. Seeds are much more transportable, not to mention far less expensive. If we can get the tetanus vaccine into rice, for example, or the pertussis vaccine into bananas, then all we have to do to inoculate entire populations is to send them the seeds, which they will cultivate and consume. The science of it shows great promise, but we have a ways to go."

I shook my head, marveling at the very thought of it. Obviously, as scientists unlocked the secrets of DNA, more and more of the impossible would become possible.

"Do you have any ideas about why Bobby was trying to look at classified information?"

It took so long for Melody to answer that for a minute I was afraid she hadn't heard the question. But then she spoke, offering a variety of suggestions.

"Maybe he wanted to blackmail someone, and he needed their medical information to do it. Maybe he wanted to buy a certain drug, but he needed the contact information for the distributor. Heck, maybe he met a pretty girl who was a patient, and he wanted to find her phone number."

"To cheat on his wife with?"

"Maybe."

"I'm sorry, but I believe he really loves

Lydia—not to mention that I just don't think he is that kind of person."

As soon as the words were out of my mouth, I regretted them. Melody had cheated on Orin Wynn, so she was that "kind of person." I met her eyes, and I could tell we were thinking the same thing.

My face flushed with heat, I quickly moved the conversation back to Dr. Updyke, asking Melody if she knew him personally and what she thought about him.

"I mean, I know he's well respected in the field, but is he a good guy? I definitely picked up a strange vibe from him last night."

Melody shrugged.

"Every brilliant researcher I know gives off a strange vibe," she said. "I wouldn't read anything into it. Let me say this unequivocally: Harold Updyke would never risk such an illustrious career by doing anything outside the bounds of the law. DNA research is so heavily regulated by the FDA that even if he tried, he couldn't get away with it. Trust me, Anna. There's too much regulation, too many watchdogs. You're barking up the wrong tree with this one."

"Maybe you're right."

"I mean, things used to be kind of lax until a man died in a gene therapy experiment in 1999. The FDA has been firmly in control ever since."

"Really?"

"Absolutely. Ask your old friend Reed Thornton. He'll tell you the same thing."

TWENTY-FOUR

My mood was somber as I left Melody's house. I was upset with myself, frustrated that the mere mention of Reed's name still caused my pulse to race. Surely there had to be an expiration date on the desires of the heart, a statute of limitations on past loves.

With a heavy sigh, I pulled out of Melody's driveway and made my way to the main road. Next stop in my investigation was a trip back to Exton, to see if I could do a little forensic accounting on the computer Bobby had used at the Internet café the night he disappeared. I flipped on the radio as I settled in for the drive, but I had the volume so low I almost missed the breaking news alert. I thought I heard the name "Doug Brown," so I turned up the volume and listened. My jaw dropped open at what was being said.

According to the reporter, a motorcycle belonging to Doug Brown had been found, wrecked and abandoned, along Dreiheit Pike in Lancaster County. Authorities believed it was the same motorcycle that was taken on Wednesday night by Robert "Bobby" Jensen, who was still being sought for questioning in the death of Mr. Brown.

I drove toward the highway as fast as I could. I wasn't sure of the exact location where the bike had been found, but I was determined to drive up and down the road as many times as necessary to find it.

As it turned out, when I reached the site there was no question about where it was. Police cars lined the road, as did a number of news vans. Averting my face as I slowly drove past a clump of reporters, I realized this was why they hadn't been out at the farm this morning. They had all been here, where the news was really happening.

Despite the risk, I had to take a look. I pulled to the very end of the line, parked my car, and got out.

Some people were standing at the railing, so I simply joined them and tried to act like a curious onlooker. From what I could see, the road made a broad curve with a steep drop-off. Looking downward, I spotted a number of policemen doing something on the side of the hill. As I watched, I realized they were taking measurements—and then I saw it, the crushed and mangled motorcycle.

Swallowing hard, I refused to allow myself to cry. Still, the sight was shocking. If Bobby had been riding that motorcycle when it crashed, then surely he was dead or at least severely injured. If he was dead, then where was his body? If he was still alive, then how had he managed to get away? On the other hand, was this some sort of setup? Had he made it look like a motorcycle crash but walked away unhurt? I just didn't know, though forensic evidence—such as the existence of blood—should answer at least one of those questions.

Running a hand through my hair, I gazed

farther down the hill to see a farm. Surely, if Bobby had survived the accident, he would have had the sense to go there for help. The answer was obvious to me, yet none of the cops seemed to have even noticed the nearby structure. Pulse surging, I decided to walk down there myself, even if it got me seen by the reporters. I knew my brother, and I knew if he survived that crash, then that is where he would have gone.

From where I stood the hill was too steep to climb down, so I made my way to the other end of the parked cars, beyond the clump of reporters and past most of the curious onlookers. As I went, my stomach churned when I saw the point of impact, a concrete retaining wall marred with thick, black tread marks exactly the width of motorcycle tires.

About twenty feet beyond that things leveled out a bit, and it looked as though there might even be a path there, leading down. Keeping my eyes to the ground, I made my way past a tall man in a charcoal grey coat and started down the hill.

"I wouldn't try that if I were you," he called after me.

"I'll be fine," I replied, not looking up. If he was a reporter, I didn't want him to get a good look at my face.

"I'm sure you will," he persisted, "but there's a cop at the bottom who's just going to send you straight back up here again, like he did to me."

"I'll take my chances," I replied, wishing the guy would leave me alone.

"Whatever you say, Annalise. You always were stubborn."

Maybe it was the way he said my name. Maybe it was the deep tones in his voice. Whatever it was, I knew instantly that he wasn't a reporter.

He was Reed Thornton.

Stunned, I turned to see him standing at the top of the path, hands in his pockets.

"Reed?"

He nodded, and then a smile broke out on his handsome face.

"I knew it was you," he said softly, walking down to meet me. "You look so different but exactly the same, if that makes sense."

"Reed?" I asked again, feeling like an idiot, but all other words escaped me. What was he doing here?

When he got to me, he opened his arms

for a hug, and I slipped into them as easily as if I belonged there. He was taller than I remembered, and the years had been incredibly good to him. Something about him was also different but exactly the same. Unbelievable.

"How are you?" he whispered into my hair, holding on to the hug a little longer than necessary.

"I'm okay," I replied, pulling away. "I'm here to find Bobby. What about you?"

"Long story. Let me buy you a late breakfast and I'll tell it to you."

I glanced down the hillside path toward the farm house and told him I'd have to take a rain check.

"Look, I know you want to investigate down there, Annalise, but we need to talk first."

His expression was so intense that I finally agreed.

"But no food for me, thanks. People have been trying to feed me all day."

He tilted his head back and laughed, and I realized that the motion was so familiar I had practically memorized it. Who was I kidding? I had dreamed about it. Longed for it.

Missed it.

Together we climbed to the top of the hill, and then Reed led me toward his car. Part of me was regretting my decision, feeling that I really did need to talk to the cops about the farmhouse as soon as possible. As if he could read my mind, Reed took my elbow as we neared the car, pulled me a little closer, and spoke softly into my ear.

"Trust me, the cops know what they're doing."

He continued to hold my elbow until he led me around to the passenger side of his car, a beautiful dark gray Lexus.

I lowered myself onto the soft leather seat and watched as he closed the door and walked around to the driver's side. Something about the entire scene was so surreal, so bizarre, that for a moment I wondered if I was asleep and this was just a dream.

"I go by Anna now, by the way," I said to him as he got in and started up the car.

"That's right. I had heard that. Okay, Anna. I'm not really hungry, either. Let's just drive instead."

He eased past the parked cars and the

people as I leaned forward to shield my face, pretending to dig through my purse. Once we were in the clear, I settled back and turned to my companion, studying him in profile. His black hair was shorter than it used to be, though it was still straight and just the slightest bit spiky. The line of his jaw was firm, his eyes a sparkling blue under thick lashes.

Amazingly, he was even more handsome than I had remembered. I couldn't help but wonder what he thought of me.

"I'd love to play catch-up with you," he said, glancing at me, "but before we do that, I think I should jump right in and tell you what's going on. I talked to Haley last night, and she said you were in town at Lydia's request, trying to find your brother."

"Yeah, he sort of vanished off the face of the earth. Do you know anything about that? Is someone targeting the Dreiheit Five?"

He seemed surprised at my question.

"Why do you think that?"

"Well, Doug's dead, Bobby's missing, I was attacked, Haley's under the protection of a bodyguard. Sure seems like it. Has anyone done anything to you?"

"Well, yeah, I had a break-in at my condo, but I'll get to that in a minute. You were attacked?"

I explained about the ski-masked intruder and his strange request for rubies. Reed had never heard the term "Beauharnais Rubies," though he seemed very concerned for my safety—and upset at the thought of someone holding a gun to my head. I wondered if that meant he still cared a little bit for me, or if his concern was more general, as in one old friend for another.

"I don't know what that has to do with any of this, but I'll explain things from my end," he said.

"Okay."

Reed turned off of the highway and onto a picturesque, winding road. The snow had almost completely melted on the blacktop, though it still remained in large patches on the dormant fields, creating yet another gorgeous winter scene.

"The day before yesterday—around noon Thursday, to be precise—I came home from a trip to find that my condo had been broken into. A glass panel on the back door was shattered, making an easy reach to the lock and the knob from the inside. None of my possessions seemed to be missing, and in fact the only sign of the break-in was the shattered glass. I couldn't figure out what had happened. I called the police anyway, but it wasn't until after they took their report and left that I listened to my phone messages. There was one from Doug from the night before, talking about the fax he had just sent. The tray in the machine was empty, though, and that's when I realized what had been taken in the break-in: Doug's fax. I looked closely, and there were a few tiny shards of glass on the floor in front of the machine. Obviously, the person who broke in had tracked them there."

"What did you do?"

"I pressed the memory button and re-printed the fax. Whoever stole the hard copy wasn't exactly tech-savvy. They must not have known I could recover it from the machine."

"What did the fax say? What was it?"

He turned again, driving us down a road that sliced between two Amish farms, a series of rambling white buildings looming up on both sides.

"First, you have to hear Doug's phone message, the one that alerted me to the presence of a fax. I recorded it."

His hands clad in black leather gloves, Reed reached into his coat pocket and pulled out a digital voice recorder. Holding it up, he pressed the play button, and soon the voice of Doug Brown filled the car.

Hey, Reed. Doug here. Listen, man, I've been thinking about the fax I just sent, and I wanted to elaborate. I'm sure you're wondering why I'm selling out my own company. There was a long pause, and then he continued. *I think you'll understand once you read the files, especially that last one. After everything they had already been through that very night—and then they had to suffer and die like they did? Ever since I read that part, I've been thinking about my own life, what it's worth.* Again, Doug was quiet, but when he spoke, his voice was firm. *Look, I need to do the right thing for once, even if it costs me my job . . . maybe my marriage . . . and probably my friendship with Bobby, who might be up to his elbows in this thing himself.*

Anyway, I'm rambling. I just wanted to explain. It was great seeing you at

the conference. I appreciate the work you're doing. Call me as soon as you get this. Bye.

The recording ended with a beep, and then the car was silent.

"The fax was sent from Doug's office at Wynn Industries headquarters in Hidden Springs at seven o'clock Wednesday night," Reed said finally. "Then his phone message followed about ten minutes later. According to Exton's coroner, Doug may have died as early as eight thirty the same night, which looks pretty cause and effect to me. He ratted out his company through a fax and a phone call, then he was dead less than two hours later, and the fax was quietly intercepted. Obviously, whoever killed him and stole the fax didn't know about the phone message or they would have erased that too."

My eyes wide, I again asked Reed what was in the fax that could have been worth killing over. Without replying, he reached down between our two seats and pulled out a file folder, which he handed to me. Holding my breath, I opened it up and studied the pages inside.

First was a fax cover sheet with the Wynn Industries logo on it. In the comments section, Doug had written a note:

Reed,

As per our recent conversation regarding unauthorized gene therapy, here's proof positive that it was happening right under our own noses. Talk to me before you act on this!

Doug

After that were what appeared to be pages of old medical files. Judging from the font, the text had been typed on a typewriter, and the first one was dated March 1991. Doug had drawn arrows pointing to the date, the patient's name, and the very first sentence of the doctor's notes: *Newborn presents with Wolfe-Kraus syndrome. Have enrolled in study.*

The rest of that page and the next two pages were simply dated entries written by a doctor that described the newborn's series of office visits that took place over the next several years. I skimmed the entries, and it looked to me as though the patient had a disorder and was given some sort of procedure that appeared to be moderately successful in treating it. The effects of the procedure seemed to fade, however, because it had to be repeated every few months, something that the doctor did not seem happy about. The final entry, which was circled, said: *Patient has been withdrawn from study due to religious objections of Amish parents, who indicate they have been feeling conflicted about "tampering with God's will" in the matter of their child (i.e., if God wanted this cure to work, we wouldn't have to keep doing it over and over). Parents have been counseled as to the effects of discontinuance, e.g., WKS symptoms will return in full. Patient discharged on this date, November 12, 1994. All data from this subject has been included in summary reports. File closed, HU, MD.*

"'HU, MD.' is that Harold Updyke, MD?"

"Yep."

"I don't quite understand. What's Wolfe-Kraus syndrome? What study is this referring to?"

"WKS is a rare genetic disorder, one that plagues some of the Amish in the area. In the late eighties, Dr. Updyke isolated the missing gene that causes the disorder, and from 1991 to 1994 he conducted an FDA-approved study that explored various treatment options."

"Treatment options. You mean tampering with genes."

"Yes. For the study described there in the file, he used the same technique that French Anderson pioneered the year before to treat SCID."

"French Anderson? SCID?" I asked, shaking my head. It was all too much, too fast.

"Sorry, French was another bigwig in the field of DNA research. In 1990, he treated some kids who had severe combined immunodeficiency by removing cells from the patients, growing them in the lab, inserting the missing genes into the cells, and then reinserting them into the patients' bodies."

"Is that what's meant by gene therapy?"

"Yes, that's the most common approach, replacing a missing or nonfunctional gene with a normal one by inserting it into a nonspecific location within the genome. Geneticists may also choose to swap genes through homologous recombination or selective reverse mutation. Or they can regulate the degree to which an abnormal gene is turned off."

"Okay. I understood about ten percent of what you just said."

"Sorry. In plain English, the hardest part of gene manipulation is getting the genes back into the body and making sure that they go to the right place and do the right thing once they get there. It's a very complex process."

His words echoed similar comments Melody had made earlier.

"So was the study described by Dr. Updyke in this file a success or a failure?"

"A little of both, I guess. It was a step in the right direction, but it wasn't a cure. The study was closed out by the end of that year. According to the FDA, that was the last approved study Dr. Updyke conducted. Now keep reading."

I glanced out of the window at the curvy road in front of us and realized I was starting to feel vaguely carsick. I told Reed as much, asking if he could pull over before I went any further.

"Sure. I think this is what I was looking

for anyway," he said, putting on his blinker and turning onto a gravel road. It led us through a field on someone's back acreage. When we reached the end, he simply stopped the car and put it in park, though he left the engine running for the heater's sake.

Hoping it was okay to be trespassing out here, I returned my attention to the pages in front of me, moving on to the next patient file. This one was dated January 1995 and began the same as the previous one, with the notation *Newborn presents with Wolfe-Kraus syndrome.* This time, however, no study was mentioned. From the series of treatment notes that followed, the child was given some sort of procedure and then seen a number of times over the next three months. Unlike the first file, however, entire paragraphs from this report had been blacked out, so it was hard to tell everything that had been done. Near the end, it was noted that the child had a "significant tumor on the pituitary." At the bottom of the page, Doug had circled the last sentence: *Tumor proved fatal. File closed on this date of April 6, 1995, HU, MD.*

"Does WKS cause tumors?" I asked Reed.

"No," he said, studying the horizon in front of us. "But gene therapy can."

I took a deep breath, trying to understand.

"So you think this file shows that Dr. Updyke tried gene therapy again on another patient, even though the study was finished?"

"Yes."

"What's wrong with that?"

"Unless it's part of an FDA-approved trial, gene therapy is unethical, not to mention illegal."

"So why try to skirt around the law? Why not just do another study?"

Reed shrugged.

"Lots of reasons. The application process is grueling. Once you submit it to the FDA, approval can take forever—if the study you're proposing even gets approved. All results have to be reported, tons of paperwork has to be done, and on and on. All deaths must be carefully autopsied. With DNA research, human trials are so heavily regulated that every time a researcher wants to modify a treatment, they practically have to start back at square one. I'm guessing that Dr. Updyke followed the rules that one time and then decided that was for the birds and just did it on the sly after that. To be honest, back then a lot of researchers were going that route. It wasn't until 1999 that the FDA really cracked down, and even then they got serious only because a young man died from a gene therapy procedure, one that had broken all sorts of rules."

"Yeah, Melody mentioned that."

Outside, a flock of birds landed in the field next to us and began pecking at the ground.

"So all the heavy regulation on DNA human trials is a bad thing?" I asked.

"On the contrary," Reed replied emphatically. "It's absolutely, vitally necessary. We can never, ever underestimate the implications of gene manipulation, especially if modified genes get into the germline. Approved studies are a lot of trouble, but considering the consequences, that trouble is worth it."

He was getting technical again, so rather

than ask what "the germline" was, I looked again at the pages from the file and the words obscured throughout.

"I wonder if there's any way to recover the text that's been blacked out."

"We should find out soon," Reed replied. "The FBI is working on that as we speak."

I gasped, putting one hand to my mouth. "You turned this over to the FBI?" I asked, wondering how Bobby was involved and if he was going to end up going back to jail—if he was ever found. I wondered if maybe that's why he had wanted to disappear, because he couldn't take the thought of yet another conviction and sentence.

"Keep reading," Reed said, gesturing toward the papers in my lap.

I did as he said, noting that there were two more patient files. One was very brief, with a single entry that indicated prenatal testing for WKS had been conducted on a twenty-one-year-old pregnant woman, one who had lost two infants to the disorder in the past. The fetus she was currently pregnant with, however, tested negative. At the end of that entry was the sentence: *Patient indicates that her mother, age forty, is also pregnant, due in August. I have recommended testing for her as well, particularly considering her age. File closed on this date of December 21, 1996, HU, MD.*

"Explain something to me," I said, glancing at Reed. "How does this disorder thing work? This woman lost two previous babies to WKS, but then her third baby apparently didn't have it. Why is that?"

"Didn't you ever have to diagram genetics in high school, back in biology class? You remember those little charts that showed dominant genes and what chance the offspring of two people would have for inheriting blue eyes or a big nose or something? It's a statistical thing. For a child to be born with WKS, both parents have to have been carriers. Even then, there's only a twenty-five percent chance that their offspring will have the disorder, but when you consider that's one in four kids, that's pretty high."

"I see what you mean."

"Keep reading."

I turned to the next page, which was apparently the file for the previous girl's mother. The forty-year-old woman had come in for testing, only her news was not so good, as the fetus did test positive for WKS. Though parts of this file had also been blacked out, it looked as if a different treatment approach had been used this time, some sort of procedure done to the fetus in utero rather than waiting to treat the child once it was born. It must not have worked though, judging by the final entry: *In-home delivery at 9:35 pm, male infant pronounced dead at 10:15 pm.* The rest of the paragraph was blacked out, and there were no other pages.

"What was it about this file that bothered Doug so much?"

"Check the name and the date."

I looked at the top of the page to see that the pregnant woman in question, the one whose baby had WKS and died shortly after it was born, was listed as "Katherine Beiler Schumann."

"Katherine Schumann . . . is that Kate Schumann? Lydia's mother?" I cried. Flipping backward, I checked the name on the previous patient, which confirmed it. The twenty-one-year-old whose fetus tested negative was listed as "Grete Schumann Stoltzfus." That must have been when she was pregnant with Tresa. Flipping forward again, I scanned all of the dates in her mother's file until I got to the one that mattered: According to the final entry, Grete's mother's baby was born and then died on August 16, 1997, the very night of the fire.

The night that changed all of our lives forever.

TWENTY-FIVE

At first, I was simply speechless. I needed to process this, to think, to walk, to *move.*

"Can I walk around out here?" I asked, nearly hyperventilating. "I need some air. I have to process."

"I don't see why not. It's just a field."

Not even waiting for him to join me, I simply got out and started running. I ran back up the gravel road the way we had come, blood rhythmically coursing through my veins like a drum. When I reached the blacktop, I turned around, slowed my pace, and jogged all the way back to the car. By the time I got there, Reed had turned off the car and was standing in the sun, leaning against the hood, his back to me. He was talking on a cell phone, and by the tone of his voice and the words I could hear, the conversation sounded personal, not business.

I walked toward him, and when he noticed me, he spoke again into the phone.

"Sorry, Heather. I have to go. I'll call you later. You too."

After he had hung up the phone, I spoke.

"First of all, this means we didn't kill three people, only two. Not that it makes that much of a difference, but in a way it does. At least in here."

I put a hand on my heart, the ache of guilt and loss fading just a little as I absorbed the realization that my actions that night hadn't helped to kill a newborn baby. By the time the fire started, that baby was already dead—and had been dead for several hours.

"Yeah, I know what you mean. Though, as Doug pointed out in his phone message, in another way this makes it worse. The Schumanns had already been through the heartbreaking death of their baby on that very night. After going through all of that, then they ended up burning to death in the fire? It's enough to make you sick. No wonder Doug was compelled to send me those records."

Reed was right. Regardless of the exact sequence of events, by the end of the night three charred bodies were found in the remains, even if one of them had been dead before it happened.

"I have questions, lots of questions," I said, pacing in front of the car. "First, what does this have to do with Bobby? These files are old. His only connection to any of those procedures is that he was an intern at the WIRE the summer that Kate Schumann was a patient. I know Bobby's smart, but you can't tell me that any of his duties there involved high-level stuff like this."

"No, of course not. I was the highest-ranking intern that summer, and even my work was pretty low level. At least I got to deal with viral vectors. Bobby's job was pretty basic. Lab cleanup, sterilizing equipment, things like that."

"So what does any of this have to do with him?"

"I'm not sure. My guess is that Dr. Updyke continued to be involved with clandestine human trials—and maybe, these days, they're still going on, only now Bobby helps in some capacity. You know how your brother always worshipped the brilliant Dr. Updyke. Maybe Doug found out about these old experiments, so he called Bobby to get more current information about what might be going on over there."

"Actually," I corrected, thinking of the phone message that night from Doug to Bobby, "Bobby is the one who asked Doug to get some information. There's a message on Bobby's machine from that night, from Doug. He said something like 'I have the info you asked for, including some you didn't expect.'"

"Maybe it was the part he didn't expect that caused the problem. Then, instead of ratting out the doctor, Bobby acted to protect him instead."

"Protect him. By killing Doug?"

"It sure could look that way."

I moved in front of him, hands on my hips.

"You think Bobby killed Doug to protect Dr. Updyke?"

Reed studied my face, the blue of his eyes almost piercing in their intensity.

"I'm afraid that's one possibility. I'm sorry, Anna, but it's a logical conclusion, given all the facts. We know for sure Updyke didn't do it himself. He was at a symposium in Pittsburgh that night, speaking to an audience of a couple hundred people."

I paced some more as my mind rolled around the possible events of last Wednesday night.

"In his phone message to you, Doug said that he was selling out his company, and that doing so was probably going to cost him his marriage and his job."

"Yes, that's what he said."

"So why would Bobby be the killer? He may be a big fan of Updyke, but he's not particularly invested in Wynn Industries, other than as a low-paid employee. I mean, haven't you heard the expression 'Follow the money'? A big medical scandal at the WIRE would be a disaster for Updyke personally, sure, but something like that would come at a much higher cost to Wynn Industries at large. The company would lose a fortune, not to mention its reputation, which in turn would further lower its value. The ripple effect could end up costing them millions—even billions. Given that, who's to say that Orin Wynn didn't kill Doug? The way I see it, that's a much more logical conclusion, especially since Orin's daughter was in a loveless marriage with Doug."

"Orin Wynn also has an ironclad alibi. At the time Doug was killed, Orin was in a board meeting at company headquarters with nine other people."

"So maybe Orin arranged to have Doug killed by someone else. Either way, I'd point the finger in his direction long before I would suspect Bobby. If we're comparing the two, Orin had a much bigger motivation. So did Updyke, who also could afford to hire someone to do his dirty work for him."

Reed folded his arms against his chest, seeming to consider my words.

"To be honest, Anna, knowing all three of these men as I do, I can't imagine any one of them doing something like this. They're honorable and kindhearted, and they live with integrity."

I waited for Reed to make his point,

gazing out at the field beside us. In the fall, they would be bursting with beautiful cornstalks. Now, however, those stalks were nothing more than ugly nubs in the ground.

"If Orin and Harold and Bobby are all good men," he continued, "then you have to think of their unique positions in this. If Orin or Harold killed Doug, it would have been a crime of calculation. But if Bobby killed Doug, it would have been a crime of passion, a coldhearted act motivated by greed. As much as you don't want to hear this, Anna, the facts do point to a hot-hearted impulse motivated by the desire to protect someone's reputation and career. Given that none of them is the type to commit a murder, which crime sounds more likely to you? I say the crime of passion makes a lot more sense. Bobby being the guilty one here."

I also folded my arms across my chest and turned to face the same direction as Reed, leaning back against the warm car. The sun was creeping toward noon overhead, and I still hadn't called the cops to tell them to check out that farmhouse. Now the man I had longed for and loved for many years was calling my own brother a murderer. Truly, at that moment, I wanted nothing more than to go home to California, sit on the rotting back porch, and forget all about any of this. Of course, given Kiki's injury and attitude, not to mention the break-in at our house, things had changed back there as much as they had here. Maybe it was time to reinvent myself yet again, only this time leaving the country and starting over somewhere else, somewhere very far away, where no one would ever figure out my true identity.

"If you really think Bobby could have killed Doug, then why did you come," I asked softly, "especially if you've already turned in your evidence to the FBI?"

Reed was quiet for a long moment, his shoulder warm against mine despite the cold air that surrounded us. When he finally spoke, his voice was gentle, the voice of a man who had suffered much and learned from his pain.

"I'm here because Bobby is my friend. Regardless of what he may have done, I came to see if I could talk him into voluntarily surrendering himself while he's still in a position to make a deal. At the very least, I came to show him I'm here for him. People sticking by you in times of trouble, that's one of the most important things in life. I think we all learned that the hard way."

I nodded, knowing I certainly had.

"Besides," Reed added, "I was worried about the impact all of this might have on you. When I heard you were in town, I had to come and see you and tell you what I knew."

"Why tell me at all?"

"Because I didn't want you hearing it somewhere else. As a friend, I thought I owed you that much."

Though I resisted the impulse, what I most wanted to do, right then, was lean more tightly against him, maybe even rest my head on his shoulder. I thought about the years that had passed since we last saw each other, about the summer I met Reed and fell in love with him. He was smart and fun and good looking, yes, but as it turned out he hadn't been the man I thought he was. Except for that one kiss, he also hadn't been the least bit interested in me as anything other than a friend. We had corresponded when he was in prison, but even then his letters weren't about us. They were about all the things that had happened and all the ways he was changing. Of course, his words had made up for what he had done that night and made me fall back in love with him again. Much to my dismay, the letters eventually came to an end, and once he got out, he never looked me up or made any effort to see me. Eventually, as I tried to nurse my twice-broken heart, I decided that I would not mistake Reed Thornton's friendship for something else ever again. Judging by the phone call I had interrupted earlier, he was involved with someone now anyway, someone named Heather.

"So how are you these days?" he asked.

"I'm doing okay. Good job, friends, church. If I could erase the fire and everything else that happened that night, things would be a lot different, obviously, but I can't complain. How about you?"

He shrugged, raising a thumb to scratch at his eyebrow, a gesture I fondly remembered.

"I probably work too much, but otherwise I'm good."

"Good."

Reed suddenly excused himself to go around to the back of his car and root around in the trunk.

"Here we go," he said, coming out with a pair of binoculars. "These have been in there since football season. A gift from my girlfriend."

He came and stood beside me and looked through the binoculars in the direction the car was facing.

"Here, take a look," he said, passing them off to me as I tried not to think about his girlfriend remark. I put the binoculars to my eyes and peered through them in the same direction.

"What am I looking at? It's all fuzzy."

He tried to make an adjustment, took off his gloves, and tried again. That time, it worked. I still wasn't sure what I was seeing, but after a minute of scanning the hillside in the distance, I realized that we were now on the opposite side of Bobby's accident site. Watching through the binoculars, I saw the crowds of people along the roadway, the cops climbing all over the hill like ants, the crumpled piece of metal that had once been a motorcycle.

"I think the police are finally checking out that farm," Reed said, and with a surge of hope I turned my attention in that direction, realizing the field we were in probably belonged to the people who lived there.

My hope faded a bit as I carefully scanned the scene and realized that the home and outbuildings looked as though they were abandoned. At least there didn't seem to be any animals to speak of, any clothes flapping on the clothesline, or toys left in the yard. Uniformed policemen were swarming the property, though, so if Bobby really had gone there, I hoped they would turn up some sign of him, of what had happened next.

Together, we watched and waited, taking turns with the binoculars, until it was clear from the policemen's movements and body language that they had discovered something. I wondered if they had found Bobby, but after a while it became obvious that their discovery wasn't nearly that monumental. Still, they knew something, and Reed promised to find out what it was and report back to me.

Finally, we decided to go. As Reed took the wheel without his gloves, I was startled to see scarring on the back of his now-bare hands. That reminded me that he had been dealt one of the biggest blows that night, receiving third-degree burns on his back, arms, and hands while saving Ezra from the fire. Now, all these years later, I wondered if he had any lingering physical problems related to the burns or the scar tissue. How sad, that all our scars were emotional, but Reed's were physical as well.

He started up the car, made a tight K-turn in the narrow space, and headed back up the gravel road. When he pulled onto the blacktop, turning to go back the way we had come, I asked him the question that was most prominent in my mind.

"So what happens next?"

"What do you mean?"

"With the FBI. I assume they'll come to the WIRE and start investigating more recent cases, to see if the doctor's illegal activity continued?"

"Yep," Reed said, turning again as he reversed our earlier route down picturesque, winding roads. "If they decide that the files I gave them provide enough evidence of wrongdoing—which they should, especially if some of the blacked-out text can be recovered—then they'll move in and subpoena other files, confiscate records, whatever is necessary to uncover the full extent of what's going on there. As they do, you need to be prepared for the possibility of Bobby being implicated."

We passed a cluster of Amish girls who were walking in single file along the side of the road. From the back, they looked like a gaggle of cute little white-topped geese. The tallest one seemed to be about eleven—the same age that the Schumann's newborn son would have been now if he had lived.

Reed and I were both quiet on the drive back. When we reached the area where my rental car was parked, I gestured toward it and told him he could drop me off there. After he pulled over, he grabbed a pen and a notepad from the glove compartment and wrote down his contact information for me, asking me to do the same for him. As we traded papers, I looked into his eyes and thanked him for coming to town, and for caring about my brother.

"And you," he added. "I care about you."

I studied his face, understanding completely why I had loved him all those years ago. I was about to say something in reply when we both noticed a commotion in front of the car. Before we could do anything about it, a bright flash went off in our faces.

We had been recognized by a photographer.

"Anna, get in your car and drive away," Reed said evenly. "I'll stall them."

Thanking him, I did as he said, moving quickly from his vehicle to mine. Other photographers and reporters seemed to be catching on, but I managed to make an escape with only a few more flashes in my face. Reed, on the other hand, sacrificed for my sake, getting out of his car and saying something to draw everyone's attention.

When I was past all of the cars and crowds, I pressed down the accelerator and went as fast as I could, away from it all. I took a few detours, just to make sure I hadn't been followed, and then I slowly let out my breath and tried to regroup.

The moment I had been dreading had now happened, which meant our photo would likely make the front page of tomorrow's newspaper—and my new identity would be blown to bits.

Please God, let the story just stay local this time.

For some reason, I had a feeling that was one prayer that wasn't going to be answered the way I wanted it to.

TWENTY-SIX

Stephanie

August 9, 1812

There are rumblings in the palace, rumblings of dissatisfaction among Karl's family. Luise is a particularly bitter pill, and she wishes nothing more than for this child of my womb to be another girl, proving yet again that I am incapable of providing a male heir to the throne.

Everything within me yearns for this child to be a boy, as that would shut up the vindictive and unpleasant Luise for good. Were it not for the vigorous kicks inside my belly that assure me of my child's good health, I do believe Luise's constant snide remarks and venomous complaints would drive me out of my mind.

As it is, the venom in her voice and eyes sometimes makes me feel not just hated but also unsafe. What could this woman's hate make her capable of?

I pray I never find out.

August 15, 1812

Today when I came upon Priscilla, her eyes were red and she clutched a handkerchief damp from tears. It took a bit of prodding for her to tell me what was wrong, as she said she never meant to share this with me for fear of casting a pall on my own delicate condition. With a fresh round of tears, my Amisch friend confided that she had had two previous children die at birth before finally having Francis, and that she has begun to feel deep in her heart that sense of foreboding that tells her the child she carries now will die as well.

Though I have not experienced the loss of a child myself, I attempted to comfort her. Sitting by her side, I patted her hand and told her that my husband's family has also had more than its share of infant deaths. The consensus we reached was that God was in charge and His will would cover whatever life or death or pain awaited.

Priscilla's grasp on God's will, however, feels much stronger than mine. Outwardly, I professed to be accepting of whatever fate awaits the fruit of my womb. Inwardly, I know that not even heaven itself would dare to rip an infant from my earthly hold.

TWENTY-SEVEN

Anna

The Internet café was sandwiched between a gas station and a hotel. Inside, the place was empty except for a group of high school girls in blue-and-white T-shirts and a family of four that seemed to be with them. I got in line behind the whole group and studied the menu for something inexpensive. It looked like my best bet would be a gourmet coffee, so when it was my turn I asked for a venti triple shot skinny sugar-free cinnamon dolce with a shot of sugar-free vanilla.

"Just have a seat and we'll bring it to you when it's ready," the woman said as she took the bill from my hand and gave me back my change.

"Thanks."

The café was named "Bites & Bytes," though there were only four desktop computers in the whole place. That led me to assume that most people came bearing their own laptops, which was a relief. With so few hard drives, it shouldn't take too long to find the one Bobby had used on Wednesday night.

I got lucky on the second try. Like many public computers, these had a wiping program to clear the decks each night, but I knew how to get around that to access the browser history anyway. When I found a long list of activity on the date and time in question, I knew I had hit the bull's-eye, especially because most of the sites matched what I already knew about Bobby's Internet activity that night.

My coffee appeared, so I took advantage of the interruption to pull out the chargers for my cell phone and my laptop and plug them both in. I didn't know how long I would be here, but I'd grab some power while I could.

Sipping my coffee, I returned to the desktop computer, went through the history, and pieced together a good list of every site Bobby had accessed. Next, I cross-referenced that list with the one I had made from my office back in California. I hadn't missed much, though at least I was now able to answer the nagging question of why Bobby had chosen Las Vegas for his decoy destination. From what I could tell, that was the only middle-of-the-night flight that went out of Philly. I did a quick search on the airport's website just to make sure, but as big as the Philadelphia airport was, I was surprised to see that all domestic departures took place between the hours of about six a.m. to midnight, with the exception of the flight he had booked to Las Vegas, which departed Philadelphia at two a.m. and had been some sort of this-month-only deal. Given the timing, the flight had been the one choice he had.

Once I finished reviewing all of the sites and made sure I had covered my bases that way, it was time to break into Bobby's email account. Lydia hadn't known his password, but I hoped to figure it out anyway. I opened up my laptop, locked into the café's wireless Internet, and opened my "Password Cracker" software, which was a nifty program that helped me take a person's known data and scramble it around, mixing relevant numbers and words to find the combination that unlocked a particular door. In my experience, the Cracker was successful about eighty percent of the time, which was better than many password finders out there. Of course, this program was designed to figure out the passwords created by the average Joe, not outsmart a random password generator or a person with superior technical knowledge.

In Bobby's case, considering he didn't even own a computer, my hopes were pretty high that my program would be able to figure out his password. I accessed the entry list and began typing every word I could think of in Bobby's life: names of family and friends, favorite places, hobbies, talents, favorite films and books, old pets, new and old addresses, and more.

At the bottom, I entered pertinent dates, such as birthdays and anniversaries.

Once I had completed the form, I set the program to work. The Internet provider

Bobby used allowed three tries before kicking out, but Cracker included as part of its protocol automatic restarting. In that way, it could cycle through a nearly infinite amount of words and word/number combinations on most ISPs, trying each one until it eventually found the password that would get me into Bobby's email account.

As the machine computed away, I sat back and stretched, feeling tension in my neck and back. I looked around the café, noticing that the teens I had stood behind in line earlier were now crammed into booths along the windows, smiling and laughing and eating their lunches. Trying not to be nosy, I watched them interact. They seemed to get along well, and they were obviously fond of the family who had brought them there, especially the woman they called Mrs. Hoffman. An attractive blonde, she was a real den mother type, warm and helpful and maternal.

She and her husband and their two children were sitting in their own booth nearby, and they formed a handsome family unit. The son was about nine or ten, tall and slim, with the same dark hair as his father. Earlier, I had pegged him as the quiet one in the bunch, member of the family, but for the moment he was going on enthusiastically about the basketball game that they had been to before coming to the café. The daughter was younger, maybe six or seven, and she was a beauty, all blonde hair and blue eyes and sparkling personality. Glancing up at her brother now and then to listen to his tale, she was doodling big, colorful flowers on the paper placemat in front of her.

A sudden beep brought my attention back to the computer screen, where the program informed me that it had succeeded in cracking the code. I watched Bobby's password appear, one character at a time, in the box at the center of my screen. When it finished typing, I smiled to see that his email password was "Ditt02268," a combination of his current extension number at work and the name of his all-time favorite pet, one of two cats we'd had as children. Bobby's choice was particularly interesting to me because at one time, before I became more tech savvy and began using a random password generator, my first email account password had been named after our other cat, Willow, who had been my favorite. I guessed great minds must truly think alike.

Once I was inside his account, I checked all of the dates of his sent emails first, not surprised to see that there had been no activity since he had gone online from here Wednesday night.

Clicking back to the roster of new mail, I scanned the full list of both opened and unopened emails, looking for anything unusual. There were a lot of confirmations of account changes from credit card companies and banks, which I had expected. Professional newsletters, some spam, and several forwards from friends were also there, but that was to be expected as well. What did surprise me were dozens of letters about geneology, ancestry, and tracing the Jensen family tree.

I sat up straight, goose bumps rising on my arms, remembering the words of the ski-masked intruder: *You are the sister of Robert "Bobby" Jensen, the daughter of Charles Jensen and a descendant of Peter and Jonas and Karl Jensen, among others. I'm in the right house, and you're the right person.* As far as I was concerned, those words showed a definite connection between what had happened to me out there and whatever had been going on with Bobby back here. Truly, I didn't see Bobby as the type of guy who would be into researching our roots just for fun; something else had propelled him to do this, something that went way beyond the average root tracing hobbyist.

For the next twenty minutes I skimmed various emails that had come in and gone out over the past few months. Judging by what I read, Bobby's interest in geneology had been going on for a while, though it had taken a sudden and extreme rise three weeks ago, right around the same time he had been suspended from work. I thought about that, wondering if this ancestry stuff had simply been a hobby that turned into an obsession once he had all that spare time. Somehow, I highly doubted it. I kept reading, trying to get a feel for the email exchanges and what Bobby had been looking for.

From what I could tell, he was interested only in our father's side of the family, not our mother's, and he had posted questions related to his search on listserves and message boards and all sorts of online sites, looking to trace back the name of Jensen. There was a receipt from about a month ago showing that he had bought a "Paternal Lineage DNA Test Kit" for two hundred dollars. He must have done the test and sent it in, because the results had come back about ten days later. I followed the link to get his test results myself, but I didn't understand most of what I was reading. The language was technical and included terms like "haplogroups" and "subclades" and "genetic signatures." The report came with explanatory information, but I didn't feel like taking the time to educate myself unnecessarily. Instead, I downloaded the whole thing to my laptop's hard drive so I could show it to Reed later and let him interpret it for me.

I was still reading through Bobby's emails and trying to put together the basics of his research when I heard the familiar "ding" of an incoming Instant Message, sent from someone who was online and wanted to talk to me—or to Bobby, actually, since I was signed on as him. A small box appeared on the upper left side of the screen, and inside was a note from the screen name "lostscholar32."

Hi, Bobby, where've you been? You haven't answered my emails!

Blinking, I hesitated only a moment before writing a message back.

Sorry, been busy. What's up?

I felt guilty for IMing with someone under false pretenses, but I needed to see who this was and if they had any connection to my brother that might be helpful to my investigation. Quickly, I sorted Bobby's mail by address and starting looking for exchanges between him and lostscholar32. Before I got too far, the reply came back.

I was able to speak with your parents before they left on their trip. Alas, they had not heard of the Beauharnais Rubies either.

My gasp was so loud that some of the teeneagers from the group across the way turned to look at me. I gave them an embarrassed wave and contemplated my reply. My mind was spinning in a hundred different directions—but mostly I was ecstatic that I now knew how to spell the word correctly, which would be invaluable for finding info on the web. Quickly, I switched to the browser on the desktop computer and did a search for "Beauharnais Rubies." Desperate to keep this guy talking, I switched back to my laptop and typed a reply.

What have you managed to learn about the rubies so far?

I glanced at my web search results, disappointed to see that there were no direct hits. There were, however, a few listings for "Beauharnais Emeralds," so I clicked on those links and was astounded by what I saw. Apparently, back in the 1800s, a woman named Stephanie de Beauharnais was given a beautiful set of emerald jewelry by her adoptive father, Napoleon Bonaparte. This set of jewelry had become known as the "Beauharnais Emeralds" and was currently on display in a museum in London. My attention from the article was diverted by a "ding" on my laptop, indicating a reply.

Your father sent along a photo that has proven quite encouraging. He also mentioned that you have a sister, though

he couldn't give me any contact info. Any chance you could put me in touch with her? Maybe she'll be able to help.

Needing to stall for time, I typed my reply.

Sure, hold on a second. Don't go away.

He responded quickly.

Don't worry, I won't!

As fast as I could, I went through Bobby's emails back to the very first communication I could find from this guy, which had been sent about two weeks ago with the subject line *Your post on the ancestry message board.* In the email, the man identified himself as Remy Villefranche, a historian and scholar and the author of the "Nowhere to Be Found" series of books, which thus far included the titles *Nowhere to Be Found: Lost Paintings of the Masters* and *Nowhere to Be Found: Missing Manuscripts.*

According to the email, he was currently working on his next book, *Nowhere to Be Found: Lost Jewels and Antiquities,* and he was researching a certain "parure of jewelry," whatever that meant, that he believed had been passed down through the generations of the Jensen family line. He said he had various forms of proof tying certain pieces of the set to Bobby's Jensen ancestors, specifically his great-great-grandfather William and his great-great-great grandfather Peter.

He concluded the email with the words *Would love to discuss this matter with you further at your earliest convenience.* That was followed by a long list of contact information, including several phone numbers, an address on Park Avenue in New York City, and a website.

I sent the guy another message.

You still there? Keep holding, I'll be just another minute.

Yep, still here. Take your time.

Turning to the desktop computer, I went to an online bookstore and did a search for this man's books. Sure enough, he seemed to be a legitimate author with a major publisher. Scanning further down, I could see that he had earned some good reviews, most of them praising the books' "thorough research," "gorgeous photos," and "attention to detail." Sounded legit enough for me.

On the laptop, I held my breath as I typed my next message:

You live in Manhattan, right?

Right. Why?

Because my sister's in town. She'd like to meet with you in person.

As I waited for his reply, I tried to calculate how long it would take me to get to New York City. If I took the train from Malvern with a switch at 30th Street Station, I could probably be at Penn Station in about three or four hours. Then again, if I drove, I could probably do it in two and a half. Though I couldn't spare the time or the money for either method, this was too important a conversation to have via the Internet or even on the phone. I needed to not just pick this man's brain but also observe his body language and facial expressions. I was also going to tell him about my intruder and see if he could help to shed some light on who the man might be who had broken into my home. By the end of the evening, if he was any help at all, then perhaps this part of the mystery would have been solved.

The computer beeped as his response popped up.

Super! Just name the place and the time and I'm there!

Even better, he was willing to come to

me. I thought for a moment and then suggested we meet tonight at a restaurant near the train station in Paoli, which should make things convenient for him.

His reply was swift as he asked me to hold on a minute and don't go away. Assuming he was checking the train tables, I replied for him to take his time. The messaging box sitting dormant, I clicked over to Bobby's Sent mail and read the reply he had given to this guy's original email.

Dear Mr. Villefranche,

I don't know anything about rubies passed down through the family, but I'd love to talk with you if you can shed some light on my paternal lineage search. I'll call you in just a bit. Which number should I use? Right now, it's a little after 2:00 p.m. here in Hershey, and I'll probably call when my computer session ends at 3:00.

Thanks,
Bobby Jensen

Hershey? Computer session? Bobby's emails were providing as many questions as they were answers! I recalled seeing another message that had the word "Hershey" in the subject line, but I had thought it was spam and hadn't bothered to read it. I found that email now, but before I could open it, another message popped up from Mr. Villefranche.

Okay, I just called some friends who live in Lititz, and they're going to pick me up at the Amtrak station in Harrisburg and drive me to our rendezvous. Should we say dinner at 8:30? How about The Olde Greenfield Inn in Lancaster? My treat, of course.

That sounds fine. She'll meet you there.

How will I recognize her?

I thought for a moment, grinned, and wrote:

Just watch for a mysterious blonde lady in a navy peacoat.

Very well. Tell her to watch for a not-so-mysterious gray-haired old man in a burgundy cravat. Must run now so I can pack and make that train.

Okay, bye.

The sound effect of a closing door indicated that Remy Villefranche was no longer online. I sat there for a minute, grateful for this monumental break in the case. Maybe the tide was finally turning, all of my questions would be answered soon, and somewhere Bobby would turn up safe and sound.

Then again, the way things had been going, maybe the whole situation was just about to become even more complicated.

TWENTY-EIGHT

Stephanie

August 30, 1812

My walks have become shorter and much slower of late, as the babe inside has made me quite cumbersome. Sadly, Priscilla was not to be seen in the fields today, though I hovered at the back fence for quite a while, waiting for her. Finally, Samuel emerged from the barn, little Francis tagging behind. He came out and told me with a heavy heart that Priscilla was not well and had taken to her bed. I asked if she had gone into labor, but he said it was quite the opposite, that her womb felt still, as if the child inside had no desire to move at all.

Concerned, I offered to have the palace doctor visit their home and do an examination, but Samuel politely refused. It was not until we had concluded our conversation and he walked away that I realized how ludicrous my offer must have sounded. Women like Priscilla do not receive visits from palace doctors, not even at the behest of a Duchess. Why must our world be so divided by class when all that really matters is what is inside the heart?

I already love the child I am carrying so deeply that I shudder to think of what it would be like to be in Priscilla's shoes, to know that my son was bound to die before he had even had a chance at life.

September 2, 1812

Today I received shocking news, shared with me in confidence by one of the palace guards. According to a conversation he overheard between Luise and Leopold, they are preparing to take action if the child I bear is a male. When I asked what sort of action, the guard would only shake his head and indicate by gesture that my child would then be killed.

Killed!

My precious son killed!

I asked why, and the guard said it is because Luise covets the throne for her own son. I wanted more of an explanation, but the guard bid me good day and took his leave, obviously in fear for his life.

Now I am supposed to be resting in my room, but I cannot rest. I cannot breathe! Here is what I do not understand. The marriage of Luise and the Grand Duke was left-handed! Everyone knows the descendant of a morganatic union carries no right to title or property or privilege. How then could Luise's son inherit the throne, even if my own child were not in the way? Tonight, I must speak to Karl in private and ask him how this could be possible.

Could my own in-laws really be plotting the murder of my son?

TWENTY-NINE

ANNA

"You type fast."

I looked up from the keyboard to see the little girl who had come there with the sports team.

"That's because I use a computer everyday. I've had a lot of practice."

"My dad uses computers everyday too."

Glancing over the girl's shoulder, I could see that the team members who had finished eating were starting to get restless.

"My favorite color is purple," the girl announced, pointing at my purple sweater, one of the ones I had borrowed from Lydia.

"Well, my favorite color is blue. I think

we're backwards," I replied. Pointing at her royal blue jersey with white letters across the front, I asked, "What does the 'CCS' stand for?"

"That's my school. I help my mom with the spirit squad. We got to use the pom-poms today."

Before I could reply, the girl's mother noticed our conversation and called out to her daughter.

"Melana! Don't bother the nice lady!"

"It's not a problem," I assured her, but the girl quickly told me goodbye and trotted off to join some of the teens who had gathered near the gumball machines behind me.

"I'm sorry," the woman said after the child was out of earshot. "She's our little spitfire."

"She's adorable," I replied. "No need to apologize."

The boy asked his father for a quarter, and then he got up and also headed for the machines. As he walked past, he gave me a shy smile, his handsome eyes a deep brown.

Gathering my thoughts, I tried to decide

what to do next. Bobby had mentioned Hershey in his email to Remy Villefranche, so I looked for emails with "Hershey" in the subject line. The first one had come in two weeks ago from an email address I didn't recognize and contained just two sentences: *I saw your note on the bulletin board at school. I never use my locker. You're welcome to it.*

Bobby had written back the very next day.

Thanks, it'll be a lot easier if I can leave my papers and stuff there and not have to lug them back and forth. I need the locker # and combination. Once I get that, I'll send you the $20 for the month. I shouldn't even need it that long, but you can keep the change.

The person had responded within the hour.

The locker is in Whitehall Commons, first floor, #329. Combination is 5475. Just send the check to the school post office, box 718.

I jotted down the information and then read the final note, which had been written by Bobby a few days later.

Thanks again. Found the locker, opened it with no problem. Check is in the mail.

As I sat there puzzling over their exchange, the little girl ran past me, bounding toward her parents with a bright yellow gumball clutched in her hand.

"Mason got purple and he won't trade!"

"Fine, here," the brother said, running after her before the parents could intervene. He grudgingly made the trade, and I smiled at their interaction, thinking how much they reminded me of Bobby and me at that age.

The rest of the group was getting up to leave, carrying their trays to the trash and making quick runs to the restroom. Finally, the two adults managed to herd the children and teens out the door, the woman giving me an apologetic smile and a wave as she went. I waved in return, hoping she knew they hadn't been a bother.

Still, the quiet left in their absence was nice. Back at the keyboard, I did a web search for "Whitehall Commons" where the locker Bobby had apparently rented was located, and it came back with the web address for the medical school in Hershey.

A medical school? Was that where Bobby had been spending his time since he got suspended? It sure sounded like it, especially if he had needed to rent a locker. Though his email made it sound as if he needed the locker for convenience, I had a feeling it had more to do with keeping certain things hidden from Lydia.

Just to make sure that I wasn't way off base, I looked up a phone number for the main administration office at the medical school, called on my cell phone without disconnecting the charger, and pressed a series of buttons until I had a human being on the phone. When I asked if there were lockers in Whitehall Commons, the woman just laughed.

"No, hon. They're all rented out for the semester. You could try putting a note on the bulletin board in the student union, asking to share. That's what some of the kids do."

"Okay. Thanks anyway," I said, thrilled to have confirmed exactly what I wanted to know.

I hung up, thinking that though there was a good chance Bobby had cleared out the locker before he disappeared, there was just as good a chance that the locker would be full, a veritable gold mine of information.

Quickly, I signed off both computers, packed up my laptop, and headed to my car, surprised as I did to see that it was after three o'clock. With slow Saturday traffic, I knew the drive from Exton to Hershey would take a while, so I got onto Horseshoe Pike and settled in for the ride, my mind rolling over and around all I had learned thus far. Reed called a while later, just as I was crossing over the Turnpike, to give me the information he had learned about the accident site.

"First of all, the police discovered tire marks that prove Bobby was forced off the road by someone else."

I shuddered, trying not to picture my poor brother fleeing in terror as some vehicle slammed up against him and tried to force him over the side of a cliff.

"There's one more thing," Reed continued. "Police found physical evidence of injury a little further down the hill from the motorcycle."

"What kind of evidence?"

"There was blood spattered out in a

pattern consistent with a body hitting the ground at a high speed. Obviously, they don't know yet if it was Bobby's blood, but that's what they're assuming for now. From there, they found signs that he made it to the farmhouse, though the family that lives there is out of town, according to a neighbor. Police say that Bobby broke in, did a few things, and then left. On the kitchen table, they found some cash and a note."

"Cash and a note? What did it say?"

"Hold on a second. I wrote it down 'cause I knew you'd want to hear it word for word."

I waited, listening as he rustled through papers.

"Here it is. 'Dear Homeowners, I'm sorry about the mess I've made. I hope this is enough to cover the broken glass, the clothes I took, and the bandages and medicine and stuff. I don't have enough to pay for the tractor, but I'll see that it gets back to you eventually. Thanks and, again, I'm really sorry.' He signed it 'B. Jensen.' "

"So he survived the accident," I said, letting out the breath that I had been holding.

"Sounds like it, yes."

"Then he made his big escape on a tractor?" I asked incredulously.

"On an Amish farm, Anna, it was probably that or a scooter."

"Don't Amish tractors have metal wheels so they can't be used as transportation?"

"Yeah. The police are thinking that because of Bobby's injuries he only used it to get as far as the nearest car or bicycle or horse or whatever else he could steal that would go faster and farther. They're conducting a pretty intense search for an abandoned tractor. They think if they can find that, that will help them narrow in on how he really got away."

"Can't they just follow the tread marks?"

"No, the ground's frozen so there weren't any. No snow that night, either, so no tracks. They can't even tell if he went onto the road or stuck with grass. They have calculated how far he could've gone on a full tank of gas, so that's the search area they're focusing on first."

"Someone must have seen him. It's not like an injured man driving around on a tractor would have gone completely unnoticed."

"That's why they're canvassing the neighborhood."

After we concluded our call and hung up, I thought about all that Reed had said. Surely, Bobby must have known that leaving a note would tip off the police and give them parameters for a search. Sick to my stomach that my brother's disappearance had now turned into a manhunt, I wondered if there had been some method to Bobby's madness in leaving that note or if his injuries had included a big knock to the head and he just wasn't thinking clearly. Either way, I couldn't help but picture my brother, bleeding and in pain, dragging himself all the way to that farmhouse only to find no one home, no phone, and no good form of transportation. I said a quick prayer once again for him and kept driving, more determined than ever to find him as quickly as I possibly could.

When the delicious smell of chocolate filled the air, I knew I was getting close to Hershey. Breathing it in as I went, I found the medical school and turned onto the campus. Soon I had parked and made my way inside and was standing in front of locker number 329, punching in the combination of 5475.

With a pop, the door unlocked, and I swung it open to reveal a notebook, file folders, and a big stack of loose papers. Pulling out a few pages, I held my breath as I flipped through them, looking for Bobby's handwriting. Sure enough, this stack of stuff belonged to him.

Heart racing, I grabbed the entire pile, but as I pulled it out, a ring of keys slid from among the papers and clattered to the floor. Picking them up, I saw that one of them wasn't a regular key, like for a house or a car. It was smaller than that and round at the bottom. Slipping the whole ring into my pocket, I closed the door of the empty locker and returned to the main lobby, where I had seen some study nooks. I chose one that was off by itself, plopped the heavy pile of papers onto the table, and pulled out the keys to study them some more.

Two were unremarkable, but the third one, the round one, had the word "Steelcase" on it, which led me to believe it was for a filing cabinet. My mind raced, wondering if that cabinet was somewhere here on campus, back at Bobby's apartment, or maybe even at the lab.

Thinking of the lab, I remembered Dr. Updyke saying Bobby had been suspended for trying to access restricted information there. In my mind, I had pictured him hacking into something off-limits in the computer, but I realized now he had probably been hunting down papers or files in the office. This very key, in fact, might be the one that unlocked drawers that held the information he sought. The question was, had Bobby found what he was looking for, or had he been caught too soon?

For now, I slipped the keys onto my key ring, tucked them away in my purse, and turned my attention to the pile of papers. I went through them carefully from top to bottom.

Just as in Bobby's email, many of his papers related to a genealogy search, including a handdrawn chart of our family tree. Bobby had written it out on a big piece of paper, and I unfolded it to see that he had tracked himself backward through our father and grandfather, on up the line to a man named Samuel Jensen, who was listed as our great-great-great-great-great-great-grandfather.

Other than the genealogical stuff, the rest of the pile consisted of handwritten notes and photocopies of textbook pages, all relating to genetic disorders that seemed to be common to the Amish—things with names like *glutaric aciduria* and *Crigler-Najjar syndrome* and *medium-chain acyl-CoA dehydrogenase deficiency.* Bobby had highlighted various paragraphs, but most of the terminology was way over my head. The best I could tell, it looked as though doctors had made progress in isolating the genes that caused such disorders and that the Amish might someday be helped by "gene therapy at the eight-cell stage." The next paragraph, however, made it sound like something they weren't likely to do even if the technology was available:

> Though in vitro fertilization is not specifically prohibited by the *Ordnung*, the practice is not common among the Amish, primarily due to the hefty price tag, the time involved, and the overriding sense of

> tampering with God's will. The far simpler process of preimplanation genetic diagnosis and selection is not an option for this population due to the subsequent destruction of unsuitable embryos.

I put that page aside and moved on to the next item, a newspaper article titled "Gene Hunters Explore Founder Effect." The article explained in simple terms the whole Amish-genetic phenomenon that Reed had told me about, saying that more than one hundred and fifty thousand Amish in America could trace their roots back to only two hundred common ancestors who had immigrated from Europe in the eighteenth century. Through generations of intermarriage among the descendants of those immigrants, the recessive genes that were diluted in general populations remained captive in the closed Amish society. With each generation, the odds increased that carriers of the same rare disorders would marry and produce afflicted children—hence the "founder effect."

Among the gene hunters who were interested in this unique population, the article said they fell into two camps: those whose research was beneficial to the Amish and those who were merely taking advantage of them for material gain. The nonprofit Clinic for Special Children, located near Strasburg and founded by a world-renowned pediatrician, was cited as "a perfect example of give-and-take between researchers and patients," ably succeeding in its dual goals of caring for the patients who suffered from rare disorders and advancing research into causes, treatments, and cures.

In contrast, the article said, some research labs that focused on the Amish were "merely take and no give," the types of places where Amish blood was collected for study and eventual profit in genetic engineering without regard to those who were currently suffering. Though the author didn't come out and say it, I had a feeling that the WIRE fell into that latter category, especially considering that the lab was primarily for research rather than treatment, not to mention that Wynn Industries was a for-profit pharmaceutical company. For them, it was all about the bottom line.

I put the article aside and picked up the last item, which looked to be a printout of some lab tests. Reading carefully, I saw that the person tested was Isaac Jensen, and that he had had a negative result for Wolfe-Kraus syndrome. I sat back, suddenly remembering the look that had passed between Grete and Lydia last night at the dinner table. A surge of nausea rose in my throat as I realized that something must be wrong with Isaac.

Did he have a rare Amish disorder despite the fact that only one of his parents was Amish? Obviously, Bobby had been concerned enough about his son's health to have him tested for WKS, and probably without Lydia's knowledge. Once the results had turned out negative, Bobby's next step must have been to come here and do research, trying to figure out what could be wrong with his son. That would explain the notes and textbook copies in the pile, but what about the genealogical stuff? Was Bobby looking for genetic clues for some disorder in our family tree? As far as I knew, there had been no Amish blood in our family's past—though considering that our forefathers had lived in Lancaster County, I supposed it could be possible.

I looked again at the names on the chart he had made.

Samuel Jensen—great-great-great-great-great-great-great-grandfather
Karl Jensen—great-great-great-great-great-great-grandfather
Jonas Jensen—great-great-great-great-grandfather
Peter Jensen—great-great-great-grandfather
William Jensen—great-great-grandfather
Otto Jensen—great-grandfather
Henry Jensen—grandfather
Charles Jensen—father
Bobby Jensen

Near the top, Bobby had drawn an arrow pointing from Karl Jensen to his father Samuel. Beside the arrow, in a small notation, he had written *Y-DNA46 says no genetic connection.*

No genetic connection between a father and son? Obviously, Bobby had run some sort of DNA test to figure that one out, but considering how many generations back that was, what difference did it make? Maybe Karl was Samuel's step-son. Maybe Samuel's wife had had an affair. Maybe Karl was adopted.

Maybe Bobby was grasping at straws from eight generations back.

Shaking my head, I decided I had learned all that I could here. I gathered up the papers and carried them to my car, dialing the number of Lydia's cell phone as I went. When she answered, I asked if she was alone, or if not that she please get herself alone. While she did that I started the car to warm up the heater.

"Go ahead, Anna. What is it?"

"I need you to talk to me about Isaac's health," I said. "I don't mean to pry, but this is relevant to my investigation. I saw a look that passed between you and your sister last night, a look of concern. Is there something wrong with him?"

Lydia replied that she didn't know how this could possibly relate to my investigation, but that she would tell me what she could. She said they had all been worried about Isaac for a while now, though they didn't know what was wrong with him.

"He seems so smart, but he is not a very good student at school, and he has a lot of trouble reading and writing. This year, we had him tested, and it turns out that he has all sorts of learning disabilities."

"Learning disabilities? That's not so bad."

"No, it is not. That we could handle. God makes all of us a little different, and if Isaac needs special help, we will get it for him. Our concern is with his language. He seems to be regressing. I am sure the other night you heard him call snow 'white cold' and the cookie sheet a 'square.' These days, cows are 'moos,' the car is a 'go far,' and so on. He is doing this more and more. I assumed it was all part of his learning disabilities, but Bobby has been extremely upset about it."

"Has Isaac been seen by a doctor?"

"Not yet. Bobby asked me to wait until he had explored some other options, and then he disappeared."

I took a deep breath and asked Lydia if she was familiar with something called Wolfe-Kraus syndrome.

"WKS? Of course. It runs in my family—my sister, my mother, my cousins. I feel sure I am a carrier as well. Why?"

"Because Bobby had Isaac tested for

it." When Lydia gasped, I added, "Don't worry, the test came back negative."

"But why would Bobby think Isaac had WKS? That disorder needs two carriers to manifest in a child and Bobby is not Amish."

"He's been doing some family research, though. I have a feeling there may have been Amish blood somewhere in our family tree, at least enough to make disorders like WKS a possibility."

"Ah," she said, and then she was quiet for a moment. "Still, WKS is fatal before or at birth. Isaac is eight years old and very much alive!"

Isaac is eight years old and very much alive.

I thought of Bobby's papers, of his family tree and genetic tests and highlighted medical texts. I thought of his suspension from work, of the old files that Doug had faxed to Reed proving that gene therapy had been going on at the WIRE years ago, before Isaac was even born.

Was it possible that Isaac was living on borrowed time, that those eight years had been bought with some sort of genetic tinkering in his past?

"Lydia, tell me something."

"Yah?"

"At any point during or after your pregnancy with Isaac, did you ever have an office visit at the WIRE with Dr. Updyke? Did he ever do any tests or procedures on you?"

Lydia was quiet for a long moment. I waited for her response, my heart in my throat, watching as a cluster of students crossed in front of my car and moved down the sidewalk toward another building.

"Yes," she finally whispered. "Isaac was conceived in vitro there. So was the baby I'm carrying now."

I sat up straight, goose bumps rising along my arms as I thought about the article I'd found in Bobby's locker, the one that said some rare Amish disorders could be treated by using in vitro fertilization and gene therapy.

"In vitro? Why?"

"Bobby insisted. We lost our first child to a miscarriage. Bobby said he never wanted to go through that heartbreak again, and that the only way he was willing to have more children was if I would conceive this way. He told me that Dr. Updyke had a new method for implantation that would make any future miscarriages much less likely."

"A method for implantation?"

"*Yah.* Bobby said the doctor told him that the kind of miscarriage I had was likely caused by the fetus never really implanting correctly onto the wall of the uterus. He said it was a simple problem he could fix. He didn't even charge us, though I know that sort of thing can be very expensive."

I was trying to form a reply when she spoke again.

"I may be naive, Anna, but I am not stupid. After hearing this, I did a lot of reading about miscarriage and fertility treatments and artificial insemination and all of that. I finally agreed to do it, as long as the doctor was willing to fertilize only one egg, not multiples as they usually do, and no preimplantation genetic diagnosis. The whole thing went exactly like the books said, and nine months later Isaac was born. It worked so well that when we decided to have another child, we went through the same process again. Why do you ask, Anna? What does this have to do with Bobby's disappearance?"

I wasn't ready to answer that, or to share the thoughts swirling around in my mind. Instead, I told her this was a side issue relating to some papers of Bobby's I had found. Fortunately, she was interrupted on her end at that point and I managed to end our call without having to explain any further.

Now, as I sat in the car and looked out at the graceful campus in front of me, at the long shadows cast by an orange sun that hung low in the winter sky, the theory that filled my mind was so sinister and dark it was almost too scary to contemplate.

What if Dr. Updyke hadn't pioneered a "new method for implantation," as Lydia had been told, but instead had only used that as an excuse for what he really wanted; the opportunity to do genetic modification of an Amish (or at least half-Amish) embryo in vitro?

From what I had read in Bobby's papers, gene therapy was best done at the eight-cell stage, prior to implantation, but that wasn't likely to be a viable option since in vitro fertilization was something most Amish people wouldn't consider. Given that, had the temptation in this situation simply been too great to resist? Had Bobby's desire for a healthy child and Lydia's willingness to be artificially inseminated been too good an opportunity for the doctor to pass up?

If so, then Isaac and the baby in Lydia's womb were both living proof that Dr. Updyke had stepped far outside the bounds of medicine and of ethics—and of the law. In the hands of the authorities, their very DNA could likely cost the man his career, his medical license, and maybe even his freedom.

No wonder Isaac and Lydia were in danger.

THIRTY

STEPHANIE

September 3, 1812

Last night's conversation with my husband has filled me with endless frustration and fear. Though Karl believed not one word of the rumor about Luise and Leopold's intentions, he said if it were true it would not be the first time a morganaut attempted to overcome his origins.

I asked for an explanation, and the best he could tell me was that the laws of succession could be altered in situations where there was a lack of a male heir to the throne. He gave the example of a firstborn female heir being substituted for a male, or a morganatic son being enfranchised and married to Royalty, so that he could then assume the throne.

So it is possible that one day Leopold could rule Baden? I demanded. My husband only laughed, saying it was either that or pass his title to our own firstborn daughter, and hope that the palace guard didn't end up in pink uniforms and the state dinners become frilly tea parties!

There is much not to like about my husband, most of all his sarcasm—and the dullness of his imagination. He sees nothing where nothing can be plainly seen. He believes rumors and threats only after they become reality.

By then it will be too late.

September 5, 1812

I have not slept for two nights. As discreetly as possible, I have attempted to confirm the rumors of Luise's planned treachery against my baby. My efforts tell me that without a doubt the rumors are true. If my child is born male, he will be killed.

Knowing that, I have begun to form a plan in my mind, a plan that would spare my son but surely rip my heart in two. Tomorrow, if I can bear it, I shall go to my Amisch friends and tell them of my proposal.

Now, hour by hour, I wrestle with the conflict that rages in my soul, the battle between needing to produce a male heir and needing to save my baby's life should he be born male.

The first choice would justify me in the eyes of my husband, the palace, and the country.

The second choice is the very opposite of self. Would I sacrifice my honor for his life? This is the question with which I wrestle.

My son, do you despise the selfishness that draws me to the easier option? Or do you intend to keep tugging at my heart even before you are born, making me fall ever more in love with you until the second option is the only one I can bear to choose?

THIRTY-ONE

Anna

It was time for me to head back to Dreiheit and get ready for my dinner with Remy Villefranche. The mystery of the Beauharnais Rubies paled in comparison to the mystery of my nephew's health, but until I had all of the facts, I couldn't know what one part of this investigation had to do with the other, so I decided to proceed as planned.

Putting the car in reverse, I started to back out of my parking space but stopped short when I realized a van was sitting directly behind me. I waited for a minute, but it didn't move, so I honked the horn, turning to give a wave to the driver. He didn't see me, so I got out and gave him a bigger wave. Rather than get out of the way, though, he rolled down the passenger window and asked me if I knew where he could find Whitehall Commons.

"This is it right here," I said, gesturing toward the building on my right.

"I don't think so," he replied, holding up what looked like a map. "Not according to this, anyway."

I didn't have time for this. I was about to tell him to look at the sign on the building when the side door of the van slid open and two men jumped out.

Before I could react, they dragged me away from my car, pulled me inside the van, and slammed the door.

Tires squealing, the van took off. As we careened around a sharp turn, I struggled to break free from the grip that pinned me to the floor. I tried to look around, but a hand clamped firmly against my eyes, blocking the view. We turned again. I tried to scream, but another hand clamped over my mouth and nose.

I couldn't breathe.

"Do you want me to take my hand away?" a voice whispered near my ear.

I nodded frantically, desperate for air.

"No screaming."

I shook my head no. When they let go, I couldn't have screamed if I wanted to. I could only breathe, sucking in deep gasps of air.

"Where are the rubies?" the voice demanded.

"The Beauharnais Rubies," a second voice added.

I was too scared to reply. Finally, I muttered that I didn't know what they were talking about.

"Are you sure she's the right one?" I heard the driver ask.

"We're gonna make sure once you stop," a voice said.

The van squealed around another turn and another and then screeched to a halt. I felt someone grip my hair and jerk my head backward. I opened my mouth to scream but instantly realized as I did that something had been thrust between my teeth and was jabbing the inside of my cheek. I let out a garbled yell as the sticklike item was just as quickly removed from my mouth.

I heard the sound of the door sliding open and then I felt myself being pushed. The hands let go of my hair, my eyes, my body, and I was falling. I landed on cold, hard pavement with a thud. Behind me, the door slammed shut and then the van screeched away, just barely missing one of my legs with a back tire.

"Whoa! Are you okay?"

I looked up to see a group of students staring at me from where they stood on the sidewalk. After a beat, they all began moving toward me. They helped me up and brushed me off and asked me what had just happened. Blinking, I looked around and realized I had been driven in a circle and that I was back where I started, directly behind my car which was still sitting in its parking space, engine running, door open.

Too dumbfounded even to reply, I let them help me to the curb where I sat, my legs suddenly too wobbly to stand. There, one of them pulled out a cell phone and called for campus security. I remained silent, still too stunned to speak, dismayed to hear my helpers argue among themselves about what they had just witnessed. They had conflicting ideas about the color of the van, what the people inside looked like, even how many there had been. About all they could agree on was that none of them had thought to look at the license plate.

Finally, one of the group sat next to me, a pretty young woman with dark hair and a calm demeanor. She gently asked if I had been violated in some way. Did we need not just campus security but the Hershey Police?

How could I respond to that?

I hadn't been raped, punched, stabbed, or shot, but I had been violated. Rubbing my tongue against the inside of my cheek, I suddenly realized what had been shoved in my mouth: a swab.

Whoever abducted me had taken a sample of my DNA.

For the next forty-five minutes my emotions vacillated between fury and terror. The campus police secured my vehicle and brought me back to the station, but other than giving them Reed's name and number, I didn't tell them much. I was simply too overwhelmed to speak.

When Reed finally came dashing into the station, eyes frantic, all I could do was collapse against his strong shoulders. He held me as I cried, and for a long time we just stood there like that in the middle of the empty waiting room, rocking back and forth, arms around each other. After a while he handed me a tissue and suggested that I clean myself up while he spoke to the people in charge.

In the station's restroom I rinsed my face, fixed my hair and makeup, and cleaned up my disheveled clothes as best I could. When I came out, I was relieved to see that Reed had taken charge of the situation and had asked for a copy of their report and my keys. Once he had those, he thanked them for their help, saying that the matter would be referred to the FBI from here.

We went out to the warmth and privacy of Reed's car, where I found my voice at last. Sitting there in the dark quiet, I described what had taken place in the parking lot as well as what I had found in

Bobby's locker and what I had learned on the phone from Lydia. When I was finished with the whole tale, Reed agreed with my conclusion that my captors had been swabbing my cheek for DNA, though he had no better idea of why someone would do that than I did.

He also agreed that the situation with Bobby and Lydia would have given Dr. Updyke a unique opportunity for gene tampering at the most opportune stage of growth. According to the medical files Doug faxed to Reed the night he was killed, the doctor's previous attempts at gene therapy had been done during pregnancy or immediately following birth—never prior to implantation. Those procedures had failed, but perhaps by treating the embryo at such an early stage, the doctor had finally managed to succeed—to a degree. What was happening to Isaac now was anybody's guess.

I listened as Reed called his friend with the FBI and relayed our conversation. It didn't sound as though they were ready to move in on the lab just yet, though he promised to get back to us as soon as he knew anything. Concerned for Isaac and

Lydia's safety, I asked Reed if they could be put into some sort of protective custody in the meantime.

"That's not a bad idea," he replied. "Let's give it an hour or two and see if we hear back. If not, I'll make another call. Bobby seemed to think they'd be safe at the farm, and I have to agree, for now."

Suddenly, I remembered my dinner in Lancaster, and I looked at my watch, relieved to see that I could still make it to the restaurant on time if I didn't go back to the farm first. Now that I had been kidnapped, albeit briefly, and once again pressured to produce the Beauharnais Rubies, my meeting with the mysterious Mr. Villefranche was more important than ever. Still, I no longer had the nerve to go alone, so Reed agreed to go with me.

Leading the way in my car with him following behind in his, I zigzagged us over to Hershey Road and got on it heading southeast. I called Remy's cell phone on the way, and though he didn't answer I left a message in his voice mail saying I was bringing a friend with me to the restaurant and that I hoped that was okay. Once we finally got there, I chose a well-lit spot in the parking lot, one with an empty place next to it for Reed to pull in. Getting out of the car, I felt myself shivering, though whether that was from the cold or my nerves I wasn't sure.

"You okay?" Reed asked as he held out his elbow. I told him I was fine as I took his arm and we walked together to the restaurant. Fine or not, at least I had him there by my side.

Hesitating at the door of the beautiful old eighteenth-century converted farmhouse, I wondered aloud whether jeans would be allowed in such a nice restaurant. I was sorry I hadn't had the chance to change for dinner, but at this point all I cared about was getting answers to my questions.

"I wouldn't worry about it," Reed replied, opening the door for me. "You're beautiful no matter what you're wearing."

Surprised by the compliment, I stepped inside, heat flushing my cheeks. As Reed stepped in behind me, I told him how stupidly I had packed for this trip, saying that my only alternative would have been a summer dress and strappy sandals anyway.

"You California girls are all alike," he teased, clicking his tongue. "Some parts of the world still have four seasons, you know."

The cozy restaurant was humming with activity. Hovering near the hostess stand was a short, silver-haired gentleman holding a leather satchel, dressed in an elegantly cut suit and wearing a maroon tie. Our eyes met and when I gave him a nod, his face burst into a broad smile.

Greeting us both with enthusiasm, the man shook our hands, thanked us for coming, and insisted that we call him by his first name. With a nod to the hostess, we were escorted through the main dining room, past a crackling fireplace, and up the stairs to the balcony. There, we were led to a table off by itself that was neatly set for three.

We sat and engaged in polite small talk until the waiter came to take our order. As Remy tried to decide between roasted halibut with hollandaise and the restaurant's signature seafood and pasta, Reed held the menu high, over his face, and gave me a wink. Our host was quite a character. Finally, Remy decided on the halibut, Reed ordered the roast pork, and I chose the filet mignon. Once the waiter departed, Remy's demeanor changed, and suddenly he was all business. He leaned forward, focusing in on me.

"Now that we're here, I must ask you the question I have asked every one of your relatives that I've been able to track down: Are you in possession of the Beauharnais Rubies, or at the very least do you know where they are?"

The man stared at me with such rapt expectation that the trauma of the last few days began roiling up within my stomach. I swallowed hard, trying not to feel again the shock of the masked intruder in my bedroom or the horror of my abduction on the campus. Those people had wanted to know the same thing, the only difference being the manner in which they had asked. Suddenly, I viewed the man across from me not as a kindly old scholar but as a similar threat. Reed put a warm hand on my arm, obviously sensing my panic and understanding I was so upset I couldn't even form a reply.

"You're not the first person to ask her that," Reed said on my behalf. "Anna has been attacked twice in the last three days, first with a gun to her head and then while being held down in the back of a van. Both times, they demanded that she hand over these rubies, whatever they are."

"Attacked?" Remy cried in dismay. "Were you hurt?"

Finding my voice, I said I was okay but that my housemate hadn't been so lucky. "Look, I don't even know what the Beauharnais Rubies are. I never even heard of them until the other day. Now people are crawling out of the woodwork trying to take them from me. I came here tonight because I want to know what's going on."

The older man seemed genuinely disturbed. He fidgeted nervously with his silverware, adjusted his tie, and accepted with relief the pot of tea the waiter brought. Dipping the tea bag up and down in the steaming water, Remy finally spoke.

"I'm afraid these attacks may have been partly my fault," he said. "Sometimes I get so caught up in the hunt, I forget that not everyone's interest is quite so . . . scholarly. In my excitement, I may have said too much on too public a forum."

I glanced at Reed as we both waited for

Remy to go on, which he did, albeit reluctantly.

"You see, in researching my latest book I have filled the Internet with queries, assigning tags to all sorts of names and terms. Whenever one of those terms pops up on a website, in an article, or even as a comment or a question to a message board, I get an electronic alert. Several weeks ago, I received a number of alerts for 'Grand Duchy of Baden,' which is one of my tags. In taking a closer look, I realized that someone was doing genealogy research and had been asking about that region of Germany in the early 1800s. That someone was Bobby. When I saw his posts, one post in particular, I was so excited that I jumped in with both feet. Eventually, I'm afraid I may have blabbed too much on my blog, putting it out there for all the world to see."

"Blabbed how?" Reed demanded. "What did you say?"

Remy left the tea bag alone and guiltily met our eyes.

"That Bobby Jensen of Dreiheit, Pennsylvania, might hold the key to a two-hundred-year-old mystery, namely whatever happened to the priceless Beauharnais Rubies, which disappeared from the royal vaults of Baden in 1830 and have never been seen again."

I sat back, trying to think of the implications of what Remy had done.

"Actually," he added, even more guiltily, "I may even have implied that Bobby or one of his family members was in possession of these priceless jewels today. I'm sorry, Anna. I realize now how ignorant that was. My blog is about scholarly research, not a how-to guide for criminals. But if strangers are accosting you and demanding the jewels, then I have a feeling they're simply picking things up where my blog left off. Bobby said he'd never heard of any such jewels, but I'm afraid I didn't quite believe him at first."

"The group that nabbed her tonight swabbed her for DNA," Reed said. "Why?"

"Oh my," Remy replied, shaking his head, "that means you have more than mere treasure hunters on your tail. I'd say they were descendents of the last documented owner of the jewels, trying to prove they have a stronger claim to them, genealogically speaking, than you do. We are talking about the resolution of one of the greatest mysteries of the jewelry world. If the Beauharnais Rubies are found, there's going to be a mad scramble for ownership rights. The fact that someone is willing to retrieve your DNA forcefully is a bad sign, as it means you probably don't have a solid claim. These thugs accosteswabbed you because they need to know who they're dealing with and how your DNA stacks up against theirs."

"Accosteswabbed?"

"Yes, I coined that word in an article I wrote for *Vanity Fair*. You can't imagine the radical steps people take in order to trace genealogy these days—from swabbing the cheeks of strangers to plucking hair from corpses."

"You've got to be kidding," I said.

"Sadly, no. Genealogy used to be a pleasant little hobby, like a guessing game or a jigsaw puzzle," Remy explained. "But once ancestral DNA testing was made available to the masses, the whole nature of things shifted. Some folks get so intent on their search that they push it too far."

I let Reed have the paper and sat back, looking at Remy.

"I know DNA is used in paternity cases, but can it really tell you all that much about your family tree?" I asked, thinking of the ancestral DNA report I had found among Bobby's email.

"Oh, my. Yes," Remy said, explaining that because markers on the Y-chromosome passed through male generations relatively unchanged, it was now possible to confirm through DNA testing all sorts of genetic connections, even distant ones. "For example, once your brother obtained his genetic signature, he used some online databases to compare it with other known male Jensen descendents and construct a family tree. That's what led him to write the post that caught my eye. You see, those comparisons showed that Bobby was a descendant of a man named Karl Jensen, but not of Karl's father, Samuel Jensen. That's what's known as a 'nonpaternal event,' when two men are not biologically related, even though they're legally considered father and son."

"But what difference does it make?" I asked. "You're talking about six, seven, eight generations ago. Who cares?"

"In your brother's case, I believe he was

trying to track down some sort of medical mystery and was hoping to go as far back as possible. The trail ended with Karl Jensen, and Bobby was trying to figure out where it went from there. That's the post that caught my eye, the one that got me so excited when I realized the implications of what he was asking. I emailed your brother and he phoned me, but he seemed to be more concerned about his paternal lineage search than he did about my story of priceless jewels."

"That's because his son is sick," Reed said, handing the article back to Remy. "That was far more important to him at the time, I'm sure."

"Yes, I know, with some rare disorder," Remy replied. "Bobby was trying to figure out if there was any Amish blood in his family tree, as that might help him narrow down what could be wrong with the boy."

"Do you know what he found out? About the Amish blood, I mean?"

Remy tucked the article back into his briefcase.

"Yes, I do. I thought if I scratched Bobby's back he would scratch mine, so I helped with his search. As it turned out, two generations of Jensen men were married to Amish women: Karl and his son Jonas. Once Bobby knew that, he no longer cared about the mystery behind Karl's nonpaternal event with Samuel. But I did. In fact, I think it's the most exciting thing I've heard in a long time."

I looked at Reed, heartbroken to know that my hunch had been correct. With Amish blood in our family tree, there was a much bigger chance that Isaac had some rare disorder—and that Dr. Updyke had tampered with his genes. Sadly, some of the pieces of this puzzle were falling into place exactly where I didn't want them to.

"Frankly," Remy continued, opening his napkin with a flourish and placing it on his lap, "I was a bit miffed when Bobby put me off and said he'd have to deal with the jewels some other time. It was just through sheer luck that I spotted him online today and he connected me with you."

I bit my lip, feeling suddenly guilty about my deception from this afternoon. Obviously, Remy didn't even know Bobby was missing. I decided I would tell him before the night was over, but for now I wanted to change gears and learn more about the Beauharnais Rubies.

The waiter arrived with our salads at that moment, and I was glad for the interruption as it gave me a moment to collect my thoughts. Picking up my fork, I realized I was hungry—which made sense, considering I'd had almost nothing to eat all day.

"All right, Remy," I said after the waiter was gone, "my brother may have been too focused on his son to think about it, but after being attacked twice by people who want these rubies, I need to know exactly what they are and what they have to do with me."

Ignoring his own salad, Remy sat back with a twinkle in his eye and began to tell us the tale of the Beauharnais Rubies, a story that started with Napoleon Bonaparte in the early 1800s.

THIRTY-TWO

Remy began with a simple history lesson, explaining about European royalty in that era and how ties between countries were often strengthened through marriage. Napoleon had no legitimate descendants of his own, Remy said, so when he wanted to align himself with the newly expanded Duchy of Baden, he decided to adopt his wife's cousin, a charming young woman named Stephanie de Beauharnais, and marry her off to Baden's hereditary Prince Karl. Karl was the reigning Grand Duke of Baden's grandson and had become next in line for the throne when his father had died a few years before.

In celebration of Stephanie's adoption, Napoleon gave his new daughter an elaborate matching set of jewelry known as the Beauharnais Emeralds. Five years later, when he learned that Karl and Stephanie were expecting their first child, Napoleon commissioned a similarly elaborate set of diamonds and rubies called the Beauharnais Rubies. The jewels were meant to celebrate the birth of a new male heir to the Baden throne, so when Stephanie ended up having a girl, Napoleon held on to them. A few years later, when she finally had a boy, Napoleon immediately sent the rubies to her as a congratulatory gift.

Sadly, by the time the jewels made it from Paris to Baden, Stephanie's newborn baby boy was dead. According to Remy, records indicated that the rubies were received at Baden's palace on the day of the infant's funeral and placed directly into the vault. Considering the situation, they were never worn publicly. Stephanie was later painted wearing them, but Remy said her expression in the portrait was not a happy one.

With only a few exceptions, the Beauharnais Rubies had never been seen since.

As our empty salad plates were taken away and delicious-looking entrees put in their place, Remy continued his tale, filling in some of the details of what we'd already learned. First, he said, the marriage of Karl and Stephanie may have produced children, but it was quite miserable. They seemed to dislike each other from the very beginning, so much so that at one point Napoleon himself had to intervene and help make peace between them.

To complicate matters further, Karl's grandfather had a second wife, a commoner named Luise, with whom he had had a son named Leopold. At that time, the laws of succession prevented Leopold from succeeding his father as Grand Duke because of his mother's nonroyal origins. Considering that there weren't many male heirs in the family, however, Luise had high hopes that eventually those laws would be changed to allow her son to ascend to the throne.

Those hopes had been dashed when Stephanie married into the family. As the royal daughter of Napoleon and a healthy young woman in her childbearing years, there was a good chance that she and Karl would produce plenty of sons, all of them legitimate heirs eligible for the throne who would take precedence over Luise's son, Leopold. Consequently, Luise hated Stephanie and made her life quite miserable.

When Stephanie's second child turned out to be a boy, everyone knew that Luise's worst fears were coming true. When that newborn boy died several days later, rumors began to circulate that Luise and/or Leopold had been responsible for his death. Though nothing was ever proven, those rumors persisted to this day.

There were other, different rumors about the baby as well, Remy said, including one that claimed that Leopold had switched the healthy infant at birth with the dead or nearly dead infant of some local peasant. Supposedly, this story went, the true heir to the throne had been taken far away and given over to a man—a former palace guard—who was instructed to kill him. Unable to carry out such a heinous crime against a defenseless child, the man had instead allowed the babe to live, though he eventually imprisoned him in a dungeon.

Those rumors took on an eerie reality sixteen years later.

Pausing to take a few bites of his halibut, Remy asked if we had ever heard of the name Kaspar Hauser. I hadn't, but Reed vaguely recalled reading something about him in one of his DNA magazines. My curiosity piqued, I ate my filet mignon and listened as Remy continued with his tale. He said that sixteen years after Karl and Stephanie's newborn son supposedly died, a strange young man appeared one day on the streets of Nuremberg. No one knew who he was or where he had come from, but there was obviously something wrong with him. He could hardly walk, and he only spoke a few intelligible words.

The young man indicated that his name was Kaspar Hauser, and eventually it was deduced that he had spent many years, possibly his entire life, as a prisoner in a small cell with almost no human contact and only a few little wooden toy horses to keep him company. Despite that, he was very intelligent, and experts were able to educate and rehabilitate him to a degree. He seemed to be about sixteen years old, and soon a rumor began to spread that Kaspar Hauser was in fact the offspring of Karl and Stephanie, the son who had supposedly died at birth sixteen years before.

That story grew, and eventually so many people believed that Kaspar Hauser was Karl and Stephanie's son whom Leopold had spirited away and left to die that he became a worldwide sensation. Soon there was talk of having him restored to his rightful place in the royal family, but before anything official could be done, Kaspar Hauser was assassinated. Even after his death, Stephanie never publicly confirmed or denied whether she thought he was her son or not. She went to her grave years later refusing to comment.

To this day, Remy said, the truth about Kaspar Hauser's origins were not known. In recent years, two separate DNA tests had been done, but they contradicted each other, one saying he definitely was the son of Karl and Stephanie, the other saying he definitely was not. As no tests were currently being allowed on his remains, the facts were still shrouded in mystery.

While I found the whole story interesting, I wasn't sure how it tied in with me or my family tree. I said as much to Remy now, but he simply grinned and told me to be patient.

Having thoroughly studied the entire situation, Remy said he had developed a theory of his own. In his opinion, the newborn boy had indeed been spirited away—but not by Luise or Leopold. Instead, Remy said, he thought that *Stephanie* had done it herself, that upon hearing rumors of her evil in-laws' intentions to kill her child if it was a male, she had made arrangements to protect him and outsmart her enemies. For years, Remy had been convinced that Stephanie somehow communicated with another pregnant woman and arranged for the exchange of their children after they were born in order to save her son's life.

His theory sounded pretty far-fetched to me. Certainly, Stephanie's motivation was understandable, but I found it hard to believe that she would have been able to locate a peasant woman who was also pregnant who also delivered around the same time who also happened to have a boy who also was willing to give her child away and take Stephanie's in exchange. As far as I was concerned, those were some pretty big leaps of faith, all in a row. Still, for the sake of argument, I went with it for now.

Remy explained that at that time Baden and the Palatinate were heavily populated with the Amish. Because of their radical belief that baptism should take place in adulthood rather than infancy, they had suffered horrendous religious persecution throughout Europe. Though Baden was more tolerant than some countries were, it was still not ideal. The Amish had been immigrating to America in search of true religious freedom for a while, many of them coming to Lancaster County. It was Remy's opinion that Stephanie de Beauharnais had traded newborn sons with an Amish woman who had then brought the child with her to America where he would be safe, his true identity never revealed.

To prove his theory, Remy had been studying Amish immigration records for years, trying to pinpoint the exact family, the exact child, but without success. When he read Bobby's post a few weeks ago, however, Remy realized that his search had been hindered by one incorrect assumption, that the Amish family in question had immigrated soon after the boy was born. Instead, Remy now realized, the family didn't leave Baden for America until many years later, when the boy was grown and married and would have been about twenty-one.

In retrospect, Remy said, the timing now made perfect sense. The child had been raised in Baden, perhaps with the hope that he might one day safely return to the palace and take his place as the rightful heir. When Kaspar Hauser showed up and everyone began saying he was Karl and Stephanie's son, Stephanie had kept mum because she knew the real truth. At that point, she may even have been laying plans to straighten things out and introduce her true son to the world. But then, on December 14, 1833, Kaspar Hauser was lured into a park and stabbed; three days later, he died. Once that happened, Remy said, Stephanie probably realized that as long as Luise or Leopold or any of their followers were around, her son would never be safe.

It was Remy's belief that at that point

Stephanie went to her son and his adoptive Amish parents, urged them to leave the country, and gave them the Beauharnais Rubies as a gift. Amish immigration records confirmed that two couples with the last name of Jensen left Europe a few weeks later, on the first day of January 1834.

At that point in Remy's long, complicated story, he sat back and dabbed at his mouth with his napkin, looking at me expectantly. I wasn't sure what he wanted me to say, but obviously I was missing something.

"Again," I said to him, "your tale is fascinating, but what does it have to do with me or my family tree?"

"Don't you get it?" he replied gleefully. "Your great-great-great-great-great-grandfather, Karl Jensen, wasn't biologically related to Samuel Jensen, the man listed in all the records as his father, because Karl was adopted. His real parents weren't Amish at all. They were royalty, the duke of Baden and his wife the duchess, Stephanie de Beauharnais."

It took a while for me to soak that in, that the elaborate tale Remy had spun about jealous in-laws and murder plots and secret heirs had to do with my family, my people, my forebears. Unbelievable.

Over a dessert of crème brûlée with fresh raspberries, Remy explained the final part of his tale, the story of what he knew about the rubies after they had been brought to America by my five-greats grandfather, Karl Jensen.

Though the full set of the Beauharnais Rubies consisted of a necklace, coronet, tiara, comb, earrings, a belt, and bracelets, only two of those pieces were ever seen again. In 1887, a jeweler in New York bought the coronet, and in 1888 a private buyer in France purchased the belt. Otherwise, Remy said it was likely that the remaining pieces had been passed down to the first-born male son of each subsequent generation of the Jensen family.

"That was my theory anyway, though your brother told me he has never heard of any jewels, and neither has your father."

Remy bent over and rummaged through his satchel again, finally pulling out some papers. He handed one to me and I looked it over as he explained that it was the receipt from the sale of the coronet in 1887.

The seller was listed as William Jensen of Pennsylvania, who sold it for $135,000.

"William Jensen? Is he one of my great-greats?"

"Yes, William would have been your grandfather's grandfather."

"My grandfather's grandfather? Wait a minute. He's the one who built the big old family home in Dreiheit, the one my grandparents lived in." I glanced at Reed and then back at Remy. "We were always told that the money for that house came from the oil boom in western Pennsylvania. I mean, the Jensen family wasn't rich, but that was a gorgeous house. The story was that it was paid for with profits made from selling land to Standard Oil."

"Yes, that's what your brother told me, so I did a search of the records of Standard Oil's bills of sale for a ten-year period during that time. There were no receipts for anyone named Jensen."

"So what you're saying," Reed interjected, "is that William lied? He went out of town for a while and came back with $135,000, saying he got it from the Pennsylvania oil boom when in fact it had come from the sale of a part of the Beauharnais Rubies?"

"Exactly!" Remy exclaimed. "William sold off those two pieces, as far as I can tell, but the rest of the set remained intact. Perhaps he just wanted enough money to build a nice home. The remainder of the set stayed in your family and continued to be passed down through the generations, at least as far as your grandfather. What happened from there is anybody's guess, but given that his death was sudden and unexpected, I have to imagine that he simply died before he had the chance to pass them along—which is why these treasure hunters are after you. If your claim is no stronger than theirs, they may be able to assert ownership once they have possession. Of course, they don't know about this photo, which could help lend credence to your own claim."

Remy handed me a family photo, one I had seen before.

"Your father faxed that to me just before he left town, saying he may have discovered a clue to the mystery but that he wouldn't have time to pursue it further until he got back from his trip."

"Who is that?" Reed asked, looking on with interest.

"My grandparents, on their honeymoon at Niagara Falls," I said. "I always loved this picture. We were told that the jewels she has on here were fake, like a joke. Are you telling me these are the Beauharnais Rubies?"

"Yes, they are," Remy replied, beaming, "and I must say, she looks quite fetching in them."

I sat back in my seat, holding the picture in my hand, gazing at the smiling face of Grandma Jensen when she was just in her early twenties. The jewels around her neck and hanging from her ears and nestled in her upswept hair were so elaborate, so gorgeous and over-the-top that we all believed the story that they were fake, mere props provided by the photographer. Suddenly, I felt angry with my grandparents that they had kept a secret of this magnitude from the rest of us all these years. I couldn't imagine where the jewels could be now. Obviously, they had been in my grandparents' possession back when the photo was taken. After that, where had they gone? Had my grandfather really died without telling anyone where they were hidden?

"How do we know for sure that my grandparents didn't sell the rest of the rubies at some point?" I asked.

"Well, other than the beautiful home they lived in, did they leave behind any large fortune or purchase anything of great value? Something that perhaps they could have afforded only by selling something else of great value?"

"No," I replied frankly. "My family has always lived very modestly. Trust me, if there was any big fortune, we didn't know about it."

"Then perhaps the jewels are hidden away in their house somewhere."

"That's not possible," I replied. "When my grandfather died and we had to sell the place, we cleared it out top to bottom. We never found anything of value—well, except for an old family quilt my parents donated to the Folk Art Museum. But even that was homemade, not store bought."

Remy said there was a possibility that when William had the house built he had installed some sort of hiding place into the walls or the foundation.

"Do you think the new owners would allow us to take a look?" he asked. "In my line of work, I've become pretty good at spotting hidey holes and secret places that a less-experienced person may never notice."

I shrugged, saying the house itself had been moved to a new location but that I could call them tomorrow and ask.

"Excellent. If they give you the green light, by all means, let me know and I'll meet you there. I'll be staying with my friends in Lititz for a few days."

Hoping it didn't sound tacky, I asked Remy what the jewels would be worth if we could find them now.

"I hesitate to put a value on them, but millions, certainly. Perhaps tens of millions if the set is still intact and in good condition."

Beside me, Reed let out a low whistle and said it was no wonder I was being attacked right and left. Remy's face colored, and again he apologized for making such a stupid blunder in discussing the situation on his blog.

"Let me ask you a question," Reed said. "If Anna's family descended from royalty, is that significant in any way? Do I need to start bowing down or calling her Princess Anna or anything?"

We all laughed.

"Not after this many generations, especially considering that that particular monarchy was dissolved in the early 1900s. The best Anna and her family get at this point is a claim to fame—and of course a priceless set of jewels, if we can find them."

THIRTY-THREE

Driving through the darkness toward Dreiheit with Reed following closely behind, I kept thinking about poor Stephanie de Beauharnais and the difficult choice she had had to make in giving up her son in order to give him life. Thinking of the other mother, the Amish woman who adopted Stephanie's son in secret, I realized now that her own child must have been born dead, or nearly so, which was why she had agreed to the trade. Had that been the beginning of one of the disorders that plagued the Amish to this day? I shuddered at the realization that the markers for

Karl's royal DNA had essentially remained unchanged through six generations—all the way down to Isaac, whose DNA had likely been altered somehow.

In the darkness, I reached for my phone and dialed Reed to ask him if the FBI had decided to bring Isaac and Lydia into protective custody. He said that he had just hung up with his buddy, who told him that there was already a "discreet presence" in place around the farm instead, which should keep them just as safe.

"The FBI is already protecting them?"

"Not exactly. They're watching the farm in case Bobby shows up, but that means they'll also be there should anything else happen."

I tried not to think about Bobby showing up in the dark of night and being shot down by a G-man with an itchy trigger finger.

"What did your friend say about Isaac's health?" I asked. "Shouldn't he be tested?"

"Yeah, we both think so. If Lydia will let me, I can do a blood draw on him to get things started. Who knows? Maybe he's not as sick as we fear. Why don't you talk to her about it, and I'll swing by with a collection kit around noon tomorrow."

"Sounds good," I said.

We continued to talk as we drove, and it was just nice to have him there on the line with me, his voice warm and deep in the cold stillness of the night. He said he had an idea about my safety, one I wasn't going to like but that might prove to be very helpful in the end.

"You've been dodging the press since you got to town," he said, "but now that we know about the rubies and everything, maybe you should be a little more available to them."

"Why?"

"Because I bet if you throw them some crumbs, they'll follow you around like your own little flock of birds. I doubt anyone would dare try to nab you or hold a gun to you if reporters and photographers are nearby. Given the potential value of those jewels, it might be the prudent thing to do."

As much as I was sickened by the thought of playing up to the press, he had a point. I felt safe when Reed was with me, but he couldn't always be there. I told him I would think about it.

"Anna, let me ask you something," Reed

said suddenly, his deep voice like velvet in the night. "How is it I haven't seen you in eleven years, but being together feels as comfortable and natural as if we'd seen each other a week ago?"

Maybe because I never stopped thinking about you, never stopped loving you, I thought but did not say.

"That's the nature of certain friendships, I guess," I ventured, gazing out at the moonlit landscape that surrounded me.

"We were more than friends, Anna, if you recall."

"Were we?"

"Are you kidding? I was crazy about you back then."

His comment was so shocking that my jaw literally dropped open.

"Crazy about *me*? Reed Thornton, I was madly in love with you, but for most of that summer you acted like I barely existed. I mean, you were nice to me and we had a lot of fun together, but there was no romance involved. Crazy about me? Yeah, right."

He was quiet for a moment, though I thought I could hear him chuckling.

"There was no romance involved, thanks to the shred of self-discipline I was able to muster. Think about it, Anna. I was twenty-one years old, and you were just seventeen. Granted, you didn't seem like any seventeen-year-old I had ever met before, but that didn't change the fact that you were too young for me. You have no idea how hard it was to remember that."

"Except when you kissed me the night of the fire, hanging out with you was like going around with my brother all summer. You're telling me now that you liked me more than you let on?"

"Oh, yeah. Way more. I thought about kissing you every time we were together. That night, I guess it was the combination of the beer and the romantic setting and the fact that we were alone, in the dark. I couldn't help myself. And then I had to do something to shift the focus, so like an idiot I whipped out a joint."

We rode along in silence for a moment before he spoke again.

"I've never forgotten the disappointment I saw in your face when I did that. It was a moment I've taken back in my mind a zillion times since, that moment when I killed any feelings you may have had for me. Your face—I can still see it. After we kissed, you looked up at me with those big, beautiful eyes filled with trust and adoration, and I had to go and blow it by offering you a toke. I knew you were different, Anna. I knew it was a dumb thing to do even as I was pulling it out of my pocket. But I was just so . . . um . . . ready to keep going, and I really didn't want to take things further. I guess it was an attempt to change the subject the best way I knew how, by getting high."

I swerved to avoid a patch of ice and lowered my speed on the hilly road.

"I'm sorry, Reed. I never understood any of that. I had put you up on such a pedestal, and when I realized you did drugs, the pedestal toppled. If I hadn't stuck you up on there in the first place, maybe I would have been more understanding when I learned you were human."

"Well, thanks for being kind, but that was more than just being human. What I did was wrong and really, really stupid. Offering pot to a minor? For that alone I deserved every minute I spent in prison. I really wasn't a very good person back then, Anna."

"Don't be too hard on yourself, Reed," I said softly. "After all, you were good enough to make me fall in love with you."

"I don't know how. I hate who I was then, always putting myself first, so spoiled and selfish and bored with life."

"You don't seem to be any of those things anymore. What changed you, Reed?"

With dismay, I realized that we had reached the farm. Slowing, I put on my blinker, turned into the driveway, and pulled toward the house.

"The same thing that changed all of us, I guess. But that's a long story, better saved for another day."

I hoped another day would come soon, because I really did want to hear about all that he had learned and done since the day he turned to look at me in the courtroom, his eyes filled with regret.

In the dark and silent driveway, I softly thanked Reed for coming to my rescue earlier tonight, not to mention joining me for dinner and safely seeing me home. Whispering in the stillness, I asked him if it felt weird to be back here, standing beside the very house we once caused to burn. He seemed surprised by the question.

"Oh, Anna, I've been back dozens of times since then. In fact, I'd say Grete and Nathaniel are among my most treasured friends."

As if to prove his point, the door suddenly opened to reveal Nathaniel, still dressed at this late hour and holding a lantern. Smiling broadly, he came out and gave Reed a warm handshake and a brotherly hug. After several minutes of quiet conversation, they said goodnight and we parted ways.

Inside, the house was quiet, everyone else in bed. At the top of the stairs, Nathaniel handed me a flashlight and bid me goodnight before opening the door to the bedroom he shared with his wife. In a whisper, I thanked him for waiting up for me.

"Think nothing of it," he replied, not seeming the least bit annoyed that it was so late, despite the fact that he had been up since before dawn, worked a full day, and would have to repeat the same thing tomorrow.

Feeling oddly nervous in the dark, silent house, I lit the lantern beside the bed and gathered my things. Holding the flashlight in slightly shaky hands, I crept back downstairs to the bathroom where I brushed my teeth and dressed for bed as quickly as I could.

Stepping back out of the bathroom, I paused in the darkness, listening to the sounds of the night. This old farmhouse creaked ever so slightly, and I could hear the gentle hiss of the woodstove, the ticking of the clock.

Despite my serious case of nerves, I wanted to take a peek inside the ceramic jar in the kitchen, the one I had seen Lydia use as a hiding place this morning. Bravely, I tiptoed across the floor, wincing at every creak my footsteps made, and as quietly as I could lifted the lid. I pointed my flashlight down inside, but I knew immediately that whatever she had put in there was gone now. The jar was empty but for a few cookie crumbs at the bottom.

Back upstairs and safely buried under the covers, my mind wandered back to the conversation Reed and I had had in the car. I was still astounded to learn that once upon a time he had cared for me too. Somehow, just knowing that, even if I never saw him again after this week, made all the difference in how I felt about him—and, more importantly, how I felt about myself. All those years ago, I hadn't been some pathetic lovelorn idiot. I had been responding in kind to a man who loved me too.

The next morning dawned less brightly than the one before. Sitting up in the bed, I pulled the simple green shade to the side and peered out at the sky. Gloomy and gray, it looked as if it might snow today. I had a lot to do, including Doug's wake this afternoon in Hidden Springs, so I really hoped it wouldn't. At least Reed had offered to drive us there together.

Gazing out at the frozen landscape, I thought of what the snow might mean for Bobby, on the chance that he was out there somewhere, cold and hurt and alone. In the past few days, so that I could better focus on my investigation, I had tried not to dwell on whatever sufferings he might be going through. But now an image suddenly filled my mind, that of him lying somewhere in the darkness, crying out for help with no one around to hear. Thinking of the keys I'd found in his locker, I decided it was time to take things up a notch.

I was ready to do whatever it took to find my brother, once and for all.

I was about to drop the shade again when I noticed movement out toward the henhouse. It was Grete, wearing a black cape over her Amish dress, and in her hand she carried what looked like the same small item I had caught her with in the kitchen yesterday. When she reached the door of the hen house, she looked to the right and then to the left, almost guiltily, as if she wanted to make sure she wasn't being observed. I pulled back from the window, afraid her eyes might travel up this way, and then peeked out again a moment later to see her slipping inside the building. Even with the window closed, I could hear the disturbance among the chickens as they clacked and squawked. A moment later, she reemerged, hands empty, and headed back toward the house. I didn't know what all of that was about, but I hoped to have the opportunity to find out later.

Despite the cold of the bathroom, I decided to take a quick shower. At least the water was nice and warm. I wasn't sure how they did that, but I had a feeling it was heated with some source of Amish-approved fuel such as propane or gasoline.

Once I was dressed in sweater and slacks, ready to go, I came downstairs to find Lydia and Isaac sitting at the kitchen table, their bodyguard standing near the window. Lydia was sipping coffee and reading her Bible, and Isaac was drawing pictures. Lydia told me that everyone else was at church.

"Church," I echoed, for the first time realizing it was a Sunday. Suddenly, more than anything, that was where I wanted to be too. For just one blessed hour, I wanted to sit in God's house and focus on nothing else but my Savior.

"We're sticking close to home today," Lydia added, giving me a knowing look over Isaac's head. We both knew that as much as she wanted to go, it wouldn't be safe.

She offered me breakfast, but I declined, saying I needed to get rolling. Outside, I spotted several cars parked at the end of the driveway, so I took Reed's advice and didn't attempt to elude the press. Instead, I gave a small wave as I pulled onto the road, and soon I realized that several of them had jumped into their cars and were following me.

I had one very private errand to run today, but before I did that, I needed the strength and encouragement a good Sunday service would provide. Not knowing where else to go, I drove to downtown Dreiheit to my grandparents' old church, one that held many happy memories for me. Once there, I pulled into the parking lot, and by the time I got out of the car, three different reporters were rushing toward me.

"Have you had contact from your brother, Miss Jensen?"

"Annalise, where have you been all these years?"

"Are you romantically involved with Reed Thornton?"

"I'm sorry, but I'll have to answer your questions later, when I have more time," I said sweetly, and then I walked toward the building and pushed through the doors, one backward glance confirming they weren't going to follow me inside. Choosing a seat near the back of the sanctuary, I forced myself to forget everything else that was going on and focus on the music, the prayers, and the sermon.

Coming to church had been the right decision, I decided as we stood to sing the closing hymn. After all I had been through in the last few days, all the questions that were swirling around in my mind, all the heartache and concern and frustration and fear, it had felt good to let that go and simply focus on God. I thanked Him for the privilege of worship and asked Him to help me remember its importance even in the midst of trouble.

When the service was over, I made my way to the front of the sanctuary and through the double doors into the Sunday school building. I felt guilty using church as a cover, but I knew the reporters were probably still waiting for me out front, and I wasn't ready to be followed again just yet.

Ducking down a side hall to avoid a group of people congregating near a coffee machine, I managed to get all the way to the back of the building without incident. Once there, I pulled my hat down over my hair, turned up my coat collar, and stepped outside, glad to see that no one was around. Trying not to look suspicious, I took off jogging.

By my calculations, the WIRE was just six blocks away.

I wasn't too winded by the time I got there, but my heart was pounding strongly, nonetheless. Trying not to look suspicious, I jogged to the back of the building, made sure there were no cars in the parking lot, and then I stopped at the door and pulled out my key ring. Hands trembling, I tried the keys I had found in Bobby's locker, gasping when the biggest one slipped easily into the lock and turned. Moving into the dark building, I quickly looked around for an alarm but didn't see one. Considering the technology housed here, I knew there had to be something. Before I could decide whether to stay or to go, a flash of light streaked through the darkness. Terrified, I spun around to see that it had come from the sun glinting off the shiny silver bumper of a black Mercedes just pulling to a stop outside.

Dr. Updyke.

Heart pounding, I opened the nearest door and slipped inside, realizing once I was there that I was in a mop closet. With the stench of cleaners burning my eyes, I forced myself to freeze. Watching through a crack in the door, I saw the doctor step inside, followed by his teenage son.

"Catch the alarm, would you?" Dr. Updyke said as he flipped on the light and moved down the hall.

"What's the code?" the boy called after him.

"Four four seven one three."

As I watched, the kid flipped open a metal box next to the telephone and punched in the numbers. Then he grabbed a magazine from the nearby counter, sat in a chair, and waited for his father.

Part of me was sighing in relief that I hadn't been caught; the other part was still holding my breath, wondering how long they would be there and if I would be able to remain hidden until they were gone.

"Hurry up, Dad! Practice starts in ten minutes!"

His father didn't reply, but after a short while he reappeared, a small stack of manila files tucked under his arm.

"All right, let's go."

After re-enabling the alarm, he flipped off the light, stepped outside, and locked the door.

I didn't know what to do next. On the one hand, I had been given the code to the security system like a free gift out of the blue. On the other hand, the doctor could just be running his son over to the high school and coming right back, in which case I could still get caught.

Summoning my nerve, I stepped out of the closet, crossed to the metal box, and punched in 44713. Then I gave myself exactly two minutes to dash through the building to see if I could locate the file cabinet my round key would unlock. Whether I found anything or not, I told myself, I wasn't sticking around.

Fortunately, I spotted a small sign on a door near the back of the first hall I went down, one that simply said "Archives." The door was locked, but the second key on Bobby's ring turned as easily as the first had on the back door.

The archive room was dark and smelled of old paper. From what I could tell by peering through the shadows, there weren't any outside windows here, so I took a chance and flipped on the light.

I quickly surveyed the room, which held rows of metal cabinets. With just a minute and a half left, I kept moving. Scanning the room, I could see that a number of the filing cabinets had no locks on them at all. Moving forward, I looked at each row until I reached the back of the room. There stood a wall of locked Steelcase filing cabinets, each with a round keyhole. As quickly as possible, I tried the key on them one by one, finally finding success on the fifth try.

With just thirty seconds left, I opened the top drawer and looked at the contents, which seemed to be organized by last name. There wasn't time to go through any files now, so I simply scanned the labels, looking for anything familiar. Under "Jensen," my heart raced to see that there was one file, which I pulled. After that, nothing else seemed relevant until I got to the name "Schumann," which was written on three different files. Grabbing all three, I slid the drawer shut. My self-appointed time was up.

As I crossed back toward the door, I

tucked all four files under the waistband of my slacks, smoothing my shirt and coat into place over them. Once I had turned off the light and locked the door, I sprinted up the hall toward the back entrance.

I stopped at the corner and peeked around it toward the door, but I didn't see anything in the parking lot outside. Steeling my nerve, I reactivated the alarm, stepped outside, pulled the door shut, and made sure it had locked behind me.

Taking off, I jogged along the back of the empty body shop next door, avoiding the main road for as long as I could. The coast seemed clear, no black Mercedes in sight, so finally I dashed across the street and ducked between two buildings to get to the next block. When I finally neared the church, I slowed my run to a walk, trying to catch my breath in the cold morning air. It wasn't until I was back inside the Sunday school building and making my way toward a front exit that the magnitude of what I had just done hit me.

In pursuit of the truth, I hadn't simply gone "sneaking and peeking," as Kiki liked to call what skip tracers did. I had actually let myself into a medical lab using keys that weren't mine, gone through restricted files, and removed four of those files from the premises. There was no other way to say it.

I had just broken the law.

THIRTY-FOUR

Considering files were tucked in my pants and pinching me at the waist, it wasn't easy to appear poised for the reporters who were still waiting by my car when I stepped out of the church. Trying to act natural, I simply walked toward my car and acknowledged the three of them with a slight nod.

As soon as they saw me, the questions started up again. Listening as they fired away, I finally responded to the man who asked how it felt to be back in Dreiheit after all these years.

"It feels a lot like coming home," I said to him, surprised to realize I meant it. After that, I got in my car and drove away, smiling at the sight of the entourage that quickly fell into place behind me. Reed was right. Finding security through my own private papparazzi had been a good idea.

When I was sure they couldn't see me, I slipped the files out from under my clothes and set them on the seat. I was dying to flip through and read them, but I didn't dare until I was somewhere much more private than this.

Turning on my phone, I saw that the battery had only two bars left. Prioritizing the calls I needed to make, I started with information, where I requested the number for the Wong family in Holtwood, Pennsylvania.

Mrs. Wong answered the phone, and once I explained who I was, I told her that it had come to my attention that a family heirloom might be hidden inside the structure of the house they had bought from my parents. I said I had an expert who wanted to wander through and take a look for possible hiding places. When I finished explaining, Mrs. Wong said she was sorry, but that would not be possible.

"I'd let you if I could," she added, "but we had the house dismantled five years ago."

"Dismantled?" I asked, incredulous.

"Yes, can you believe that, after all the trouble we went through to have it moved here? My husband's an architect, you know, and he always has to be changing, evolving, improving. We kept some of it, like the paneling from the downstairs study and the marble bathtub. But everything else was disposed of or sold off and taken elsewhere five years ago."

I thanked her for her trouble and hung up the phone, disappointed but not devastated. I felt sure that if a secret hiding place had been built into that house, Bobby and I would have found it as children. Considering all the games of hide-and-seek we played, all the cupboards and cabinets and closets we had hidden in, if there had been some sort of secret latch or door, I just *knew* we would have run across it. The house that was no more had been a lovely home in its day, but I didn't think it had held the Beauharnais Rubies in my lifetime.

Back on the road, I called Remy and left a message with the bad news on his voice mail. As I finished, my phone sounded a little warning jingle and then it died. I tucked it into my purse, hoping I could find somewhere to charge it again soon.

Except for the reporters who once again lined up at the end of the driveway, things were quiet at the farm when I returned, as Grete and her family still had not returned from church. I spotted Lydia and Isaac and the ever-present bodyguard out in the field, Isaac sitting comfortably atop a horse as Lydia led it around the path. I gave them a wave and went inside, my heart beating quickly as I carried the pilfered files up to my bedroom.

There was no lock on the door, so I rolled up the window shade and kept one eye on Lydia and Isaac outside as I took a look at what I had managed to acquire. Saving the Jensen folder for last, I first flipped through the ones labeled "Schumann."

Two of those files were for Schumanns I didn't know with addresses I didn't recognize. The third file, however, was the one I had been hoping to find: that of Katherine Beiler Schumann, Lydia's mother. My hope was that the file would contain her full medical record without anything blacked out as it had been in the version Doug faxed to Reed.

Flipping through several pages, I was disappointed to see that the typed office visit notes weren't there at all. Instead, the folder only held lab test results and signed legal consent forms. I was no doctor, but even I could tell that this information showed nothing of importance, as if someone had stripped out the good stuff and left only filler.

Bracing myself for more disappointment with the next folder, I tossed this one aside, but as it hit the bed, something slid forward and poked out from the edge. Picking up the file again, I realized a photograph must have popped loose from inside the folder's front pocket.

I picked up the picture and studied it, not quite sure what I was looking at. I heard a loud squeal outside, and I glanced up to see that Isaac was much closer to the house now. Turning my attention again to the photo, I decided that it was a close-up of someone's skin—someone's very diseased skin. There was a gray pallor to it, and the surface was dotted with puffy, pustule-like globs.

Bile burning at my throat, I held the photo out at arm's length, trying to make sure that was what I was seeing. The scene reminded me of something familiar, some Third World documentary I had seen about smallpox.

"I fed the horse an apple!" Isaac cried suddenly from the doorway of the bedroom, startling me so thoroughly that I dropped the photo and knocked the file folders on the floor.

As Isaac proceeded into the room without invitation, jabbering about the horse, I scrambled around to pick up the papers and the photo, tuck everything together, and shove it into a nearby tote bag.

"What do you need, Isaac?" I asked, my voice a little too sharp.

"My mom is making potato soup and wants to know if you'll be here for dinner."

"Well, why don't you run down and tell your mom I'll be right there and we can talk about it?" I replied in a nicer tone.

"Okay."

Just as quickly as he had appeared, Isaac turned and left. To the sound of his feet clunking down the stairs, I pulled the papers from the tote bag, neatened them into a pile, and slid them between the mattress and box spring. After smoothing out the covers, I grabbed my purse and slipped the photo into an inside, zippered pocket.

"Are you coming, Aunt Anna?" Isaac called.

"Just a second."

Leaving things as they were for now, I forced myself to head downstairs. From the sound of a male voice and the excited exchange of greetings between old friends, I realized that Reed was here.

Spotting him as I neared the bottom of the stairs, I couldn't help but think how handsome he looked in black slacks and a maroon sweater. As he caught me looking at him and returned my gaze, I felt heat suddenly flushing my face. The moment was not lost on Lydia, who smiled shyly and averted her eyes.

Now that he was there, what I most wanted to do was fly into his arms, show him the photo and the files, and tell him about the illegal thing I had done. Resisting the urge, I simply gave him a hug so that I could softly ask if he would take Isaac out to the barn for a few minutes while I explained to Lydia what was going on.

"No problem," he replied, and soon the two fellows were bundled up and out the door. At my urging, the bodyguard followed along behind as well.

Lydia was sitting at the table, peeling potatoes, so I joined her there, trying to think how to say all I needed to say. Before I could even put together the words, she spoke.

"You have news of some kind," she said, more of a weary statement than a question.

"Yes, I do."

As gently as possible, I explained to Lydia the medical portion of what I had learned at dinner last night, that apparently two generations of Jensen ancestors had been married to Amish women. Before I went any further, Lydia held up a hand to stop me, fully aware of what I was getting at.

"For what it's worth," I added, "Reed is very optimistic about Isaac's health. He just wants to run some blood tests to rule things out, if you're willing. Right now in fact, if you don't mind."

"Reed can do this here? Today?"

I nodded, saying that was why he had come.

Lydia set her peeler and potato down on the table and walked to the window. There, she stood for a long time, hands on her hips, looking outside, silently thinking or maybe praying. I gave her some space, not speaking, picking up a potato and slowly peeling it myself.

Finally, she turned to look at me, her eyes filled with tears.

"Had I known Bobby carried these genes, I would have done nothing differently. I would still have married him. I would still have had children with him. The women in this community know the risks of having children, but this does not stop them. God's will always prevails. Who are we to say exactly how a child should be? Who am I to think I have a right to a perfect child and a perfect life? What is perfect, anyway? In the eyes of God, all of us are. Even the children with disorders. Maybe especially the children with disorders."

As she returned to the table, I couldn't help thinking what a wise, wise woman my brother had married. As she had said the day before, she might be naive, but she certainly was not stupid.

I decided to tell her a little bit more about what I knew.

"When you and I spoke on the phone yesterday, Lydia, I asked you if you had ever been seen at the WIRE by Dr. Updike. Are you aware that both your sister and your mother also went there during their pregnancies?"

"*Yah,* of course. That was how I first reconnected with Bobby. I went with my mother to the WIRE for her testing, and I recognized him as the boy I used to play with. Of course, I hadn't seen him since we were children and your grandparents sold their house, but I would have known that face and smile anywhere."

"What kind of testing did your mother have done there? Blood work?"

"More than blood work. I think it was an amniocentesis. Whatever involves sticking a long needle through the abdomen."

I shook my head.

"I'm sorry, Lydia. She wasn't having an amniocentesis. By what we can tell from the lab's records, gene therapy was being done to the fetus."

Lydia shook her head firmly.

"She would not have done that, trust me. You did not know my mother like I did."

"Then it's quite possible that she was lied to by the doctor. After all, you probably were."

Lydia's eyes widened as she took in what I had said. I had a feeling she was right, that her mother had not known what was really going on. Kate had gone to the WIRE at the urging of her daughter Grete, and though she had agreed to an amniocentesis—or at least what she had thought was an amniocentesis—Dr. Updike obviously had had other plans in mind.

Clearly disturbed, Lydia gathered up the potatoes and carried them to the sink. Trying to be a comfort, I joined her there, and as I rinsed and she sliced, Reed and Isaac came out of the stable and started walking toward the house. I couldn't help but be warmed by the site of the two of them together, the handsome man and the lanky little boy.

"You still love him, don't you?" Lydia asked, startling me.

I was going to deny it, but she had been

so honest with me I felt I owed her the same.

"It doesn't matter. He has a girlfriend and a whole life separate from mine."

"That may be, but I wonder if he looks at her the way he looks at you."

Reed and Isaac came in the back door at that point and our conversation ended. After they took their coats off and Isaac chattered on excitedly about the horse, Reed looked at me over his head and I nodded. He turned his attention to Lydia, who also nodded, and then he said he had to get some things from the car but he'd be back in a minute. While he was out there, Lydia sat down with Isaac and explained to him that Reed needed to take a blood sample from his arm. She explained how that was done, saying that it was just like what Daddy did all day at work, taking people's blood. Isaac didn't look too happy about it, but he didn't bolt from the room, either. I excused myself, saying I needed to take a little walk and I'd be back in a while. I was just putting on my coat when Reed came in the door, a white shopping bag in one hand and small black satchel in the other. We shared grave looks, and then he came on into the house as I went outside.

It struck me that if I wanted to get a look at whatever Grete had hidden in the kitchen canister yesterday morning and carried into the henhouse this morning, now might be the perfect time. I knew that the Amish church service went on for a while and was usually followed by a community meal. I wasn't sure how much time I had, but they weren't here right now, so I thought I would take the chance. Hands in my pockets, I strolled up to the henhouse, swung open the door, and stepped inside.

Immediately the chickens went crazy, cackling and squawking and making such a ruckus that I wasn't sure what to do. Quickly I made a cursory inspection of the whole interior, my eyes finally lighting on what looked like a loose square of wood with a knot hole right in the center on the floor. Just on a hunch, ignoring the squawking and the flying feathers and the musty stench of the chicken coop, I squatted down, stuck my finger in the little hole, and lifted. Much to my surprise, as the wood came up it revealed a hiding spot below. There, in a shallow space under the floor, was a metal fireproof box. I didn't know what was inside, but my heart pounded at the sudden thought that it could be the Beauharnais Rubies. I had no idea why Grete would have them, but then again there were a lot of things I hadn't yet figured out. Reaching into the hole, I grabbed the handle of the box. I was about to lift it up out of the floor when the door to the chicken coop swung open.

Caleb stood there in the doorway looking at me, his eyes wide.

THIRTY-FIVE

"Anna?" Caleb demanded. "What are you doing in there? I thought a fox was attacking the chickens!"

Mortified, I had to make a quick decision. Acting as if it was the most natural thing in the world, I let the box drop back down into the hole, slid the board on top, and stood, brushing the straw and dirt from my knees.

"Sorry, I was just looking for something. I thought maybe it had fallen under a loose board."

Eager to get out of there, I moved past him and into the sunlight, and then I held the door open for him to do the same. He came readily, asking what I was looking for and if he could help.

"It's a long story," I said. "Don't worry about it."

He didn't press the issue. Thinking of my conversation with Lydia about Caleb and drugs, I wanted to ask where he had been since he snuck out Friday night. Dressed as he was now, handsome in jeans and a leather jacket, he looked quite different from the Amish fellow who had carried my suitcase in from the car just two nights before. I said as much to him now.

"*Yah,* I wanted to get home while the family was still out at church. I need to change back into my Plain clothes."

Together, the two of us walked toward the house. I wanted to scold him for leaving like that, for shirking his duties, for possibly getting involved with drugs. Instead I just told him I hoped he wasn't getting mixed up with the wrong people.

"The wrong people. Englishers, you mean?"

"I'm talking about drugs."

Caleb stopped short and looked at me.

"Drugs?"

I glanced around and lowered my voice. "Your sisters may be fairly sheltered, Caleb, but they're not dumb. They know what kinds of things go on in the outside world—especially over by the Quarry." His eyes widened, so I added, "Bobby saw you there a few weeks ago."

Caleb's face turned bright red, but the expression in his eyes was one of hurt, not anger.

"Bobby saw me near the Quarry, so he assumed I was taking drugs?"

"Or selling them."

Looking stunned, Caleb finally tilted his head back and let out a giant groan of frustration.

"Unbelievable!" he cried, shaking his head and looking at me. "Why did no one say anything to me? I mean, they are always nagging, always complaining. But no one ever looked me in the eye and said, 'Caleb, are you mixed up with drugs?' No one. If they had, I would have told them the truth."

"Fine. Caleb, are you mixed up with drugs?"

"No," he replied, looking me straight in the eye. "I . . . I am a musician."

"A musician?"

"I play guitar in a band. *Electric* guitar."

Suddenly I realized why he lived such a secret life. A guitar was one thing; for all I knew, the *Ordnung* might even allow that. But an electric guitar would probably be a no-no on several levels as far as the Amish were concerned.

"We practice on Saturday mornings, but the only way I can get out of here on time and not get stuck doing my chores is by not coming home Friday night. I usually stay at a buddy's house in town. We do two gigs every weekend: Saturday nights at The Alternative and Sunday mornings at church."

"Church?"

He nodded.

"It is a praise band," he said guiltily, as if that was an even bigger crime. "If Bobby saw me near the Quarry, that is because I play at The Alternative every Saturday night, a coffeehouse run by the church and located right in the thick of things. We play music to draw in the crowds, and then the pastor gets up and talks about addiction and recovery, forgiveness and restoration, things like that. They give out free coffee and donuts along with brochures about the twelve-step programs the church offers."

I was so speechless that I didn't even know how to respond.

"I know I was wrong to keep it a secret, Anna. I want to tell Grete and Nathaniel, but it is going to break their hearts. I will have to do as Lydia did and leave home, and then what will that do to them, to this farm? They need my help here. Ezra is not old enough to shoulder my load."

I told Caleb that while I understood his problem, deceiving his family and ignoring his responsibilites wasn't the solution.

"'Tis wrong to lie, *yah,* but to think that Bobby's mind went to drugs, that hurts. I would not take drugs. My whole calling is to help kids get *off* of drugs. Does he think I learned nothing from what happened the night my parents died? If the Dreiheit Five had not been drinking and smoking marijuana back there, maybe *Daed* and *Mamm* would still be alive."

My eyes widened, dismayed that he had swallowed the line about the "Wild Teen Party" that predicated the tragedy. Then again, he had a point. If my friends hadn't been pressuring me to drink, I wouldn't have led them to the hidden fireworks. If Reed hadn't pulled out a joint, I wouldn't have marched off and fallen asleep in the car and missed the first signs of the fire, before it was too late to save them.

Finally, I could do nothing except exhale deeply and apologize for my brother's misperception. I also suggested to Caleb that he pray about this, that if God was leading him in a certain direction, He could certainly help him find a way to make it happen.

Together, we moved toward the house. I would have to find another chance to get back to the henhouse later and look inside that strongbox, but for now I was just glad that Caleb and I had had the opportunity to talk in private.

At least that was one mystery solved.

When we stepped inside, it was to find Reed sitting at the kitchen table all alone. Caleb greeted him and then headed off to his bedroom to change clothes. I sat down next to Reed, noting that he had a potato in one hand and a peeler in the other, but he didn't quite seem to know what he was doing. He was running the peeler blade over the brown skin, but at the wrong angle and without enough force. Putting my hands on top of his, I showed him how to do it. As we moved our hands rhythmically together, I asked how it had gone with Isaac. Reed shook his head, smiling ruefully.

"About like you'd expect. Isaac cried, his mother cried, we all cried." With a grin and a wink, I could tell he was kidding, at least about that last part. "I think Lydia is fixing him a hot bath. That should help him calm down."

"Good."

When I thought Reed had the hang of using the peeler, I let go of his hands, though I didn't really want to. Unfortunately, he glanced up at me just then, and I knew he caught the hesitation and the longing in my eyes.

"Anna," he said, his voice soft, almost like a whisper.

Summoning my nerve, I smoothed a lock of hair into place behind my ear and then met his gaze, trying to understand the emotion on his face, trying not to be ashamed of the love that must be clearly visible on mine. Slowly, Reed reached up with one hand and flicked at my hair, at a small piece of potato peeling that was lodged there.

Embarrassed, I looked away, but with the same hand he gently grabbed my chin and tilted my face to look at him again. We sat like that for a long moment, my heart beating, my lips aching for his kiss, my brain reminding me he was involved with someone else.

I also could not forget that he had spurned me in the past—not once, but twice. Suddenly, more than anything, I wanted an explanation for his actions.

"Why did you stop writing to me from prison, Reed? I treasured your letters and then they just ended, for no reason. What happened? Was it the age difference again?"

He shook his head.

"No, that was all me. Prison was . . . well, it was a nightmare, but one I knew I deserved. When I wrote to you, I was looking for absolution, I guess. At the very least, I needed your forgiveness. Once you gave me that and we kept writing back and forth, you seemed to be falling for me again, but I wasn't ready. I had a long road ahead of me, a tough path of finding God and learning about grace. I cut things off with you because at that point I had a lot of things to sort out. It's hard to let someone else love you when you completely hate yourself."

"I'm so sorry you felt that way, but I know what you mean. I had to deal with my own demons too." I blinked, a single tear slipping down my cheek, though I wasn't even sure which one of us I was crying for. "But what about later? You never contacted me once after you got out."

He shrugged and looked away before bringing his gaze back to me.

"It was a good while before I was finally ready, but by then you had taken off," he said simply. "Bobby told me you wanted a fresh start, so I let it go. I thought I owed you that."

I blinked again, this time sending twin tracks of tears down my face. He reached up and brushed those tears away with his starchy potato hands. Smiling despite my tears, I grabbed one of those hands in mine, turned it over, and slowly kissed it, right where the scar peeked out from under his cuff. Tears filled his eyes then too. With both arms, he reached out and pulled me close and just held me, rocking back and forth right there, pressing my face tightly against his strong shoulder.

For some reason, I wanted to sob, to let out all the pain of all the years we had spent apart. But I had already stepped over the bounds with that kiss. Now that I understood we had truly gone our separate ways, my sobbing was best reserved for when I was alone, for my own private mourning.

Lydia came back into the room at that moment, startled when she spotted us in an embrace. Flustered, she excused herself again, but Reed and I pulled apart, and he called her back in as I used a corner of a napkin to wipe the tears—and the potato starch—from my cheeks.

When she returned, she was blushing, but she tried to act nonchalant as she gathered up the rest of the potatoes, carried them to the sink, and began to rinse them.

"How's Isaac?"

"He will be okay," Lydia said, her back to us as she worked. "Though I don't know if he'll ever get over the realization that that is what his father does for a living, sticking people with needles and taking out their blood."

We all chuckled.

"By the way, Caleb's here," I said. "He's in his room."

"Oh! I didn't even hear him. Did you fuss at him for disappearing like that?"

"We had a nice talk, actually. I wouldn't be so quick to jump to the wrong conclusions with him, if I were you. He's a good kid."

An electronic tone went off in Reed's pocket. He pulled out his cell phone, looked at the number, and excused himself. From the expression on his face, it was a call he didn't want to take.

"Hi, Heather," he said as he stood and began walking toward the door. As he went, I could hear the vocal tones of a female voice come through, and she sounded very angry. "I know. Yeah. I told you how the press is with us. They always say things like that."

He stepped outside, softly closing the

door behind him, to continue his conversation in private. As he did, I asked Lydia if she had a copy of today's newspaper.

"*Yah.* 'Tis right there in front of you."

I realized she had spread the paper on the table to catch the mess from the potato peelings. I pushed some of those peelings aside to get a look at the front page. Just as I had suspected, the photo of Reed and me in his car was front and center. It wasn't bad as photos go. In fact, the photographer had caught us in such an intimate gaze that I didn't blame his girlfriend for being angry. In this paper, at least, the lead story focused more on us than on Bobby's disappearance or Doug's death. Then again, this was an old familiar tale around here, and if Reed and I were somehow an item, that was just the type of juicy tidbit that sold newspapers. The headline said "Old Flame Rekindled As Search Intensifies?" At least they put a question mark at the end. In the old days, we wouldn't even have been offered that courtesy.

Reed came back inside, but this time he didn't sit down. Instead, he said he was going to deliver Isaac's blood samples to the Clinic for Special Children, change into a suit at the hotel, and then he would be back to pick me up for the drive to Doug's wake in Hidden Springs.

"What about Heather? Didn't you just get in trouble for hanging out with me?"

"Heather's fine. It's the paparazzi she can't stand."

"Well, that makes two of us," I replied as I walked him to the door.

"By the way, that's for you," Reed told me, gesturing toward a white shopping bag sitting on the floor under the coat pegs. "See you in a bit."

Before I had even picked up the bag, he was gone.

I finished helping Lydia with the soup, and then I carried the bag upstairs, where I looked inside and pulled out what felt like fabric wrapped in tissue paper. Gently tearing off the paper, I unfolded a beautiful black sweater dress. It was gorgeous, long-sleeved and knee length, with a tag that identified it as a Nicole Miller. I had no idea what it had cost, but it had to be several hundred dollars at least. There were two more items in the bag as well, and I took them out each in turn to discover a classic gold-plated chunky necklace and a lovely pair of black pumps with a modest gold buckle at each toe.

I sat on the side of the bed, stunned. In his kindness, Reed had taken the time to go shopping for me, to buy me something more appropriate for a January wake than a summer dress and strappy sandals. If I wasn't so tired of being embarrassed, not to mention cold, I would have refused such a generous gift. As it was, I needed this dress more than I had wanted to admit. Maybe I would accept it but insist on reimbursing him for it later. It was a size smaller than I usually wore, but when I tried it on it fit just fine, and the necklace and shoes would be the perfect addition.

I brushed my hair and fixed my makeup as quickly as possible, so that I would have time to look at the file I hadn't yet seen, the one marked "Jensen" that I had stolen today from the lab. Pulling the papers out from under the mattress, I put the Schumann files aside and held my breath as I opened the Jensen one, hoping to learn the truth about Isaac.

Instead, my heart skipped at beat at what I saw. There, printed clearly across the label, wasn't Isaac's name at all.

It was my own name: Annalise Bailey Jensen.

THIRTY-SIX

In Reed's car, driving toward the wake, I was so upset and distracted I could hardly breathe. He knew something was wrong but didn't press me to talk, and I was glad. As we sped through the patchwork-quilt hills of Lancaster County, I couldn't stop thinking about the file, about the words I had read over and over, terms I didn't understand like "protease," "DNase," and "chelation."

More than anything, I wanted to tell Reed about it and have him explain it all to me, but I remained silent. It wasn't just that I had stolen the files and committed a crime. It was that I truly didn't want him to know if I was some sort of genetic freak, that my body had apparently been genetically tampered with at some point in the past.

I couldn't bear the thought of him seeing me as damaged goods.

As I was wrestling with these things in my mind, Reed's phone rang, and I was glad when he answered it and talked for a while. I didn't even listen to his half of the conversation. I just stared out the window and asked God to give me some clarity and direction in this moment.

I was so lost, so utterly scared and confused. Closing my eyes, I couldn't help but picture Bobby, who was also very likely lost and scared and confused. Silently, I prayed for God to protect and guide him as well.

Once Reed finally hung up the phone, he tried to lighten the mood by telling me about his life in DC, his work, his girlfriend. I feigned an interest in her, and though part of me didn't want to hear, another part of me needed to hear.

Reed explained that he and Heather had met last year at a dinner party and had begun dating soon after that. Heather was a lobbyist for the banking industry, brilliant, graduated magna cum laude from Princeton. As he talked, I got the feeling they didn't see each other all that much, even though their relationship was exclusive. I thought of his comment the other day, that he probably worked too much, and I wondered if maybe she did too. That couldn't be good for any relationship.

"We're at that point where she's pushing me to meet her parents," he said, flashing me a grin. "I know what that means. She says I keep finding excuses not to."

"Do you?"

He drove for a while, considering my question. As soon as we passed the welcome sign for Hidden Springs, I knew we were close. Reed made a left turn and drove to the end of the block.

"I suppose I have been wondering if I have a problem with commitment," he finally replied, slowing to turn again, this time into the parking lot of the funeral home. "Now I'm starting to wonder if it's commitment that I have a problem with . . . or just commitment to her."

With that, he pulled into the first available space and turned off the car. Across the street from the funeral home, I could see several yellow sawhorses lined up in a row, a police barricade, forming to keep the press at bay.

As we got out of the car and headed up the wide front steps toward the door, I thought about what Reed had just said. I kept wondering exactly when he had begun to ask himself that question about commitment. Had he been rethinking their relationship before coming here? Or had those questions started only after he had spent time with me? I may still love him, and I may still think we belonged together, but the last thing on earth I wanted to do was break up his relationship with someone else.

The press was out in full force, but with a heavy police presence there, the best they could do was snap photos from afar and shout questions to us that we didn't answer. Reed and I both ignored the hoopla, and as we stepped into the hushed dignity of the funeral home, I was relieved to know we had at least crossed the first hurdle unscathed. Glancing at my watch, I saw we were a few minutes early, which was probably a good thing. I still hadn't seen Haley since coming to town, and I had hoped to have a quiet moment with her before the crowd grew too big.

At a rack near the door, Reed helped me off with my coat, and I realized that I hadn't yet thanked him for the outfit. I did so now, apologizing that I had been too distracted to mention it before. "You'll have to let me pay you back, though," I added.

His response surprised me by its gravity.

"Please don't, Anna. When I woke up this morning, it struck me that our attendance at Doug's wake is going to be all over the news, probably for days to come. I know how much you hate seeing yourself in the media, so at the very least I thought you should feel confident with how you're dressed."

"But it must have cost—"

"It doesn't matter. What matters is that I had a few spare minutes and my hotel is right near the outlet mall and I just wanted to do this, one friend for another. Okay?"

Looking into his handsome blue eyes, I could tell it was important to him that I accept his kindness as a gift, no reimbursement allowed.

"Okay," I said, sliding my coat onto a hanger and placing it on the rack. "For what it's worth, I needed this more than you could imagine. Thank you."

"Well, for what it's worth," Reed replied in a soft voice as he placed his coat on the rack beside mine, "you look quite incredible, if I do say so myself."

Smiling shyly at the compliment, I turned my attention back to the reason why we were here.

Moving toward the closed casket at the front of the room, I spotted Haley when I was halfway there. Her arms flew open when I was still a good ten feet away, and I moved quickly into her hug. She smelled vaguely of Scotch, but at least she seemed sober for now.

"Wow, California must suit you, Anna. You're so tanned and healthy looking," she said as we pulled apart.

I wanted to give her a compliment in return, but the truth was that she looked terrible. Of course, she was here for her husband's funeral, so I hadn't expected her to look great. But I was still taken aback by her appearance. At just twenty-nine, there were already lines around her mouth and beside her eyes. Always petite, now she was positively skeletal. The skin-and-bones look did not become her, not even dressed up in couture clothes and an expensive haircut.

"I've missed you so much," I said finally. "How are you doing? Are you okay?"

She nodded, though it was obvious this hadn't been the best week of her life. More people began coming in, and after she and Reed greeted each other with a hug, I told her we would get out of the way.

"We'll talk later," she whispered to me just before she was descended upon by a pack of blubbering relatives.

Reed and I respectfully filed past the coffin and then made our way to Mr. Wynn, who was standing at the other side, talking with a small cluster of people. Still robust and handsome in his sixties, when Mr. Wynn realized that the tall blonde waiting to speak to him was his daughter's old best friend, his eyes filled with tears.

"Annalise Jensen, aren't you a sight for sore eyes. What are you, a fashion model now? Look at you!"

"Thank you. You look great too, sir."

I gave him a warm hug, remembering as I did the conversation Reed and I had had just yesterday, when I suggested that Mr. Wynn could have killed Doug. I knew now I didn't believe it, not for a minute. He was rich and powerful, yes, but he was not a killer, not even close. He was more like a well-dressed, well-heeled teddy bear.

"Reed, how are you, son?" he said, shaking Reed's hand and patting him on the shoulder. They chatted like the old friends they were, and I remembered how very present Mr. Wynn had been after the fire and through all our trials. Because he had recruited and hired the three interns, he had seemed to feel personally responsible in a way, and he had even offered to pay the legal expenses of any of us who couldn't afford to cover our own.

It had been his fancy lawyer who convinced the police to drop charges against Lydia, and as far as I knew he had funded most of Doug's defense team. My parents had refused to accept his help, probably out of sheer pride, but I had always thought it awfully decent of him to offer.

As more people lined up behind us, we finished conversing with him and stepped out of the way. Next stop was Haley's mom, Melody, who looked a little lost. She was standing near the back of the room, clad in a filmy blue-and-green dress, her blond hair clipped up on one side with a pearl clasp. When we reached her, after hugs and hellos, she kept hold of my hand for a while. Inwardly smiling, I thought of my old nickname for Melody: The Floater. It certainly seemed as if she was about to float away now, and that she was clinging to me like a helium balloon fighting against its own string.

"Are you okay?" I finally asked, and she shook her head.

"Haley doesn't want me to stand with her, so I went and stood over there. But then Orin wanted to stand there, so I came over here. I don't know where I'm supposed to be. I feel so stupid."

Kindly, Reed suggested that Melody could man the guest register near the door, saying that way she could greet people and make sure they signed the book while staying clearly out of the way of her daughter or ex-husband.

"Thank you, Reed!" Melody cried, letting go of my hand to kiss his cheek. "You always were the brilliant one in the bunch."

At that, Melody floated across the room to her new post, the eyes of several male guests noticeably turning to watch as she passed by.

"Boy, even at fifty-something, she's still the best-looking gal in the room," I said.

"Present company excluded, of course," Reed wisely replied.

Once I forced myself to stop thinking about the file with my name on it that was hidden back at the farm, the next two hours passed quickly. I was surprised at how many people I recognized. Some of our old friends from high school had come, as had various friends of Haley's family I had met over the years. Doug's parents were also there, of course, though they were even less sociable at their son's wake than they had been at his trial.

The biggest surprise was how many Amish people had turned out for this, despite the fact that many of them had had to hire drivers to get here because it was a little far to come via horse and buggy. I saw a lot of old Amish friends, the same ones who had rallied around us in the wake of the fire. Near the end of the afternoon, I was even more surprised to see Nathaniel, Grete, Caleb, Rebecca, Ezra, and even Tresa all come filing in. Seeing them there, I realized I should have known they would be coming—and offered them a ride. As the surviving children of the couple Doug helped to kill in the fire eleven years ago, their presence spoke volumes about forgiveness and faith in action.

At one point, I simply stood to the side of the room and scanned all of the faces around me. As I did, I couldn't help but wonder if we would ever know who pushed Doug Brown to his death. In truth, it could have been almost anyone, even someone in this room.

The bigger question, to my mind anyway, was if whoever killed Doug had succeeded in killing Bobby as well.

"Have you seen the ladies' room in this joint? It's humongous," Haley said to me once the crowd had dwindled down.

Grabbing my arm, she pulled me toward a side door as I gave Reed a look of general helplessness. There was an empty sitting area in the front half of the bathroom, so Haley and I sat on two overstuffed chairs in the corner and talked. Soon, she lit up a cigarette, even though there were No Smoking signs everywhere. She always had been a rebel.

Except for the smoke, it actually was a pleasure just to sit for a bit and catch up with each other in private. Haley still had a wicked sense of humor and a way of blurting out exactly what was on her mind. She told me a bit about her life and how unhappy she and Doug had been. Now that he was dead, she said, all she could do was lament that she hadn't tried harder to be a good wife and to make the marriage work.

She asked about Bobby and where I thought he had gone and what I had been able to figure out, but I kept the conversation vague, not wanting to divulge too much at that point about my investigation. I had her describe for me their strange encounter the night he took the motorcycle, but from the way she talked, it sounded to me that she had been pretty drunk at the time—and that the story had become embellished in the retelling.

Eventually she asked about Reed and me, as I had known she would. I told her we were spending a lot of time together trying to find Bobby, but that we were just friends now and always would be just friends.

"Well, poo, that's no fun. He's still so hot and totally loaded. He has, like, tripled his family's wealth in the last few years just by wise investing. Did you know that?"

I shook my head and tried to think of a tactful way to say that Reed's money had never been a big selling point for me. Rich or poor, I loved who he was on the inside.

"Daddy said he's got a lot of WYI in his portfolio."

"WYI?"

"Stock. Wynn Industries stock."

I sat up straight, a chill racing down my spine.

"Reed owns stock in Wynn Industries?"

"A boatload."

"How? I mean, isn't he on some big DNA ethics board? How can he serve on that if he's invested in a company that deals with DNA?"

She shrugged.

Our conversation ended there as a female employee of the funeral home stuck her head in the door and told us they were closing up for the evening.

"And there is no smoking in here, *ever.*"

"I'm so sorry," Haley replied with a catch in her voice. "It's just that I miss my late husband so much . . ."

As her eyes grew wide and full of tears, the woman backed off, the door bouncing shut with a quiet thud.

"You're worse than ever," I said, shaking my head, remembering the drama that Haley loved to create everywhere she went.

"Not really," she replied calmly, tucking away her cigarettes. "I'm just older than ever and skinnier than ever and uglier than ever."

"Haley . . ."

"Oh, come on. I saw your face when you came in. You never could lie."

"All right. You don't look healthy to me."

With that, Haley reached up, grabbed the top of her hair, and pulled off what turned out to be not a pricey haircut but an expensive wig. Underneath, her head was completely bald.

"Yeah, well, chemo does that to a person."

THIRTY-SEVEN

Haley and I parted ways at the front door of the funeral home, her wig secured back on her head, the knowledge that she would likely follow her husband to the grave within the year almost too much for me to bear. According to her, she was enduring the chemo for her father's sake, as he refused to let her give up, but she felt sure it wasn't going to make much difference in the long run. At her request, no one outside of the immediately family even knew she was sick, and she asked me to please keep it that way.

"What about your drinking?" I asked,

knowing the time for being delicate had passed. "Doesn't that interfere with your treatments?"

"Honey, I probably won't make it to Easter," she said as we pulled on our coats. "Do you really think it matters if I self-medicate now and then?"

On the drive back to the house, I closed my eyes and pretended to rest, though my mind was reeling from too many devastating things: the news that Haley had cancer, the discovery of a file with my name on it, the knowledge that Reed owned stock in Wynn Industries.

Once again, Reed Thornton had turned out not to be the man I thought he was at all. How many more times in life would I have to be burned before I got wise to the fact that he was bad news?

Twice during the drive home he asked me if I was okay, but I just mumbled something about having a headache and being emotionally exhausted.

We drove the rest of the way in silence, and when he pulled to a stop in the driveway of the farmhouse, I jumped out of the car before he even had a chance to turn it off.

"Thanks for the ride," I said, relieved to see that the whole family was just now getting home as well. A big twelve-passenger van pulled up behind us, and people began popping out, one by one. Further back, along the road, a coterie of paparazzi was lining up as well.

"Anna," Reed said, calling to me in a low voice.

I wanted to pretend I hadn't heard him, but it was kind of obvious that I had. I walked back to where he was standing in the open doorway of his car.

"What?"

"Did I do something to offend you?"

I looked at his face, at the gorgeous blue eyes, the chiseled jaw, the perfect mouth. Had I really made no progress in the past eleven years when it came to evaluating people? Or was my problem more specific than that, one of simply not being able to evaluate this particular man who stood in front of me?

"It's all about the pedestal, Reed. Whenever I put you up on one, it topples over. I'm just trying to keep things from toppling too far."

And I'm just praying the person who

killed Doug and ran Bobby off the road wasn't you, I thought but did not say.

"Fine. Give me a call." Reed obviously didn't know all that I was thinking, but he could tell the subject was closed. With a resigned expression on his face, he got back in his car and pulled out of the driveway right behind the big van.

Swallowing hard, I turned my attention to the family, who seemed to be in very good spirits despite the fact they had just come from a wake. They filed into the house, but as they did, I reached out and grabbed Grete by the sleeve of her coat and asked her if we could talk.

"I should put dinner on," she said, but I told her Lydia had already made dinner, a nice pot of potato soup that should be ready by now.

Grete then nodded at Nathaniel, who herded the kids inside and closed the door, leaving us out in the cold, alone. Glancing toward the photographers at the end of the drive, I led her around the corner of the house, behind the enclosed back porch, where we couldn't be observed quite so easily.

"What is it, Anna? Is something wrong?"

She rubbed her hands together and blew on them as I nodded, all of my angst about Haley's cancer and the genetics file and Reed's stocks boiling up inside of me. With an anger I didn't know I possessed, I demanded for Grete to tell me what she was hiding in the floor of the henhouse.

She took a step back and put a hand to her mouth.

"How do you know about that?" she whispered, looking back and forth as if to make sure I hadn't been overheard by anyone else.

"I saw you, remember? I saw you hide something in the cookie jar yesterday and then take it out in the henhouse today. It didn't take long to find your secret stash, but unfortunately Caleb showed up before I could look inside. I'm thinking now might be a good time to go take a look together. We can use your flashlight."

"Why is this your concern?" she whispered. "What could this possibly have to do with you?"

"It has everything to do with me. Let's go."

Together, we walked toward the henhouse, me holding firmly to Grete's elbow, her shining a flashlight on the ground in front of us. When we got there, I held the door as she stepped inside, quickly opened the floor, and pulled out the metal box. The chickens squawked furiously, and soon I could see Nathaniel standing at the back door with a flashlight, pointing our way.

"It's okay, it's just us," I called to him. "Don't worry about it."

He hesitated and then went back inside, closing the door behind him.

Grete thrust the box in my hands, put the flashlight on top of it, spun on her heels, and marched away. I stayed where I was, daring to hope that I had my family's priceless jewels in my possession at last. The best I could figure, Grete must have found them at the old homesite, probably after the house had been moved away—though why she had taken them out of hiding yesterday, I wasn't quite sure.

Carefully, I pointed the flashlight at the box and lifted the lid. I had expected to see a velvet case or perhaps a smaller wooden box inside. Instead, I found myself looking down at the square object I had seen Grete with yesterday.

It wasn't a jewelry case; it was a camera.

Underneath the camera were photos, lots of photos, mostly of Tresa and Ezra when they were younger, but also candid shots around the house and the farm, pictures of the entire family. No one ever looked directly at the lens, and Nathaniel, especially, was seen only in profile or from the back. The only shot of his face was of him lying on the couch, sound asleep.

Confused, I swallowed hard, wondering what I had done.

Quickly, I stepped into the henhouse and put the box back where it belonged, under the floor. Once it was in hiding, I made my way to the house, shining the flashlight on the ground in front of me as I went. When I got there, I spotted Grete sitting on the steps of the back stoop, clutching at her stomach and crying.

Mortified, I knelt down in front of her.

"I am so sorry," I whispered. "That's not what I was expecting to find, Grete. You were right. That's none of my business. Please, please let's just forget this happened."

She looked at me, her eyes red, her nose runny.

"You have found my secret sin," she whispered. "Now everyone will know. I will be disciplined. It will be taken from me."

I took a deep breath and let it out slowly, wondering how on earth I could make this right.

"It's just a camera and some pictures," I said softly. "I promise I won't ever tell anyone."

"These things, they are not allowed. The *Ordnung* strictly forbids it."

I stood up and turned so that I could sit next to her on the stoop.

"If they are forbidden, why do you have them?" I asked.

She dabbed at her eyes with the hem of her sleeve.

"Because," she said, sniffling, "about a year after my parents died, I realized that I could not remember my mother's face. With no photos for reference, her image was lost to me forever. I knew my *daed* would eventually disappear from my mind as well. Right then, I decided I needed a way to remember, a way to see the faces of my loved ones whether they are here with me or not."

Heartbroken for the pain I could hear in

her voice, I put an arm around Grete's shoulders as she explained that yesterday morning she had the camera out because she had been snapping pictures through the window of the kids and Lydia playing in the snow. She said that all of her photos were taken that way, when the subjects had no idea they were being recorded on film. If I hadn't come down when I did, I would never have known. Again, I apologized for poking my nose in where it didn't belong, and then as simply as I could I explained what I had thought was in there, a set of priceless ruby-and-diamond jewels that had been handed down through my family but disappeared somewhere along the way.

"Rubies and diamonds?" she asked, clearly astounded. "In a chicken coop?"

For some reason, her question struck me as funny. I giggled. That, in turn, made her giggle, despite her tears. Soon, she laughed, then I laughed, and as we fed off of each other, we got to laughing so hard that our sides were hurting. Finally, as we both calmed down and grew quiet, I promised her, yet again, that her secret was safe with me, though I added that she might want to relocate the box to a different hiding spot, because Caleb had seen me fooling with the loose board earlier.

After that, Grete and I went inside the house, though when she told me to "butz" my "gums," I couldn't help but start laughing again. She laughed too as she explained that she'd merely been suggesting that I clean the mud from my shoes.

Upstairs, I hung up my sweater dress and changed into jeans, and then I went back downstairs and joined the family at the dinner table. There, they were just about to have prayer and enjoy Lydia's soup, homemade biscuits, and a delicious-looking fruit salad.

Over dinner, somehow we began talking about the old days, about how Grete and Lydia and Bobby and I had been such constant companions whenever we visited our grandparents in Dreiheit as children. Once Caleb was born, the girls usually brought him along as well. I still remembered being astounded by that, by the sight of my peers, mere children themselves, caring for their younger sibling with all the expertise and confidence of young mothers.

Lydia talked about the noisy games of Dutch Blitz we had played on rainy days, and Grete shared with the younger ones about how Lydia and Bobby were the biggest pranksters ever born—and even worse when they were together to egg each other on. I reminisced about the old games of sardines and hide-and-seek, all the hours we had spent playing in our big old family house.

"Remember Bobby's favorite trick with hide-and-seek?" Lydia asked, eyes twinkling. "You think we would have wised up after a while."

"That's right," I said, grinning as it came back to me, "he would hide near the person who was counting, and then as soon as they were finished and set off to find everybody, he would slip out of his hiding place and go put himself right where the counter had stood when they were counting."

"*Yah,* I remember that," Grete added with a laugh. "No one ever thought to look in the place they started from, the place they had already been, because they didn't think anyone would be there. Bobby was always so smart."

Lydia moved on to describe some adventure we'd had out in the tree house, but my mind stopped where it was, right at that point in the conversation. There was something about what we'd said, something about Bobby, that suddenly clicked in my brain like the biggest, most powerful light switch in the world.

"Wait!" I said, but because they were laughing and talking they didn't hear me. "Wait! Guys!" That time I seemed to draw everyone's attention. Startled, they all turned to look at me. "It's Bobby. I know where he is."

I looked at Lydia, the one who had called me with such urgency in her voice four days ago and begged me to help her find him.

"Really," I said, my heart pounding, my hopes soaring for the first time in days. "I think I know where we can find Bobby."

I had never driven so fast in my life.

Crammed into my little four-seater rental car was me at the wheel, Nathaniel in the passenger seat, and Caleb, Rebecca, and Lydia squeezed tightly in the back. Grete had wanted to come too, but as there literally hadn't been room for one more, she offered to stay back with the kids and with the neighbors who had come to stand guard while we were gone. As we flew down the dark and hilly roads with four vehicles of paparazzi in pursuit, I tried to explain my theory, one that Bobby had probably been counting on me to figure out a lot sooner than this. Just as in hide-and-seek, I explained, he had hidden himself right where it began.

I didn't know if I could find in the dark the gravel road Reed had driven us down, so instead I just headed to the high, sharp curve of the highway. Once there, I pulled over, turned off the car, and we all spilled out, flicking on flashlights as we did. Leading the way, I practically ran down the steep hill, past the sight where the motorcycle had crashed, past the place where spattered blood had been found. At the bottom of the hill, in a full-out run, I headed for the empty farmhouse, the one where Bobby had left some cash and a note saying he had taken the tractor.

There probably hadn't even been a tractor.

In fact, he likely hadn't ever left.

Knowing my brother as I did, if he had been extremely injured in that crash but still coherent, he would have dragged himself here, bandaged himself up, done something to make it look as if he had left, and then simply found a safe hiding place to lie in wait until the threat was gone or until I found him, whichever came first.

Given that he hadn't yet resurfaced, I had to conclude that either he knew he was still in danger from a killer who hadn't yet been caught, or he was so hurt that once he got into his hiding place he couldn't get back out.

I had explained all of this to the family in the car on the way over, and now with shouts of Bobby's name, we fanned out, each of us looking for where he could have hidden himself. The press was going nuts, trying to decide which person to follow, shouting questions about what we were doing and why. Finally, I stopped and turned around, facing the whole lot of them.

"My brother is here somewhere," I said with certainty. "He's here and he's hurt and he needs us to find him. You guys can either jump in and help or get out of the way."

"Hey, I'm just a stringer," one reporter

said. "Whatever you've got going on, my job is to write about it."

"You want something to write about?" I demanded, advancing toward him, my hands clenched into fists at my sides. "Write about how a herd of bloodsucking, tabloid-writing leeches did something decent for a change and helped us find an innocent and injured man." By then, there were at least ten people in my audience, each of them staring at me as if I had gone nuts. I took a deep breath and told myself to calm down. "Let's try it this way. The sooner you guys pitch in, the sooner we can find him, and the more likely you are to get an exclusive before even more reporters and photographers show up here."

That seemed to work. Suddenly, they all sprang into action, going where I dictated, doing what I said to do. I pointed out the gravel road behind us and sent three of them back up to their cars, telling them to go the long way around and see if they could drive up in here on the gravel road, so that we could use their headlights to see better.

Even with everyone searching, we still

couldn't find him. We broke into the house and checked the attic, the basement, and every nook and cranny of every room and cabinet and closet. We scoured the barn and the silo and the washhouse and the other structures that dotted the land, even the older structures that were no longer in use. Finally, when some were giving up hope, I said that if I knew Bobby, he would have put himself someplace smart, someplace underground, maybe, where the temperature wouldn't get down to freezing.

"A good root cellar would do it," Nathaniel told me. "The temperature is more or less constant year round."

"*Yah,*" Rebecca added, "if the cabbages do not freeze all winter, then Bobby could have survived for a few days."

"But we already checked the basement and the springhouse," Lydia cried, her voice thick with despair.

"The barn!" one of the photographers said suddenly.

"*Yah,* the barn," Nathaniel nodded. "Sometimes there is a second root cellar in the barn!"

En masse, we ran into the big red barn with its graceful, curved roof. Nathaniel led the way, scanning the dark, cavernous room with his flashlight. Finally, he paused, training the vivid beam upon a large rectangle of wood flooring over in the corner. On one end of the long, door-sized board were hinges; on the other was what looked like a handle—a blessed, beautiful, black, wrought iron handle.

Holding my breath, I half clung to Lydia, half held her up as we watched Caleb grab that handle and lift open the door.

THIRTY-EIGHT

Bobby

The angels were calling his name.

He could hear them, their voices urgent, crying "Bobby! Bobby!"

He wanted to respond, wanted to tell them not to carry him away to heaven just yet. He still had others to save here on earth first.

Surely, they would understand. Surely, God would give him a little more time to get to his wife, his son, his unborn child. Bobby opened his mouth to cry out in return, to explain, but no sound came.

The water was all gone, had been gone

since morning. His throat felt like sandpaper against raw, bleeding tissue.

He was cold, the shivers wracking his frame like seizures.

He was dying, he knew that, but he fought it. He wasn't *ready* to die.

Lydia. He still had to get to Lydia.

Funny how one of the angels sounded just like her. Was that God's idea of a joke—or was it meant to be a comfort? As the bright light came—and he had known it would, eventually—he didn't even have the strength to shield his eyes. He simply opened the one good eye and looked up to see the heavenly beings that had finally arrived to carry him off before his time.

He had always thought that the light at death would be a single, divine illumination. This wasn't like that at all. This light came from many different sources, beams and flashes and every one of them causing him immense, wincing pain.

Wasn't there supposed to be no pain in heaven?

Funny, but one of the angels even looked like Lydia, smelled like Lydia.

Wept like Lydia.

He blinked, wanting to understand why this moment was nothing like what he had expected of death. It was far more painful, far more real, far more desperate.

Angels looking like men came down and surrounded him and scooped him up, their faces those of his loved ones, their arms strong and sure. As he braced himself for their flight to heaven, instead he felt himself being carried sideways, toward more lights, another softer pair of hands supporting the back of his head. The lights they were approaching looked like the twin headlights of a car.

Were there cars in heaven? Were there sirens? Because he could hear sirens in the distance, no doubt.

He was being lowered down then, lowered onto what smelled and felt like the soft fabric of auto upholstery. He braced himself for what was apparently going to be a drive, rather than a flight, to meet his Maker. He was confused, because surely the Bible had never said anything about getting to the Promised Land this way!

He braced himself for the journey, but nothing happened. His heavenly transport didn't move at all. Instead, the angels all seemed to be waiting for something as the sirens grew louder, closer.

He was lifted again, put down on a bed or a pad of some kind. Someone grabbed his wrist and held it. Another slid something hard and plastic around his neck. Yet another poked him with a pin on the back of his hand and then strapped down his arm with the harsh, scritchy sound of Velcro. They all kept trying to talk to him, but he couldn't understand the words now. They were a jumble in his brain, a wave of discord and confusion to his ears.

Soon a new sound was added to the mix, a rhythmic putter-putter that blew wind in his face and shone a beam down to earth from the sky.

Finally, the true light of heaven had come.

Again, as he felt his body being moved sideways one more time, Bobby opened his good eye.

There he saw the Lydia-angel again, running alongside, still crying. To his right, also running, was an Anna-angel as well—only this version had long blond hair and a face covered in tears.

"It's okay, Bobby," the Anna-angel was saying. "You're gonna be okay."

He swallowed, an act fraught with pain, and tried once more to speak.

"I knew you would come," he finally managed to rasp.

Then he closed his eye as the forward movement stopped short and the clang of metal slamming shut against metal assaulted his ears. As he felt his body lifting high and then higher, he thought of that old expression, of shuffling off this mortal coil. Sailing into the sky, he knew this was his time to shuffle. Slowly, Bobby let go.

As he raced toward heaven, he smiled, his body given up to God, his mind sliding into the dark, soft embrace of unconsciousness.

THIRTY-NINE

Stephanie

September 6, 1812

Love has won over pride.

Tonight, with the guard's help, I slipped from the palace and made my way to the home of the Jensens. My dear friend Priscilla did not look well. Her face was pale. Despite the cool night, sweat beaded along her brow.

Samuel provided a stool next to the bed, and that was where I sat as I proposed my plan. If my child is born male and their child is born dead, or sickly and likely to die soon, there would be a secret trade, her child for mine. To all eyes, it would look as if my child had died and their child had lived, nothing more than that.

They could raise my son as their own. I would in no way interfere, but I asked that I be allowed to see him once a year, if only from afar. Upon his eighteenth birthday, the truth would be revealed to him and he would return to the palace and his rightful place on the throne.

That was my plan, but as the Jensens are strongly religious, I expected to have a bit of trouble persuading them. After certain assurances, however, they acted amenable to the idea and promised to put it to prayer.

There seemed to be two reasons for their acceptance of my proposal:

—They did not want to face the heartache of losing another child. By raising my son, by nursing him at her breast, by training him in the way he should go, it would be like getting a second chance with their own child.

—They likened my story to that of Moses, in the Bible. Priscilla said that Moses also had been slated to die because he was born a male. To save his life, his mother told his older sister to put the baby in a reed basket and let the basket float to the Pharoah's daughter in the river. Priscilla said that when the Pharoah's daughter saw the babe, she decided to raise him as her own. He grew up to be a great hero for his own people.

This story deeply heartened me. I had heard of Moses, of course, but hadn't known the details of his life story. With tears in my eyes, I told Priscilla that this was exactly like Moses, except in reverse. This time, the princess was giving the babe to the commoner.

Samuel and Priscilla wanted some time to pray and talk, so we have made a plan for Samuel to bring a basket of schnitz pies to the palace tomorrow, as a gift to me. Samuel knows how to read and write, and at the bottom of the basket will be a letter revealing their decision, along with his plan for how we can pull off the trade.

As I wait for their answer, there is such peace in my heart about it. I know one thing for sure. This was the right decision.

Now I can only hope that my precious Amisch friends think so as well.

FORTY

Anna

Our time at the hospital consisted of sitting, waiting, pacing, and getting periodic updates from the RN about Bobby's condition. She threw a lot of things at us at first: dehydration, exposure, hypothermia, gangrene, fractures, internal bleeding. As the evening wore on, more and more family members came, mostly from Lydia's side of the family. Given that Bobby had been airlifted to Philly, I wasn't sure how all of these Amish people were getting here. Again, they had probably either hired taxis or taken the train.

Eventually, the group grew so large that

we were moved to a different waiting room, one big enough to hold the cousins and coworkers and friends and loved ones who continued to make their way to us for hours on end. Though it was good to see how many people really cared about my brother, I kept thinking how tactless some of them were, how much better I liked the Amish way of handling tragedy. They didn't offer stupid platitudes or empty statements. They didn't try to put words in God's mouth nor motivations behind His actions.

They simply prayed in silence, sat in quiet companionship, comforted with hugs and pats and gentle, soothing sounds.

Lydia seemed oblivious to almost everything that happened outside of those much-anticipated medical updates from the charge nurse. Never making much noise or fuss, every so often Lydia would simply start crying again, and once in a while those tears turned to sobs.

At one point I felt a familiar hand on my shoulder, and I looked up to see that Haley was there. Of all the non-Amish people in the room, she turned out to be the best at simply knowing what I needed. Surely, that kind, instinctive competence had risen up out of her own battle with cancer; she didn't give me any empty platitudes because she knew from her own experience that they were meaningless and sometimes even hurtful. Instead, she made sure Lydia and I always had a water or coffee or tea at hand, that we ate an occasional piece of fruit or cracker, that we had both a Bible and a blanket nearby. When the nurses pulled Lydia and me aside to give us updates, Haley came with us and made sure we understood exactly what they were saying.

Most amazing of all, as far as I could tell, Haley didn't sneak a drink the entire time. She slipped away for a smoke now and then, but she always came back ready to do whatever needed doing next—even if that was just to sit in the seat beside mine and let me rest my head on her shoulder.

Despite the large number of people who waited there with us, there was one glaring absence in the room: Reed Thornton. I took that as a very bad sign. Reed had a close working relationship with the police on this investigation, so there was no way he couldn't have known by now that Bobby had been found. In my opinion, Reed's not showing up here at the hospital spoke volumes about what was really going on. I didn't know why, but he had to have been the one who murdered Doug and tried to murder Bobby. He wasn't here now because he was already on the run, afraid that Bobby had been coherent enough to provide the name of his attacker before losing consciousness.

I had said as much to the cluster of law enforcement officials who seemed to be keeping an eye on the situation. They wrote down the information I gave them about my suspicion of Reed's conflict of interest with the stocks, and though they thanked me for the input, they didn't exactly keep me informed of what they did with that knowledge or how their own investigation was progressing.

Sadly, Bobby had been so out of his head when we found him that he had only managed to mutter one intelligible sentence the entire time. Tears filled my eyes now as I remembered it, that moment when they were loading him onto the helicopter and he opened one eye and saw me. *I knew you would come,* he had whispered, and all I could think of now was that his faith in me had been utterly misguided. I hadn't done a very good job of finding him at all—especially considering the fact that his life still hung in the balance. He had already gone into cardiac arrest once, on the helicopter, though they had been able to jolt him back to life with the onboard defibrillator. We could only pray that he would make it through the night, because according to the nurse, that would go a long way in helping to get him from critical to stable.

As the hour grew later, the crowd began to dwindle until it was down to a handful. Worried about her health, I finally insisted that Haley go home. She agreed but promised to return the next day once she was finished with Doug's private funeral. Nathaniel was offered a ride back to Dreiheit with a cousin, and we urged him to take it, to go to his family and his farm. Caleb had stayed here as protection for Lydia, and Rebecca remained simply for support.

Somehow, the four of us—Caleb, Lydia, Rebecca, and I—managed to make it through the night, stretching out on the chairs in the quiet waiting room and sleeping fitfully between updates. Just after dawn, the nurse came and told us that for the first time since he arrived last night, Bobby's vital signs were looking good. The doctors still weren't sure if they would be able to save his leg, but at least it looked as if they had managed to save his life.

Breathing a deep sigh of relief, the four of us simply fell together into a big group hug. Blinking away the tears, I didn't know what I would have done if Bobby hadn't made it.

We still wouldn't be allowed to see him for at least another hour, so I suggested that we go down to the cafeteria and get some breakfast. Lydia insisted she wasn't hungry, so Caleb said he would stay there with her if we would bring him back something. After freshening up in the restroom, Rebecca and I walked together through the maze of hallways until we found the half-empty cafeteria. Grabbing trays, we went down the line and served ourselves and then chose a table by the window. As I sat there sipping coffee and watching the sun rise above the horizon, I felt much better.

Bobby was alive.

Soon, all of our questions would be answered.

As we made our way back to the waiting room, Rebecca carrying the box that held Caleb's breakfast, our small talk turned to quilts. I asked Rebecca if she did much quilting, and if she enjoyed it.

"*Yah,* I like it, but more for the company than anything else," she replied. "It is hard to make myself sit down and do it all alone."

I told her about the family quilt we had discovered when we cleared out my grandparents' belongings in Dreiheit. It had been in the bottom of a trunk, and once we got a good look at it, everyone in the family had been excited about it except me. When the appraiser shared that excitement and suggested that we try to place it with a collector or a museum, I was glad to see it go.

"Why did you not like it?" Rebecca asked. "Was the needlework poor?"

I shook my head, wondering how to explain.

"No, the needlework was fine. And despite its age the fabric was still in pretty good shape. It was the way they carried out the design. The thing had six squares, with a scene in each square. They were supposed to be Bible scenes, but whoever made it had gotten the stories kind of wrong. It bugged me. Like, the first one was obviously supposed to be the story of Moses, but instead of the Jewish girl floating her brother in a basket to Pharoah's daughter, it looked like Pharoah's daughter had put the baby in a basket, covered it up with rocks or something, and was handing it over to the Jewish girl. It was just very, very strange."

Rebecca giggled.

"That was not an Amish quilt. We would never show scenes with people."

"I know. I think that's why it was valuable, because it was so unique."

We reached the waiting room and came around the corner to see Lydia and Caleb sitting together and talking in hushed tones, having what looked to be a very serious conversation. Rebecca had stopped at the water fountain, but I stepped toward them, my stomach clenching at the thought that Bobby had taken a turn for the worse.

When I asked what was going on, they both looked up at me, surprised.

"We are discussing my . . . situation," Caleb said, and then as if to demonstrate he strummed a few licks of air guitar.

I glanced at Lydia, who had tears in her eyes but was smiling.

"Let me just say that many of my prayers have been answered today," she told me.

Just then, the nurse appeared in the doorway to tell us we could see Bobby for five minutes each hour, one at a time. Of course, I deferred to Lydia, but she shook her head.

"I can wait until the next hour," she told me. "You go now. Is more important that you get the answers you need, to find out who did this to Bobby and why."

She was right. I went with the nurse, following as she led me into the intensive care unit and past a nurses' station so high tech that it looked like a NASA Command Center. When we reached a glass door, she opened it to reveal my brother, much cleaner than he had been last night, practically swathed in bandages from head to toe and looking like someone who had just narrowly escaped death. Tears filled my eyes immediately.

"That bad, huh?" he rasped.

Crossing to the bed, I wanted to embrace him but didn't dare. Instead, I just leaned in close and patted the only unbandaged place I could find on his arm.

"No, not that bad. You're alive, that's what counts."

"Ah, Bobanna," he whispered, closing one eye, the other covered with a bandage. "Somehow, I knew you'd grab the first visitation slot."

We both smiled.

"Lydia seemed to think it would be more prudent, considering that we've only got five minutes and a ton of questions for you."

He took a deep breath, the beeps on one of his monitors picking up and then slowing down again.

"No pleasantries, then?" he teased, opening his eye again.

"Sure. You look great, how've you been, done anything interesting lately?" I teased back, twin tears spilling over my smile.

"Ha-ha," he whispered, and I could tell that it hurt for him to talk. "Point taken. And you do look great, by the way. When I saw you last night, I thought you were an angel, there to take me to heaven."

"Sorry. Just a sister, there to get you to the hospital."

He took a few deep breaths, and I used the moment to look around and see the various machines and contraptions that were hooked up to him.

"Who ran you off the road, Bobby?"

"I don't know. A dark car, not too big."

"Who killed Doug?"

"I don't know that, either. He called and told me to meet him there, but when I came in . . ." His voice trailed off as he took another deep breath. "When I came in, he was lying on the floor. Dead. I was checking his pulse just to make sure. Then I heard a noise above me and looked up to see a big box falling toward me. I rolled out of the way in time. And then I left. Fast as I could. But you already knew all of that."

I shook my head.

"No, I didn't know that. I'm sorry Bobby, but I couldn't remember how we were supposed to communicate. I never read whatever you left for me."

He was quiet for a moment and then finally, surprisingly, lifted his pointer fingers and scraped one across the other in a "tsk-tsk" motion.

"You don't remember? You said hide it in plain site. Obscure any words that might flag and post it to a blog or a MySpace or a Facebook."

"What title did you use?"

"What else? It's on Blogspot, under 'bananafanafofana.' "

The door opened, and the nurse peeked inside, warning me that I only had one more minute. When she was gone, I leaned closer to Bobby and spoke in a hurried whisper.

"Did Dr. Updyke modify Isaac's genes?"

Bobby nodded.

"And the new baby's too?"

He shook his head no.

"The embryo tested negative, so he didn't have to."

"Did the doctor do what he did to Isaac with your knowledge, Bobby? Or was he acting on his own?"

"It's all on the blog. Why don't you read that and get back to me?"

"I found your keys, broke into the archives, and stole a file with the name of

'Jensen' on it. I thought it would be about Isaac, but instead it was about me."

"You?" Bobby asked, so startled that he jerked his head up off the pillow. Wincing sharply, he lowered it back down. "Why you?"

"I was hoping you could tell me. I was never treated at the WIRE in my life."

"Sorry, sis. I have no idea."

I could see the nurse hovering, but I wasn't ready to go.

"Who do you think did this to you, Bobby? Who do you suspect?"

He closed his eye and exhaled a ragged breath.

"I spent four days in that black pit with nothing to do but think. Even after all of that, your guess is as good as mine. All I know is it had to be someone who would—"

"Time's up," the nurse said, opening the door.

"Someone who would benefit heavily from keeping things quiet," he finished.

"Updyke?" I asked.

"I hope not."

"Mr. Wynn?"

"I doubt it."

"Reed Thornton?" I suggested.

Bobby's eye flew open on that one. But before he could say anything else, the nurse took me by the elbow and escorted me from the room.

FORTY-ONE

Back in the waiting room, Lydia peppered me with questions, but I didn't want to take the time to respond. More than anything, I needed access to the Internet, to find the letter Bobby had posted on an anonymous blog that had been intended for me.

I answered what I could for Lydia about how Bobby looked and sounded, but then I told her I had to do something and that I would be back soon. Without waiting for her reply, I raced to the elevator and took it to the first floor. At the information desk, I asked where I could find a computer to go online. The woman gestured toward a single workstation in the corner.

There, I accessed the Internet and typed in the web address where I would find Bobby's secret message to me. As one simple blog among hundreds of thousands, it could have sat unnoticed by anyone else forever. As he said, it was hidden in plain sight.

When the page pulled up, it featured exactly one post, albeit a long one. I skimmed it quickly in its entirely and then went back and reread it again, more slowly. For security reasons, Bobby had used a lot of initials and abbreviations. To make it easier to understand, I copied the post and pasted it into a text file, and then I inserted my guesses as to what he meant by each abbreviation. Once I had done that, it was easier to read, and I studied the letter carefully.

Hey sis, glad you found me! If you're here, you know I managed to use your suggestions to go under.

Here's the deal: Dr. Updyke has been going outside the bounds ethically

and legally with his work at the WIRE for a long time. I figured it out 10 yrs. ago, after Lydia had a miscarriage at 11 weeks. Being an employee at the WIRE, prenatal testing was free and easy, so before we tried again, I did basic work-ups on both of us. Not surprised to find that Lydia was a carrier for WKS, but shocked to learn that I WAS TOO! Couldn't figure that one out, but now I have. Long story, bottom line, several generations in our family tree married into the Lancaster County Amish, and the bad gene got passed down. You might want to get checked too.

Anyway, I wanted to try again at having children, but what to do? Couldn't take another miscarriage, much less still-born from WKS. Talked to Dr. Updyke, who offered to use gene therapy on the next one. He said past experiments had failed, but that was because he could only treat after the child was born or in utero. He said if he could modify at the eight-cell level and inseminate artificially, we could have a child free from WKS.

At that point, after what he told me, I'd like to say that I blew the whistle, but I didn't. Instead, I took advantage of his knowledge so that our next one could have a chance at a normal life. Don't judge me too harshly—when you want kids as badly as we did, you're willing to do a lot of things you wouldn't think of otherwise. Here's the part even I can't justify: Lydia doesn't know, never did. We tricked her. Going to explain it to her tonight, hope she'll find some way to forgive me.

Anyway, Dr. Updyke was right, Isaac was born disorder free. He's been healthy for 8 yrs. Was ready to repeat the procedure with the child Lydia carries now, but as it turned out, we didn't need to.

But then a few months ago, Isaac's health started failing. Did a swab while he was sleeping, and he tested negative for WKS. So what is it? What's wrong with him? I don't know! Dr. Updyke says not to worry, but I can't help it.

A few weeks ago, I thought if I could get a look at the experiments that had gone wrong in the past, that I could maybe talk to the families or at least read the case notes and figure out some way to help my son. Dr. Updyke wouldn't let me access those files, though, so I broke into the archives and tried to take them anyway. Big mistake. Not only was I caught and suspended, but the only information I was able to get were dates of the procedures, not names.

Once I was on suspension, I spent a lot of time studying the problem, first trying to trace our roots so I could know where the WKS had come from, and then trying to study the variations and mutations of the disorder. Lots of work but turned up nothing. Finally, last week I called Doug. Met him for lunch, told him the whole truth, asked if he could use his security clearance to get the info for me on those other patients.

When I got home tonight there were two messages from Doug on the phone,

both pretty urgent. He said he had gotten the info I wanted, plus some I didn't expect. I don't know what he meant by that. His message said to meet at the new Wynn Industries building, but when I got there, he was dead, and then somebody tried to do me in as well. Don't know who, never saw a face, took off running.

That's where I am now. Anna, you know I can't go to the authorities on this. They're not going to listen to an ex-con, especially one previously convicted of involuntary manslaughter! They're not going to take my word against a world-renowned scientist or the owner of the company or whoever killed Doug and tried to kill me. Afraid I may even be framed for his death.

All I know is that by stirring the pot in an attempt to save my son, it looks like the secret of Dr. Updyke's work is getting out—and things are dangerous. Right now, because Isaac is the only living proof of Dr. Updyke's illegal gene therapy, I have no choice but to take him and Lydia out of here and keep them safe until I can get real proof and make that whistle blow loud and clear.

If for some reason we don't make it, you have to take it from here. Tell the authorities that we know there's proof at Wynn headquarters because Doug found it and tried to bring it to me. He died for it, in fact. Tell them to exhume the bodies of the babies from the failed experiments, and all the proof they need will be there in their messed-up DNA.

Talk to Reed Thornton about it. This is what he does, hunts down the rule breakers like Dr. Updyke. Trust no one else but Reed!

Sorry to throw all this on you, Bobanna, but it's life or death right now. Am using what you taught me to create a very confusing mess and buy time. When I get back to Dreiheit tonight, I'm going to take Lydia and Isaac and disappear.

Respond in kind, I'll know where to look. Sorry for being so obscure, but I learned from the best. Be careful. Stay in touch you-know-how.

Bobby

There was a printer connected to the computer, so I printed out the entire thing, folded it, and put it in my purse. Before I walked away from the computer, however, I erased all of the browser history, including the hidden cache. That post really had been for my eyes only.

Though Bobby's letter certainly fleshed things out, it still didn't answer some of my most fundamental questions. Thinking about all we still didn't know, I stood and was about to move to the elevator when the lobby doors whooshed open and Reed Thornton came walking in. With him was the man of the hour himself, Dr. Updyke.

Shrinking back as much as possible, I watched as the two men walked purposefully across the lobby and down a hallway. They talked as they went, and though I would have given anything to hear what they were saying, I didn't know how I could get close enough without being seen.

Still, I had to know what they were doing and where they were going. As discreetly as possible, I tagged along behind, slipping around corners and hiding behind vending machines. When they went through a "Staff

Only" door, I waited a beat and then went through it too, just in time to see them step into a room off to the right. Inching forward, I read the sign on the door they had gone through: Department of Neurogenetics, Diagnostic Laboratory.

Taking a chance, I looked in the window. The room was like a big lab, though it seemed to be empty except for the two of them. They were at the far end and were obviously discussing a piece of equipment, one that looked like a small, black copy machine connected to a computer workstation.

Watching the backs of both of their heads, I pushed lightly on the door. It opened without making a sound, so I slipped inside and easily moved behind a large metal cabinet. From there, I could hear what they were saying, and as long as no one else came walking into the room, I didn't think they would ever realize I was there.

Pressing myself into the tight space, I listened carefully, though most of what they were saying was so technical that I didn't understand it. From what I could tell, they had come in there to look at a specific piece of equipment similar to one Dr. Updyke was thinking about getting for the WIRE. He wanted to show Reed a few things about it, and it sounded as though the lab coordinator had given them permission to be there since they were coming to the hospital anyway to visit Bobby.

Dr. Updyke was describing some of the WIRE's plans to Reed, rhapsodizing about the various ways that new equipment could enhance their work. The two men talked money for a while, the doctor saying that he could buy a new house with what some of the machines in this lab cost.

"They are worth it, though," Reed replied, "especially when you compare what you're saving in man-hours."

"Oh, yeah. Remember the old days? What we had to go through for sequencing? This baby can handle almost four hundred samples at a time."

"Impressive."

"Then there was the amount of time spent disabling viruses," the doctor said with a laugh. "Remember that?"

"Remember? Are you kidding? That's mostly what I did the whole summer I worked for you."

"That's right. What were we using back then? Pox?"

"Primarily, yes. Cowpox."

The doctor went on to talk about more ways technology had improved, but all I could think was *cowpox*?

That must have been what was on the person's skin in the photo.

Cowpox.

So many questions were racing through my mind that I didn't hear much of what they said next until Bobby's name was mentioned. Perking up, I listened as the two men came walking closer, and it sounded as though they were now going upstairs to see him.

Considering what I knew—and didn't know—about Dr. Updyke and the WIRE and Reed, there was simply no way these men were going to get anywhere near my brother, not if I could help it. I thought about pushing over the cabinet to block them, or running into the hall to shout for the police. Instead, before I could do either, the door suddenly swung open and a man in a white lab coat came into the room.

He smiled at the two men but then did a double take when he saw me hiding nearby. Before he could react, I had no choice but to step out from my hiding place. Grabbing the nearest thing I could find, a square metal box, I held it up in the air and told the man in the lab coat to go get security or I would throw the box on the floor. My hope was that it was a ten-thousand-dollar piece of equipment or something, and that he would be so startled and compliant that the situation would soon be under control.

Instead, he just looked at me as though I were crazy and said that if I wanted to throw his lunchbox on the floor, could he please take his soda out first?

Feeling my face flush, I set the box on the counter and asked him to please, please go get hospital security. With a glance from me to the other two men, he left.

"Anna, what are you doing?" Reed asked.

Instead of replying, I simply reached into my purse, unzipped the inner pocket, and pulled out the photo.

"This was in Kate Schumann's medical file from 1997," I said, holding it up so that they could both see. "Would one of you like to tell me what sort of genetic engineering you were involved with back then, and what cowpox had to do with it?"

Both men were quite startled. Reed held out a hand and I reluctantly gave him the photo, though I lied and said I had already made a bunch of copies and put them in a safe place. As he studied the picture, he explained that disabled viruses were often used in gene therapy, to help carry new genes into cells and then replicate.

"You're saying that a person is intentionally injected with a virus?" I asked incredulously.

"A disabled virus," Reed corrected.

"The virus in that picture doesn't look too disabled to me," I said.

Reed looked questioningly at Dr. Updyke, who merely pursed his lips and shook his head as if to say he wasn't talking.

"What did you do to Isaac Jensen?" I demanded of the doctor, a surge of anger rising up inside of me. "Is he going to die? Was whatever you're doing down at the WIRE worth killing Doug for and trying to kill Bobby for?"

"Whoa," the doctor said, holding up both hands. "Nobody killed anybody here."

"Stop lying! You're out of control, doctor. You have to be stopped! What's wrong with Isaac? Why did you kill Doug? Why was that photo in Kate Schumann's file?"

I thought maybe if I kept questioning him around in circles, eventually he would break. Before I had that chance, however, the door burst open and a number of men came spilling in, each of them bearing guns pointed firmly at the doctor.

Somehow, I didn't think they were mere hospital security.

As Dr. Updyke raised both hands into the air, the main gunman held up a badge and announced they were with the FBI. From the look on Updyke's face, he was disdainful of the entire situation and quite irritated by all the fuss. That irritation seemed to fade into resignation, however, as he slowly seemed to understand that the jig was finally up.

"Oh, fine," the doctor said, speaking directly to me. "Kate Schumann's fetus had WKS, which I attempted to remedy in utero via gene therapy. Unfortunately, at some point during gestation, the disabled virus re-enabled itself. The infant carried to term but wasn't viable at birth. That's a photo of the baby. It was born dead, covered with pox."

I gasped, realizing that the situation the night of the fire had been even more tragic than we'd thought. Not only had Lydia's mother delivered her child stillborn, but the infant's body had been horribly riddled with cowpox.

Now it was Reed's turn to look angry.

"You really used the viruses we were disabling for human trials? Illegal human trials?"

"I was making progress. At least the genetic material didn't integrate into the wrong place in the genome."

"You mean like it did the time before," Reed demanded, "when it landed on the tumor suppressor gene and induced a fatal tumor in a three-month-old baby?"

"Yes. That was unfortunate."

While I was relieved to hear the doctor confess, I was more concerned about what was going on in the here and now.

"What did you do to Isaac?" I demanded.

"The in vitro procedure done to Isaac

Jensen was one hundred percent successful," the doctor announced haughtily. "I have been telling Bobby for weeks that his son's problems are medically predictable and not progressive. He just wouldn't believe me."

"That's because the child has obvious complications," Reed said.

"Those complications are a necessary evil, a side effect of protecting the germline. Say what you will, at least I acted responsibly."

I looked from the doctor to Reed.

"What's the germline?" I asked.

Reed explained that it had to do with subsequent generations of genetically modified people. According to him, that was the biggest unknown in genetic tampering, how genes that were altered now might manifest themselves in future generations.

"How can you say that you acted responsibly?" I demanded of the doctor.

"I inserted an extra chromosome along the X axis. Isaac is XXY."

Reed's eyes narrowed as he glared at the doctor.

"Klinefelter's?" he whispered incredulously. "You gave that child Klinefelter's syndrome on purpose?"

"Most men with Klinefelter's grow up perfectly normal and never even know they have it. In many cases, symptoms can be mild or even nonexistent," Dr. Updyke said.

"What's Klinefelter's?" I asked, my heart in my throat.

"It's is a chromosomal disorder that can cause difficulty with speech, reading, and writing," Reed explained. "Dr. Updyke is correct in saying that Isaac won't degenerate into a worse state, but he will always have to live with the hurdles he is dealing with now."

"But why?" I demanded, looking from Reed to Dr. Updyke. "Why give someone a disorder that would do that to him?"

"To make sure he'll be sterile," Reed said sadly, shaking his head. "Men with Klinefelter's syndrome usually can't have children. This way, Isaac won't pass on his altered genes to the next generation."

The doctor nodded, a noble smirk on his face. I simply stared at him in shock. This man was nothing less than a monster.

"What gives you the right to play God this way?" I whispered.

"I have dueled with the double helix and won," Dr. Updyke replied. "For all intents and purposes, my dear, I *am* God."

FORTY-TWO

After meeting with the FBI, Dr. Updyke confessed to having conducted illegal genetic modification on three different patients: the infant who lived for three months but then died of a tumor, Kate Schumann's stillborn baby, and Isaac Jensen. He refused to confess to the murder of Doug Brown or the attempted murder of Bobby Jensen, but I felt sure the FBI would get that out of him eventually as well.

By the time they led him away in handcuffs, I still hadn't had the nerve to ask about the file I had found with my name on it. I simply couldn't bring it up in front of so many people. I hoped to deal with it soon more privately, beyond Reed's listening ears.

As for Reed, I was astounded to see that the remaining members of the FBI were treating him like a hero, patting his back and shaking his hand and saying it looked like a job well done. I started to object, to tell them about the stocks, but when I did, they just laughed.

"So this is her, huh?" one of the men asked Reed. "The one you were talking about?"

"Yep. Can't you tell by the obstinate posture? The suspicious glare? The judgmental scowl? This is her all right, and if you don't mind, Lieutenant, we'd like a moment alone."

With a wink, the man slipped from the lab. As the door shut behind him, Reed began pacing in anger.

"Honestly, Anna, I don't know what to do with you. Stocks? You thought I was a murderer because I bought stock in Wynn Industries?"

"I didn't go that far with it. I just told the police—"

"Yeah, the police! Did it ever cross your

mind to come to me and ask me about things first? I would have gladly explained. But no! You had to jump to all sorts of horrible conclusions. I was dumbfounded when they told me. I thought we knew each other. I thought we—" He stopped short and simply looked at me.

"You thought we what?"

"Nothing. It doesn't matter. The case is wrapping up nicely now. The FBI has it under control. You don't need to play detective anymore."

It was my turn to be appalled.

"'Play detective?' You think I was *playing* when I found my brother? When I went back to the very place where the police missed him, only I found him?"

Reed shook his head.

"That's not what I meant. I just—" Again, he stopped short, looked at me sharply, and folded his arms across his chest. "Fine. You want to know about the stocks? I'll tell you. I started buying stock in Wynn Industries two months ago as part of a joint investigation between my office and the FBI. We knew that becoming a large minority stockholder would give me access to the things we needed to see from the inside. Yes, I own stock there—but as part of this investigation. Don't believe me? Fine."

Before I could say whether I did or not, Reed opened the door and waved his buddy back in. From the look on the man's face, I could tell he was trying to suppress a smile as he verified what Reed had just told me, assuring me that the entire transaction was on the up and up.

"Why are you trying so hard not to smile?" I asked the man. "This is funny to you?"

"No, ma'am," he said, allowing the grin to break out in full force. "We've just never seen Dr. Thornton get quite so . . . worked up . . . over a woman before. If I didn't know better, I'd swear you hurt his feelings."

"Thank you, Lieutenant. That will be all," Reed said, nearly pushing him back out of the room. As the door swung closed again, I realized that what the guy had said was true. By doubting Reed's integrity, I had hurt his feelings.

"Reed, please don't be angry. This is what I do. I'm a skip tracer. I have to think the worst of people sometimes. That's how I'm able to dig out the truth."

"I understand that," he replied. "But this is me, Anna. You thought the worst of me."

I stepped closer.

"Years ago, I did the opposite, Reed. I thought only the best of you, and look where that got me. Isn't it time I looked at you with my eyes wide open, able to see both the good and the bad? I really am sorry I hurt your feelings. But I still think this was a step in the right direction for me. For us."

We looked at each other for a long moment.

"Is there an us?" he asked.

"I don't know. Is there?"

How can there be an us if there's still a her?

Slowly, Reed reached up and placed a hand on the side of my face.

"I have a lot of flaws, Anna. I leave wet towels on the floor. Sometimes I get so caught up in my work I don't get home till midnight. I've even been known to wear the same shirt for three days in a row on vacation."

His movements deliberate, Reed placed the other hand on the opposite side of my face, his fingers weaving themselves aggressively into my hair. Suddenly, I wanted nothing more than for him to kiss me, to mold his mouth hungrily against mine.

"Just don't ever, ever question my integrity again, okay?" he asked softly, and I nodded as he moved his lips so close to mine I could almost taste them. "If I had no integrity, Anna, don't you think I would have kissed you by now?"

He held his pose for a long moment. Then, finally, he pulled back and slid his hands from my hair, leaving me to stand there in surprise.

"See? Integrity. I've got tons of it," he said, and then he turned and left the room.

I didn't see him after that. The place was simply buzzing with FBI agents, and when I found Lydia upstairs, she had just learned the truth about Dr. Updyke and what he had done to Isaac. She was weeping in her brother's arms, probably tears of sadness and joy all rolled into one.

Feeling suddenly claustrophobic, I knew I needed to get out of the hospital. I wanted to be alone for a while in the quiet, where I could think. After making sure Lydia was okay, I told her I was going to run back to the farm for a while. Caleb opted to stay at the hospital, but Rebecca asked if she could catch a ride with me.

All the way back to the farm, as I drove, I kept thinking about the things I had learned today. My emotions flitted from relief that Isaac wasn't dying to anger that he would never be able to father children to joy that at least he hadn't died of WKS as an infant to frustration at Bobby for letting Dr. Updyke play God on his own offspring. I didn't know how things were going at the hospital between Bobby and Lydia, but he had a lot of explaining to do. Given that she was a woman of character, not to mention raised Amish, I had no doubt that she would find it in her heart to forgive him. My bigger concern was that they needed to deal with the fact that Bobby had willingly deceived his wife, an act that had resulted in nearly fatal consequences.

Rebecca had questions about what had happened, so I recapped the whole story for her. When I got to the part about the Amish infant who died from a tumor, I was surprised to hear that Rebecca knew who I was talking about.

"*Yah,* I think I remember that," she said.

"Weren't those the parents who stole their own baby's body?"

When she said that, something clicked in my memory and the whole fuzzy situation came sharply into focus. Of course! There had been a big scandal when that baby died, not because of the tumor but because the state required an autopsy whenever a death was sudden and unexplained. The Amish didn't believe in autopsies, however, and had tried to prevent it. When the court ruled in favor of the coroner, the baby's body disappeared before the autopsy could be done. All that had been left behind was an anonymous note, one that said that because of their religion, they could not in good conscience allow the baby's body to be violated.

That case had made the papers all the way over in Hidden Springs. From what I could recall, everyone suspected the parents of having stolen their own child's body, though they repeatedly denied it. The last thing I had heard, the couple had ended up moving out to Ohio, and the body had never been found. Once again, Dr. Updyke's genetic tampering had led to much heartbreak and misery.

It was almost one p.m. by the time we got to the farm. As we climbed out of the car, we could see Grete and Isaac out by the washhouse, working to hang their colorful laundry on the line, the ever-present bodyguard standing nearby. I thought of my dream, the recurring nightmare that had seemed to come and go over the years. There was always a clothesline in the dream, the deep maroons, purples, and blues of Amish laundry flapping in the wind. I hadn't had the dream since coming here, and I had to wonder if it would return now that I had been back and faced my past.

Rebecca went out to join them, but I proceeded into the house. It was quiet and empty, the kitchen cozy and warm as usual. I was just hungry enough to make myself at home, so I peeked in the propane-powered refrigerator and grabbed some cheese and a handful of grapes before going upstairs to change clothes and freshen up. Once I was dressed, I leaned across the bed to raise the window blinds and let in the brilliant winter sun. From my vantage point there, I could see the roofs of several of the smaller outbuildings and beyond that the back fields. In the distance were the trees on the land that had once belonged to my grandparents.

As I stood and looked out at the serene landscape, I thought about those two babies from long ago, the one whose body was stolen and the other whose body was burned. Gazing at the scene outside, thinking about the distance between where I stood now and where our group had been when we shot off the Roman candles that fateful night eleven years ago, it suddenly seemed incredulous to me that the fire had, indeed, been an accident.

In most of our trials, the distance had been a key point in our defense. But every time it came up, the prosecution would trot out an expert witness who would testify that such a long-distance spark from a roman candle would be “possible, though not probable.” That element of possibility, along with the irrefutable evidence of spent casings, had been enough to bring about convictions across the board. But that was when we all thought it had been an accident.

Now that there could have been a motive for the fire that night, the entire course of events seemed to shift before my eyes.

The realization hit me now with such force that I actually had to sit down on the edge of the bed.

What if we hadn't caused the fire that killed Lydia's parents after all?

What if the fire had been set intentionally by Dr. Updyke to hide the fact that the baby's body was covered with cowpox?

What if he had seized the opportunity of our reckless behavior by using a Roman candle as the source of ignition to start the fire at the *Dawdy Haus* on purpose?

I knew I had to talk to someone about this, someone else who had suffered as I had for the past eleven years, burdened with guilt and self-hate and grief and shame for a tragedy that we may not have caused after all.

I needed to talk to someone from the Dreiheit Five.

My cell phone was still dead, so I decided to go out into the field and use the phone shanty. I practically ran, skirting past the washhouse and the barn, dialing Reed's cell phone as soon as I got inside. My call went straight into his cell phone's voice mail, so I left a message, one that grew more excited as I talked, telling him my theory.

There was no way to reach Bobby, of course, and Lydia couldn't have her phone on in the hospital.

That left Haley. I didn't know her number by heart, but I called information and they put me through. When she answered, she said she had just arrived at home from Doug's funeral and was thinking about heading back over to the hospital to sit with me and Lydia. I told her to come out here instead, as there was something extremely important we needed to discuss.

"Of course, Anna. I can do that. What's this all about?"

"Wait till you get here. I'll explain it then."

Back in the house, as I waited for Haley to drive over from Hidden Springs, I was practically jumping out of my skin. I should have calmed my nervous energy by helping the others with the laundry outside, but I needed some time of solitude to wrap my head around this shocking new reality. Instead, I grabbed a broom and a dustpan and went to work, sweeping the entire downstairs.

Eventually, Grete came inside by herself to make some tea and learn more about what had happened down at the hospital. Rebecca had tried to fill her in outside but hadn't wanted to say much in front of Isaac. I hated the thought of having to go through the story twice, so I was glad when Haley showed up then and I could tell them both together.

Haley seemed uncomfortable coming into the house after all these years, but the warmth with which Grete welcomed her was both commendable and touching. Over mugs of hot tea, the three of us sat at the table as I recounted for them much of what we had learned today. When I got to the part about the night of the fire, about Grete's mother delivering the child and it being born dead and covered in cowpox, I was afraid the very thought might be too upsetting for Grete, but she seemed to take it okay. I explained that the procedure Dr. Updyke had claimed was an amniocentesis all those years ago had in fact been a genetic modification of the fetus that had gone terribly wrong.

I went on to tell them about the other genetically modified Amish baby, the one who had died of a tumor at three months and whose body disappeared in anticipation of a court-ordered autopsy. Both of them remembered that incident well.

Glancing at Haley, I told her that this next part was why I had asked her to come here.

"I have a theory," I said, "one that just came to me a little while ago. I don't think that child's parents stole that body so that it couldn't be autopsied. I think Dr. Updyke took it instead and left that note to cast suspicion away from himself by mentioning the Amish religion."

"That's terrible."

"Furthermore," I continued, looking at Grete, "I'm beginning to believe that the fire that burned down the *Dawdy Haus* and killed your parents was not started by a bunch of Roman candles that we set off way out in the back of the back fields. I think someone needed to destroy that newborn's body too, and so they took advantage of the situation and set this house on fire intentionally, making it look like an accident when in fact it was intentional. It was arson."

The news hit Grete and Haley in completely opposite ways. Grete seemed deeply disturbed by it, and I couldn't blame her. Where before the fire had been a tragic mistake, now her parents had been the victims of an intentional evil.

To Haley, the news came as the stunning, incredible realization that maybe, just maybe the biggest mistake of her life had not really played out the way everyone assumed that it had. Suddenly, an agonized sob burst from her throat.

"To think, poor Doug never had the chance to know this before he died," she cried.

"I wouldn't be so sure, Haley. The night Doug died, he was the one who discovered all of this evidence and even faxed a copy of it down to Reed in Washington. Then he offered to meet Bobby and give the information to him as well. I know you and Doug had your moments, but I have to say, I believe he died knowing this. To be honest, he died a hero."

Haley was so overcome with emotion, she excused herself and went to the restroom. She stayed there for a while, the sink running to drown out the sound of her sobs. I hoped that they were good sobs, tears of relief and not just of grief.

Grete handled her emotions in a different way. She simply got up from the table, excused herself, and went to her room.

Left there alone, I busied myself in the kitchen, washing our mugs at the sink, wiping the water from the counter. With Haley still crying in the bathroom, I moved on to the sitting area and straightened the slipcover on the couch, picked up some of Isaac's toys, and gathered his storybooks into a pile.

One was a book of Bible stories, and I absently flipped through it, looking at the vivid pictures, thinking how God always had things under control even when it didn't feel like it. Turning the pages through the story of Moses brought to mind the conversation I had had with Rebecca early this morning at the hospital, about the family quilt that had been discovered among my grandparents' possessions and was now housed in the Folk Art Museum in Lancaster.

Maybe it was my afternoon for epiphanies, but suddenly I had another realization, and this one seemed almost too incredible to be true. I put down the book, called to Haley that I'd be back in a minute, and ran full speed out to the phone shanty. There, I dialed the number for Remy Villefranche and excitedly told him that I may have a lead on the Beauharnais Rubies at last.

"Do you remember the quilt I told you about? The handmade one that my family donated to the Folk Art Museum?"

"Yes."

"Remy, it's just a hunch, but I think the quilt might lead us to the rubies. Are you still in town? Are you free right now?"

"Yes, I'm still in town. And as to whether or not I'm free, do you even have to ask?"

With so much going on, I didn't want to leave the farm and take time to meet him at the museum, but I asked Remy if he could run over there by himself with a camera, snap some pictures of the quilt, and then come here. I thought we could study the images together and see if they didn't give us some sort of lead—if not to where the rubies were now, at least to where they had been once upon a time. Without hesitation, Remy agreed to hit the road right away. After hanging up, I ran back toward the house and past the clothesline, ducking under a big sheet that was flapping noisily in the wind. Rebecca and Isaac were nearby, and as I passed them I grabbed their hands and spun them around.

I didn't know why I was so happy. I didn't know why I suddenly felt as though weights were lifting off of me. All I knew was that my brother had been found, I had a lead on the jewels, and most important of all, there was a very real chance that the truth I had believed about myself for the past eleven years had, in fact, been a lie.

FORTY-THREE

STEPHANIE

September 7, 1812

To Your Highness, Duchess Stephanie de Beauharnais:

It is with warm greetings that my wife and I write this letter. Our answer is yes. We accept with great honor and humility the responsibility that is being bestowed upon us. As for details, perhaps the same method of conveyance for this letter could be employed to convey the "item" in question. It is our sincere prediction that after you give birth to your son, you will develop a deep craving for schnitz pie, and that you will insist on at least seven or eight pounds' worth. I would be grateful to deliver that basket to you myself, as I would like to meet the new prince or princess in person and pay to him or her my deepest respects.

In Christ's Name,
Samuel Jensen

FORTY-FOUR

Anna

There was still a little juice left in my laptop, so when Remy finally arrived an hour later, we uploaded his photos of the quilt. Both Haley and Grete had rejoined me in the kitchen by then, and though Grete busied herself with making dinner, Haley sat with Remy and me at the table. For a moment, I wondered if I was being disrespectful to my hosts by using a computer in their home, but I then decided that it was probably okay for the time being since it was running off of battery power.

When the pictures finished loading, we studied them on the screen, zooming in wherever necessary. Suddenly, the quilt that had seemed so unattractive and incompetent before took on an entirely different luster in this new light.

The first panel featured the Moses scene, including a river, a princess, a commoner, a baby in a basket, and even bullrushes. On the river bank to the right was embroidered a small, red fire. I still didn't understand why there were brown rocks on top of the baby in the basket, but I had to assume that had something to do with how Stephanie de Beauharnais and the Jensen family had made the switch.

Without knowing the truth behind the picture, it really did look as though it had been designed to tell the story of Moses. Looking at it with new eyes, however, the babe in the basket clearly wasn't Moses at all, but the son of Stephanie de Beauharnais and her husband, Karl Friedrich, Grand Duke of Baden.

The second panel, which we had always thought was supposed to represent Noah's ark, was instead the scene of the two couples on a ship as they sailed across the ocean to America. This time, the red fire was shown burning on the bottom deck of the ship, inside a wooden box.

The third panel, which we had assumed represented David tending his sheep on a hillside in Bethlehem was probably the newly located Amish farmer, Karl Jensen, tending his sheep in Lancaster County. The red fire in that square burned just under the roof of the house, along a dotted line surely meant to represent the attic.

The fourth panel, which we had taken to be the story of the Prodigal Son leaving home was more than likely either a depiction of Peter Jensen leaving the Amish religion, or his son William Jensen heading off to sell some of the jewels. Either way, in that picture the man carried the red fire with him, burning brightly from a lantern he held in his hand as he waved goodbye.

The fifth panel looked to be an Amish barn raising, the bare skeleton of a house just going up. Under the house was a large gray square, and we had assumed that it represented Jesus' admonition that a wise man builds his house upon a rock. In that panel, the fire burned under a nearby tree.

The sixth and final panel featured a man

standing with his arms outstretched, surrounded on all sides by odd red columns. That had always been the hardest one to decipher, but by the positioning of the man's arms, he seemed to represent Christ on the cross.

Instead, I realized now, the man was simply holding out his hands to emphasize what surrounded him: five fireplaces. In the center fireplace burned the red fire.

"The rubies were hidden in a fireplace," I said.

"But that doesn't make sense," Remy replied, shaking his head. "Extreme fluctuations of heat can damage jewels. No one would ever use a fireplace to store such a valuable treasure."

Remy clicked to the next picture. "This was the write-up on the wall plaque beside the quilt," he said.

I skimmed the text that thanked our family for the acquisition, though I was surprised to read that the museum's curators had determined that each panel had been sewn by a different person. As the various fabrics traced back to a wide range of dates, they had concluded that the quilt was assembled over several generations.

Perhaps each time the oldest Jensen son took a bride, she was given the opportunity and the responsibility to add her favorite Bible story to the montage, the write-up said.

What it should have said was that each time the oldest Jensen son took a bride, she was given the news about the priceless set of rubies that were being passed down through the family, and it was her responsibility to identify the rubies' hiding place by sewing it onto the quilt in the guise of a Bible story.

We all stared at that photo, trying to make sense of it. "Go back to the fireplace scene again," I said.

Remy did as I asked, and again we stared at the image, trying to make sense of it. Even Grete finally joined us to take a peek.

"This is supposed to represent your grandparents' old house? Because I do not know why there are five fireplaces in the picture when there were only four chimneys on the house."

Stunned, Remy and I looked at each other and then at Grete.

"Are you sure?" Remy asked.

"*Yah.* I grew up in the bedroom at the top of the stairs here and looked out my window at the silhouette of that house every day of my life until they took it away."

I stood and grabbed my coat, urging the others to do the same.

"Where are we going?" Haley asked.

"On a treasure hunt. Come on."

Outside, the four of us stopped at the toolshed to gather a sledgehammer, a chisel, and a crowbar, and then I called out for Rebecca and Isaac to come with us. Our actions caught the attention of the press as well, and soon they were skirting around the edges of the property, trying to see where we were going in such a hurry. Nathaniel was working on his tractor out in the field, and when he saw us, he came along too.

We quickly marched as a group across the fields to the old homestead and down into the open-air basement. Just as in the picture, there were five fireplaces down there, remnants of the house's old heating system. Only four of them were stained with soot.

Handing Remy the sledgehammer, I offered him the first whack. His gleeful blows didn't do much to advance our cause, however, so eventually he handed the heavy tool over to Nathaniel, who attacked the chimney with gusto once Grete explained that an old family treasure might be hidden inside.

We all moved back and watched with rapt attention as the structure began to crumble brick by brick, each piece falling to the ground with a plink. Finally, when I was starting to give up hope, a different sound made a hollow thunk, and then suddenly a square wooden box dropped from inside the remaining structure. Hands shaking, I knelt down and grabbed the box, lifted it up, and dusted it off. Opening the lid revealed soft fabric inside. Carefully, I raised a corner of the fabric and gasped. Nestled among the folds was the most astonishing, sparkly, brilliant, glittery diamond-and-ruby necklace I had ever seen.

"There's something else!" Remy whispered, pointing at a square of paper that poked up from the corner.

Breathlessly, and with as much care as possible, Remy rooted down through the box, proclaiming that under the jewels there looked to be some documents and letters. He slipped out the top one and gingerly unfolded it.

"It's dated July 21, 1831, to 'My Dearest Son' and signed at the bottom, 'Sincerely, Your mother, SdB'!" Remy looked at me, his eyes filled with the glow of our reward. The treasure hunter had persisted all the way to the prize.

"What does it say?" Haley asked.

"'My Dearest Son, I have received your latest communication, and I find it as baffling as your previous missives. While I appreciate that you are a man of the land, a worker, and a husband, I also do not think you appreciate the extent to which I have sacrificed in order to keep you safe until this time. Worker or not, husband or not, whether you want to or not, it is time to assume the throne!'" Remy paused in his reading, swallowed hard, and kept going. "Next paragraph says, 'I truly thought that once you read my journal entries from all those years ago, you would understand and accept your duty in this matter. Leopold now has plans to marry a princess of Badenese descent, which will be the final step in making him eligible for the crown. His coronation will likely begin soon after that, the event that Luise has plotted and schemed over for many years. All it will take to stop it, my son, is for the truth of your birthright to be revealed. I do not understand your refusal in this matter! You speak of being content with the life you lead now. Need I remind you that a royal's first obligation is not to his own contentment but to the service of his people?' "

Again, Remy stopped reading, almost as if to let his brain catch up with the words that spelled out the exact theory he had held about the fate of Karl and Stephanie's firstborn male son since the beginning.

" 'To make matters more complicated,' " Remy continued, " 'Kaspar Hauser continues to gain popularity each day, and all the world awaits for me to weigh in on this matter of whether or not he is my son. He is a sad creature and an oddity for sure, but he is not the man who needs to come home and take up his grandfather's legacy. Make no mistake, Karl Stephan: You are. Please, do the honorable thing and come back to us now. Sincerely, Your mother, SdB.' "

When Remy set the letter down, his eyes were shining, and we were all speechless.

In a way, I was more excited about the letters than I was about the jewels. Just looking at them there, sitting in their folded, beribboned pile inside the jewelry box, I felt a connection to the past, a link to Stephanie de Beauharnais, the woman who had been my six-greats grandmother. I wanted to read them all, and right away, but Remy begged me not to touch them, saying that they needed to be handled in the proper conditions or they could disintegrate in our hands.

Finally, with a deep sigh of satisfaction, he closed the lid.

"I do believe," Remy said, "that not only do I now have what I need for the last chapter of *Nowhere to Be Found: Lost Jewels and Antiquities,* I also have the first chapter for my next book: *Nowhere to Be Found: Missing Missives.*"

Climbing up out of the basement, I was amazed to see a whole line of cars and people watching from the road. As much as I hated the press, when I spotted a dark green van driving slowly past, I couldn't have loved them more. Cupping my hands around my mouth, I shouted out to the whole lot of them, asking who wanted an exclusive.

They all cheered and waved their arms, so I yelled again.

"I'll give a full interview, with pictures, to whoever can stop that van and keep those people captive until the police get here. They're criminals!"

En masse, the crowd moved in, so many bodies blocking the way that the driver of the van had no choice but to surrender. Considering how many reporters it took to subdue the people inside, I wasn't sure how I would sort out my promised reward, but I was just relieved that for now we were safe.

With the "accosteswabbers'" plan for sweeping in and taking the jewels obviously foiled, for the first time in my life I could honestly say I absolutely loved the press.

FORTY-FIVE

At Remy's suggestion, I borrowed Isaac's bodyguard and drove into town to a bank, where I rented a safety deposit box for the jewels and the documents. Back at the house, Remy had thoroughly photographed and cataloged the entire set, but the letters remained in their bundle until such time as we could meet with an expert and have them safely duplicated so they could be read without damaging them. I had no idea how our family would be proceeding with the jewels, but that was a question better left for another day.

With all the fun of our discovery, it had been easy to forget that Bobby was still suffering greatly at the hospital, Lydia was grappling with the hard truths about her child's health and her husband's deception, and Reed and the FBI were still working to extract the whole truth from Dr. Updyke.

When I returned from the bank, I was pleased to see that Haley was still there. She was reclining on the couch, simultaneously playing Mancala with Isaac and talking on her cell phone. I knew that Grete would be uncomfortable with having a phone in the house, so finally I gave a few hand signals to Haley and she sat up, suddenly realizing the rudeness of her ways.

"Oh, sorry, duh," she said, holding one hand over the mouthpiece. "I'll hang up now. It's my mom. She wants to know if she can swing by later and drop off some of this leftover funeral food."

"Funeral food?"

"Yeah, we had a catered lunch with Doug's parents after the funeral this morning, but there's a shrimp platter, two pies, and a cake that never even got opened, if you guys would like them."

"That would be lovely," Grete said, so Haley told her mother yes and then ended her call.

I wasn't sure what to do with myself next. I wanted to get back to the hospital to see Bobby and maybe even relieve Lydia for a few hours, but I kept delaying in the hopes that Reed would stop by. Looking at my watch, I decided I would give it one more hour, and if he hadn't appeared by then, I would head to the hospital and catch up with him later.

Grete and Rebecca chatted easily as they worked at the sewing machine by the window, and when I asked if there was anything I could do to help out around the house for an hour or so, Grete asked if I knew how to make egg noodles.

"I do," said Haley. "Can I help?"

"You direct, I'll help. I've never made noodles in my life."

"Okay. Grete, do you mind if we make ourselves at home in your kitchen?"

"Please, feel free. Seeing the photos of that quilt has made me very much in the mood for sewing today, not cooking."

Haley and I washed our hands at the sink, and then she began listing the ingredients and utensils that we needed as I retrieved them from the pantry and put them together in a collection on the counter. I didn't understand my old friend at all. Just this morning, she had attended her husband's funeral. Considering that, where was her good humor and energy coming from?

Fifteen minutes later, as we were up to our wrists in dough, I came out and asked her. Lowering her voice, Haley replied she wasn't sure, but there was something so incredibly healing about being here in this house and being back together with her old best friend that she felt better today than she had in weeks.

"What about the life insurance mess your mom was telling me about?" I asked, also keeping my voice low. "Did the police drop that?"

"I'm not sure. I'm not worried about it."

"You sound pretty cavalier for a woman with involuntary manslaughter on her record. Don't you remember the horror of that whole time? The possibility of juvie or jail hanging on your shoulders like a million-pound weight?"

She shrugged.

"What difference does it make? I won't live long enough to get to trial anyway."

As I processed that thought, Haley assembled the pasta maker, though she seemed a bit perplexed that it had no wire or plug. When I reminded her that this was an Amish house and that most of their appliances used elbow grease, she studied the contraption for a minute, figured out which way to turn the handle and where to load the dough, and then got down to business. We were really getting the hang of it when there was a knock at the door and Melody stuck her head inside.

"Anybody home?"

Grete met her at the door and took from her two big pie boxes, and Rebecca went out and helped bring in the rest from the car.

As good as Haley was looking today, especially compared to yesterday at the wake, Melody was almost the opposite. At the wake, she had looked her usual stunning self; today, she was a mess, her hair askew, her outfit looking thrown together and rather wrinkled.

I asked her if she was doing okay, but she shook her head and said that it had been a difficult day, what with having to get through the funeral, host Doug's obnoxious parents at lunch, and figure out how to unload all this food, all the while catching whispers of rumors about Dr. Updyke having been arrested by the FBI.

"And what about Bobby?" Melody asked. "Does he know who ran him off the road?"

I told her no and then caught her up on what we did know about what he had been through. Haley and I finished with the noodles, and as she cleaned up our mess, I made a pot of tea, hoping that would help Melody relax. Everyone seemed ready to take a break, so finally we all sat at the table and chatted as we sipped, talking about Bobby's situation and Doug's death. Grete made the very wise observation that healing usually began with forgiveness, even when you didn't know whom you needed to forgive.

"I never got into the whole Amish forgiveness thing the way Anna and Reed did," Haley said suddenly to Grete and Rebecca, surprising me with her frankness. "I had a hard time believing it was genuine. I guess it wasn't until the school shooting that I really started to get it. You people don't just put on an act or say the right things. You genuinely, truly forgive."

Rebecca and Grete nodded as if they didn't even quite understand there was another alternative.

"Have you worried that our family did not fully forgive you for the fire?" Grete asked as Melody stood and walked to the stove to pour herself one more cup of tea.

Haley shrugged.

"I suppose so. It's hard to believe the people you wronged have forgiven you when you haven't forgiven yourself."

"We forgave you, Haley. As soon as it was done, it was given over to God. We forgave Anna too," said Rebecca.

"And Bobby and Reed and Doug," Grete said.

"And Melody," Rebecca added.

"And Melody?" I chuckled. "What did you forgive her for?"

"For starting the fire at the *Dawdy Haus,*" Rebecca said.

I looked up to see Melody at the stove, her shoulders suddenly taut.

"What do you mean, Rebecca?" I asked,

wondering if I had misunderstood what she said.

"Melody started the fire at the *Dawdy Haus,* the one that killed my parents."

Now everyone except Melody was staring at Rebecca.

"What are you talking about?" Grete demanded of her sister.

"That night I knew *Mamm* was having the baby because I heard her tell *Daed* to boil some water and call the doctor. I stayed up, waiting for the news of a brother or sister. From my bedroom window, I got to see the whole big fireworks show way out back that you folks made. Then later Melody came tiptoeing around closer, just before the fire. But it was okay. We all forgave. It is the Amish way."

Next to me, Haley began to tremble with emotion.

"The Amish way? To witness a crime and keep your mouth shut for eleven years?"

Rebecca was so startled by Haley's questions, she couldn't even reply.

Incredulous, Haley, Grete, and I all looked over at Melody, who was slowly pouring hot water into a cup. Suddenly, there was a commotion at the back door as Isaac came bounding in, followed by the bodyguard. Melody leapt toward the huge man, swinging the hot, heavy teapot around in a wide arc as she went, landing it against the side of the bodyguard's head with a sickening thunk. We all screamed, but in the time it took for me to grab Isaac and whip him around behind me, the bodyguard was lying in an unconscious heap on the floor and Melody had managed to get the gun out of his ankle holster. Now, she had it trained on all of us.

"Mom, what are you doing? Have you cracked?"

"Come on, Melody," I said in a much calmer, more soothing voice. "You don't want to do this. Don't add a new crime to an old one."

Melody shook her head sadly and told us that she had already added several new crimes, so what difference did it make? "In for a penny, in for a pound."

The gun still gripped firmly in her hand, Melody herded us toward the sitting area. The main light fixture in the room was a floor lamp powered by a propane tank that was tucked neatly inside a large, round wooden base. Gesturing with the gun, Melody made the five of us sit around that base now, our backs to each other. Her eyes scanned the room and soon landed on Grete.

"Get some rope," Melody said, and Grete did as she asked, walking calmly to the pantry, reaching inside, and coming out with a new package of clothesline cord. She carried it over to Melody and handed it to her.

"Open it," Melody commanded.

Grete did as she said, and though her hands were steady, I could see the fear in her eyes, especially when Melody told her to tie us up. Reluctantly, Grete secured one end of the rope to the pole and began wrapping it around us.

"You're my mother," Haley cried. "I can't believe you let me blame myself all these years for a fire you started."

"Well, for what it's worth, I never meant to frame you or your friends—or to kill the Schumanns. That all just sort of happened."

"Sort of happened?" I demanded. "How?"

Tightening her grip on the gun, Melody kept one eye on Grete's movements as she explained.

"Harold—Dr. Updyke—asked if I wanted to meet him out here that night for the delivery, and of course I said yes. I wanted to see if his in utero gene therapy procedure had worked."

"Wait," I said, shaking my head. "How did you know about it? What did that have to do with you?"

Melody seemed surprised by my question at first, but then her eyes narrowed.

"Well, it's not something I tell people, dear, but as part of my divorce settlement I arranged to receive a large block of stock in the WIRE. As a major stockholder as well as a scientist working in the field of DNA myself, I had a significant interest in their work. Harold understood that, and he kept me apprised of his experiments—including the ones done without the FDA's knowledge. We even conducted a few top secret experiments together, ones that combined my work with plant DNA and his with human DNA. It was a win-win situation for both of us, as you can imagine."

I finally understood why Melody had never seemed bitter about the division of assets in her divorce. Because she lived in a small house and wore secondhand clothes, I always assumed she had received the short end of the stick; now I realized that her holdings simply hadn't been liquidated. Mr. Wynn may have kept their big fancy house, but Melody was given stock in the one branch of the company that held all the promise of DNA itself.

"Anyway," she continued, "when the baby was stillborn and covered with pox, I knew what had gone wrong, and I had to think fast. An autopsy would have ruined everything, don't you see? I sent Harold on his way and helped the Schumanns clean up the baby, and we even tucked it in a cradle out in the *Dawdy Haus.* Then I told them to go back to the main house and stay away from the body less they contract pox themselves. I thought they would do as I said."

Grete paused in her tying to look at Melody in astonishment.

"There is not a mother alive who would walk away from her newborn child, dead or not, contagious or not," she said. "You are a parent. You should have known they would not leave."

Melody looked surprised, and I realized that she didn't get it and never had, as if she lacked the very essence of motherhood itself.

"Keep tying," Melody instructed gruffly. "Look, that wasn't my fault. I just knew I had to come up with some way to get rid of that body. I had a feeling Bobby and Lydia were out there in the dark, and everybody knew he used to send up fireworks as the signal to get her to join him. I left the *Dawdy Haus* and snuck around back and took a Roman candle from his truck. Once I found a good patch of dry grass behind the *Dawdy Haus,* it wasn't hard to get the fire started, and I made sure to leave some casings a little further out, where they would show up as evidence if necessary. My plan was to make it look like a simple accident, a misfire from a Roman candle. I had no idea the Schumanns would be killed, nor that the police would treat it as a crime scene."

"You sure kept your mouth shut afterward, though, didn't you?" Haley cried.

"By then the Schumanns were dead, honey. Nothing I could say or do would have brought them back to life."

"You could have taken responsibility for what you did instead of making us pay for your crime!"

"Oh, please. You got involuntary manslaughter. If they had known the truth, I would have gotten first degree murder."

"What about Dr. Updyke?" I asked. "He didn't start the fire. Why was he willing to stand by and watch five people get sentenced for a crime he knew they didn't commit?"

"He didn't know," Melody said. "For all his brilliance, Harold Updyke can be an idiot. My actions saved him from having his patients autopsied twice in a row; first when I took the body of the baby who had died from a tumor and made it look as though the Amish parents had done it, and then when I started the fire here. Both times Harold actually thought he'd been lucky, the simple benefactor of convenient circumstances. I let him think whatever he wanted, but I made sure he stopped doing any more experiments that were outside of the law. He complied for a few years, until Bobby came to him asking for help in conceiving a healthy child. Considering that the procedure could be done at the in vitro level, Harold thought it was too good of an opportunity to pass up." She gestured toward Isaac. "Obviously, things went fine that time. It's just too bad Bobby got all panicky about a few little symptoms that had a perfectly logical explanation."

Haley and I looked at each other, eyes wide.

"You tried to kill Bobby by running him off the road," I said.

"You killed Doug," Haley added.

"It's not as though I wanted to," Melody answered. "If the two of them hadn't been poking around in things that weren't their business, none of this would have happened."

"How did you know they were poking around?" I asked.

"Bobby was caught red-handed trying to break the lock on a file cabinet at the WIRE. Harold gave him a warning, but when his own key to that file cabinet disappeared, he had no choice but to put Bobby on suspension. After that, Bobby obviously went to Doug for help, because Doug tried to access the archived files via computer. What he didn't know was that those files are tied into an electronic alert system, which sent Harold an emergency notification. As soon as he told me Doug had been going into those old files, I knew we had a problem. Everything I've done since has been damage control."

"Damage control? Killing my husband was *damage control*?" Haley shrieked.

"Like you even cared about him. I figured I was doing you a favor."

"How did you do it?" I asked.

"Doug was easy. Thanks to those electronic alerts, I made sure I was waiting in the parking lot when he came out of Wynn headquarters that night. He was so worked up, he didn't even ask me why I was there. It wasn't hard to get him to talk to me and tell me what was going on. He said he'd found two files that proved Dr. Updyke had done illegal gene therapy in the late nineties, and one file in particular that made him question whether the big fire that killed the Schumanns had been an accident. Of course, at that point I knew I had no choice but to kill him."

Melody told Grete to hurry it up and then continued her tale.

"Doug had left a message for Bobby and sent a fax down to Reed, but otherwise he hadn't actually spoken to anyone. That was all I needed to know. I said I had an idea where we could find more proof, over at the new building. Like a lamb to slaughter, Doug followed me there, all the way up to the eighth floor. In the elevator, he told me that he had called Bobby's house again from the car and left a second message, this one saying he should meet him there. I made sure I hadn't been mentioned in that message and then proceeded as planned, relieved that this was going to be a two-for-one deal."

"Unbelievable," I whispered. At some point since the accidental murders in the fire, Melody had gone off the deep end. Where before she had killed by accident, now she was murdering by intention, just to cover up the original crime. I had to wonder if her precarious mental state had somehow been distorted these past years by working in the field of DNA, by manipulating living organisms at will. I thought of Dr. Updyke's comment that for all intents and purposes, he was God. Melody now had that same, crazed look in her eye, that same arrogance that surely came from confusing genetic manipulation with the very act of creation—an act that could only be performed by God Himself.

"Up on the eighth floor, I led Doug near the edge, and when he turned his back, I was able to push him to his death. When Bobby got there, I was waiting for him. I dropped a box of tiles, but he managed to roll out of the way before they hit."

"How did you catch up with him later to run him off the road?" I asked, wincing at the knot Grete was tightening around my wrists.

"I didn't. Bobby took off so fast, there was no way I could catch up. I figured I was done for. I went home and packed my bags and headed to the Philadelphia airport, wondering how long it would be before someone realized that *I* had set that fire that killed the Schumanns. I thought I might get a few days' head start anyway, enough time to go somewhere far away and start over."

"The airport," I whispered.

"Yeah, dumb luck, huh, that Bobby and I ended up in the same terminal at the same time?"

I didn't reply, knowing that luck hadn't had much to do with it. Given that there was only one flight out at that hour of the night, it wasn't surprising that they had ended up in the same place at the same time.

"I was just glad I spotted Bobby before I bought my ticket—and before he spotted me," Melody continued. "I knew he was up to something fishy, and I wasn't sure what to do until Haley called all worked up over the stolen motorcycle and I put two and two together. On a hunch, I hid outside airport security and waited. Sure enough, about a half hour later Bobby came walking out. He hadn't boarded that plane after all. When he took the train right at the airport, I knew for sure that he was headed to wherever he'd stashed that motorcycle, probably in Hidden Springs. To get there, he'd have to change trains at least once, which would give me enough time to race ahead in my car and wait for him along the highway. I had no doubt he was going back to get his wife and kid. People like Bobby always do the right thing."

"You can do the right thing too, Melody. It's not too late."

Ignoring my comment, she told Grete to stop tying and sit down with the rest of us, and then Melody used one hand to tie her in as well.

"Once I took care of Bobby, the only variable left was Reed. All I had to do was drive down to DC, break into his condo, and take the fax Doug told me he had sent. Lucky for me, Reed wasn't even home that night. I got the fax without any problems, and I even made it back in time for work the next morning."

"Except Doug never thought to mention that he'd left a message for Reed on his phone, telling him about the fax," I said. "When Reed heard that message, he was able to reprint the fax, and then he brought it straight to the FBI."

"Yes, I have been concerned about that. But the files only implicate Harold. My name is nowhere to be found. It seems incredible to me, but I think I just might squeak through after all."

"You don't think they'll figure it out? Eventually, Updyke is going to tell them you were here with him the night of the fire."

"Maybe. But it'll be his word against mine. Not another living soul knows I was here."

There was a small ax beside the wood stove, and I was startled when she walked over and picked it up.

"But I know," Rebecca said softly. "I saw you."

"Like I said," Melody shrugged. "Not another *living* soul."

Suddenly, as fiercely as she had swung the teapot against the bodyguard's head, Melody swung the ax in a broad arc, slicing across the pole above our heads, the top of the lamp clattering to the floor. We all screamed and then screamed again as the smell of rotten eggs filled our nostrils.

Propane.

"You'll blow the whole house up!" Haley exclaimed.

"Grete, tell me about your woodstove," Melody said calmly. "Is there a timer on the igniter?"

Grete didn't answer her, but her silence spoke volumes.

"Okay, then," Melody said, moving toward the stove and fiddling with the knobs on the top. We could hear the clack as she set the knob, then she calmly put the ax down where she had found it and headed for the back door, still holding the gun.

"I set it to go off in three minutes," she told us calmly, "which should give me enough time to get out of here. Sorry it had to be this way. Think of this as a simple sacrifice toward the greater good."

Melody set the gun down on the table and gingerly stepped over the bodyguard, who was still lying so still that if his broad chest hadn't been rising and falling ever so slightly, I would have thought he was dead. Next to me, Haley began screaming at her mother, demanding to know how she could do this to her own flesh and blood, her own child.

"I'm sorry, Haley," Melody said in reply

to her daughter, and when she turned around, tears were in her eyes. "For what it's worth, I basically killed you eleven years ago anyway."

"By making me think I was at fault for the fire and deaths?"

"No, I mean literally, I killed you. That summer, Harold and I were experimenting on you and Anna. I'm afraid the cancer you have now may have come from back then, much like the baby with the tumors."

Haley was speechless, but I wasn't.

"You *experimented* on us? *How?"* I demanded.

Glancing at the timer on the stove, Melody quickly explained that Haley's allergy injections had been, in fact, test doses for gene therapy. For comparison, I had not been subjected to injections but instead to edible gene therapy—or at least that had been their goal, though the experiment didn't work.

"Remember how much you always loved my tomatoes, Anna? Back then, we didn't realize that ordinary stomach acid would kill off the genes before they ever had a chance to enter the bloodstream. You never absorbed a thing."

"How do you know? Did you test me?"

"Of course, dear, once a week, when you were sleeping. When your mouth was open, I'd do a swab."

"I don't believe this," Haley finally managed to mutter.

"Look on the bright side, darling. You're going to be dead soon anyway, but at least now your suffering won't be prolonged the way it would with cancer."

With that, Melody opened the door, stepped out, and pulled it quietly shut behind her.

FORTY-SIX

Immediately, we all sprang into action. The sulfur smell of the leaking propane was overwhelming, and from the top of the woodstove we could hear the ticking of the timer as it measured out the few minutes we had to get free and get outside before the whole place would blow up. I suggested that we all try to rise upward, that if we could get high enough—if we could actually get our feet under us and stand on the wooden base—then we could slide the rope up over the pole and then we would be loose.

It wasn't easy, especially because Isaac

was so much smaller than the rest of us. The wooden base wasn't balanced well enough for this many people to try climbing up on it at once, all while being simultaneously bound together with rope. Still, we finally managed to get our balance and then together, as one, we stood.

The plan worked in a way, though as we pushed the rope over the top of the pole, the whole contraption began to fall sideways, and we landed in a big heap on the floor. Relieved that no sparks had ignited an explosion, we quickly wiggled free of the ropes that were now loose on all of us. Gripping Isaac under the arms, I whipped him up onto my hip and ran for the back door, nearly throwing him out onto the ground once I got there. Haley made it outside next, and then Rebecca. Finally, with perhaps fifteen seconds left before the stove would ignite and the house would blow up, Grete and I each took a hand of the unconscious bodyguard and pulled. We weren't strong enough to drag the massive fellow, and I knew we needed to give up and run for our own lives.

At the last moment, seeing we weren't going to get him out in time, Haley ran back into the house with a yell. Seconds later, Grete and I dove for cover as we heard the telltale click of the woodstove igniter.

There was a "kaboom," but it wasn't as loud as either of us had expected. Still, smoke began pouring from the door, and there was no way to go inside and see if Haley had survived. Nathaniel came running from the barn, saw what was going on, and reached for the bodyguard's hands. With one giant tug, he dragged him all the way out of the house and onto the frozen ground outside.

With the noise and confusion and smoke that followed, I was living in real life the nightmare that had plagued my sleep all these years. Soon there were sirens and firemen and neighbors, and the best I could do was stay out of the way and pull my nephew on my lap and hold him as tightly as I possibly could while he cried deep, heaving sobs into my shoulder.

Later, I came to understand what Haley had done in those last few seconds, when she sacrificed her life to save a man she didn't even know. In the moment before ignition, she had run into the room, grabbed cushions off of the couch, and thrown them and then herself down on top of the propane tank in an effort to contain the explosion. According to the coroner, she probably felt no pain. She had also likely died instantly, her body absorbing most of the force of the aluminum tank as it blew.

By the time Reed got there, I was all cried out. Still, I allowed him to hold me as I had held Isaac, and together we stood and watched the activity that swarmed around us.

There was something about fire and this house that would always go together in my mind. But at least now I knew, for certain, that eleven years ago a group of stupid kids around a little bonfire in the back field with some fireworks hadn't done the unthinkable, hadn't caught a house on fire, hadn't taken any lives.

For now, that would have to be enough.

FORTY-SEVEN

Stephanie

December 18, 1830

My Dearest Son,

This will be the last communication between us. Enclosed please find the remaining pieces of the Beauharnais Rubies. You should now have possession of the entire parure. These magnificent jewels were given to me in honor of your birth. It seems only fitting that they now belong to you.

It is with a wounded and aching heart that I surrender this battle of wills between us and beg of you to depart for the safety of America with my blessing. As you may know, less than a week ago, Kaspar Hauser was attacked and stabbed in the chest. Word has now reached the palace that yesterday he died of that wound.

My son, the forces that threatened your life at birth persist even now, in your adulthood. I once made a choice between honor and love. I understand now that in choosing love, I actually chose both. It is with honor that I again sacrifice and send you on your way. Godspeed, my son. I will keep to my death the secret of your true identity. May you live a long and healthy life, prosper in all that you do, and find much peace and happiness far away from the dark clouds of evil ambition that hover over Baden.

You never knew me as a mother, but I knew you as my son. From afar, every year on the anniversary of your birth, I would stand atop the castle wall and the Jensens would bring you to play in the nearby pasture, the one with the gnarled apple trees along one side. Over the years, I have watched you grow in health and love and goodness.

May this be my greatest legacy, even though 'twas done in secret. By giving you up, I gave you life.

No greater love hath any man than that.

Your mother, always and forever,
Stephanie de Beauharnais

EPILOGUE

Anna
Six Months Later

"Does it fit?" Lydia asked, hovering on the other side of the dressing room curtain. "It may need taking in at the shoulders."

I stood in front of the mirror and looked at the dress, a perfect reproduction of the one worn by Stephanie de Beauharnais in the portrait that had been painted of her by François Gérard. In that portrait, she was posed in a beautiful floral summer dress, holding a small fan and wearing the Beauharnais Emeralds. Today, the photographer was going to attempt to recreate that painting on film with me, only I would be wearing the Beauharnais Rubies instead.

More than likely, this would be the last time I would ever have the chance to wear them. The buyer had been incredibly patient, but tomorrow he would finally be whisking them away to a collection in Europe, where they would be joined with their sister set, the Beauharnais Emeralds. Already, my family and I were soaking up the last moments we would have with this treasured piece of our heritage, one that had become so much more to us than a sparkly windfall. In fact, at first we had hoped to keep the magnificent heirlooms in the family, but the cost of insurance was prohibitive. At least we had the contents of Stephanie's letters, which no one could ever take away—even if the originals had been moved to the Smithsonian.

Besides Stephanie's letters, there had been other documents in with the jewels, documents that had proved conclusively the succession of ownership from Karl Jensen all the way down the line of firstborn male sons to my grandfather. Those documents had saved us from having to endure prolonged court battles with other Jensen descendants, including my nefarious accosteswabbers.

One by one, other possible claimants had been ruled out as well. The couple who bought the house might have a legitimate claim, but a review of their contract showed that they had specifically purchased the "above ground" portion of the dwelling only. That left Lydia's family, who owned the land where the jewels had been hidden, but they had no interest in claiming them.

Thus, because my grandfather's will had left all of his worldly possessions to his only child, my father ended up being the sole owner of the Beauharnais Rubies. Upon selling them, he had paid out a generous finder's fee to Remy and then split the remaining proceeds into four equal shares: one for himself and my mother, one for Bobby, one for me, and one for Grete and her siblings. They had resisted at first, but in the end agreed that the money could be used to help each of the kids establish themselves once they were married, not to mention the large tithe that would bless their entire community.

"Anna? Are you coming out?" Lydia

asked, and I whispered my reply through the curtain.

"If this article wasn't for *National Geographic,* I wouldn't be doing this. I mean, it sounded like a good idea at the time, but now I'm feeling kind of stupid."

"*Ach,* Anna, please let us see."

Summoning my nerve, I finally slid open the curtain that separated me from Lydia. Behind her stood Bobby and Isaac, and when I stepped out of the dressing room, everyone's eyes widened.

"That's just freaky," Bobby said, shaking his head at the resemblance between me and our six-greats grandmother.

"It's the dress and the hair, that's all," I said, but as I stepped out to look again at the life-sized blowup they had made in preparation for the shoot, I had to admit that we did look somewhat alike. My lips were fuller than hers, and her neck had been longer than mine, but we both had the same eyes, the same figure, the same hands.

"Is it Anna, or is it Stephanie?" Remy cried, coming across the studio to get a better look.

These days, Remy was positively floating on air as the story of the priceless treasure he had helped to recover was one of the hottest topics in the media. He and I had been interviewed on *Good Morning America* together the same week we showed up on the cover of *People* magazine, and after those two simple appearances, the sales of his books had skyrocketed, going into subsequent printings and making Remy Villefranche practically a household name.

I had been a household name before then, of course, only nowadays people didn't look at me with scorn or judgment, but instead with curiosity, sometimes envy, and almost always a little grace. As much as I hated the media, when the entire story about Melody and the WIRE and the Dreiheit Five and the Beauharnais Rubies and everything all came out, I decided to fight fire with fire, so to speak. After fulfilling my promise of an exclusive to the reporters who helped capture the accosteswabbers, I hit the circuit, telling the truth about what had happened, sharing the exciting story of the jewels, and repeating over and over my main point, which was that we Americans are too cruel to each other, too quick to judge, too willing to accept the lies masquerading as truth in the tabloids.

And though I had been offered several ongoing media-related opportunities, I had turned them all down. Today was my final official public appearance, and then I would return to California, for a time at least. More and more, I had been thinking about drawing that chapter of my life to a close and moving back home to the East Coast.

Kiki and I had fully reconciled, but her life was changing too. Somehow in the aftermath of all that happened, she and Norman had fallen in love and were now engaged to be married. Their ultimate plan was to sell his house in town, use the proceeds to renovate her house at the beach, and then live there together. Though I couldn't be happier for them, it was clear that my time as Kiki's housemate was coming to an end. I was just glad I had been able to pay for all of the repairs that had been needed in the wake of our ski-masked intruder—and throw in a little extra besides, for good measure.

As for that intruder, Remy's hunch had been correct. The man who had broken into the beach house and demanded the rubies at gunpoint was a direct descendant of Karl Friedrich, Grand Duke of Baden. The man had planned to use his DNA results to defend his claim to the jewels, but of course my father's DNA held the more significant link, not to mention that the documents found with the jewels provided all the proof we needed. Once he learned that, the man gave up, pled guilty for his crimes, and was currently serving his sentence at the prison in Chino.

"Miss Jensen?" the production assistant said, waving me over. "Let's touch up the makeup and then we'll start putting on the jewels. If you don't mind, the writer would like to ask you some questions at the same time."

Mindful of the dress, I climbed up into the canvas-backed chair and let the makeup artists go to work on my face as the man who was writing the accompanying article scooted over a chair from the corner of the studio and sat.

He and I had already spoken several times, and though I knew the focus of his piece was the jewels and the documents, he was also hoping to include a sidebar about the adventure that had led us to discover them at last.

In that vein, he asked me now if I could tell him a bit more about the various players in the events that had unfolded during that difficult week in Pennsylvania last January. He wanted to know how everyone was doing six months later.

"Well, you can see that my brother's up and around," I said, gesturing toward Bobby, who was chatting with Remy. "He'll have some lingering health issues, but at least the doctors were able to save his leg."

"What about his job? With the WIRE closed down, was he able to find another position in the Dreiheit area?"

"Actually," I said, beaming with sisterly pride, "he's decided to go back to school instead for speech therapy. Bobby was always so smart, you know. It was just a tragedy that his education was derailed by the original fire."

I had to stop talking for a minute as the makeup artist worked on my mouth with a lipstick pencil. As I sat there mum, I thought about one of Bobby's smartest tricks ever, the mysterious ATM withdrawal in Las Vegas the night he disappeared.

All he had done to make that happen was write his PIN number on a yellow sticky note and attach it to his ATM card. At the airport, he had acted as though he was waiting for the flight to Las Vegas, when in fact he had been studying the other passengers, trying to pick out someone who seemed just a little bit shady. Once he had chosen his mark, Bobby had gotten in line behind the guy, tapped him on the shoulder, and held out the ATM card.

"Hey, buddy, I think you dropped this," Bobby had said, and then he added, "If I were you, though, I wouldn't keep my pin number attached to the actual card, you know? Somebody could find this and rip you off."

Without missing a beat, the man had simply thanked him, taken the card, and tucked it into his pocket. Obviously, at the other end of that flight, the guy had jumped on the first ATM machine he had come to. He'd probably been hoping for a lot more than what he found in the account, but a hundred bucks was better than nothing.

"How about your nephew?" the writer asked. "Isaac, is it?"

"Yes, he's doing well," I said as the

makeup artist finished her work. "He was pretty traumatized by the whole propane thing, especially coming on the heels of his father's disappearance and all of that. But he's getting better. He has great parents and a wonderful new school, so we're all quite confident that he'll continue to blossom. And, of course, he loves being a big brother."

Glancing back at Lydia, who was bouncing little Samuel on her hip, I didn't mention how relieved we had been to confirm through genetic testing that Dr. Updyke's tampering had not extended to this second son. Though we would always grieve for what had been done to Isaac, somehow Lydia had found it in her heart to forgive Bobby for his deception. Lately, they had both been working hard to put the past behind them and focus on the future.

"And Bobby's Amish in-laws? Whatever happened to their house?"

The hairstylist entered then, trailed by the representative of Lloyd's of London, the company who was currently in charge of protecting the rubies. With a little bit of fanfare, the Lloyd's man came and stood beside my chair and opened the lid of the jewels' case so that the hairdresser could take out the tiara and arrange it just so with the hairstyle she had already swept into an updo.

"There was a lot of smoke damage," I said to the writer as the stylist worked, "so repairs needed doing, but they're up and running with it now. We correspond regularly, and the whole family is getting along just fine."

I didn't add that with their share of the rubies they could have afforded to rebuild from the ground up, many times over. In truth, we were all quite rich now. Bobby and I were still trying to figure out how to be good stewards of our own money, but already my dad was scaring my mother with his dreams of hunting down Red-Rumped Swallows in the Canary Islands.

"I spoke to the Lancaster County police to get the current status of Harold Updyke and Melody Wynn. It looks like neither one of them will be back in their own homes any time soon."

I nodded, watching as the hairdresser again reached into the jewel case and came out with the earrings, which she let me put on myself.

"Is it true you were the one who tipped off the police to search for that infant's body in Melody Wynn's backyard, the one who died from tumors induced by illegal gene therapy?" the writer asked.

"Yes. Given the facts, I had a feeling Melody had buried the child in her yard and covered it up by planting the tree directly on top."

"And the infant's remains have now been laid to rest in an Amish cemetery?"

"Yes, after a lovely re-internment ceremony. I'm glad to say that the Amish community in Dreiheit has gone out of their way to make amends to the parents of the baby, and from what I understand there has been a lot of healing there."

The hairdresser pulled out the necklace, carefully draped it across my chest, and fastened it at the back of my neck. With the jewels slowly being added to my frame, I couldn't help but feel a surge of excitement. The stylist took out the bracelets next, and as she fastened them at my wrists, I couldn't wait to look in the mirror for the full effect. Already, I felt connected to Stephanie somehow, her very blood coursing through my veins.

"Speaking of making amends, the three surviving Dreiheit Five members received full pardons for their alleged crimes. Is that correct?"

"Yes, our slates have been wiped clean. We can't get those years back, you know, but it does feel good moving forward without having to carry such heavy burdens from the past." He didn't ask, but I had also been cleared for breaking into the lab, a crime the DA had decided not to prosecute considering the extenuating circumstances.

"So what will your name be now?" the writer asked. "Anna Bailey? Or will you go back to Jensen?"

The stylist reached into the box for one more piece of jewelry, but I didn't know what it could be because I thought they had already put everything on me. Turning, she held out a ring, one I had not seen before. It was stunning, though, a huge white diamond in the center surrounded by a circle of rubies.

I held it up to the light, wondering how this piece could have gone unnoticed thus far. I was about to call Remy over when a familiar movement caught my eye. There, standing quietly in the background, was the one person I most wanted to see in the world.

Reed Thornton.

Reed and I had moved our relationship along quite carefully since January. He and Heather had broken up by mid-February, and though I had found that news heartening, I hadn't wanted to rush into anything in the wake of that long-term relationship.

Instead, we started writing and emailing and calling—getting to know each other all over again. As the calls got longer and more frequent, Reed finally began coming out for visits to California. We hadn't even kissed until his last visit two weeks ago, when we went for a long stroll on the beach near his hotel. There, to the glow of a warm California sunset, he had taken me in his arms at last and told me the words that I had longed to hear from him since I was seventeen: *I love you, Anna.*

Now, here he was at the photo shoot, looking even more striking to me than he ever had before.

"Anna?" the writer repeated. "What will your name be now?"

Slowly, Reed walked forward, took the ring from me, and held it at the tip of the fourth finger of my left hand.

"How about Thornton?" he asked me. "Anna Thornton sounds good, don't you think?"

Gasping, I looked down at the ring, understanding finally what he had done. I was stunned, not just that he had found such a romantic way to propose, but that he would choose a ring for the occasion that was similar in look and feel to the heirloom jewels that had been in my family for almost two hundred years.

Then again, I shouldn't have been surprised. Any guy who went shopping for a sweater dress in an outlet mall in January just to keep a girl warm and confident was the kind of man who would spend a lifetime showing love in action.

"Yes," I whispered, tears filling my eyes as Reed slipped the ring all the way onto my finger. "Anna Thornton sounds perfect."

I blinked, sending twin tears down my cheeks as Reed leaned in for a kiss.

"Don't mess up the mascara!" the makeup person cried.

"Don't smudge the lipstick!" the stylist said.

Reed stopped just before touching his lips to mine. Instead, he simply whispered, "I love you" and reluctantly moved back out of the way, his deep blue eyes holding the promise of later kisses, of our beautiful future together. Once I was ready, he offered me his arm like a gentleman. Dressed as quite the lady, I slipped my hand into the crook of his elbow.

"Shall we proceed?" Reed said, gesturing toward the cameras that were waiting to take my portrait.

"Let's," I replied, somehow standing taller with the weight of my heritage sparkling in my hair and around my neck.

Reed led me to where I was supposed to stand, posed just as Stephanie had posed, in front of a curving golden couch.

"Like this?" I asked the photographer, placing my hands just so.

The stylists ran forward and adjusted my hands, my skirt, my hair. As all of them flitted around me, I looked out at the small group of people who were my family and friends, who had come all this way today just to lend moral support.

Six months ago, my world had been much smaller, and Kiki had urged me to take some chances. Now, not only did I have the reconnection of my family and my past, I had the glorious hope of a future filled with promise and light.

My heart soaring, I suddenly understood the truth that Stephanie had come to know: Love was about letting go of self.

Holding my chin high, I looked directly into the camera and smiled, knowing that my Amish friends had been showing me what that looked like all along.

ABOUT THE AUTHOR

Shadows of Lancaster County is Mindy's tenth novel for Harvest House Publishers. Previous books include the bestselling *Whispers of the Bayou* as well as the Million Dollar Mysteries and The Smart Chick Mystery series, which includes *The Trouble with Tulip, Blind Dates Can Be Murder,* and *Elementary, My Dear Watkins.*

Mindy is also the author of the nonfiction guide *The House That Cleans Itself* as well as numerous plays and musicals. A popular speaker and former stand-up comedian, Mindy lives with her husband and two daughters near Valley Forge, Pennsylvania.

In any story, where facts are used to mold and shape fiction, sometimes it becomes hard for readers to tell the two apart, particularly when learning about a history or culture that isn't overly familiar. For more information and to find out which elements of this story are fictional and which are based on fact, visit Mindy's website at:

www.mindystarnsclark.com.